Kith and Kin

Richard Denning

Kith and Kin
Written by Richard Denning
Copyright 2020 Richard Denning.
First Published 2020.
ISBN: 978-1-9996562-1-8
Published by Mercia Books

A catalogue record for this book is available from the British Library

Book Jacket design and layout by Cathy Helms
www.avalongraphics.org

Editing by Nicky Galliers

Author website:
www.richarddenning.co.uk
Publisher website:
www.merciabooks.co.uk

Dedication

The title of this book is of Old English origin. It derives from ancient words *cythth* and *cynn*. These words expressed the meaning of 'one's native land'. Thus, the original historical meaning of '*kith and kin*' was one's country and family. Over the years, '*kith*' has been taken to mean something like '*one's close friends*', so 'kith and kin' means 'one's friends and relatives.'

Whether it means native land, family or friends, this title summarises significant elements of this story. The phrase at the same time works well as a dedication.

This book is dedicated to my family and also this land I live in whose complex and varied history lead to the nations of England, Wales, Scotland and Ireland which in their varied ways have had a profound impact on the world we all live in, perhaps more than one would expect from such a tiny set of islands surrounded by an at times wild and hostile sea.

The Author

Richard Denning was born in Ilkeston in Derbyshire and lives in Sutton Coldfield in the West Midlands, where he worked as a General Practitioner until retiring from the NHS to focus on other work. He is married and has two children. He has always been fascinated by historical settings as well as horror and fantasy. Other than writing, his main interests are games of all types. He runs the largest tabletop games event in the UK and is the designer of several board game based on the Great Fire of London and others historical themes.

Author website:

www.richarddenning.co.uk

Also by the author:

Northern Crown Series

(Historical fiction)

1. The Amber Treasure

2. Child of Loki

3. Princes in Exile

4. The White Chariot

5. Kith and Kin

Hourglass Institute Series

(Young Adult Science Fiction)

1. Tomorrow's Guardian

2. Yesterday's Treasures

3. Today's Sacrifice

The Praesidium Series

(Historical Fantasy)

The Last Seal

The Nine Worlds Series

(Children's Historical Fantasy)

1. Shield Maiden

2. The Catacombs of Vanaheim

3. Frost Giants of Jotunheim

Britain in AD 610 to 612

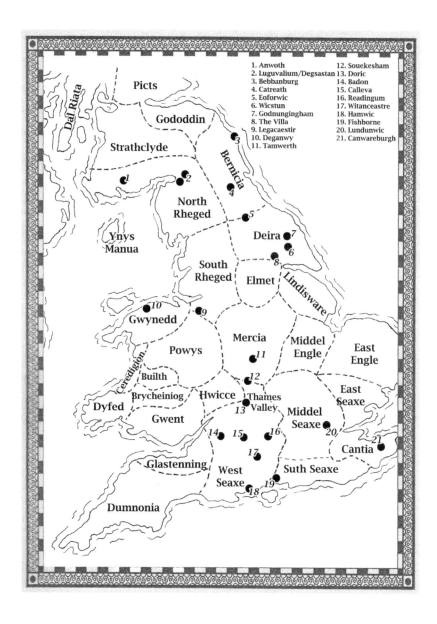

Dal Riata

Picts

Gododdin

Strathclyde

Bernicia

1. Anwoth
2. Luguvalium/Degsastan
3. Bebbanburg
4. Catreath
5. Eoforwic
6. Wicstun
7. Godnungingham
8. The Villa
9. Legacaestir
10. Deganwy
11. Tamwerth

12. Souekesham
13. Doric
14. Badon
15. Calleva
16. Readingum
17. Witanceastre
18. Hamwic
19. Fishborne
20. Lundunwic
21. Canwareburgh

North Rheged

Ynys Manua

Deira

South Rheged

Elmet

Lindisware

Gwynedd

Powys

Mercia

Middel Engle

East Engle

Ceredigion

Builth

Brycheiniog

Dyfed

Hwicce

Thames Valley

Gwent

East Seaxe

Middel Seaxe

Cantia

Glastenning

West Seaxe

Suth Seaxe

Dumnonia

Names of nations, cities and towns

Here is a glossary of the main locations referred to in Kith and Kin and what they are called today. Place names often have a great variance in spelling, so I have tried to settle on a version that seems to have been most often used. In some cases, I have corrected and updated spellings in this novel from the earlier books to reflect my ongoing research.

Anwoth – Trusty Hill in Dumfies and Galloway

Badon – The modern-day city of Bath

Bebbanburg – Fortress and capital of Bernica, today called Bamburgh

Bernicia – Anglo –Saxon kingdom in Northumbria

Boseham – Bosham, a coastal village in Suth Seaxe (Sussex)

Calleva – Roman city of Calleva Atrebatum or Silchester

Cantia – Kent

Cantwareburh – Modern day Canterbury

Catraeth – Catterick, site of a significant battle in c 597

Dál Riata – Kingdom of the Irish Scots from Ulster in what is now Kintyre, Argyle and Butte

Deganwy – Ancient hill fort in the modern town of the same name near Conwy and Llandudno

Degsastan – Battlefield in 603. Uncertain location, possibly Dawstone in Liddesdale

Deira – Anglo–Saxon kingdom north of the Humber

Din Eidyn – Ancient capital of Manau Gododdin, modern day Edinburgh

Doric – The town of Dorchester-on-Thames

Eoforwic – York

Elmet – Welsh/British kingdom around the modern-day city of Leeds

Godmunddingaham – Site of Deiran royal palace, modern–day Goodmanham

Gwynedd – Kingdom of north Wales encompassing what is now Clwyd as well as Gwynedd

Hamwic – Port in West Seaxe, modern-day Southhampton

Legacaestir – Chester

Lundunwic – London

Luguvalium – Carlisle

Manau Gododdin – Welsh/British kingdom around what is now Edinburgh

Powys – Ancient Kingdom of central and eastern Wales, covering what is today the modern county of Powys but also parts of Shropshire, Cheshire and Flintshire

Readingum – Reading

Souekesham – Abingdon

Tamwerth – Capital of Mercia, modern-day Tamworth

'The Villa' – Cerdic's home at Cerdham. Today called Holme-on-Spalding-Moor

West Seaxe – Anglo–Saxon kingdom around Wessex and surrounding districts

Wicstun – Market Weighton

Witanceastre – Winchester, capital of West Seax (Wessex)

Wochinoes – Woking

List of named characters

* Denotes historical figure

Acha* – Wife to Aethelfrith, sister to Edwin of Deira

Aedann – Once Cerdic's family slave but now his companion

Aelle* – Former king of Deira

Aethelberht* – King of Cantia, Bretwalda

Aethelfrith* – King of Bernicia

Aethelric* – Late king of Deira

Aidith – Cerdic's wife

Aneirin* – Welsh bard and poet

Boyden – A lord in Wessex

Breguswith* – Princess of Sussex

Bridget – Maid and household slave of Cerdic and Aidith

Cadfan* – Son of Iago, prince of Gwynedd

Cadwallon* – Grandson to Iago, Cadfan's son

Cenred – Father to Cerdic. Lord of Wicstun and earl of the Southern Marches

Coerl* – Lord in Mercia and one day king

Ceolwulf* – King in West Seaxe

Cerdic – Main character, Lord of the Villa and son of Cenred

Cuthbert – Childhood friend of Cerdic

Cuthwine – Cerdic's son, named for his deceased brother

Cwenburg* – Princess of Mercia

Ealdwig – Monk in Aebbadun and friend to Cerdic

Eanfrith* – Son of Aethelfrith

Edwin* – Younger son of Aelle

Eduard – Childhood friend of Cerdic

Grettir – Cerdic's family retainer

Guthred – Former Lord of Bursea to the south of the Villa

Hal – Son of Rowenna

Hereric* – Son of Aethelric, grandson of Aelle

Hussa – Cerdic's half brother

Iago* – King of Gwynedd

Lilla – Bard and friend of Cerdic's family

Mildrith – Cerdic's younger sister

Pybba* – Former king of Mercia

Rolf – Friend and huscarl of Hussa

Rowenna – Hussa's wife

Rhoerth* – King of Rheged

Rhun* – Bishop in Gywnedd, former king of Rheged

Sabert – Former earl of the Eastern Marches of Deira and leader of Edwin's royal guard

Sogor – Nephew to Aethelfrith

Theobald* – Brother to Aethelfrith, father to Sogor. Died at Degsastan.

Chapter One
Bride-gift
Spring 611

"**N**o, Cerdic, for the last time, no! You can't go!" Edwin said and stormed off towards his hall in the centre of the town.

I went to follow him but Sabert stepped in front of me, flashed me a stern glance, shook his head and then, without saying any words, turned and followed the prince.

"Woden's buttocks!" I cursed as I watched Edwin's oldest advisor follow the twenty-five-year-old prince. Then, turning the other way, I clambered up a flight of steps cut into the earthen embankment to reach a rampart that looked out over the palisades across the river Temese, past the low rolling countryside of Southern Mercia towards the border with West Seaxe that lay just a few miles away.

Reaching the ramparts, I located Eduard who was on watch with Cuthbert. I was their lord, but the pair were my oldest friends. Our friendship went back to the days when we were mere infants playing in the mud of the family estate that my father, Cenred, had been master of and my friends' families had worked on.

All that was in the distant past, of course – a time and place we had left behind when we had accompanied Edwin, brother to the murdered last king of Deira, into his enforced exile. It was an exile that had seen us travel through many English and Welsh nations, seeking allies that might help Edwin claim a throne we believed he was entitled to, help us gain revenge on many enemies and maybe, one day, go back to that childhood home.

"Well," Eduard asked, "what did he say?" His breath hung in the air on this cold spring morning. He was a tall, muscular man, the ideal form for a warrior, a profession which he both enjoyed and excelled at.

I scowled at him and did not reply.

"I think that means he said no," Cuthbert my brother –in – law suggested. In contrast to Eduard, he was thin and agile. His sharp eyes and swift reflexes made him a superb scout and one of the most skilled archers I have ever seen. He was married to Mildrith, my sister. He had grown up a nervous and often shy individual, particularly around women, but was loyal and a gentle, kind soul. So whilst it sometimes seemed a miracle that he had proposed to Mildrith, the result was a happy marriage. He was also rather more observant than my larger friend.

"It means no!" I said, agreeing with him.

That is the problem with plans. You make them, but the gods and fate intervene and throw you in other directions you were neither planning on going nor believed you needed to go.

My plan started a year or two before, when I had discovered that a boy, whom I later found out was called Hal, had been born to a woman with whom I had had the briefest of liaisons. You could hardly call it even a night of passion. I had been drunk and Rowenna, for that was her name, had sneaked into a Roman villa on the south coast of Suth Seaxe. She had been a spy for my half–brother, Hussa. He and I shared the same father, but Cenred had rejected both Hussa and his mother when my own mother discovered the affair he was having. The action had condemned Hussa to a pauper's childhood and an upbringing without a father.

Resentment had grown in him, like a disease. In revenge, Hussa had murdered my mother and, taking up arms with a foreign king, had eventually betrayed our country, Deira - an act which had forced most of what remained of the kingdom's royal bloodline, Edwin and his nephew Hereric, into exile with just a few dozen followers.

Over the following years, chance and design had brought Hussa and I together more than once. One such time was at Boseham, where my company had defended the ruins of a large Roman palace to help the kingdom of Suth Seaxe, and Hussa, leading forces from neighbouring West Seaxe, had attacked. We had won that battle and Hussa and his men had been forced to flee. As a result, we celebrated well that night. In my case, perhaps too well. I was exceedingly drunk when the spy, courtesan and whore, Rowenna had come to me in the night – some ploy of Hussa's to tempt me into the betrayal of my wife, Aidith. She had arrived with other prostitutes and dancing girls but had avoided the rest of our men and sought me out and well ... she had her way with me.

If I am being honest, I did not exactly resist. I was drunk and had not seen Aidith for quite a few weeks and ... well, I am a man, after all. It was fun ... I think. What I remember of it, that is. In the morning, she had gone. I thought I had imagined it, but Cuthbert had seen something and had said enough to make me realise it had happened.

I chose to forget all about it. I put it away and ignored it, but Aidith knew something, or suspected something, and her suspicions tainted our relationship and threatened, for a while, to destroy our marriage. Then one day Lilla, the bard and itinerant storyteller and also my friend, drew me to one side and told me that Hussa had revealed to him that Rowenna had given birth to a son around nine months after that drunken liaison and that it appeared I was the father.

Aidith had been upset when I finally confessed. Well, more than just upset. If truth be told, she was very upset but, in the

3

end, she accepted what was the truth. I loved only her. Yet, I felt a responsibility to the boy, too. We had worked our way through all of that and we had decided that I needed to find Hal and protect him from Hussa. He had burnt my mother alive – so only the gods knew what he would do to my son. The decision made I had planned to leave the next day.

That was before Ceorl and Edwin intervened.

We had all been present at the marriage between Edwin and Cwenburg that autumn of the year 610 in the Christian calendar which I have grown used to in my old age. Cwenburg was the daughter of Ceorl who was king of Mercia. It was a celebration of a tentative alliance between the Angles of Mercia and the Welsh of Gwynedd and Powys. This was an alliance which attempted to offset and protect against the rising power of Bernicia and its king Aethelfrith who, aided by my treacherous brother, now ruled all of the English –speaking lands north of the Humber, including my own land of Deira. Aethelfrith had seized Deira, killed its king, Edwin's father, and added it to his own land of Bernicia to create one powerful kingdom – Northumbria.

We had fled with Edwin into exile and, in the six years since, had striven hard to create an alliance to challenge Aethelfrith. That dream – of killing Aethelfrith and reclaiming his own land – burned in Edwin. I was sworn to Edwin and so served that goal too but, if I am honest with myself, my own primary goal was revenge on Hussa for his betrayal and the destruction he had unleashed upon my family.

After that, I hoped for a fertile bit of land to live out my life quietly and grow old with my family around me. Maybe even that cluster of fields and orchards that I had grown up upon. The Villa and its village might be a charred ruin, but a house can be rebuilt, can't it?

But these dreams required alliances to come to fruition and the wedding between Edwin and Cwenburg was an important part of that effort. On the night of that wedding I had agreed with Aidith that I would leave the next day in pursuit of Hal. I had gotten as far as packing my travelling chest and had told my friends of my plans.

The next morning, out of courtesy, I visited Edwin to ask permission to leave on my own business. Winter was not far off and it was unlikely that any threat would come at us either from Northumbria in the north or from Athelfrith's ally West Seaxe in the south before the spring. So, I did not expect any problem with my request. I found him with Ceorl in the great hall that the kings of Mercia owned at Tamwerth. The pair were sipping ale and warming themselves by a fire pit. Thinking this would allow me a chance to give my farewell to both of them at the same time, I greeted them cheerfully. Edwin turned and spotted me.

"Ah, Cerdic. I was just about to send for you," he said. "Join us, please."

"My lord," I bowed my head towards him and then also to Ceorl.

Ceorl waved at a servant who brought another drinking horn and poured me some ale that smelt strong and bitter. Ceorl nodded at me to sip it. I did.

"Delicious," I said

"One of our best, I think," he said proudly.

I glanced at Edwin.

"I would have thought you would be drinking mead," I said, after all, he was on his hunigmonap, or honeymoon, and it was traditional to drink mead at that time.

"I prefer ale," he said.

I nodded.

"My lords, I just wanted to tell you…" I started with my request, but I was cut off by Edwin.

"Let me speak first, my lord earl," he said. "I have news."

He glanced at Ceorl before continuing.

"King Ceorl has gifted to Cwenburg an estate in southern Mercia, in the Temese Valley, as part of the brýdgifu. He has asked me to see to the security of it, on my wife's behalf, of course."

"Oh," I said in surprise. I was slightly taken aback because the brýdgifu, or bride gift, was the dowry paid over by the bride's family to belong to her and to be untouched by her husband. Its purpose was to ensure, in the event of abandonment or the husband's death, that she and her children were provided for. That Ceorl had asked Edwin to arrange its defence clearly meant something more than just the usual exchanging of presents was going on.

Ceorl saw my reaction and nodded.

"Yes, it might be a bit unusual, Cerdic, but I have my reasons. The border between Mercia and the Temese Valley Saxons ran through that area but as the latter had been, until recently, only a minor kingdom and no threat to us, I had not bothered to enforce the border, nor maintain a significant garrison down there. I had much greater concerns over the Welsh to the west and Northumbria to the north.

Now, of course, the situation has changed. The Temese Valley Saxons have become part of a larger West Seaxe kingdom. In addition, as you know, West Seaxe has become an ally of Northumbria. So, I can no longer afford a weak border. I have taken all the lands in that area under my direct rule. West Seaxe has warriors as far north as Doric, thanks to the actions of your brother."

6

I was aware, through Lilla and others, that Hussa had been busy in the area the last few years and, in fact, his efforts had been pivotal in West Seaxe gaining the lands in the Temese Valley. I was also aware that Hussa had negotiated with Ceorl an agreement that Mercia and West Seaxe leave each other alone. At the time, it had suited both sides. Ceorl was looking north and west and West Seaxe wanted to consolidate its gains. Now, though, West Seaxe and Mercia were staring at each other along the upper Temese valley and a confrontation would surely not be long in coming.

"So, you need to garrison the border and prepare for an attack?" I asked.

Ceorl nodded.

"There are no Roman roads heading up the valley. They either go west or north and east. So, West Seaxe will need to use the river to open up a route into Mercia. The next two important locations upriver are Souekesham and Oxenaforda. Cwenburg will act as my representative as the lady of that earldom of South Mercia. However, Cwenburg is young and will need guidance and protection. She will take some of my own household troops and hold Oxenaforda. Edwin will see to the defence of the first likely target, Souekesham."

I had a sudden very nasty feeling that I now knew exactly where this conversation was going.

"Your own men would not be enough, then, I expect." I said, referring to Edwin's own huscarls under Earl Sabert's command.

Edwin shook his head.

"No, Cerdic. We need the Wicstun company there."

The Wicstun company: that had been the name of the local fyrd formed from villagers around the market town of Wicstun which, under my command, accompanied the princes, Edwin and Hereric, alongside Sabert's company. There were other groups of warriors who had been loyal to Edwin and his nephew, including warriors led by Guthred, a lord who had owned lands near to the Villa, and Harald, former earl of Eoforwic, but they were both in Cantia with Prince Hereric who had chosen to try to gain support from the oldest Saxon kingdom for an attempt to challenge Aethelfrith. So, as they were hundreds of miles away, they were no immediate use and, as a result, if Edwin was being asked to garrison this Souekesham, he needed me to do it.

"When do we leave?" I asked.

"Soon. Cwenburg and I will spend the rest of our hunigmonap between the estates. Then, I imagine, I will reside at Souekesham and she in Oxenaforda."

He did not seem bothered about being separated a lot of the time. Then again, this was a political marriage and, whilst the two appeared content enough, no one was pretending there had been a romance involved.

I stood up and pushed my stool backwards.

"Very well. I will get ready."

Edwin leant over and put a hand on my arm.

"A moment, Cerdic., You wanted to mention something, didn't you?"

I stared at him as I pondered asking him if I might be allowed to go and search for my son. Now did not seem an appoiate time, however. I shook my head.

"It will wait. I will talk to you about it later," I said.

'Later' was in fact a good few weeks later, after we marched to Souekesham and settled into our new home. At first it had been just the men of the Wictsun Company and the Royal Guard but then, as there was land to farm on the fertile plains on either side of the river Temese and an estate to manage, we had sent for our families. Our entourage had grown considerably in the years of our exile and I was not the only man who was married. Many of the company had either taken families along when we fled Deira, as had I, or met and married Welsh or Angle women they met on our travels. Some of the boys who had been just eight years old when we left the Villa were now warriors in the ranks alongside their fathers or older brothers. We had all found a home in Gwynedd but now the same families had moved into the farmsteads and villages of Cwenburg's earldom in southern Mercia.

At the heart of the estate, and indeed the reason we had come, was the crossing over the Temese. The river left Oxenaforda and headed south before, a few miles east of Souekesham, dividing into two. One loop of the river went off to the south whilst the main waterway headed west past Souekesham which lay along the north bank of the Temese. Numerous streams and lesser rivers fed into it, including the River Ock which emptied its waters into the Temese just west of Souekesham.

Beyond the Ock, the Temese turned south between a hamlet called Cullaham on the east bank and Sudstone on the west and then eastwards to eventually reach Doric. A few miles south of Souekesham, it was joined by that other loop or branch of the river. Thus, much of the land between Doric and Souekesham consisted of a large island called Andersey. The island was partially a marshland along the riverbanks, which proved to be an ideal home for waterfowl. In the centre of the island the land was dotted with copses and woodland thick with undergrowth. It was no use for crops but made an enjoyable hunting site. The Mercian kings had even built a small hunting lodge there which Cwenburg made use of.

As Ceorl had explained to me, there were no Roman roads between Doric and Souekesham. The loop of river that had now become a frontier was, in those ancient times, literally a back water of no significance deep inside Roman held Britain. The plains here were frequently flooded, very marshy and unsuited to the types of roads the Romans used to build. The river was the easiest route between the two and, as a result, the back water was now fortified borderland. Any attempt to expand northwards towards Oxenaforda would necessitate the capture of Souekesham. Approaching the town via the direct route would mean crossing the Temese twice: once into Andersey island and then, having crossed the marshes, again across the ford between Souekesham and Andersey. The ford was narrow, making an attack difficult.

There were two other possible angles of approach. One would be to come by boat and then storm the town from the river, but that would be easily foiled by the use of a chain of tree trunks floated out across the river which we indeed constructed and deployed shortly after our arrival.

So, that left the option of following the river along the western side through the settlement of Sudstone and so coming to Souekesham from the west – the inland side. This route would allow an army to deploy more easily, less impeded by marshes and woodland than in an assault over Andersey.

Generations that had gone before us had spotted that weakness and had come up with a solution. A series of three defensive ditches and an earthern embankment had been constructed. The fortifications were very old, we learnt. Lilla, who had been at the wedding and accompanied us to Souekesham, introduced me to a monk who was in the town acting as a healer to a household where several children were suffering from a fever. We had met him when we visited one of the two taverns in the town.

"This is Ealdwig. He is a brother at a monastery called Abbedun which is a few miles away. Ealdwig, tell Lord Cerdic what you told me about this place."

Ealdwig was a friendly – looking fellow, somewhat overweight with a cheerful smile but little hair. What hair he did have was now turning grey.

He nodded enthusiastically.

"Well, as I was saying to your young friend here," he nodded at Lilla, "there has been a town here since even before the Romans came, and the locals boast that it is the oldest town in Britain."

I snorted dismissively.

"Locals will say anything they think might sell more ale or mead," I said. "How long have you monks been here, then?"

"Now, there is a story there, too," he said.

I grunted. "I thought there might be."

"I will tell it you, if you buy me a beer." Ealdwig said with another beaming smile.

"Don't you monks have any money?" I asked.

"Well, I was once a hunter and a trapper in the woods around here before I became a monk. So, in those days, I did have some. Now, however, I am sworn to poverty."

Lilla laughed.

"Which does not seem to prevent you finding ways to acquire refreshment when you want it," he said passing a tankard to the monk.

There was something likeable about the man, so I handed over some copper pieces to the tavern keeper and soon another round of ale was slapped down on our table.

I pulled a stool forward, took a long gulp from my tankard and nodded at the monk to go on.

"My brethren founded our house up on the hills north of here over one hundred and fifty years ago. His name was Aebbe and he was one of the few men to survive the Treachery of the Long Knives?"

I burped. "What is that, then?"

"Well, have you heard of King Hengist?"

"Vaguely. A king in Cantia, I think, some time ago," I said.

"Cerdic, I am shocked," Lilla said, hurt. "Have you not listened to my stories? Did you not pay attention when we were in Cantia to their bards?"

I shrugged. "Well, a little, yes."

"Not enough, it seems. I apologise for my ignorant companion, brother. Please, go on."

"Well, Hengist was the first of your peoples to step foot in Britannia, down in Cantia. He came at the invitation of the High King Vortigern, but, later, Hengist fought Vortigern and killed his son. There was an attempt at peace instigated, so it is said, by Hengist, but he was, again, being treacherous because, before he and his men went to the meeting at the great stone circle, he told them to hide small blades in their shoes.

Then, in the middle of the feast, the Saxon warriors produced their knives and slew all the British lords, sparing only Vortigern who was ransomed. Few others survived, but one of them was a monk, Aebbe, who had been present, blessing the food. He escaped and fled here and founded our house up on its hill. The place was named after him from then on, but the town, here by the river, existed already.

Indeed, soon afterwards, your own people arrived led by a warlord called Soueke. Aebba would have a good reason to fear this, given what had happened, but he welcomed Soueke and, despite the Saxon lord being a pagan and he a Christian, they found common ground. The Saxons provided fish from the river and grain from the fields."

"As well as ale?" I put in.

"As well as ale," the monk smiled. "In return, we monks had skills in healing the newcomers found of value. In addition, the new lord may have been pagan, but he now ruled a population mostly of British Christians that we could provide with spiritual sustenance. The Saxons in the town and we monks on the hill have gotten on well ever since."

I glanced around at the non-descript tavern thinking how strange things happen in the most unassuming places.

Chapter Two
Getting to work
Spring 611

Whether all that Ealdwig told me was true or not, our role was to garrison these defences – the ditch and embankment, whatever its age, and also the ford. It would be across one or the other that any attack from West Seaxe must occur. After arriving, I had ordered that a wooden palisade be built on the embankment and the men had been busy for a couple of weeks felling trees in woodland nearby and building the fortifications.

Here Ealdwig proved quite useful. In leading us to the best locations of suitable trees, he saved us days of searching.

"For a monk, you know the land pretty well," I commented.

"The woodland and forests, yes. It was my job before I became a monk to know them, so I could track game and feed my family," he said with a shrug.

"So, why did you become a monk?" I asked as we watched Eduard and Aedann chop up the trunk of an ancient oak tree. "Were you not happy as a hunter, providing for your family?"

When he did not reply I turned to glance at him. His expression was distant.

"Did I ask the wrong question?"

"I had a son and a wife. They both died in the plagues. Do you remember the plagues, they were about about eight years ago?"

I nodded. I remembered them all too well.

"My father died at that time and others, too, in my village. I am sorry, Ealdwig, to bring back painful memories."

"Don't worry. You were not to know. Anyway, I was unable to do anything to help them. So, I decided then that I wanted to learn healing, so I might help other families. The abbey had a reputation for healing the sick, so I became a novice. Now, I seem to be the man they send out when the villagers and the woodsmen fall sick. So, I would say God has me in the place he wants me to be."

Not knowing how to respond, I patted him on the shoulder.

"Well, I don't know about your God or my gods, but I certainly think you are in the right place to help me. For that, I am thankful," I said.

After we had fortified the town, we had seen to provisioning the garrison and had taken over several large huts and, in particular, an ale hall which became Edwin's dwelling. Aidith had taken a liking to the hunting lodge and, after we arrived, had spent the first few weeks, whilst I was building walls and getting to know Ealdwig, getting the place organised according to her liking. The wife of the lord was, for our people, the head of the household. It was she that took charge of the provisioning of the estate, the storage, preservation and rationing of the food stuffs. It was she that wore the keys – the keys to the storerooms which were kept locked. They were both how she exercised her power and, at the same time, the very symbols of her authority. Somehow, I felt she would be one day buried with her keys.

What do I mean by that?

Well, usually, when one such lady died, the keys were given to her successor just as a warrior's sword would be passed on to his heir. Sometimes, in the case of a warrior, when one dies who had been significantly powerful, their sword would, instead, be buried with them.

Rarely too, when a lady of significance died, her keys would be buried with her. In such a case, we were telling the gods that here lay a woman of power and strength who should be permitted to join them. I always believed that Aidith was such a woman.

So, Aidith took command of the estate at Andersley, royal lodge of the kings of Mercia, and soon everything was running smoothly.

Which was fine until Cwenburg first visited the garrison bringing with her two companies of her father's warriors which had been allocated to the southern earldom and so to her service. Cwenburg's family owned the estate and so, of course, as the most senior lady present, she was, by right, the head of the household. As such, she would give orders to the servants and stewards. It was small things to begin with – at Aidith's request Ealdwig had located for her some juniper branches with which she set to smoking joints of ham from pigs that had been slaughtered that autumn. This coincided with the arrival of the Mercian princess.

"What is that awful smell?" she asked.

"Ham smoking over juniper. It will make a nice, sweet –tasting meat come Yuletide, my lady," Aidith replied.

"Stop it at once! You will use beechwood for hams and bacon. I don't like the flavour you get from juniper," Cwenburg replied and flounced off to her chambers.

She was not there long before she emerged carrying bundle of rosemary as well as the last of the autumnal flowers and river plants.

"What is this?" she asked.

"Its to make your room smell pleasant, my lady," Aidith said patiently.

"Well, remove them all. They make me sneeze!" Cwenburg commanded.

"As you wish," Aidith said in a particular tone of voice that made me look up at her. I knew that tone. It sounds very polite and proper, but it is a warning sign that, deep down, the cooking pot of her emotions is starting to boil. If it was a pot of briw, now would be the time to move it away from the heat. The trouble was, I was uncertain if that would be possible in this case. I tried, anyway.

"My love, you seem to be getting a bit agitated," I said that night when we were in bed. "You just need to endure the princess for a little longer. She won't always be here."

"I will try," Aidith said wearily.

"Maybe she won't be as much of a pain in the neck tomorrow," I said hopefully.

Hope however can be easily dashed.

The pot boiled over the following day.

It was pepper that was the cause of the problem. Aidith was, again, supervising the preserving of meat – pork, in this case. This was being rubbed with a mixture of rock salt, sea salt, honey and a tiny amount of black pepper. This last ingredient was rare, exotic and expensive, as it was not grown in Britannia and had to be purchased from traders who brought it from Frankia, who in turn got it via Byzantium from the fabled lands of Arabia and even further east. As such, conscious of the costs, Aidith was being frugal with its use. Sabert happened to be in the room as he had come to visit the estate to discuss rations for the company and I was showing him the progress we were making.

Cwenburg interrupted the process when a dozen hams had been rubbed in the mixture. She entered the outhouse that was being used for the process and dipped a finger in the powder and tasted it.

17

"Why are you not using enough pepper?" she asked.

"I did not want to use too much," my wife told her.

"Why on earth not? Pepper gives the meat more flavour."

"I know that," Aidith replied through gritted teeth. "But we only have a few ounces, my lady."

"Why have you not bought more, then?" Cwenburg demanded. "Surely, that was the obvious thing to do?"

Which is when Aidth lost her temper.

"I did not buy anymore because I am not a blasted, fussy princess with more money than sense!" she spat out. "If you want me to buy more of the blasted stuff, give me some more blasted silver."

We all fell silent and stared at Aidith, and then at Cwenburg. Sabert went quite pale and seemed ready to say something when, quite unexpectantly, Cwenburg laughed. We all watched her in astonishment. Finally, she stopped and looked at me and Sabert.

"I like her, Lord Cerdic, Lord Sabert. She says what she is thinking… eventually, anyway. I want her to run my household here, if that is acceptable to you all."

Sabert and I were lost for words so just nodded.

"As for you, my dear, I will do as you say and give you control of my purse in this estate. You can run it as you see fit. What do you say?" Cwenburg asked.

Aidith looked thoughtful.

"If I do so, I will still be careful with the pepper."

Cwenburg smiled.

"I should think so, too. It is blasted expensive stuff, you know."

So, that is how Aidith ended up running the household at the hunting lodge. The Mercian princess had brought few companions and, as she appreciated frankness, with which

18

Aidith was well equipped, the two moved on from this un-promising and rather awkward beginning to a companion-ship.

Cwenburg was often away at Oxenaforda and so, whilst the lodge was hers, in effect, it became ours. A sizeable hall of our own, affording a degree of independence and yet close enough to a substantial settlement nearby, brought back echoes of our childhoods spent in the Villa and nearby Wicstun and so became home to us quickly enough.

Once the defences were addressed and the men and their fam-ilies accommodated, we settled down to watch for movement from the south, but as the days shortened and the leaves fell, it became apparent that no attack from West Seaxe was forthcom-ing. So, I decided it was now time to ask Edwin for permission to leave, confident that little would happen in my absence.

The conversation did not go well.

"You want to go where?" had been Edwin's reply.

We were in his hall and had just gone over reports from scouts who had worked their way down the Temese as well as over to-wards the Codswald hills. To a man, they had come back with the same news. Or rather the same lack of news. There was no sign of an army gathering. No camps had been spotted, nor clouds of dust on the horizon, nor any smudge of smoke above watchfires. Nei-ther was there any evidence of supplies being stockpiled. All was peaceful and quiet along the frontier between Mercia and West Saexe.

"I need to go wherever my son might be. West Saexe, per-haps, to start with. Whilst the truce lasts between Ceolwulf and Ceorl, it should be safe enough to go to Witancaestre."

"Cerdic, you can't leave. Not now," Edwin said with a shake of the head.

19

"Now is exactly the time to go. There was frost last night and storms are coming. There surely won't be an attack now. Not until spring, at the earliest."

"You don't know that for certain, Cerdic," Sabert said wearily. "Ceolwulf of West Saexe is an ally of Aethelfrith, and we all know how cunning he can be. He caught us all by surprise in Deira and I don't plan for that to happen again."

Edwin was nodding vigoursly.

"Exactly! I would not put it past him to talk Ceolwulf into a winter attack."

"With what?" I asked, exasperated. "There is no phantom army out there."

"Even so, I have made a decision. You will stay."

I stared at them both and said no more. Well, not until the next day when I tried again. Then again, the week after – all with the same outcome. Winter had come in earnest and Yuletide had been celebrated and was long past, and still there was no sign of an attack. I had ended up sitting out the short days and long nights in that town watching the snow come and go and ice forming on the Temese. The ice was so thick that a man in armour could walk on it. Well, most men, anyway. Eduard proved a bit too heavy and the ice cracked under him, plunging the oaf into the cold waters where he almost drowned before we had managed to drag him back out.

"What did you do that for, you idiot?" I had asked him when we lay panting by the fire, Eduard stripped naked and wrapped in furs.

"I saw Cuthbert and Mildrith having fun on the river, so, thought I should join them," he managed to gasp between shivers.

"Cuthbert and Mildrith combined probably weigh less than you, you great auroch," I replied.

Eduard said nothing and just sneezed.

The fact that I recall that incident goes to show how little else happened that winter. Certainly, no attack. We just sat about, tried to keep warm and waited for spring. My impatience grew with each passing week.

Gradually, the snow vanished, the ice melted, and the first signs of life returned to the barren land – early spring flowers like thimbleweeds and daffodils nudging their way out into the light accompanied by the songs of the robins, doves and sparrows greeting the sun. Even then, I felt it too early for an attack and tried my luck with Edwin again failing to get the answer I wanted. We had been seeing to the storage of supplies of flour and salted meat that Ceorl had sent to us. Edwin had again denied my request and now, finally, my temper snapped.

"All through this cursed winter we have been stuck in this dung heap of a place. We have seen neither sight nor heard sound of any enemy. I could have been gone and back weeks ago!"

"Calm yourself, Cerdic," Sabert said.

"Calm myself! It's my son I am worried about, and I am stuck here and not searching for him! Why, I ask you?"

"You know why, my lord earl," Edwin replied. "We have to do this. Then, maybe, Ceorl will be persuaded to help us challenge Aethelfrith and I can regain my crown."

"That is all you bother about, that damned crown!" I shouted. "Does it ever occur to you that there are others here, apart from you, who have our own dreams and concerns? Or are you too wound up with your own importance?"

"Cerdic, that is enough!" Sabert said. "Mind your words when you talk to your king."

His chastisement pulled me up. Maybe I had spoken in haste and let my temper get the best of me.

"I am sorry, Lord, but if I could just have a few days to look for him. That is all…"

"No, Cerdic. For the last time, no! You can't go!" Edwin said and stomped off towards his hall.

Which is how I found myself on this cold battlement looking out over ploughed fields, still waiting for the seed, explaining to Cuthbert and Eduard that I had failed to get permission to leave.

"Cheer up, Cerdic," my other friend, Aedann, said as he joined us. "We will find Hal in time."

I stared at him.

"Would that satisfy you? Did it when it was your own family?"

He pursed his lips as he thought about that, his dark eyes and dark hair enhancing the natural brooding nature he had. As a youth, he had hung about the village, standing in shadows of trees and the eaves of houses watching us and saying little. I gather from what Aidith told me that some of the girls had found his behaviour mysterious and even enticing. My friends and I just found it annoying.

"You are right, of course," he replied after a moment, looking distant, and I knew he was thinking of his father Caerfydd. Aedann, like his parents Caerfydd and Gwen, had been slaves at the Villa, my family home in the Northumbrian kingdom of Deira. It was a crumbling Roman house and my grandfather, rather unusually for my people, had moved into it when he had arrived, leading a party of Angles from across the sea.

Aedann's family had been living there and were taken as slaves. The winters had been harsh and the harvests poor, not helped by the incessant raids and warfare between our peoples, and my grandfather's huscarls provided protection and stability, and so, whilst they could not have been happy about it,

Caerfydd and Gwen had accepted their fate stoically. But Ae-dann, growing up as a slave, knowing that his people had once ruled the land that my people had taken from him, had resented it.

We had been just seventeen when there was a raid on the Villa by the Welsh tribes of nearby Elmet. Many of our people had been dragged away, including my sister, Mildrith, and Ae-dann's parents. Aedann had broken the rules and, as a slave, taken up arms to try to rescue his own family. He had run away and, for a while, it was thought he was actually a spy or agent for the Elmetae. The local warriors of the Wicstun company with myself, Eduard and Cuthbert in the ranks, had pursued them to an old Roman fort and, in the end, we had rescued our people.

In the process we had seen that Aedann was brave and he-roic and, indeed, had it not been for him, we might not have gotten away – any of us. It had all been in vain, however, as his father died at the fort, though we had managed to find Gwen. Afterwards, I had freed him and as a free man he had sworn allegiance to my family and now served as a trusted huscarl or house warrior – one of my very best swordsmen and now com-mander of a company of his own.

"Sorry… I spoke in haste," I said.

He shook his head. "No need to apologise. I know you are worried about Hal."

I reached out and squeezed his shoulder and was about to reply but Eduard shouted out a warning that interrupted me.

"Scouts in the trees!" he bellowed and pointed out over the palisade, across the bare fields towards the narrow River Ock which flowed into the Temese a hundred paces away.

Over the other side of the little river was a stretch of more barren fields. Beyond them were several copses, some of which we had visited to find our timber for the freshly constructed palisade. There was also a small cemetery amongst those trees where the first Angles to reach this far upriver had been buried.

I leant over the new fortifications and squinted. He was right. There were men there, between the trees and around the low mounds that lay over the ancient bones. At least twenty figures, in fact. I could see no shields and no sign of mail. These were armed with javelins, slings, seaxes and bows: light troops able to move stealthily forward and just as quickly withdraw if we threatened them. A reconnaissance force, perhaps? If so, they might just observe us and move away again when they had assessed the strength of our position.

But they did not pull back. Instead, they held their ground whilst some of their number scampered back into the trees. I sent for Edwin, and he and Sabert joined us as ox horns were sounded, summoning the Wicstun company and the king's company, who now assembled all around us. Our standard of the running wolf on a field of green was placed above us and flapped about in the cool spring breeze.

Over the other side of the river, I could hear more horns beyond the trees and then I saw a company of spearmen emerge between the copses and begin to form up two hundred paces away from us. After a few moments, a second and then a third company joined the first, spreading out the line further west and away from the Temese.

Whoever was commanding the warriors did not wait for much of a build –up. The horns sounded out loud and strident, and the companies advanced towards us. It was a strong force. Including the scouts they had, maybe, double our number. They came on at us, clearly relying on these superior numbers to win the day.

"Form up!" I shouted. "Shield wall!" I looked at Edwin and shrugged.

"Looks like I was wrong. It was not too early for an attack!" I said by way of apology and then drew Catraeth.

I led Eduard, Cerdic and Aedann towards the gateway that pierced the palisade. It was the weak spot in our defences and Cerdic son of Cenred was going to have to hold it. Or die trying...

Chapter Three
Sword or Axe?
Spring 611

The Wicstun company was the name given to the fyrd that would gather from the town of Wicstun and the surrounding villages at the call of the earl of the southern marches of Deira when he, in turn, was so ordered by the king. In my childhood the company had formed only briefly to see off bandits and raiders under the command of the then earl, Lord Wallace, a friend of my father. Wallace had taken the company into battle at Catraeth, where he had died, leaving me in temporary command. The company and I had held the gates against the might of Owain of Rheged and it was there that the beginning of a reputation had been forged, both, I suppose for the company for myself.

That reputation was added to at the great battle of Degsastan where we had been part of the victory over the Scots, Picts and British under Mac Gabhráin alongside our then allies, the Bernicians. Allies became enemies when Bernicia attacked Godmundingham, the Deiran king's fortress, and killed our king, Aethelric. A remnant of the Wicstun company had been some of the few to escape that catastrophe along with the two princes – Edwin who was brother to the king, and Hereric, the king's son, both of whom we accompanied into exile. During our exile, we had fought with the Welsh of Gwyedd at the City of the Giants, against West Seaxe at Boseham Villa, and once more with Gwynedd against the usurper Haiarme at Mathrafal, and many other times in raids and skirmishes. The thirteen years of experience since Catraeth had made those of us who survived strong.

Through that time, others had come to join the company. Firstly, a number of the Wicstun company, who had been separated from us at Godmundingham but managed to escape after a series of adventures, had made their own way out of Deira and found us. Other men came, too, whose own lords had lost lands and rank in Northumbria or others who wandered as leaderless and masterless men which is a terrible fate for a warrior. Having a lord means you have a name and a place to live and food and ale from his table. You have companions and you have a purpose and, of course, a chance for wealth and glory. Masterless men have none of that and are typically despised. From the lowliest farmer to the highest lord, we all need our own lord to swear loyalty to, to fight for and to receive gifts from and to be answerable to. Apart from the king, I suppose, and even they answer to the gods, as must we all. So, men had come to fight under the running wolf, the banner of the Wicstun company.

In addition to the wandering veterans and the new recruits, we had young men of our own. Some of the sons of the villagers were now old enough to take up arms. Cuthwine, my own son, was now almost fourteen and was training under the watchful eye of the now sixty years old Grettir. He and three other boys had just this year become old enough to be inducted into the company, although we had not yet held the ceremony when they would place a hand on the sword of their lord or the captain of their company and swear fealty and allegiance. Traditionally, in the days of my youth, we did this in the spring as companies assembled to train together. In our exile, we had often done this before a battle or a campaign. This surprise attack had happened before we had the chance. I hoped the youths would survive the day, for they would have to fight despite not yet being sworn into our ranks.

So, over the years the company had grown in strength and now numbered more than a hundred men. Enough that, at times, we would split the company, when Eduard might lead almost half on one flank and Aedann the other flank, and I would keep a reserve with me in the centre. The previous winter I had decided to formalise this. I had presented both with their own banner which Aidith had embroidered for me. Both had the running wolf on as both were part of the greater Wicstun company and men need to know from where their fighting spirit and legacy comes. Eduard's, though, showed an axe beneath the wolf, whilst Aedann's portrayed a sword. The companies already had started talking about belonging to Eduard's Axes or Aedann's Swords and I had even had to break up the first fight that erupted from a discussion about who was better and ended up with broken noses and blackened eyes. Both men had, I noticed, started giving their own gifts to their men. They were sharing a little of their own wealth which they had, in turn, gained from me, just as I had from Edwin as a result of the booty of battle and the generosity of our host nations. Here, far from home, that same system of loyalty and gifts was creating a little bit of Deira in the army we were building.

Sabert commanded Edwin's bodyguard company which was formed around the original ten or so men that had fled with him and met up with me and the princes during the fall of Deira. These were other men sworn to the house of Aelle and so to his slain son, King Aethelric, and who had come to believe their oath now was held by Edwin or Hereric. From these we had created a company of royal huscarls to accompany Edwin. Others had gone with Hereric who, at present, was in Cantia.

Along the palisade our little army gathered under five banners – Eduard's axe banner, Aedann's sword, the Wictsun company's running wolf, Sabert's pennant and, bigger than all these, the royal flag of Deira, flapping in the strong cool breeze and signalling to West Seaxe that here a king of Deira stood and was not moving.

From the trees, skirmishers emerged. Men armed with slings, angon short spears or bows. They spread out across the fields on the far side of the river Ock. Some took cover behind a tree stump here or a hedgerow there whilst others knelt down to present a smaller target. For a while, they just stood or crouched and looked at us as we stared back at them. Then I heard a horn sounding from the trees and one of the men stood up from where he had been kneeling out of sight in a ditch, dropped a stone into his sling and whirled it around his head before releasing it at us. The stone flew across the hundred paces or so to bounce off Aedann's shield. A moment later another stone followed and, as if this was the signal to join in, the fifty or so other missile troops began pummelling us with stone or arrow.

A few men armed with javelins crept within range and released their weapons. Most fell short, sailed overhead or, like the stone aimed at Aedann, impacted harmlessly upon the shields of our company, earning them shouts of derision from our ranks. One or two of our men, confident that there was little danger, turned their backs on the enemy, lifted their tunics and dropped their britches to show their arses. One of them even did a little dance, waving his rear end around like a bucking horse. This continued until a more accurate angon pieced the shoulder of the man next to him, Alfred, who had been with me since we left Deira. With a shout of pain mixed with outrage, he fell back, and I thought he had been killed but he was soon back on his feet, blood surging from a wound that was not mortal though clearly painful. He cursed and fell back to have it bound

29

by Aidith, Mildrith and the other women who were gathered just behind the men with dressings for the wounded and ale for the fit. I noticed that Ealdwig and one of the other monks from the nearby abbey were helping them. He seemed to spend a lot of time down from his hilltop retreat on errands in the town or, I thought to myself, more likely visiting the alehouse. I nodded at him and he returned the gesture.

I turned my attention back to the fighting. The man who had drawn the ire of the enemy skirmishers now looked a little pale and elected, wisely, to get dressed again and take cover behind his shield. He shot me an embarrassed smile and I shook my head at him but with no particular venom. After all, we all deal with the tension in different ways.

Close by me was Cuthwine, standing in the second rank with other untried youths. His eyes were wide, though whether this was through excitement or fear, I could not tell.

"You alright, son?" I asked.

He turned to me and nodded.

"Yes… it's just so… real," he said and then smiled at me. A moment later he brandished his spear aggressively to show me he was fine.

I knew how he felt. Looking at him, I was taken back fourteen years and was suddenly a young lad again, standing in that field near the village where Cuthbert, Eduard and I fought our first fight. I was, at that time, a few years older than Cuthwine but no less callow. We had listened to the tales of the bards and poets like Lilla for years. Heroic tales they were, indeed, full of warrior kings and amazing, monstrous beasts or mighty champions. The heroes were figures to admire, some decended from the gods, some with the strength of giants or with skills to rival Tiw the warrior god, Thunor the god of thunder or Woden the father of the gods. In those stories, warfare was exciting and thrilling and the true test of a man's courage and honour. Then, like me in that field near a smoking village standing over the body of a raider I had killed with the crackle of burning hovels close at hand, or Cuthwine here in this small town a long way from home with an enemy about to descend on us, it is then that you realise that it is not just a story. The spears are sharp and the enemy warriors strong, and you are mortal. Reality floods in upon you. Men would die here this day.

Circling above us, invisible to mortal eyes but as real as the earth beneath my feet or the sword in my hand, the Valkyrie would have already arrived. Their job was to choose the fated amongst us. Men whose time has come. These men would die today in the glory of battle and this night would dine at Woden's table alongside those who, in life, were enemies but would then be united as the glorious dead.

Some men, like Eduard, glory in that reality. Eduard's view was, 'why worry about dying?' If today was the day that a Valkyrie would reach down and carry his soul to Valhalla, nothing he did could prevent that. If, however, he was not fated to die, then nothing mere men could do would harm him.

Others of us were not quite so sanguine. Some panic and run, most of us just try to stay alive. Cuthwine gulped as an arrow sped past his head a mere four inches away. Then he shrugged, grasped his spear harder and hunkered down behind his shield, waiting for whatever happened next.

The bombardement with stone, arrow and javelin continued for a time but with diminishing returns as we took what shelter we could behind our shields and endured the fussilade.

"Get a bloody move on!" Eduard shouted.

31

There was a grunt of agreement from most of the men. We all knew what he meant. We were pretty safe whilst this shower of missiles continued. But, eventually, they would move forward and attack and it would be that moment, when their shield wall met our shield wall, that the battle would be decided. The waiting for that moment to arrive was sometimes worse than the clattering of stone and dart on our shields.

I sighed as things dragged on. We took it in turns to leave the lines and find the barrels of ale setup on tables behind the walls. Ealdwig was supervising the distribution with Lilla assisting and I gave them both a sceptical look.

"How surprising to find you two where there is beer," I said as the monk poured me half a cup.

Lilla just winked at me but the monk, holding his hands out in supplication, adopted an innocent tone.

"I am just a humble servant, Lord."

I snorted.

"A humble servant who likes beer. I thought you Christians were supposed to be holy all the time. You know – give glory to God and all that kind of thing."

The monk nodded.

"I am doing. After all, the good book says, 'Whether therefore ye eat, or drink, or whatsoever ye do, do all to the glory of God'. That's in Corinthians, that is."

"Well, Cerdic, you have to admit that, if that is the man's philosophy, he certainly is doing it properly," Lilla said.

I laughed and sipped my ale.

Ale helped steady the nerves and give fire to our courage. There was some bread and cheese and I wolfed some down and then finished my ale. I ate too quickly, and a crumb of cheese found its way into my windpipe. I coughed and spluttered.

"Swallow properly or you will choke on it!" Aidith shouted from where she was tying off the dressing of the man who had taken the angon in the shoulder. "And wipe those crumbs from your tunic," she added.

"You do realise this might be covered in blood in a short while?" I shouted back, pointing at my tunic.

"That is not the point," she said, walking over to brush me down.

"Of course not, dear," I replied.

She poked me in the shoulder.

"Ouch."

"Don't be a baby," she said, but then gave me a quick kiss on the cheek. She did not tell me to keep safe, though. We always felt it was best to not tempt fate. I looked at her. She was wearing a sturdy green tunic and pinafore, and, at her belt, she had her small seax. A tool she needed when cutting dressings to size. She also had a pouch which contained copper needles and thread, ready for repairing the wounds we might receive. She would do her bit during the battle, but I suddenly was afraid for her. What if we lost the battle and the enemy broke in? What would be her fate, and what would be that of Mildrith, my sister, and Sian, my daughter. Despite the stories of the Valkyries, there were few warrior women amongst our race. Maybe wives of nobles and kings whose husband had died and were strong enough or had enough support to rule in their stead would fit this mould. These women were rare and most never learnt the way of the warrior or trained for battle. I glanced down at Aidith's seax. It would not be a defence if an enemy came at her with sword and shield. If we survived the battle, I would rectify that.

A few moments later, horns sounded from the enemy army and I pushed back through the ranks and retrieved shield and spear from Grettir. I risked a peek around the edge of my shield. The skirmishers were wading across the shallow River Ock not far from its confluence with the Temese, a short way down river from the obstacle of our floating tree trunks which, having been chained together, blocked the river and would prevent a water-borne assault.

Once over the river, the skirmishers spread out and took cover whilst they continued to shower us with missiles and Cuthbert and his own light troops replied in kind. Although outnumbered, Cuthbert and his men were protected by the palisade. The enemy conversely only had any scattered cover they might find. As a result, the exchange was relatively ineffectual, but several enemy skirmishers lay dead or wounded outside our fortifications. The enemy commander must have decided these losses were unnecessary and that the fight would, after all, be decided by the clash of shield wall as a horn now tooted out a series of notes, and, cautiously, their skirmishers withdrew back across the stream, leaving their fallen behind.

We cheered this minor victory, but the cheer died on our breath as we saw what was now crossing the same stream. A large body of warriors were approaching in a dense shield wall. Once across our side of the Ock, they halted to reform and then began clattering spear against shield and chanting, calling on Tiw, the one –handed warrior god, to give them victory. Our own men were now calling on the same god, or maybe Woden or Thunor, to grant us favour. Not far away, I could hear Aedann praying to his Christian God and I wondered if any of the men that opposed us were Christian. I had met the missionaries from Rome who were already at work in West Saexe and elsewhere, and Abbedunne was not the only abbey or monastery dotted around the land where the British still followed their religion.

An idle thought came to me as to what factors the gods used when hearing our prayers. How did they decide who to grant favour to, who to save, and who would die?

Another strident signal echoed out across the meadow and such philosophical thoughts left me as I prepared to defend the battlements.

You would think that each battle would be difficult to forget. Each would have enough horror, bloodshed and death that they would leave a memory forever embedded in my mind. Certainly, it was the case that the battles of Catraeth and Degsastan, which we had fought long before this day by the river, were so firmly written with runes of bloody red in my memory as to be impossible to forget. Likewise, later occasions, like the battles of Chester and the River Idle, still, at that stage, in my future also are as clear today as in those far off days.

But that battle, which we never really gave a name to, is almost forgotten. Its details indistinct save for one moment, which I see with clarity back through forty years. It was the moment that Cuthwine earned his place in the company.

As much as I can remember, after a build up where horn blows and drumbeats intensified until finally reaching a thunderous peak, the West Seaxe had charged the pallisade. The attack was led by a confident –looking red –headed veteran under the griffin banner showing that at least one of the enemy warbands present belonged to the king. Ceolwulf himself was not here, I was sure of that, but had sent a trusted lieutenant to command the assault. He seemed to have taken personal responsibility to heart because he was at the head of the attack about to fall upon us.

A company of big bastards in full mail armour and sturdy steel helms, and wielding huge axes or wide-bladed swords and massive shields, each rather heavier than I would wish to lift, formed up into a wedge and assaulted the gateway. Here, sheltered under the shields of their comrades from the intense rain of stones, rocks and missiles we directed at them, they set to with their axes and soon turned the sturdy gates we had built the previous autumn into firewood.

With the red –headed warrior still at their head, they then reformed and surged through the gates, smashing into Eduard's men holding the gateway. So fierce was that charge that they had actually broken through and threatened to envelop our lines from behind. Eduard himself was up on the palisade to one side of the gate and, seeing the danger, moved at once to the gap and threw himself off the palisade, right on to the front rank of the enemy, just missing the redhead but still breaking the neck of the man he landed on, and then cut several down before the sheer numbers overwhelmed him.

I saw him fall and, in an instant, his foes were swarming about him like ants around a piece of rotten fruit fallen from a tree. Spears and swords were lifted, and I felt sure he would die that day. I called out his name, began to move towards the gate. I tried to reach him but there were just too many of our men and the enemy between us and, despite pushing and shoving and a liberal use of my elbows, I just could not break through.

"Bugger!" I said.

That was when I heard the blowing of an ox horn behind me. I looked around to see that Cuthwine had spotted the threat and was leading a small group of youths the same age, the youngest and most inexperienced of the warriors at the battle, straight into the attack. They were trained with weapons but had not fought before. As a result, they had no experience and had not yet learnt the trade of a warrior. It also meant they did not know

36

when an action was wreckless and likely to lead to their deaths. What they lacked in wisdom and skill, they made up for in courage and youthful vigour.

Their attack took the enemy by complete surprise and I saw Cuthwine thrust a spear at a warrior bent over Eduard and pierce the man's throat. He fell, allowing Eduard to roll towards Cuthwine. A sword was raised by another warrior, the red – headed champion who had reached my friend and my son and who clearly intended landing a killing blow upon the still prone Eduard. Cuthwine knelt and raised his shield over both himself and Eduard so that the sword blow merely clattered off the board.

He had, by now, dropped his spear and drawn his seax which he thust up into the belly of the redhead. The man groaned and collapsed, drenching both Eduard and Cuthwine in blood. Eduard seized the dead man's fallen sword and now, coming up into a crouch, knelt beside my son and slew another man. That let Cuthwine scuttle forward, pick up Eduard's dropped axe and swing it wildly around, scattering the assailants who lost heart and hesitated.

There is a moment in battle when the outcome is uncertain. The fates may decide who will live and die but I still believe that a man's actions can influence that outcome. The scales of fate can be swung one way or another. The norns were watching and weaved their threads, and the West Seaxe hesitated. A strong leader on their side might still this day have been able to rally them and bring them back to the offensive, kill Eduard and Cuthwine, and even now break out into the town. The enemy had lost their commander when Cuthwine had killed the redhead and no one else amongst the company seemed to be a leader. Thus, the moment was passing without action on part of

West Seaxe. The opportunity to rally the men who had breached the gates seemed to have slipped away. Indeed, action right now might sway matters the other way.

I raised Catraeth and brought it down with a clatter on the rim of my shield. I repeated the action, again and again.

"Ut, Ut, Ut!!" I began chanting and, next to me, Grettir took up the old battle cry and the beat, as did Aedann with his men further down the palisade and Sabert and Edwin's men beyond them.

"Out, out, out!" it meant. 'Get out, save yourselves, run away for we are coming to get you!' We bellowed it and it echoed down from that palisade and over the fields.

The shock of the counterattack Cuthwine had led and the loss of their commander, as well as some of their best men at the gate, had shaken the enemy from their own certainty of purpose. Now, the thunderous pounding of blade on shield and the threat of that ancient war cry was too much for the West Seaxe. The enemy morale shattered. One man dropped a shield, followed by a second. In an instant, dozens had dropped shield and sword and they were now running back towards the stream, across the fields and into the woods, past the cemetry and out of sight.

The battle, whose name I still can't recall, was won at that moment and the West Seaxe were fleeing. Let us call it the Battle of Souekesham. Whatever the name, we had won it. I left the men cheering on the battlements and made my way over to Eduard who was being helped to his feet by Cuthwine. Cuthwine handed him back his axe.

Eduard took the axe, appeared to think about it for a moment, and then handed it back.

"Keep it, Cuthwine, with my thanks."

Cuthwine smiled and hefted the heavy axe from hand to hand.

Eduard reached over and patted him on the shoulder.

"With your father's permission, I would be honoured if you would join my company."

Cuthwine grinned at Eduard and nodded.

"Yes...yes I will." he managed at last.

Around us, the companies cheered, and my son was declared a warrior and a member of Eduard's Axes on the very battlefield where he had fought his first battle. The other boys who Cuthwine had led on that counterattack were also inducted into the company, some in Eduard's warband and others in Aedann's.

I stood there still with memories of my own first battle, the day of that raid on the Villa, playing across my mind. In some ways, I know I should have taken the axe from him and told him to refuse Eduard's offer. But you know what, I was bloody proud. Would this prove to be a fateful day? Do I look back from old age and regret not intervening? This is my story and you will have to wait to find out when I am ready to tell you. Anyway, it was not my choice to make. Cuthwine was becoming a man and a man makes his own decisions.

Lilla, I noticed, was already strumming his lyre and tapping his feet as he hummed to himself. He saw me looking at him and winked.

"Got an idea for a new song I am going to call the Warrior's First Battle. I will sing it tonight after everyone has had their fill of ale."

"Hopefully, that will make the singing not seem so bad," I replied but I was only joking. Somehow, the fact that Cuthwine would soon have a song about him composed and sung by Lilla made me even prouder.

Ealdwig and his brother monk and Aidith and her ladies set to treating the wounded. Aidith herself found us and saw to dressing scratches and wounds that Eduard and Cuthwine had received. Watching her work, I considered again my thoughts before the battle. I had always believed it was my job to protect my family, it was, indeed, the promise implicit in our vows when we married, and I would never break those vows. I would protect them all as long as I could. Yet, there was more to protecting her than standing between her and the enemy. My sword alone may not be enough. She should be able to defend herself, and so should Sian. I would start the following day, that is, if she wanted to, of course.

She saw me looking at her.

"What is it?" she asked.

"Aidith, I need to ask you something." I said.

Chapter Four
A family man
Spring 611

Rolf turned to stare at his companion. "What do you mean, it does not matter to you anymore?" he asked, incredulous.

Hussa shrugged and did not reply. A strong wind coming in off the German sea buffeted them both, as well as the king's banners above them, but they ignored it. Rolf was the larger of the two, a man with a sour expression and a face full of scars. He now scowled down at the smaller of the pair, whose hair was a shade that suggested he had once been a redhead, but his thirty years had now faded it to a deeper brown colour. A lighter, more agile man with clever eyes.

"How long have I known you?" Rolf asked, at last.

Hussa frowned as he thought over the question. He lent on the wooden palisade of the fortress they were patrolling and stared out at a pair of seagulls who called to each other harshly as they circled the harbour far below them. One spotted the remains of a fish on the deck of a boat and dived upon it.

"I don't know. Ten years, maybe. Ever since I found you in that shitheap village that stank of damp wool. Thought I was doing you a favour, taking you away from all those sheep. A decade or more you have dragged your sorry hide after me all over the length of Britannia from Alt Clut to the narrow sea."

Rolf nodded. The first seagull had now been joined by the other and they each tugged at the dead fish as well as snapping angrily at each other. Rolf turned away from the entertainment and leant back against the palisade, tilting his head to ask another question.

41

"In all that time, you have had drive, purpose and ambition. You have burned with a lust for the fire of glory, like a bird flying toward the sun, a moth toward a candle flame, a hound running after its prey. And all those years I have flown behind you and run beside you, hunting, too, for that glory."

"So?" Hussa replied absently.

Rolf lifted his hands to rub his head in frustration.

"So? So, you have been Aethelfrith's lieutenant. Second to the most powerful man in the land. A man destined to become Bretwalda and dominate all the English lands. It was you that suggested some of the plan that gave him Deira. It was you that snuck in and helped his army take Godmundingham. We, practically on our own, got him to the walls of Din Eidyn. When we left Northmbria and travelled south, no man was more powerful than you, save the king. In the south, you gave Ceolwulf the Thames Valley and destroyed the last British enclave there. What we did in West Saexe gave Aethelfrith the ally in Ceolwulf he needs to destroy Mercia and those Deiran princes. He should have been falling over himself to give you lands and even more power. Yet, now what are you?"

Now Hussa glared at him.

"He still listens to me, Rolf. I am as powerful as I was before."

Rolf snorted

"Woden's balls, you are!"

"I am still with Aethelfrith. Nothing has changed."

"Well, alright, you are here in Bebbanburg, but can you truly say nothing has changed and you hold as much influence over him as you did before we left for the south? We were away for several years. In that time others came to power and drew close to him."

Hussa shrugged and, upon seeing that gesture, a furious expression leapt into Rolf's eyes.

"You truly don't care, do you?"

Hussa said nothing. Rolf almost screamed in exasperation.

"There was a time when the man I knew would have acted swiftly to restore his influence over the king. Yet, now you seem to just let it pass. You have changed – since you have been married and since you recognised Hal as your son."

Hussa frowned. "As I recall, you were all for it when I said I planned to marry Rowenna, and you also seemed to approve of my actions over Hal."

Rolf nodded. "Yes, I was, and I am still very fond of them both. But there has to be a balance between home and hearth and our pursuit of rank, power and glory. Ten years we have been on this path and now you turn away from it."

Hussa shrugged and still said nothing.

"Oh, very well, have it your own way. You don't want to talk about this right now, then fine, but you are going to have to deal with it one day." This said, Rolf stomped away from Hussa around the palisade and then down the steps toward Aethelfrith's hall which lay in the centre of the fortress.

Hussa watched him go. He thought about catching up with his friend but, just then, from further around the fortress, Hussa heard the sound of a child's laughter. Hal, his only son who was now three, was playing with Rowenna, Hussa's wife. Hal had a head full of red hair, whilst Rowenna was a raven –haired beauty. They were accompanied by Rowenna's new maid Bridget. When he had first suggested it, Rowenna had been reluctant to have a maid but Hussa had insisted, saying that a lady should have a household to run. Over the last few days since commencing her work, Bridget had proved a good choice, both capable in her duties but also an amiable companion with a lively sense of humour and an easy conversational style. At the same time, she was not shy with her opinions and very content to return an ill -advised bawdy comment or insult from any of the fighting men with a barbed reply. Appreciative of strong women and despite her misgivings, Rowenna clearly enjoyed her company. Hal liked her too particularly some of the faces she pulled which made him laugh. He was chortling now and Hussa smiled at the sound as he moved towards them. Then he paused a moment and frowned.

That moment he had felt joy and contentment. He had a family that cared about him and he realised that these last few months since they had arrived back in the fortress following his years in West Seaxe had been for him the happiest ever. His own childhood had been most unhappy. Born the bastard son of Lord Cenred, Cerdic's father, and a poor villager, he and his mother had soon been rejected by his father on the insistence of Cerdic's mother, Sunniva. They were forced to survive on the charity of others, including much needed, but equally just as resented, gifts of food from Cenred. His mother had died of the fever when he was little more than a youth, and he had been forced to fend for himself. A deep resentment for Cenred, Cerdic and Cerdic's mother had grown within him, the flames growing until he had had his revenge – fittingly in fire as Sunniva had died in the conflagration Hussa had started, a blaze that had destroyed the Villa that Cerdic and his family had always held so dear. Cenred himself was, by then, dead also, from a plague that had swept through the region. That just left Cerdic for Hussa's vengeance to be complete.

He had always striven for influence and power. Never particularly for wealth. Wealth simply served that quest for power and glory. Nothing else had mattered and, if he was aware of the happiness others enjoyed, he had never given it much thought.

44

Domestic bliss and the happiness of family life seemed feeble and weak rewards compared with the opportunities for advancement that serving Aethelfrith afforded and the triumphs they had together shared.

So, how had Hussa the warrior lord and leader of companies of the great King Aethelfrith come to be Hussa the father and Hussa the husband? How was it that, when before he would while away a spare moment planning revenge on Cerdic and plotting the triumphs he knew were in store, now he hated being away from Rowenna and dreamt up little games and gifts to bring to Hal?

Well, it had happened anyway and, as he resumed his route to join his family, he realised that he really did no longer care. He was content.

"My Lord Hussa," a voice addressed him. He turned and spotted Wilf, one of Aethelfrith's huscarls.

"The king wishes you to join him in his hall."

Hussa glanced over at Rowenna and at Hal who, seeing him coming, was waving excitedly. "When?"

"Straightaway, my lord," Wilf said haughtily as he turned to retrace his steps to the hall.

Hussa nodded and went to follow. He glanced over at Hal and saw the boy frowning now that his father was not going to join him. Hussa felt an ache of regret as he trotted down the steps towards the hall. The thought occurred that the boy that had grown up in that poor hut in Wicstun would not recognise the man he had become and would not understand the change.

The king's hall at Bebbanburg was a huge timber structure built on a scale befitting the most powerful king in the north. The pair of sturdy oaken doors that protected the occupants from the early spring winds were engraved with symbols of fierce beasts and mighty warriors. As Hussa approached, the guards pulled on great iron rings, opening the portal so he could enter.

Inside, the roof which arched thirty feet above their heads was supported by pillars that had once been tree trunks. Fire pits were cut into the ground all along the length, several now crackling and popping, warming the king's company on this cold day. Smoke rising from the fires mingled under the roof and found escape through holes at either end of the hall. Tables ran on either side of the fire pits, occupying much of the length of the hall. The benches that accompanied them allowed as many as two hundred warriors to feast with the king. Most of the benches were empty, with just a few clusters of warriors here and there chewing at bread and cheese and washing their meal down with ale or mead.

Looking towards the end of the hall, beyond the benches, he saw a gathering. He could hear that one of the men was addressing the others. Hussa hurried along to join them.

When he reached the end of the king's hall, he found Aethelfrith siting in his high –backed chair with the bulk of his witan, or king's council, already present. Close by on his right sat Eanfrith, the son he had from his first wife, Bebba. When Bebba had married Aethelfrith early in the king's reign, the fortress that the kings of Bernicia had seized only a few decades before was called Din Guarie. Whether through affection or political necessity, Aethelfrith had renamed it after his new bride. So, Din Guarie became Bebbanburg. Bebba had died some years before and Aethelfrith had married Acha, sister to Aethelric, king of Deira, and to Edwin the exiled prince. Whilst Acha had given Aethlefrith a son, Eanfrith was the oldest of the king's sons. Now Eanfrith sat at his father's side in council in the great fortress named after his mother from which his father ruled Northumbria. This seating arrangement, given he was the king's heir, did not worry Hussa. It was the man who sat to Eanfrith's right and, as such, in a position of precedence in the council's eyes, that gave him a feeling of unease.

This man was Sogor, nephew to Aethelfrith and cousin to Eanfrith.

Hussa's own seat was a little to the left of the king. This position was still prominent but there was a time when he sat where Eanfrith did and so had been seen as the most trusted and most influential of Aethelfrith's lords. In those days, both Eanfrith and his companion were youths and too young to take part in proceedings. Now, though, the years he had been away in Suth Seaxe and West Seaxe had matured the pair and his absence in the south had eroded his influence whilst increasing theirs. Maybe Rolf was right, after all. Maybe he had allowed things to get out of hand and had not done anything about it.

"Ah, Hussa, nice of you to join us," Sogor said. "We were missing your wisdom." The words were polite but the tone acidic.

Sogor was a stocky man with fair hair and sharp blue eyes that always seemed to mock anyone he spoke to as if he were the better man, or at least, he felt himself to be so. For Hussa, though, the gaze always held something more. It was hatred that he saw in those eyes. Hussa could understand this because Sogor's father had been Theobold, the younger brother to Aethelfrith. Theobold had died at Degsastan fighting the Scots and Picts. Hussa had a significant influence in the plan that had led to the battle: a plan that meant that most of the risk and brunt had fallen upon Theobald's companies who had drawn in the enemy upon them, allowing Aethelfrith to outflank the Scots and win the day. It had been a high –risk gambit that had not been

47

without sacrifice. Upon the moor at Degsastan, a stone marked the spot where Theobald had died. Sogor would have been, perhaps, thirteen at the time. He had been left behind at Bebbanburg when the spears marched forth. When, finally, the armies had returned home full of pride in their victory, he would have seen Hussa lauded with honours for his part in that victory and the defeat of Deira that followed. Hatred had taken hold in him then, and now that he was a man with influence over both king and the king's Aetheling or heir, Prince Eanfrith, he was finally in a position to make life difficult for Hussa and, perhaps, one day, to have his revenge on him.

Hussa nodded briefly in Sogor's direction but did not respond to the barbed comments. He then turned and bowed towards Aethelfrith.

"My king, how may I serve?" he said, ignoring Sogor as he took his seat.

Aethelfrith, though now forty –three, was not showing any signs of age. A great warrior king who ruled from the Firth of Forth near the mountain fortress city of Din Eidyn to beyond the Humber in the south, and from the German Sea in the east to deep into the mountains and vales of Rheged. Whilst Aethelbert of Cantia might still hold the title of Bretwalda or Lord of Britain, Aethelfrith was stronger. Hussa and Aethelfrith had long spoken of a campaign to the south to destroy his rival, Edwin and Edwin's ally Mercia and then ... who knows what future conquests lay in store. Perhaps the Bretwalda would fall to Northumbrian swords and the northern crown would rule all the English lands. The king glanced at Hussa and something in that glance suggested the day may have arrived.

"It is spring, my lords. Gododdin are hiding in their rock – top fortress just as Strathclyde and Rheged are dispersed around their lakes and hills. They sow their wheat and plough their fields and so none of these threaten us. The time has come to go south. We will root out the pretender prince, Edwin, and destroy his allies, then all of Britannia will be open to us. I will be Bretwalda and you will share in that power, that glory and the fruits of that victory."

Everyone in the hall cheered this news. At last they were going south. It had been seven long years since they had defeated Deira. Hussa's half-brother had fled with the Deiran princes and Hussa had been keen to confront them. Now, at last, it seemed that the moment had come.

"Therefore," the king continued, "we must give thought to the distribution of the army."

Hussa listened expectantly.

"My son, Eanfrith, is now of age for command and it is time he led men in battle."

That made sense, Hussa thought. A future king would want to gain a reputation so that men would follow him in battle when the time came for him to be king. He glanced over at Eanfrith and saw that he was nodding his head and looking pleased at the prospect. Then he flicked his gaze across at Sogor and saw that he was smiling, but this was more than a mere smile of satisfaction that his cousin was having his due recognition. There was something else in that smile, he was sure. With a jolt, he realised that Sogor was, in fact, staring at him. He suddenly felt that there was more going on here and that he was about to learn something he would not be happy about.

"So," the king went on, "Eanfrith will command half the army. As for the other half..." Aethelfrith paused and, for a moment, Hussa thought he was about to look over at him. However, he instead patted himself on the chest. "I will command that directly," he continued.

Hussa frowned. So, Eanfrith and Aethelfrith would share command of the army. Where would he, Hussa, be in this plan? It did not take long for him to find out.

"So, with my son and me away from Bebbanburg, there is a need for a trusted lieutenant to remain here with his own companies to watch the north," the king said and now at last he turned to look at Hussa.

"Lord Hussa, you will remain here and protect our lands, watch Gododdin and Rheged and hold Bebbanburg for us until we come back."

All around the hall the members of the council bent heads to whisper to each other. More than one glanced over at Hussa, perhaps curious to see how he would react. Hussa frowned and cleared his throat loudly.

"Lord king, may I speak?"

Aethelfrith nodded his head that he should do so. Many of the whispers died away as the council waited to see how he would react.

"I would ask to accompany you into Mercia," Hussa said.

Aethelfrith shook his head and pointed at the reed strewn floor of his hall. "I want you here."

"But why, Lord? I have been to those lands, whilst none of you have, so it is only logical that I should be there."

"Hussa..." Aethelfrith started to speak.

Hussa had a thought and waggled his finger. "My own brother is in those lands advising Edwin. If he is there, I am best placed to defeat him. I know how he thinks!"

"Hussa!" Aethelfrith shouted and his voice echoed around the room. As the sound died, away the silence that followed

50

was absolute. It seemed the council's appetite for idle gossip had faded and been replaced by curiosity as to how this exchange between the great king and his once mightly lieutenant would play out.

Hussa also fell silent and let the king speak.

"It is precisely because of your brother that I don't want you there," the king said after a moment.

Hussa shook his head. "I don't understand; what do you mean?"

"I mean that I can't have individual grudges confusing matters."

"Lord king, I assure you my dispute with Cerdic would not confuse the matter. What makes you feel that it would?"

Aethelfrith paused a moment. "It has been suggested and the suggestion has some merit to it."

"Suggested by whom?" Hussa asked, once more staring over at at Sogor. Was that a hint of a smile again playing at the edges of his lips?

"That is not important," Aethelfrith went on. "My decision is made. You and your men will stay here and protect the north."

"My king, if I am accused of bad judgement or weakness, I feel I have the right to know by whom."

Aethelfrith glared at him. "I said that I have made my decision. The matter is over."

Hussa bit back a further response. He simply nodded obediently, knowing that it was pointless to argue with the king. So, with a glare at Sogor he sat back whilst the council continued with a discussion of the campaign into Mercia. It became rapidly apparent that his own companies, those who were personally loyal to him, would remain with him in Bernicia and, as a result, there was little in the discussions of relevance.

As the voices droned on about plans for provisioning a force of three thousand spearmen along with several hundred horses, Hussa let his mind drift from the conversation as he thought about what Rolf had said. He was being sidelined, and effectively removed from power and influence in stages. Should he just accept this? After all, staying at Bebbanburg meant more time with Rowenna and Hal. Would it be that bad to let others fight and intrigue and plot, and just accept a quieter life?

His youth had been hard. Coping with rejection by his father and the jealousy he had felt for his half –brother, Cerdic, along with the hatred he had harboured for Cerdic's monther who had denied him the family he should have known, had made him a bitter man. It had turned him away from his own people and into the service first of Elmet and then Aethelfrith's Bernicia. There, the chase for glory and power that he had pursued had born fruit and he had risen far higher than he may ever have done in Deira. Perhaps, if he was being honest with himself, he had known that there must be more to life than just power and glory, yet, if that was to be found with a woman, he had not found it despite many opportunities along the way. Not, that was, until Rowenna had come along. Now that she had, what did he feel about the ambitions of his younger self? To be the right –hand man of a Bretwalda or lord of Britain was an aim he had long striven to accomplish. In that cause, he had led Rolf and others all over Britannia. Was he now, finally, putting aside that ambition for simpler, more domestic goals?

Maybe, he was.

After a while, he had the feeling that someone was watching him. He looked over at Sogor but the prince was listening to Eanfrith describe the condition of his huscarls. Aethelfrith was paying attention to his son and asking about the numbers of mail shirts his companies owned. None of them had their eyes on him.

He glanced around the hall trying to see who it was that was looking at him. All the other lords were focused on the council, either listening to the discussion or else whispering to each other. Hussa was on none of their minds at present.

He still had that feeling and was about to turn around to see if there was someone behind the bench on which he sat when he spotted movement beyond the king's highchair in the shadows behind. There, near the door that led to the king's private chambers, he spotted Acha. She noticed that he had seen her and did not turn away. Instead, she beckoned to him. Did she want to talk to him? What on earth about, he wondered? He carefully inclined his head to show he had seen her signal. She moved away, but not into the king's chambers. Rather, she drifted over to another door that lead out of the hall towards rooms of her own. She glanced once more at him and he once more nodded, then he turned his attention back to the council.

The conversation still droned on but Hussa heard none of it. Acha, queen of Bernicia, wanted to speak to him. Should he try and join her when an opportunity arose? He supposed he should.

Chapter Five
The Queen
Spring 611

Acha had her own smaller audience chamber close to the king's hall. There the women of the court would gather in what would often be a quieter, less chaotic atmosphere than that which prevailed in Aethelfrith's mead hall. Often, when great feasts occurred, the men alone attended, and few women would be present save for cup bearers. At times like that, or else when embassies from other lands were being welcomed, or appeals were being heard, justice being dispensed or such as when the king was meeting his witan or spending time with his huscarls, the ladies would come together in this side chamber if their presence was not required.

After the Witan had ended, Hussa went to the queen's hall, taking caution that, as far as he was aware, no one had seen him. When she had travelled north from her native Deira, the queen had brought with her from Godmundingaham a small group of servants and companions as well as half a dozen warriors gifted to her by her brother, Deira's then king, Aethelric. It was one of these warriors who now guided him through the hall towards the far end where he could see a number of ladies of the court were gathered.

Hussa glanced at the man. "I remember you. Ecgfirth isn't it? You were with Aethelric at Catraeth, weren't you?"

The man, a serious looking very tall dark -haired fellow, grunted. "I was. I was one of his huscarls, but I was honoured to be sent as escort for my lady."

It may have been an hounor then, when the two kingdoms were at peace, but what about now," Hussa asked.

"What do you mean by that?" Ecgrith replied tersely.

Hussa puffed out his cheeks.

"I mean to say, back then she was the centre of attention. Princess of a friendly nation, brother to its king and so on. Aethelfrith needed Aethelric, or rather he needed Deiran spears to deal with the Scots and Picts, so he made Acha feel like a queen and made sure we all treated her that way. But once the threat from the north was dealt with and he had taken Deira and Aethelric was dead her influence at court was over. Oh, he needs her around to hold on to some legitimate claim to Deira alright but that is all. I have never had the chance to ask any of you, but how do you reconcile being here in this court when Deira is occupied by Bernicia?"

The man halted, glanced around the hall before turning to face Hussa and replying. "How do you reconcile betraying Deira to Bernicia?"

Hussa shrugged. "I have my reasons which I won't bore you with. Suffice it to say that I feel little or no loyalty to Deira. So, in my case, there is no reconciling needed. You were a loyal warrior, who swore on the sword blade of Aethelric to serve him. So, how can you serve the queen of an enemy to your kingdom?"

The man spat down onto Hussa's boot. "I serve a princess of Deira. King Aethelric released me from my oath to him so that I could swear fealty to my lady. I swore to serve and protect her. That was my oath and I won't break it now."

Hussa nodded. "Commendable, I am sure. But how is it that you are permitted to live by Aethlfrith? Surely, by now, a dagger thrust from the shadows one winter's night would have been your fate. I wonder why the king has not isolated her from any allies or friends. That would have been the safest option."

Ecgfrith inclined his head towards the far end of the hall.

"The queen had something to do with that, I believe. Despite all appearances to the contrary, she has quite a hold on the king. He may have isolated her politically to satisfy the court, but, in private, he is quite infatuated by her."

"Well he is a man, after all, and Acha is a beauty."

Ecgfrith's face darkened. "It is more than just a man's lust. She has a way with words that exerts influence on a man without it being about physical attraction. She persuaded him to let her warriors live in her service."

Hussa considered this. "I can see why you are loyal to her, then."

"Indeed."

They resumed their progress up the hall.

"Do you know why she has summoned me?"

Ecgfrith shook his head. "No, Lord Hussa. I do not."

Well, thought Hussa as they arrived at their destination, I will soon find out.

It was late afternoon and the lengthening daylight of spring was now waning with little penetrating the shuttered windows high up in the south wall. Most of the chamber was therefore poorly lit, save occasional torches and candles, but the far end was illuminated by a ring of torches as well as firelight from a welcoming hearth close to which was set a small table around which sat Acha and four of her companions. On the table were the remnants of a meal – roasted chicken, by the evidence of a carcass on a platter – and horn goblets full of wine or mead.

It had been seven years since Acha daughter of Aelle of Deira had come to be queen of Bernicia. In that time, she had borne Aethelfrith an heir, Oswald, who was now five years old and, so rumours around the court said, she was pregnant once more.

The young princess had become a mature woman who now beckoned Hussa to take a seat on a stool opposite her.

Ecgfrith took up a position close by, one hand resting idly on a sword pommel. A thought came to Hussa that this would be the moment when his crimes against Deira would come home to roost. He had stood on a dozen battlefields with little fear and yet, at that moment, he felt an anxiety that he had never before experienced. He became all too aware that he was unarmed. Having come here direct from the king's hall, where no weapons were permitted, he had neither sword nor axe nor anything save a small seax that would be little use against the great long sword the veteran Ecgfrith carried. Would Deira's vengeance upon him be enacted this day by these women and their single warrior guard?

"My queen," he addressed Acha as he took a seat.

One of the ladies poured him a goblet of mead.

Is it poison, then, that they will end me with, rather than blade? he thought. It was, so men said, a woman's weapon, after all.

The queen studied him for a long time.

Finally, she spoke. "To whom does your loyalty lie, Lord Hussa?"

He blinked. Was this a test set by Aetheflrith? Or Sogor, perhaps, and more likely. Was this a way to trick him somehow into saying something Sogor would then use to destroy him?

"The king has my oath, my lady, you surely know that..."

"Which king?"

He looked at her. "I don't understand..."

"Didn't you swear allegiance to my father once... and to Lord Wallace?"

Thirteen years before, Hussa had been called up as part of the Wicstun company. He had trained with it, and even answered the muster of the entire company that had taken place at the Villa. During the training sessions in Wicstun, oaths were sworn to Lord Wallace – the then earl of the Southern Marches – and through him to King Aelle. Hussa had sworn them even though he had not believed in them and, indeed, had taken the first opportunity to renege on them and take up service with, first, One Eye of Elmet, and, eventually, Aethelfrith.

He nodded. "I did, but I never felt bound by them."

Her eyebrows rose slightly. "Really… so oaths mean little to you, nor loyalty?"

He considered this. "I made the decision to renege on the oaths as I had already been betrayed by my father, by my people. Now I serve the one who I most believe can win power and so, in turn, let me share it. This would give me fair reward for my services and be a recompense for what fate, Deira and my father did to me."

Ecgfrith snorted in disgust.

"It is as I said, my queen, the Lord Hussa has no honour. He serves his narrow self –interest and whoever gives him the best chance for his own glorification."

Hussa glared at the warrior before shrugging and returning his attention to the queen.

"Ecgfrith speaks a degree of truth. I do look out for myself and those loyal to me and, in so doing, I place my abilities and skills in the service of the one most likely to reward them. That was never going to be your father or brother, my lady. Your father was great once, but those days were far behind him in my youth. Your brother, let us be honest, never had that greatness. I was, in any event, a fatherless bastard without the benefit and reputation of a family name. My father, and so, in turn, Deira had abandoned me."

"Yes, we have all heard the story of the poor rejected bastard son of one of Deira's lords, forced to scrape by whilst his brother lived in luxury," Ecgfrith said snidely. "Other men deal with the situation they are left with. I … we had to."

Hussa's head whipped around. "What, by serving the king who destroyed your people? Who now is the one who acted purely for self-interest and self-preservation?"

Ecgfrith's face reddened and he stepped towards Hussa. "I serve my queen and I still serve Deira…" He spat out the words.

"Enough!" Acha commanded and both men fell silent.

Still serve Deira… Hussa thought to himself. What did he mean by that exactly?

"Compromises and accommodations have had to be made by us all, let us just leave it at that," Acha said and glanced at them each in turn. Hussa nodded. Acha glared at a hesitant Ecgfrith who, after a moment, also nodded.

Hussa took a deep breath before asking the question that was uppermost in his mind.

"Why did you ask to see me, my lady?"

Acha paused a while before replying. Was that her lip she was biting? Was there anxiety there? Perhaps asking herself how far he could be trusted.

"I have noticed that you and Sogor do not exactly get on."

Hussa nodded. "His father died at Degsastan. Soon afterwards, I became more influential over the king. I think he blamed me for his father's death, and even came to believe I had engineered it to gain power."

"But he could do little about it, young as he was at the time." Acha observed.

"Then I was absent for a few years…"

"Years in which he grew to maturity and also gained influence over Eanfrith, the king's oldest son and heir," she went on.

"You have been passed over, Hussa. Ignored, even. You are almost irrelevant, in fact," Ecgfrith commented in a tone that sounded so much like that used earlier by Rolf that it was unsettling. There was a touch of triumph in those words as if reminding Hussa of the irony of his own questions about the queen's diminished influence.

Hussa glared at the huscarl again.

"Am I called here just to be made fun of?"

Acha held up a consoling hand. "Not at all, Lord Hussa. We merely wish to show you that we know what you are feeling. Understand it, even." She paused again, still hesitant it seemed. "Aethelfrith is now forty –three. Perhaps, for a king, not that old."

Hussa nodded. "Your father was much older when he died."

"Yes, he was. But my father, whilst a warrior in his youth, died in a time of peace. He died in his bed. Aethelfrith is a warrior king who still leads his men in battle. Men grow slower as they get old. It is not unlikely he may fall one day. If he did, who would succeed him?"

"Probably Eanfrith, unless your brother, Edwin, could return."

Acha nodded. "In either event, my own son, and any others that came along, would not be seen favourably. To Eanfrith, they would be children of a different mother to his own. To Edwin, the children of his bitter rival."

Hussa thought about that for a moment. "Yes, they may not be safe in Northumbria."

"Yet, if you step back a moment and think about it, Oswald has the best claim to the throne of a unified Northumbria. He has both Bernician and Deiran blood in his veins. Both kingdom's royal houses represented in one line. A line that may be acceptable to both peoples."

Hussa gave her an appraising look. This is what Ecgfrith meant when he spoke about serving Deira. For Oswald to one day be king would unite the kingdoms in a way that neither Eanfrith nor Edwin could hope to do.

It made sense and yet there were obstacles in the form of Eanfrith and Edwin who would pursue their own claims and, if Oswald got in the way, he may not live long, whoever became king.

He tapped his fingers on the rim of his goblet as he thought about that. Then he had another thought and looked up sharply at the queen.

"Why are you telling me this? I could go to Aethelfrith with what you have said. Or Sogor."

"You could, but you need an ally, Lord Hussa. You need a route back to power. I could be that route."

Hussa shrugged. "Perhaps you could, but what would you need from me in return?"

"For now, nothing, except your ears and eyes. Keep me informed of whatever information you feel would be relevant and I would do the same, as well as watch over you. If my patronage would be of value at any time, I can extend that. Not publicly, perhaps, but in private with the king, I mean."

"Do you need me to swear an oath?"

Ecgfrith snorted. "What would be the point?"

Acha shook her head and reached over to lay a hand on Hussa's forearm.

"Not yet, and not to me in any event. One day, though, I will, and it would be to my son. You will swear to help him gain his throne. When the moment comes, I will call on that oath and you will swear it."

61

Hussa thought about it. "As Ecgfrith says, what would be the point? What would stop me just breaking it when the moment suited me?" Acha bent forward so their noses almost touched and looked into his eyes. Close at hand, the fire in the hearth crackled and popped and sparks rose. Smoke drifted over them and in that firelight, the queen worked her sorcery upon him.

"The point would be, on that day I asked for that oath, I would believe you because you will want to swear loyalty to Aelle's line. Finally, at last, you would have a reason to do so."

Those eyes held him in their gaze for an age. There was something in them that he had never seen in Aethelric, but had, he accepted reluctantly, seen an echo of in Edwin. Here it was present in a pure form in this woman, this queen. It was as if the old king Aelle was alive. The stories of the origins of the royal houses told of how they were descended from the gods, from giants and from spirits of ice and fire. In his youth, Aelle had apparently been fond of claiming that the fire spirit Sutyr was amongst his ancestors and that flames burnt in his veins. That fire had driven him on to claim a kingdom. A part of his spirit, the spirit that had forged a kingdom, was not dead. The spark was still there. It might burn in Edwin, but it blazed with the fury of a funeral pyre in this woman.

Hussa nodded, then said, "Yes, my lady." And he believed it.

Chapter Six
Departure
Spring 611

The day following the war council brought a bitterly cold wind from the north accompanied by hail and torrents of rain. The high fortress of Bebbanburg was lashed mercilessly and everyone from the king down hid from the inclement weather, huddling close to fires that spat and flickered whenever the doors opened to admit warriors along with the storm. Water gushed down every path and, in some places, newly created waterfalls plunged from the high rocks into the surging waves far below. There was little to do save drink mead and ale and tell each other stories of how Thunor, god of lightning and thunder, was angry with men and was punishing them all for whatever insult he perceived he had received. It seemed that any campaign south into Mercia would never be possible.

Yet, if Thunor had been angry, he must have forgiven the inhabitants of Midgard, for as suddenly as the gales and rains had come, they were gone. Over the next few days, the cold winter weather finally retreated and the seas around Bebbanburg became placid whilst, overhead, the first sun of springtime warmed the fortress. Beneath the citadel, fishermen were preparing their boats for putting out to sea. Inside the citadel, the companies of Aethelfrith, Sogor and Eanfrith, and the king's other lords were gathering. Riders galloped out to carry a summons from the king to every village and settlement within a day's ride. The fyrd was being called out to bolster the ranks of veterans. As they arrived in twos and threes, carrying spear and shield and some of them with rusty but still serviceable mail shirts and good steel helmets, they joined the professional soldiers who ran experienced eyes over the part –timer's equipment, usually accompanied by disparaging remarks.

The forges of Aethelfrith burned late each night as spearheads were replaced, shield bosses and armour repaired, and swords sharped on whetstones in the ward. The citadel became acclimatised to a constant cacophony of hammering and banging. In the past, that noise had always been a comfort to Hussa. It usually accompanied the start of a new campaign which promised glory and wealth and the chance to grow in his power and influence. Now, though, the noise brought mixed feelings to him. Each hammer blow sounded out like a signal to anyone who would listen that he was not going along, had been rejected and was being left behind. He might enjoy the time with his family and, perhaps, that now meant more to him than his status. Yet, he knew that any glory and any wealth to be had was for others to share; other heroes would shine this summer and it was not going to be Hussa. He felt like the only man not invited to a friend's wedding, or a tenant whose lord has neglected to ask him to the harvest feast, and he was forced to watch everyone else laughing and joking as they entered the lord's mead hall.

"Well, this is not exactly going well, is it?" Rolf grumbled as he stood next to Hussa on the western palisade and looked down at the camp that had sprung up at the bottom of the rock upon which Bebbanburg was built. The growing army was now almost a thousand strong and, so, too large to billet in the citadel or the village that was located along the west and northern sides of the rocky promontory.

One of Sogor's companies was engaged in a mock battle with one of the king's own companies. From up here, the two men could hear the clatter of wooden swords on wicker shields. Hussa grunted and turned to look at his companion.

"Why are you moaning? They are off to war whilst you get to stay safe and sound here, drinking ale and with the pick of Bebbanburg's women to choose from. You should be happy!"

Rolf snorted. "Really, happy? How happy are you about it?"

"I am fine."

"Bollocks, you are! When we attack Mercia and the rest, it will be one of the biggest battles in our lifetime."

Hussa shook his head.

"We don't know that."

"Come on... think about it. Edwin has allies in three Welsh lands – Mercia, Gwynedd and Powys. They are not just going to sit around and let us go where we want. There is going to be a big battle and one that men will talk about for generations – bound to be. I want to be there. "

"You would get yourself killed. You should think about that."

"I am thinking about the loot and the glory."

Hussa waved his hand dismissively. "Well, sorry. Someone has to watch the north when the army is away in the south."

"I don't see why. There are very few buggers left to fight up here. We have already killed most of them. Or else, those we have not killed are very conveniently fighting each other and it would be rude to interefere. We saw to that at Degsastan and all those campaigns since. Rheged's towns are occupied by us and their lords mostly sworn to Aethelfrith. The bits we don't control we don't care about and the handful of lords not loyal to us are weaklings whose straggle of warriors are left skulking in mountains or up some tree in the forest bothering birds. The Gododdin hide on their rock, and very welcome to that they are too, whilst Strathclyde has been fighting the Picts and

65

the Scots. It is over up here. Its going to be a bloody boring few months."

"Don't do that," Hussa said, finding his fingers had drifted to the serpent's symbol at his throat – the symbol of Loki the trickster god whom Hussa was most loyal to.

"Don't what?"

"Don't tempt the Norns," Hussa muttered.

Rolf laughed. "I hardly think the Norns take much notice of me. Those hags might weave man's fate, but I thought you believe that a man makes his own fate. Since when have you been worried about the Norns? Or the gods for that matter, apart from Loki that is," he gestured at the snake symbol on its chain at Hussa's neck.

Hussa once more moved his hand to the symbol. He always trusted that the trickster god would protect him and guide him. So, what twist of fate was being played out now? What purpose was there in him sitting out this great war and this, possibly the greatest battle in a generation.

"I do, but it is best to keep out of the gaze of both Norns and gods."

They stood for a while watching the mock fighting below. Finally, Hussa turned and led the way down the steps to the ward where some of his company were practising sword play. He picked up a dummy blade and shield and threw them at Rolf before getting a set for himself. Rolf looked down at them with disinterest. Then Hussa noticed Rolf's gaze fix on something across the other side of the ward. He glanced that way and saw that Bridget was walking from the laundry buildings to Hussa and Rowenna's quarters carrying a basket of Rowenna's dresses and Hussa's shirts.

"Who is she?" Rolf said. "I can't recall seeing her before.

"She is new. Come to think of it, I don't think you have met her yet. She is called Bridget and is Rowenna's maid. She only started work a week or so ago. I think you were away at my estates at the time."

"She is a fine -looking lass, that one. Red hair, green eyes and shapely, too. Mind if I go say hello?"

Hussa shrugged. "Be my guest," he said. "Although I should warn you…" he started to say but Rolf had already jogged off across the fortress. Bridget must have heard him coming as she turned to face him.

Hussa could not hear what Rolf said, nor Bridget's reply, but it was not long before Rolf came back across to him with a wry smile on his face.

"Well, how did it go?"

"I asked if she had plans for tonight or would she like me to help her out in the laundry with a scrubbing brush. She told me to shove this wooden sword somewhere unpleasant," he reported.

Hussa grunted. "Sounds like an auspicious start then and up to your usual standards. I was going to warn you that she has a bit of a temper if she does not like how someone talks to her, but you ran off."

Rolf nodded. "Yes, I picked up on that. Strong accent, though. Where is she from?"

"She is a Scots woman captured by Aethelfrith's raiders tangling with the Dal Riada up near Alt Clut. I bought her from him when Rowenna agreed to have a maid."

"Scots, eh? I heard they could have a fierce temper. I will remember that when I talk to her again."

Hussa's eyes widened. "So, you are not giving up?" he asked.

Rolf shook his head. "If I am stuck here with nothing to do, I might as well have a quest to pass the time."

Hussa pointed at Rolf. "Just you be careful quite how well you get to know her. Get her with child and you owe me twenty shillings!"

Rolf nodded. "Might be worth it at twice that price," he muttered under his breath and accompanied the words with a sly grin. Hissa heard him nonetheless and the remark earned Rolf a glare from his companion.

"Anyway, speaking of passing the time, come, let us practice," Hussa said, sliding his hand into the straps behind his shield and then twisting his body to present the shield to his friend. He raised his other arm and bent the elbow, readying the sword for a strike.

Rolf shrugged. "Can't see the point," he said with a bored yawn, back in the doldrums it seemed.

Hussa lunged with his blade at Rolf who had to step away sharply to avoid a blow to the face.

"The point is to always be ready!" Hussa said with a smirk.

Rolf frowned. "Ready for what?"

"How in the name of Freya's tits should I know. Anything might happen."

Rolf laughed. "Oh yes? Well, get ready for this then!" he replied as he leapt towards Hussa with a roar.

Several weeks later the king decided it was time to begin the campaign. The spring weather had continued to improve. The month of the festival of the goddess Eostre, had seen feasts in the citadel to celebrate the life and fertility that returned to the fields in the villages around. In time, the fourth month gave way to the fifth month of the year, Trimilce – the month of the three milkings. Hussa had always found that name amusing. Then again, he had never been a farmer. His mother had made a living mending clothes and making new tunics and shirts for the inhabitants of Wicstun so Hussa had not learnt about animals and the ways of the farmyard. Cerdic, no doubt, knew all about cows and could have explained about the milking traditions. Not that he would ever ask his brother, of course. Rolf was from a farm and when Hussa had absently commented that the month's name was a bit silly had been forced to listen as the man told him all about cow's udders filling with milk intended to feed their newborn calves. So much milk, indeed, that they needed milking three times every day.

"Fascinating," Hussa had commented.

"Well, you asked," Rolf had replied.

It was now a fine, very warm and dry, spring day. Only a scatter of clouds was visible in an otherwise blue sky. The household of the king gathered on the battlements as, down below, Eanfrith took charge of his first command. After a bellow of ox horns, the young prince led the army towards Eoforwic. Other companies from further south, including companies recruited from Deira and the area around the ancient Roman city, were gathering there and, as the time for the assault into Mercia approached, the time had come for the companies from Bernicia to join them. The column headed west away from the sun rising behind the fortress of Bebbanburg and down the path through woodlands that would take them to the Roman road which led south towards the old wall and distant Eoforwic.

Once Eanfrith was out of sight, Aethelfrith and Acha, along with most of the court, left the battlements but Hussa lingered and watched the rest of the column marching off to war, leaving him behind. Now, all that remained in Bebbanburg was Hussa's companies along with those of Sogor and the king's own companies. There were enough ponies and horses for Aethelfrith's men as well as Sogor's to travel mounted and thus these could depart a little later than Eanfrith's men who had to march to Eoforwic.

The spring was full advanced when Hussa attended Aethelfrith's final council meeting in Bebbanburg before he and Sogor were due to depart for Eoforwic. Most of the thegns and earls were away with the forces in Eoforwic and so the gathering was a smaller one. Aethelfrith chose to hold it at a table in his mead hall. Hussa was using a crude map drawn on hide to help give his report on the readiness of his command to protect the northern part of the Northumbrian kingdom along with occupied lands taken from the Goddodin and the lands of Rheged captured by Northumbrians after the victories of Catraeth and Degsastan.

"I have a full company at Jedworth with patrols from there regularly passing within a half day's march of Din Eidyn. There is another company over at Luguvalium watching over Rheged and two reserve companies here at Bebbanburg, one of whom can be mounted on horses from my own estates if the need arises," Hussa explained. "I can concentrate the four companies on any given location in the north of your lands within four or five days at the most. There are depots of food and fodder sufficient to keep all of the companies in the field for several weeks if we had to fight."

Aethelfrith nodded.

"That all looks adequate. Any reports of trouble?"

Hussa shook his head. "Nothing out of the ordinary. There have been the usual raids by the Gododdin which have been repelled easily enough and with mimimal losses. The Picts and Scots seems to be at odds with each other and we hear rumours of fighting in the mountains and islands but not anything that need worry us."

"Very well, I will leave the north in your hands. We ride tomorrow at dawn. Is there anything else you need me to decide?"

Hussa scratched his head. "I had given thought to beginning work on a new well. The old well is giving poor water and in small volumes. As a result, we have to rely on water from outside the fortress. In the event of a siege that would prove a problem. A new well might be sensible."

The king frowned. "Hard work digging through the rock beneath us," he said.

Hussa nodded. "Yes, but I have a few ideas about that."

"Go ahead and try them, then."

"I will, lord king."

The following morning, Aethelfrith and Sogor led their companies out of the fortress, down the steep path that descended from the gateway at the northern tip, past the harbour below and on through the village that was inland of the citadel. Hussa and Rolf watched them leave. Rolf looked sullen.

"So, why did you suggest we dig a well?"

"Mainly to stop your moaning and sulking about not being with the army. Come on, get the men to collect axes and go out into the forests. I want large boughs and logs. Bring the timbers up here."

Bebbanburg was built on a massive slab of rock dozens of feet deep. It was part of the reason that the British tribes had built a fortress on it –Din Guarie they had called it. Ida, the first Bernician king, Aethelfrith's grandfather, had conquered it maybe seventy years before. That rock may have been the source of its strength and yet it was also as Aethelfrith himself had suggested, a problem when it came to building wells. An old well, dug back before Ida had taken the citadel, still was used but no

71

one now alive could recall when it had been created or how. In his travels, Hussa had visited other fortresses built on rocks and had even been a prisoner with his brother in one in the lands of the Scots. He had talked to some of the inhabitants and picked up an idea or two and now he planned to put these ideas into practice.

Rolf did as he was told and led a party into the woodlands inland from the coast. They returned with two carts piled high with thickly cut oak and beech trunks. These were built into a pyre on an area of rock which Hussa had ordered cleared of the thin covering of grass and earth. He had a fire started and they stood back and watched as the flames engulfed the towering structure. Everyone came out to observe the spectacle including Acha and Rowenna, accompanied by Bridget who was struggling to hold back a wide -eyed, overly excited Hal.

"Woden's sweaty bollocks but that is hot," Rolf remarked as they stood thirty yards away. Hussa nodded. The heat was, indeed, intense. Some enterprising sorts had placed fish impaled on sharpened sticks close by or flat bread on stones but had to rush in to retrieve them as they blackened quickly, earning them the good -natured abuse and cat calls from their comrades.

As the fire burnt on, Hussa sent the carts back down the hill, this time to the harbour where they collected gallons of cold sea water. When they returned, he had men clear the ashes away from the rock surface. Then, before the rock could begin to cool, the barrels of water were tipped over and the water gushed over the glowing stone. With a whoosh, billowing clouds of steam erupted into the sky and as their gaze moved upwards, they all heard it: a mighty crack that echoed across the whole fortress and rumbled beneath their feet.

As the steam cleared away, everyone crept forward and inspected the result. There, where solid rock had been two hours before, a wide crack ran five feet across its surface.

"Stay back!" Hussa shouted and then just he and Rolf walked over and, treading carefully on the still warm stone, to peer down. The crevace, perhaps a natural fault in the rock, snapped open by the heat and then the sudden cooling of the rock, plunged deep into the bedrock.

Hussa smiled at Rolf.

Rolf shrugged. "Alright, I will say it. You are not completely stupid!"

"Thank you for the support," Hussa said dryly.

"Don't mention it," Rolf said absently as he waved over at Bridget and winked at her.

Bridget glared at him but then led Hal along behind Rowenna and Acha as they came closer.

"Careful, my lady," Hussa said. "It is a little unstable."

Acha came closer even so and looked down into the chasm.

"Merciful Woden, but that goes down quite a way," she said and then smilled at him. "Very clever what you did there. The king will be pleased."

"Can you feel the heat?" Rolf said to Bridget. "In the air between us, I mean."

"I would agree that some objects around here would benefit from a bucket of cold water," Bridget replied, but this time rather than a glare, it was a slight smile that passed over her face.

"Come along, let us retire to my hall. It is cooler there," Acha said, oblivious to some of the finer points of the exchange and led the ladies away from the rock. As they moved away, Bridget glanced back at Rolf before looking away again.

"Think I am making progress there," he said.

Hussa shook his head and turned to study the smouldering chasm.

"We will let it cool tonight and see about widening that tomorrow…" Hussa started to say and then noticed a messenger was making his way up to the fortress from the gateway on horseback. He was wearing a cloak that was damp suggesting he had ridden through a rain shower and looked travel weary. Hussa recognised that the young man, whose name was Edgar, was from the company that he had deployed in Luguvalium. So, anxious to hear the man's news, he jogged over to him followed by Rolf.

The man slid off his horse and raised his hand in greeting. Rolf took the horse's reins and passed them to a stable boy. The messenger took a moment to catch his breath and Hussa waved at a servant to bring him ale which Edgar accepted with a nod of thanks. He took a swig and then inclined his head at Hussa.

"My, lord. I bring urgent news from Luguvalium. Rheged is in rebellion. There has been an uprising…"

"What, when?" Rolf asked but Hussa silenced him with a gesture and nodded at Edgar to continue. He listened carefully as Edgar made the rest of his report. Then he turned to Rolf.

"Send riders at once, south. The king must be told today. He will not yet have reached his first stop on the way to Eorforwic. Tell him the news and ask for instructions. Tell him I am mustering the garrison and calling in the fyrd."

The riders departed at once and the fortress was thrown into frantic activity as Hussa made it as ready as he could for whatever Aethelfrith's orders would be. Hussa had expected a reply the following day with his instructions but it was not long after dusk that riders could be heard approaching the citadel. Exercising due caution, he called out the guard but almost at once he spotted that Aethelfrith and Sogor accompanied by Eanfrith were leading a small group of mounted men. He rushed over to the gate to meet the king.

Aethelfrith looked tired and angry as he entered the citadel, dismounted and then stomped over to his hall.

"My lord king, will you want food and ale in your rooms before my man reports his message?"

Aethelfrith shook his head and just sat down on his throne and waved at Hussa. "He can give us his news right here – we might as well all hear it."

Hussa turned to the messenger who was near at hand. "You heard the king, Edgar. Make your report."

"Yes, my lord."

Edgar stepped forward and took a deep breath.

"Sometime before winter comes again, please!" the king said impatiently.

"Yes…my king, of course. I have come from Luguvalium with urgent news. A week ago, there was a revolt led by King Rhoerth of Rheged. It happened in the Novantae lands to the north west of Luguvalium, my lord. We only maintain a small warband there and it was attacked by a large force. Since then, there has been a general uprising, swelling the numbers. The enemy now hold everything west and north of Luguvalium – all of the northern part of Rheged."

"Where are they based?" Sogor asked.

"The fortress of Anwoth, lord," Edgar replied. "They have smaller garrisons in other strong holds but Rhoerth, his family and the bulk of his strength is there."

"What is their strength?" Aethelfrith asked.

"They have at least three companies, lord king… but more join them daily."

"I don't know Anwoth fort. How large is it?" Aethelfrith asked.

"Not that big, my lord king. It's a steep sided hill, well protected by ditches and palisades."

"So, a defensive location to gather a force, but they will soon be looking to march on to something larger, like Luguvalium," Hussa suggested.

"That must be prevented," Aethelfrith said. "Those western lands are remote and have few fortresses and what they have are not going to hold a large army. However, if they take the fortifications at Luguvalium, they would be able to call on all the warriors in southern Reged, too."

They considered that prospect in silence for a while. A light pattering on the roof told them that the rain which Edgar had ridden through earlier in the day had reached them.

"Why do they attack now I wonder?" Sogor asked.

Chapter Seven
Response
Spring 611

"Lord," Edgar answered, "we captured a messenger from Mercia passing through Rheged. He was made to talk and confessed that news of the concentration of our men at Eoforwic has been passed by the Eboracci to Mercia."

This was no surprise to anyone at the table. The Eboracci were the British tribesmen who lived around Eoforwic and who had been conquered first by Deira and then passed into the domination of Bernicia. Passing on information of Angle armies to kingdoms who were no friend, and possibly enemies of Bernicia like Mercia, made sense. What was a surprise, however, was the revolt of subjugated Rheged.

"Looks like Ceorl of Mercia relayed the news of our gathering army far and wide – to his allies Gwynedd and Powys, but also further afield. Rhoerth must have decided to take advantage of the bulk of our strength being in the south to try to throw us out," Hussa surmised.

"Maybe you should have seen this coming," Sogor suggested. "You are earl of the Northern Marches, after all."

"I have only had that role a few weeks, Lord Sogor, as you know very well. Indeed, I was expecting to be at Eoforwic or wherever the army is at this time. I have only just got back from a few years away in West Seaxe, how was I supposed to know what Rhoerth is up to? Correct me if I am wrong, but were you not earl of the North before the witan appointed me? You are the one with spies up here, not I! It would have been appropriate to give me access to those spies, don't you think? Or do you plan to use them to spy on me?"

Sogor leapt to his feet, hand moving to the hilt of his seax. "Find your own spies!" Sogor hissed.

"Stop this bickering," Aethelfrith commanded in a low voice. "Sit down, nephew!"

He glared at his brother's son until Sogor reluctantly resumed his seat. Then, reaching for the map, he studied it for a while before finally throwing it back onto the table and glanced up at them all.

"Very well, I will now tell you what we are going to do…" He paused to gather his thoughts then continued.

"I am determined to crush this rebellion quickly," Aethelfrith said. "We must make an example that all of Rheged, indeed all of the lands we occupy, will take note of. They will learn that if they rebel against me then they will suffer the consequences. To do that, we need speed, and that means riding hard and fast to Anwoth.

"Now, the only companies we have sufficient mounts for are Hussa's two, if I lend him my own huscarl's horses for the duration of the expedition, and Sogor's companies."

Sogor frowned. "My companies? My lord king, if I go to Anwoth and your mounts are used there, too, we can't leave for Eoforwic."

"We can't launch a campaign in the south at the same time as fighting in the north. So, the campaign into Mercia is delayed until I am happy the north is secure. The army will remain at Eoforwic. It may be a late summer campaign is possible. In any event, I do not wish to alert Rheged or anyone else that our plans are changing. So, we send a rider to the army to order it to raid Mercia. Make that bastard Ceorl think we are coming. Keep his eyes fixed on his border so any reports he sends Rhoerth suggest that we are still intent on a campaign down there."

Hussa nodded. This made sense.

"As for Anwoth, we will send a force there to assess the situation with the aim of capturing it and destroying or dispersing the forces it holds." Athelfrith looked at Hussa and Sogor. "All my other captains are at Eoforwic except the pair of you."

Sogor glanced over at Hussa. "So, which of us will you send?"

"I want to make sure this is done, so, you will both go with your companies and you can pick up the garrison at Luguvalium on the way. My own company will hold Bebbanburg."

"Who will command the army you are sending to Novantae?"

Aethelfrith paused a moment whilst he studied them both.

"Sogor will command. Hussa you will follow his orders." The king nodded at his son. "Eanfrith will accompany you to learn what he can, but I place the command under an experienced and reliable captain."

Hussa ground his teeth together. This was not an unexpected decision, yet it still rankled.

Sogor smirked but then bowed his head. "Thank you, lord king," he said. Then he looked up again. "I am unfamiliar with Anworth and I am sure Hussa is, too. Do you know anything about it?" he said to Edgar.

"Not much, my lord. It was a hill fort which was little used when Rheged was independant. When we took over Rheged, we made Rhoerth remove his garrisons from there as with his other forts."

"It would be helpful to have the aid of a spy who knows the fortress or can get in," Sogor said.

Aethelfrith shrugged. "Maybe, but I don't have any agents over there, and from what he has said, I don't think that Hussa does either," he replied.

Hussa shook his head.

"Then if you don't either, Sogor, we must do without the luxury of a man with inside knowledge."

"What about a woman with inside knowledge?" a woman's voice sounded out from the side of the hall. Recognising it, Hussa turned sharply, it was Rowenna's voice. "Let me come along and I will find out what you need to know."

"What are you doing here, woman?" he asked her.

"Hal had wandered in during the council. I came to get him back and overheard what you were all talking about."

Hussa spotted Hal peering at him from beneath a nearby bench. He smiled at his father and then bit into a bread roll he must have scavenged from the remains of the meal left on the table.

"Well, take him and get out – this does not concern you ... or him."

"You need a spy to infiltrate the enemy fortress. That is what I do..."

Hussa interrupted her. "It is what you used to do. You are a mother now... go back to our room and take Hal and we will speak later."

"I can speak Welsh and I even know something about Rheged as I was sent there once. Before I worked for the kings of West Seaxe, I served Pybba of Mercia for a while who had me spy on Owain and Urien, former kings of Rheged."

Hussa glared at her. "You never told me any of this."

Rowenna shrugged. "I was a spy. It pays to keep quiet about my past."

Sogor laughed. "Maybe Hussa should not go along. He clearly does not have much control over his wife, my lord king. I think he needs to stay at home to sort out his own house."

Aethelfrith ignored him. "My lady, did you ever go to this place, Anwoth?"

Rowenna smiled. "Yes… lord king. Owain used it as a hunting lodge. It was some fifteen years ago, I think, but I remember something about the place including a seldom used trail that Owain used to use when trying to avoid the court if he wanted to go hunting quietly."

"How well did you know Owain?" Hussa asked.

"Jealous are we, Hussa?" Sogor asked him.

Rowenna shrugged. "It was long before we met, husband and I was very young. You would be best not knowing about those times."

"Oh, this is funny," Sogar teased. "Our lord Hussa's wife used to be Owain's lover!" Aethelfrith held up a hand to silence Sogor. "I apologise, lord king," Sogor said, as he struggled to siffle his sniggers.

"Well," the king said, "It seems you have your agent."

"Highness… please, no." Hussa said. "Think of my son."

"Your son can stay here – he will be safe enough."

Rowenna shook her head. "He comes with me. Hussa can look after him when I scout the fortress."

Sogar lost control completely at this and let forth a roar of laughter as he pounded on the table. The sudden noise started Hal who dropped the roll. Showing the survival instincts of a three –year –old, he reached up to the table and, finding an abandoned chicken leg, retrieved it and sat back down, biting into it with satisfaction.

"Nursemaid Hussa!" Sogor said. A glare from the king finally silenced him.

"I am not sure that taking the boy is wise…" Aethelfrith said.

"Maybe not, but I insist, lord king" Rowenna said, and fixed the king with one of her glares. Hussa shook his head. Might as well surrender now, highness, he thought. Once she looks at you like that, you have no hope.

Aethelfrith held up both hands.

"As you wish," Aethelfrith said to Rowenna, then turned his attention back to the men. "Lord Sogor, Lord Hussa, you have your agent. She knows the land, speaks the language, has skills we all know about that make her ideal, and seems to be able to get her way. The decision is made. Make preparations for departure within the day."

The king turned away to his chambers. Sogor, still chuckling, passed Hussa and left the other way through the main doors.

Hussa turned to Rowenna.

"Well, that's just great. You and Hal along? How am I supposed to concentrate on what I have to do now?"

"We'll take Bridget. She can look after Hal when we are busy."

Double the joy, then. How will Rolf concentrate with that distraction? Hussa thought to himself.

A week later, the companies under Sogor and Hussa left Bebbanburg, heading out along the same track Eanfrith had followed and, like him, turned south on the Roman road. This ancient road, whilst crumbling and in terrible repair, was still the quickest way to travel over land and took them swiftly to the old stone wall that stretched from the German sea in the east to the Irish sea west of Luguvalium. They passed through a decaying gatehouse, then turned west to follow the great wall, an easier path than following the valley up through the border hills. This southerly route also took them in a loop further away from any scouts that may have strayed east from Anwoth and past Luguvallium, or, more likely, scouts from the Gododdin or Kingdom of Strathclyde who might pass news of their coming on to the King of Rheged.

82

Three days' ride brought them to Luguvalium. After resting there two days, they left the old Roman city accompanied by another company of men comprising most of the garrison. Together, the little army of about three hundred spears headed further west along a narrow Roman road that led through a chain of old fortresses where, centuries before, Roman legionaries would have dwelt when these lands were part of that great empire. The remains of Roman settlement was much less obvious here, north of the great wall, than it was to the south, Hussa knew though that the Romans had settled this land, indeed, for a while, pushing as far north as a great earth embankment Hussa had passed once when travelling with Cerdic to Dal Riata.

Holding on to the Pict lands had proven hard and the Romans had fallen back from the earth wall to hide behind their stone frontier. As a result, the roads, as well as the occasional remains of their forts between the walls, were in much worse decay than those Hussa was familiar with in Deira and elsewhere. But you could still see those remains if you looked out for them.

They were camping in one of the old forts – which contained little more than space for Hussa, Rowenna, Bridget, Rolf and a few of his huscarls, with most of their companies in the fields around. Sogor had taken billets in a town they had passed through, telling Hussa to find his own shelter. Hussa did not mind. It meant he did not have to talk to Sogor tonight. Hussa was poking at the fire, stirring it into life. Rowenna brought Hal and sat down by the fireside. They had spoken little since that day in the council chamber at Bebbanburg. Partially, this was because Hussa had been very busy getting his companies ready for the road. They had not intended leaving Bebbanburg and all the provisions for an army on the march were in Eoforwic or in garrisons to the north where he had expected trouble might come from. Thus, he had been forced to scour the area for sufficient grain and dried meat to feed his men. Somehow, Sogor had managed to obtain the best pick of the provisions still left in Bebbanburg, a fact that annoyed Rolf no end. At least, until he had taken three men and returned from the sheds where Sogor's companies were piling up their food with several barrels of good mead and some salted pork.

"You don't think that he will miss it, do you?" he had asked Bridget who just shrugged but accepted a cup of mead from him.

"Here's to you two fair ladies," Rolf toasted, tipping his cup towards first Rowenna and then, with a wink, at Bridget.

"You don't give up, do you? Do you think to wear down my defences like a fortress by repeated assaults, despite the odds against success?"

Rolf shrugged. "Such a citadel would be worthy of a hundred attacks or more."

"You can be charming at times, I will give you that," remarked Bridget.

Hussa was feeling sour so moved away from the fire and drank his mead alone. He had no excuse for not talking to Rowenna, if truth be told. He was just angry with her, with Aethelfrith, with Sogor even, for how it had all turned out. Was it more than that? Was it jealousy, too?

"So, what did you get up to with Owain?" he had asked one night, just before they left Bebbanburg.

She glared at him. "Does it matter? Have I asked you about what you did before we met? They don't matter to me, why should Owain matter to you?"

"That is different," he said.

"Why?"

To that he had no answer, because there was none. The fact that it was really none of his business what she had done before they had married only made him even more angry.

After that, he had not asked her any more questions. Hardly spoke to her, in fact.

This night at the camp, she sat down on a low section of wall, with Hal now dozing on her lap.

"Hussa, I need to tell you something. Something you should know before we get to the fortress."

He looked up. "Yes. What is it?" he said.

"I'm with child," she said.

He stared at her, his mind totally blank for a moment. He suddenly felt a bit like Hal must do when he would point upwards and ask why was the sky blue or why was it dark at night-time? Everything was confusing. She was with child? A thought now formed in his head and, thanks be to the gods, he managed to stifle it before it reached his mouth: was he the father? He must be. Yet this was quite a surprise.

He had never had a child before, at least, that is what he believed. He had known many women. After all he was handsome enough, and powerful, and, whilst he knew he could be cruel in the cause of revenge when he felt justified, as with Cerdic's family, he never was so to women or people he had power over on a whim or for pleasure. Some women had been with him for just a night, others for weeks or months, but no news had reached him that he had ever fathered a child. When Hal had come along, he had assumed, as had Rowenna, that Cerdic was the father. He had even used this fact to disturb the perfect happiness he saw in his brother's marriage. Even when he accepted Hal as a son and married Rowenna, he still believed that Cerdic was the boy's father. But now…

Now those few words, that short phrase 'I'm with child' changed everything. If Rowenna was carrying his child and thus he was to become a father, did that mean he already was? He looked down at the small form asleep on her lap. Did that mean that Hal truly was his son?

He gulped.

"Oh," he said. "I didn't expect you to say that."

Chapter Eight
Replacements
Spring 611

In the fields that ran along the west bank of the river near Souekesham, farmers were sowing the seeds that would grow into this year's wheat which, in turn, would be threshed to release grain. The grain would be fed into a pair of huge stone querns in the miller's house in the town to be ground into flour which would serve to make a year's worth of bread. In the orchards and hedgerows, the early buds showed where, that autumn, a harvest of berries and apples would be picked. The newborn lambs gambolled in the meadows and young calves followed their mothers across the pastures. With the raid from West Seaxe defeated and the coming of spring, the company had celebrated the festival of the goddess Esotre and she had been merciful and granted us new life and blessed us in sending, once more, the sun to warm our newly –sown crops.

I had given thought to asking Edwin for leave again to search of my son, yet a conversation with Sabert had persuaded me that this was futile.

"You have got to be joking, Cerdic,"

"Why? The raid was defeated. Surely, now, there is little chance of another attack. Why can't I go?"

"You know what he will say. He will point out that it is spring. The winter is behind us and the campaign season begins. What we defeated may have been but a scouting party to test our strength in advance of the main attack."

I shrugged.

"Maybe, but the thing is…"

Sabert sighed.

"Do you know what he will do if you ask him?"

I shook my head.

"He will ask me, and I will tell him that you should not go. Like it or not, we need you here. Not galivanting about on some wild goose chase."

That had me riled and I clenched my fists, and through gritted teeth spat out the words, "Now, just you wait a moment, Sabert..."

I did not finish the sentence, however, because an ox horn sounded loud and strident from the north gate – the road that led to Oxenaforda.

"Now what? Have they gone around us and are attacking from the north?" Sabert said.

I did not answer because I was already running that way, passing Edwin who had emerged from his hall in the centre of the village, pulling a cloak around his shoulders.

"What is it?" he asked Sabert and I.

"We don't know," I shouted back over my shoulder.

At the gate we were met by Aedann and the three men on guard there. He was gesturing up the road that ran north about half a mile before bending north east towards Oxenaforda which lay some eight miles away, hidden beyond the woodlands and the high ground to the north and upon which lay the abbey at Aebbedun.

Round the bend, a column of spearmen came in to view, marching behind a slender, mounted lord. Behind him a pennant flapped above the column. I squinted at it and made out the image of a silver Wyvern on a green flag – symbols I recognised.

"These are men of Mercia. It might be Ceorl." I said.

"No, not the king," Cuthbert said. "Look again."

I did and realised that the rider was not the lord I thought I had seen leading the company but a lady – Cwenburg. She was travelling together with several monks in long brown tunics. The first monk made a comment and Cwenburg laughed in response. The monk turned his head and I realised it was Ealdwig. He looked up at me and waved and I returned the gestured.

"Open the gate!" Edwin ordered and, with a creak and a shudder, the wooden gate we had built swung open.

We waited until they passed through it before we scampered down the steps we had cut into the embankment to meet her.

Cwenburg held up a hand to halt the company.

"Wife," said Edwin in greeting as he pushed past me.

"Husband," she said and allowed him to assist her as she dismounted.

"Why are you here?" he asked. "Are these reinforcements?" he added looking at the spearman under the green and silver flag.

"Not reinforcements, but replacements."

"We are being replaced?" I asked. "My lady," I added.

She shook her head. "Not permanently," she admitted "Just for a few months. Do you have somewhere we can talk?"

"This way," Edwin said as he led her to the hall. Sabert accompanied them. I held back a moment to shake Ealdwig's hand. He told me he was going to visit the ale house with Lilla, which proved no surprise to anyone.

"Is that the only reason you came?" I asked him.

He looked hurt.

"Actually, Cwenburg and her father recognise our skills in healing, even if certain thick –headed lords are less perceptive," he said with a gesture in my direction.

I glared at him, but he just smiled.

89

"Anyway, she, on the king's behalf, has asked us to set up a healer's house, an infirmary if you like, in the town, to treat the garrison."

"Well, that is actually a good idea," I acknowledged.

"I am so glad you approve. So, when my Lord Abbot asked me to escort the royal party safely from the abbey to the town and look into the matter, I naturally agreed to do my duty."

"He asked or you volunteered?" Lilla asked.

The monk turned to him with a weary glance. "Details, details. Do you want an ale or not?" he asked. I shook my head at Lilla and as they walked over to the tavern went the other way to Edwin's hall.

Once inside, we all waited until Cwenburg had removed her own rain -soaked cloak. She sat down and we joined her at benches close to the fire. Looking up at me asked, "Is Aidith well, Cerdic?"

I nodded. "She is my lady," I replied. "I think she was going to buy some more pepper today," I added mischievously.

Cwenburg gave my hand a gentle slap and she laughed. "I don't imagine I will be allowed to forget that incident."

"I also tease her about it most days, if it makes you feel better, my lady," I said.

"I am looking forward to spending some time with her."

"I am sure she will enjoy that," I replied.

She did not speak again until some mead had been served. Then the princess began her explanation.

"Over the last few weeks, Aethelfrith has been concentrating a large army at Eoforwic. My father believed that he was getting ready to strike on Mercia. We had been about to call on you to march to Tamwerth as part of a general mobilisation and were also preparing to ask Gwynedd and Powys to come to our aid.

But, before we could, news reached us a few days ago from Iago of Gwynedd that there has been an uprising in Rheged. Iago's spies report that Aethelfrith is not, in fact, at Eoforwic but still at Bebbanburg, and he is responding to the uprising by sending a force under his nephew Sogor to crush the rebellion. Iago has agreed with Selyf of Powys and my father that we will aid Rheged against Aethelfrith."

"Well, aiding one's enemies' enemy makes sense, but how?" Edwin asked.

"That is where you come in, husband."

Edwin looked surprised at that. "What do you mean?"

"I mean, this is what I am doing here. I am replacing you, so you can march first to Gwynedd and then take a boat to Rheged. You are going to help Rheged, husband. I will look after the border and care for the families of your men whilst you are away."

"Why us?" I asked. "Why doesn't Iago just send Cadfan or Cadwallon?" Iago was now an old man but both his son, Cadfan, and his grandson, Cadwallon, who was only a little younger than Edwin, were capable warriors.

"That I do not know," the princess said, shaking her head. "I imagine you can find that out in Gwyedd."

"You are going where?" Aidith asked. We were in the hunting lodge that we had taken as our own house. She and Mildrith were supervising the preparations for Cwenburg to live in the lodge whilst she stayed here. Although, whilst Edwin was also here, she would join him in his hall in the town. After the company left for Gwynedd, Aidith would host her in the lodge.

"What was that?" I asked absently and looked over at her from where I was sitting with Cuthbert, sharpening our swords and seaxes on a whetstone.

91

Aidith was stirring a pot of briw – the pottage of barley, leeks, onions, carrots and chunks of pork. It was bubbling away, and she added a scatter of herbs for flavour. Mildrith was chopping thyme and rosemary close by. The aroma was pleasant, and my stomach rumbled as I remembered I was feeling hungry.

I wandered over to the hearth, picked up a horn spoon and went to scoop up a spoonful. With a tutting noise, Aidith slapped my hand away.

"It's not ready yet," she chided.

"Sorry," I mumbled.

"You have not answered me. Where are you going now?"

"Rheged, somewhere," I said absently.

"Don't you even know where in Rheged?" Mildrith asked.

I shook my head.

"A warrior does not always know where he is going, my dear," Cuthbert replied before I could answer.

She snorted. "I don't think any of you ever know where you are going," she said.

"That is not entirely fair," he said, hurt.

Mildrith laughed at that and then looked thoughtful. "Woden's beard, Cerdic, but didn't you kill their king? Rheged's king, I mean. What was his name?"

"Owain. Well, yes, but…"

"And you are going to the land whose king you killed?" Aidith said.

I nodded.

She shook her head in exasperation then pointed her spoon at me. "I have given up asking why you do things, although, I do wonder why they asked you to go. Does it not sound a bit odd to you?"

I thought about that. Now that she put it that way, it did seem a bit odd.

I pursed my lips. "Maybe it is a bit strange…"

She shrugged and went back to stirring the pot.

"Just don't die, alright? Either of you, I mean," she said gesturing at Cuthbert and me.

I took her hand and pulled her over from the hearth to my lap and hugged then kissed her.

"That is the basic plan. Beyond that, I have not really worked anything out," I said.

"Well, you might want to give it some thought. Kings rarely do things without a reason."

She rose from my lap and, after kissing me on the forehead, returned to her work.

She had a point. Why was I going? Why send for a bunch of Angles? Angles who were traditional enemies of Rheged. Why summon them from southern Mercia and send them all the way to Rheged? If Iago had a reason for this request, I needed to know it. I made up my mind to ask in Gwynedd as Cwenburg had suggested.

Lilla and Ealdwig came to see me as we prepared to depart.

"How are the plans for that infirmary coming along?" I asked the monk.

"I think we have a house we can make into a sick house," he said with some satisfaction. "I am going to return to the abbey to talk to the abbot about a stock of healing herbs along with some surgical tools, as well as making sure we have at least one brother here at any time."

"Can I ask you to keep an eye on my family, then?" I asked.

"I am happy to do so," he answered.

"Good luck in Gwyedd," Lilla said.

"Are you not coming along with us?" I asked.

He shook his head. "Not this time. I am heading south to see what is going on down there. Hope to be back this way for Yuletide. If not, then I will see you next spring."

"Aren't you afraid you will miss out on an exciting story?"

"It is always a risk wherever you are concerned," he said with a laugh, "but if something interesting happens, I am sure you will tell me when we meet again."

He made his farewells, started whisting a cheerful tune as he clambered into a small skiff and rowed off down the river.

The following day the company set out heading northwest towards Gwynedd.

A week later we stood in the court of Iago, king of Gwynedd. We were in his fortress of Deganwy which was nestled between two hilltops close to the sea. Cadfan, Iago's son, had adopted Edwin and so, I expected, that made Iago legally his grandfather. Iago was old now and had announced just the week before that he would retire to a monastery within a year, making Cadfan king. This pleased Edwin as he felt it increased his power in Gwynedd – and as the adopted son of the king, would help his cause.

One man who did not approve of this was Cadfan's natural son, Cadwallon. A year or so younger than Edwin, the boy had taken an increasingly intense dislike to Edwin and resented his hold over Cadfan. Whilst, as first –born natural son of Cadfan, Cadwallon would inherit Gwynedd one day, he still felt threatened by Edwin.

We had arrived, paid our respect to Iago, and then I had asked why we had been sent for.

"With Prince Edwin's permission, of course, it has been proposed that you will be part of an armed force we will send to the hill fort of Anwoth to aid their king in their uprising." Iago replied.

94

"Surely, there are companies from Gwynedd and Powys, or perhaps even Mercia, which could go?" I suggested.

"It was I that asked that you go," a familiar voice answered from the side of the chamber.

"You asked for us to go, Rhun? Can I ask why?" Edwin demanded.

"Politics, my dear prince," Rhun answered.

"What do you mean?"

Rhun swept his hand over Edwin's party. He lingered over me.

"My brother Owain was slain by Deira at Catraeth. Killed, in fact, by Earl Cerdic here."

I said nothing. As Mildrith had recalled, what he said was entirely true. Rheged had attacked Deira but had been defeated at Catraeth. I had killed Owain at the gates of the fortress of Stanwick Camp. Rhun had been briefly king but, wishing to remain a churchman, had stood aside for his own son, Rhoerth, who now led the rebellion against Bernicia.

"We of Deira were your enemies then," Prince Edwin said. "But now, Prince Cadfan is my adopted father and Gwynedd supports my claim to Deira. We are allies."

Rhun nodded and rose to his feet to walk across the hall.

"Allies of Gwynedd, perhaps, but many in Rheged would see you as enemies still. Yet, if you were to help in the rebellion ... if you were to stand against Bernicia, that would do much to help heal old wounds," Rhun said.

Edwin glanced at Sabert who was shaking his head.

"Lord prince, our place is to be here, or in Mercia waiting for Aethelfrith's attack," he said.

"I would agree," I said.

95

Now was no time to be campaigning in the far north when the great battle against Aethelfrith, the battle we had been preparing for these many years, was finally imminent. Fighting in this remote land, far from Mercia and Aethelfrith, would, at the very least, weaken us and, if it went badly wrong, might be the end of us.

"There is an additional reason for why you, Earl Cerdic, should go in particular," Rhun said, leaning on a stick as he moved towards me.

"And what is that?"

"We received a report this morning from a spy in Luguvalium. Do you know who leads about half the force being sent by Aethelfrith to crush the rebellion?"

I shrugged, not knowing, not sure I cared.

"Lord Hussa."

"My brother?"

"Yes. Reports say he is accompanied by a raven –haired lady who rides dressed for war. Do you know who that is?"

"I think I do…" I trailed off because a thought had just occurred to me.

Hussa was going there with Rowenna. If she was there, did that mean my son would be there, too?

"Even so," Sabert said, interrupting my thoughts, "just because Cerdic's brother is there, does not mean he has to go."

"I'll go," I said. Then, looking at Edwin, I added, "With your permission, my prince, let me take the Wictsun company."

"Lord prince, with the king's permission, of course, we should discuss this in private before we respond," Sabert said.

Iago nodded and he, Edwin and I, withdrew to the side of the room. I was aware that many pairs of eyes were turned in our direction. Many ears, no doubt, straining to hear what we were saying. Rhun, in particular, was studying us carefully, although the old man could not hope to hear us from the far side of the chamber.

"Lord prince, I should go." I said as quietly as I could, once we had reached the shadows alongside the king's hall.

"Lord prince, with all due respect to Earl Cerdic, I believe his judgement might be impaired," Sabert said.

"Sabert …." I started to say but did not get far.

"Oh, come on, Cerdic, Hussa is there. That woman Rowenna is there. That means the boy you believe to be your son may be there, too. Tell me honestly that that is not on your mind."

I did not know what to say.

Edwin studied me. "Cerdic, you have badgered me all winter to let you go after this boy. I am unsure that your judgment in this matter can be trusted," he said. "I don't know, but maybe I should send Sabert."

I shook my head. "If Hussa is there then I am best placed to defeat him. I know him better than any of you. Yes, if the boy is there, I would want to know about it. Is that a surprise? Of course, I want to know. But hear me now – I swear on Thunor's hammer that I will do my best to defeat Bernicia. Have I ever not done that?"

Sabert looked at Edwin and shrugged. "I can't say otherwise. I am still uncertain however…" Sabert said.

"I trust Cerdic," Edwin said, nodding at me. "I will send him."

He stepped back into the centre of the hall. Conversations that had started up whilst we talked died away. Iago looked up from where he had been reading a report Rhun had handed him.

"Well, Prince Edwin. Have you made a decision?"

"I have, lord king. I can see the political merits here in our supporting your allies and trying to make them our allies. In addition, if Cerdic's brother leads the enemy force or a large part of it, that may give us a tactical advantage. His presence can make a difference."

Iago nodded. "Gwynedd will send support, too," he assured us.

"Who will come with me, Lord?" I asked.

"I am going!" announced a young voice. Turning, I saw Prince Cadwallon emerge from beside the throne, surrounded by his house guards "I will take a company."

"Earl Cerdic," Iago said, "it is my wish that my grandson commands the forces we send. It is fitting that a prince leads them. Do you agree?"

I glanced at Edwin and Sabert but knew that there was only one answer I could give.

"As you wish, Lord. It will be an honour to serve the prince," I replied through gritted teeth.

I bowed and then turned to add something that only Sabert could hear.

"Just great." I muttered under my breath. "I have to take orders from the royal brat of Gwynedd."

Trusty's Hill

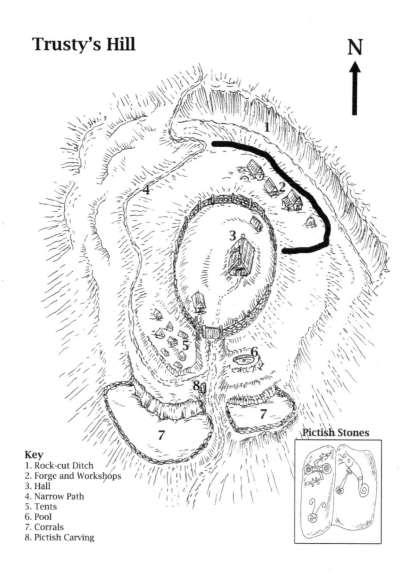

N

Pictish Stones

Key
1. Rock-cut Ditch
2. Forge and Workshops
3. Hall
4. Narrow Path
5. Tents
6. Pool
7. Corrals
8. Pictish Carving

Chapter Nine
Anwoth
Spring 611

I thought it would take us a few days to organise the boats to take us across the short sea crossing to a small fishing village not far from Anwoth. However, Cadfan had not been idle whilst he waited for our arrival, and the fully provisioned boats, along with crews and captains, were ready when we arrived in Deganwy. If anything was to be done to intervene in the fate of the uprising, it must be done quickly and so, with only a night's rest in Deganwy, we set off before dawn the following morning when the tides were favourable, and a southerly breeze filled our sails.

The actual sea crossing itself took little more than a day, passing first up the rugged coast of Rheged with its peaks and moors, and then crossing the same waters I had sailed through with Hussa when escaping from the Scots on the way to that fateful battle of Degsastan. On that journey we had been apparent allies, but we had been only a couple of weeks away from his bretrayal of Deira, the murder of my mother and the burning of the Villa.

I was standing at the prow of the ship staring out over the sea and thinking about that betrayal when Eduard punched my shoulder.

"What did you do that for?"

"To get your attention. You were miles away – you alright?"

"Years ago, not miles away, but yes, I'm fine – it's nothing. Were you asking me something?"

He gave me one of his *'I don't believe you'* looks but left matters alone.

"I was just saying that I can't say I am eager about the idea of Cadwallon being in charge, he is not exactly keen on us, is he?" Eduard commented as he sat down next to me and looked over at Cadwallon's vessel as it cut through the waves a little seaward of us. To our front we were closing in on the coastline of northern Rheged, the part to the north and west of Luguvalium.

"That is true," I said, nodding in agreement. "Just have to keep an eye on him and make sure none of us lose our heads, won't we?" I gave him a hard look as I said this.

"Me? Why me? Calmest person around, me."

On my other side, Cuthbert snorted.

"Oh, sure you are. Remember that time you got into a fight with about five Bernicians after Degsastan and ended up breaking several noses. All because of what they said about your mother."

He held his hands out to express his innocence. "I love my mother. They had it coming."

"Then there was that time you slept with that lass at the tavern in Tamwerth after Edwin's wedding and her husband came in and you threw him out the window!" Aedann shouted from where he was sitting on a barrel next to the front mast, needle and thread in one hand and a tunic he had ripped when loading the ship in the other.

"He interrupted me at a rather delicate moment. You go back to your blasted sewing!"

"It was a top floor window, with the shutters closed. He smashed through the shutters and then fell fifteen feet. Luckily, he did not break his neck. It was only the fact that he landed in the privy pit outside that saved him."

Eduard shook his head.

101

"I don't know. You do one or two things wrong in the heat of the moment and no one ever forgets."

"I think the point is," I said, trying to bring the conversation back under control, "that we just need to remember we don't have any friends here. Our job, however, is to show that we are Rheged's allies. So, no cavorting with the local women. Keep sober, no fighting and try not to start a war or anything like that."

"You can trust us, Cerdic," Eduard said earnestly. I spotted Cuthbert glance at Aedann and exchange a doubtful look.

The following morning, the Novantae coast of North Rheged was close at hand and so, following Cadwallon's vessel, we nudged up the River Fleet and into the small harbour. There we docked and disembarked and were met by a squad of spearmen. Their leader greeted Cadwallon.

"My name is Gurci – huscarl to King Rhoerth. You are welcome Lord Prince. I am asked to request that you and your men should hurry along to Anwoth Fort."

"Why the rush?" I asked. Gurci looked over at me and then he gestured eastward along the road that led towards Luguvalium. Smoke could be seen rising from some miles away.

"Bernician campfires?" I asked.

He nodded. "They are as little as a day's march away. Likely to arrive by tomorrow night, we believe. They might have scouts ahead of the main party, perhaps mounted, so we are looking to get all the men inside the fortress today."

"Lead on then," Cadwallon ordered. Then he turned to me and added. "Let's unfurl our standards, make an impression."

"You're sure?" I said.

"Yes. It's just what they need to see."

Cadwallon organised his company and headed off with them in the lead. The Wicstun company assembled next. When the running wolf banner, as well as Aedann and Edwuard's banners were raised, I saw Gurci study it intently and then stare at me.

"I have seen that banner before, a long time ago – at the battle of Catraeth."

"You were there?"

He nodded.

"I was a young huscarl in my first battle."

"You chose a pretty terrible battle for your first. Yet for me, too, it was my first proper fight."

He studied me.

"Your face is familiar…" Then his eyes widened. "I remember now. I was at the gate, close to King Owain. We were forcing our way in. Thought we had won the day, in fact. Then you were there and Owain fell. You killed him… didn't you?"

The question hung in the air. Around him his men were staring at me. Next to me, I felt movement. Aedann's hand had drifted across to rest on his sword pommel. On the other side, Eduard had his axe held in his hand. It had been on his back a moment before. I glanced at him and shook my head and he lowered the weapon. Then I turned back to Gurci.

"Yes, that was me. I was your enemy that day but hope this year to fight on your side."

"So, you are Earl Cerdic. The man who killed Owain and held the gate against us at Catraeth. The same man who helped defeat us at Degsastan."

"Yes, I was there …"

He studied me for a long moment and then finally nodded. "Some of my kindred would consider you the devil himself, or maybe a demon incarnated in human form and come to torment us."

"You met this bloke before?" Eduard muttered. "He is not far wrong"

I ignored him.

"What do you think?"

He stepped closed and looked me in the eye.

"You are no demon. You are just a man, which can be worse. It does not really matter for, at any other time, my oath to Owain would oblige me to kill you. But I have sworn another oath to his grandson, Rhoerth. So, today, with the Bernicians just hours away, I welcome any help I can get from man or devil. So, at least until this war is over, neither me nor my men will harm you."

"I am relieved to hear that," I said.

"Follow me, then," Gurci said and marched off after Cadwallon.

Eduard let out a whistle. "Touchy folk, eh?"

I turned to Eduard to reply but Aedann beat me to it

"About the death of their former king? There is a surprise!"

Eduard nodded at him. "See, even Aedann agrees they are overreacting."

Aedann blustered, "You idiot! Of course, they are touchy! Half the poetry written by Aneirin and Taliessen was about Owain or his father Urien of Rheged. They are seen as valiant defenders of the Britons and valiant in their defiant fight against you English. How do you think they feel about the man who killed Owain?"

"That was years ago!" Eduard said.

Aedann shook his head. "My people, the Welsh, don't forget things in a dozen years. They will still be singing songs about the fight against the English in a dozen centuries!"

"Alright," I said. "let's put the flags away for now. And when we arrive at this fortress, Eduard, keep your gob shut. No tirades about them needing to 'move on' Let's go." I said and headed out after Gurci. As we marched along, I silently cursed Cadwallon for suggesting I unfurl those banners.

We followed Cadwallon and Gurci along the north side of the Fleet estuary. Presently, the path turned eastwards in the direction of a crossing over the river and those distant Bernician campfires.

"Not that way," Gurci said. "We might run into the Bernicians. Follow me."

We all veered off northwards heading upriver and further inland. The ground rose gently into a terrain of low hills and rolling countryside, thickly forested and cut by streams. We splashed through one such stream just shy of where it flowed into the Fleet and then turned to follow the track as it ran along the side of the stream north and westwards, further into the hills. Visible now over the trees to the north of us was our destination – a hill fort that rose a good two hundred feet above the level of the river and the sea.

We climbed until we were level with the fort and then headed more directly towards it along a track that curved around the southern side of the hill, following the walls of a stone enclosure that housed over forty cattle including many young calves. The enclosure backed on to the exposed face of a rocky outcrop. On the far side of the enclosure, the path switched back to turn uphill above the outcrop. This gave us access to a terrace where more cattle as well as sheep and pigs were kept. A cow herder watched us pass and then returned to minding his charges.

Onward, the path climbed up to a further higher terrace with an outer defensive wall enclosing a number of dwellings to the left side and a well on the right before passing up a steep slope that led to the summit.

"What's that?" Eduard asked pointing to a rock slab that leant against the side of the passageway through which we were passing. Its surface was carved with elaborate symbols. I could make out the figure of some form of sea creature, its body bent forward over what looked like a pin or a brooch. Further over was a series of more abstract designs – full of circles and swirling lines.

"No idea," I said. "Where is Lilla when you need him, eh?"

Once we passed the stone, we were directed to lead the companies into the terraced area behind its protective wall. Here we found several temporary lean –to shelters erected against the slope of the hill and Gurci directed me to leave the company to settle in whilst he led Cadwallon and myself up the slope through a gateway in the wall that ran around the summit. It was made of stone laced with a timber framework. The enclosure was quite small. There was just enough space for a fair – sized hall and a few outbuildings. Above the hall, the banner of the royal house of Rheged flew. It was the first time I had seen it since Degsastan. There it had been somewhere in the distance. The last time I had been this close to a king of Rheged was when I killed Owain at Catraeth fourteen years before.

Two mail –shirted guards stood on either side of the hall doorway. Next to them were baskets where Gurci now pointed.

"Please leave your weapons here," he instructed.

Cadwallon appeared to be about to argue.

"Prince, we should do as we are asked. After all, this is a fortress preparing for war and caution is quite understandable," I suggested.

As I said this, I removed my weapons. One was Wreccan, my long sword. The other was Catraeth, the roman shortsword with which I had slain Owain.

"Indeed, I can understand why," Cadwallon said eyeing the blade. "That weapon in particular can hardly be popular here."

Gurci followed his gaze and stiffened slightly. One of the guards caught sight of the blade as I placed it in the basket. He said nothing but his expression was dark.

"I expect these to be here when I return." I said.

"They will be, Lord. None of my men would want to touch that particular weapon, you can be sure of that," Gurci said and led us into the hall.

Word of our arrival had clearly reached the court as inside the hall we were greeted with silence and a hundred pairs of eyes, all staring at me. The deepest frost of winter would have difficulty competing with that welcome.

Gurci led us past the benches, each lined with warriors, to the far end where a young king sat at the high table flanked by his lords. Platters of roast game steamed on the tables and several men were sipping at goblets or gulping down ale from drinking horns. We had arrived during a meal. Gurci bowed his head followed by Cadwallon and myself.

"Lord, may I present Prince Cadwallon ap Cadfan ap Iago who is king in Gwynedd."

Cadwallon stepped forward and with a flourish produced an ornate cross on a silver chain.

"My grandfather bids me present this gift as a sign of his goodwill and his admiration of you, lord king."

Rhoerth bent forward to take the item and examined it.

"A fine gift indeed. My thanks to your grandfather for sending you and your men to our aid. Come, sit by me so we can talk more."

A chair was pushed up to the table by Rhoerth's side and Cadwallon went around the tables, took his seat and accepted a goblet of ale.

That left me standing beside Gurci who now gestured at me.

"May I also present Earl Cerdic ap Cenred of Deira and companion to Prince Edwin."

Rhoerth nodded and studied me.

"So, this is the great Lord Cerdic. The man who held the gate at Catraeth, who slew my uncle, King Owain, and thwarted our efforts to drive your race into the sea. I must say, you do not lack for courage, Earl Cerdic. There are many men here who would be glad if I had you thown from our fortress, so your body was dashed against the rocks below. Or hanged, so the Northumbrian army that is but hours away can see."

Around me there was a rumble of assent at these words.

"I, for one, would find that amusing," Cadwallon said.

I glared at him before turning back to the king.

"Believe me, lord king that to do so would only suit the purposes of my enemies and yours in that same army."

Rhoerth titled his head. "Oh? How so?"

I hesitated. I could see Cadwallon smile and lean back, sipping at his goblet as if he was enjoying the show.

"My brother leads part of that force."

I might as well have set fire to the bloody hall. Half the men leapt to their feet. Despite the prescription on weapons in the king's presence, a dozen swords were brandished in my direction. The words 'spy' and 'kill him' rumbled across the mob. I raised my hands.

"Lord, believe me, Hussa is no ally of mine. We share a father but have different mothers. He murdered my mother And one day I will kill him for it. He serves Aethelfrith, enemy to my own lord, Edwin."

"So, your enemy is my enemy," Rhoerth said, nodding as he understood. "So much is clear, son of Cenred. What I need to know, though, is why I should not treat you as my enemy also. You killed my uncle, one of the great warrior kings of my people. Would it not be fitting for me to have you slain in turn?"

Around me the bellows and catcalls demanded exactly that.

What should I have replied? Should I have threatened him – pointed out that the very company who had defeated his people at Catraeth were encamped outside the gates? Should I have begged for mercy?

What I said was, "Kill me if you like, but not tonight. Let us defeat my brother and Bernicia. Then after that, if you still wish it, you can kill me…"

Rhoerth stared at me for a long moment and then, finally, he laughed.

"Come, sit on my other side, Lord Cerdic, and let us be friends tonight."

I did so, happy to be further away from the hostile glares directed at me from most men in that hall.

"What do you say to that, Prince Cadwallon?"

"Oh, Lord Cerdic and I are already are the greatest of friends." Cadwallon said, fixing me with a glare as unwelcoming as that of the king's men.

Chapter Ten
Too tough a nut
Summer 611

"You should go back. Return to Luguvalium with Bridget, at least. Better still, I will send Rolf back with you all to Bebbanburg," Hussa had insisted. He looked along the path, searching for a sight of the big warrior amongst the backs of the company riding away from him.

"Why?" Rowenna asked arching her eyebrows.

He turned to look at her again. "You are with child, woman," he said, tapping the hilt of his sword. "We are going into battle. It is hardly the right place for you."

Rowenna glared at him. "I am many months away from having the child, Hussa. I have a job to do here. It is a job I am good at. Besides, the king would not be pleased if I disobeyed his orders, would he? Think how that would look for you."

"Balls to the king," Hussa said, shaking his head. "I don't care what he will say, I won't take a risk with you."

"It's not your choice to make, husband. I also gave the king my word and once I agree to do something, I see it through."

"But..." he started to say but withered under her glare. He had led men in a shield wall and assaulted the walls of a fortress and his resolve had held strong. On that crumbling pathway, with no enemy in sight and with hundreds of his men not far away, he should have been at ease and full of confidence. He should have been able to put his foot down and insist that he got his way with this woman.

"But what?" she asked.

"Nothing dear..." was all he could manage.

"That's better," she said with a sweet smile on her lips. She leant over and kissed him then leant back and laughed at his bewildered expression.

"Well now, stop dawdling beside the path, the company is getting ahead of us," she said and with a kick of her heels, trotted her horse along after the army.

Hussa stared at her, cursed and followed in her wake.

The route they took meandered through low rolling hills, heavily forrested and thick with undergrowth. Here and there they passed old hill forts which they were obliged to check. None of them showed signs of recent occupation, however, so they reformed the column and pressed on. A few days later the column emerged from woodland close to the River Fleet.

Across the river, they could see their objective – a fortress on a hill maybe two hundred feet above the river and about half a mile from it. At the river crossing a small town had grown up which offered shelter and the opportunity to sleep indoors after several damp nights under the stars. Most of the inhabitants had fled so there was plenty of room and an enterprising merchant who had followed the army from Luguvalium set up in the abandoned inn and soon had a thriving business going as the men, thirsty from the hours on the road, were happy to pay for an ale or mead.

Night was drawing near, so Sogor and Hussa agreed to billet the men as best they could in the settlement. Then they set off with the captains of the companies to scout out the fortress. Despite Hussa's disapproving glare, Rowenna accompanied them. Hal was left with Garrett, one of the men from Hussa's company who had been with Hussa almost as long as Rolf and who Hal found amusing. The humour they shared was predominantly based on Garrett's ability to emit a variety of loud noises from

111

various parts of his body. Rowenna was not entirely pleased with Hal's choice of company but as it kept him happy, she let it go. Three –year –old boys do need lots of entertainment, after all.

They crossed the river, passed through a narrow strip of farmland and then exited into the undulating hillocks and moorland that lay beyond. They finally halted in some woodland a few hundred yards from Anwoth and looked up at the fortress.

"Steep, ain't it," Rolf observed, taking in the hillside that rose at a severe angle to the hilltop. Climbing up the sides of the hill would be hard work for men, particularly labouring under the weight of mail shirts, heavy wooden shields and weaponry. At several levels, terraces had been cut into the hillside above ditches and either earthen embankments or stone walls added.

"Looks like the only accessible route is the path that leads between those terraces to the gates..." Sogor observed.

"That is a slaughterhouse waiting to happen," Hussa argued.

"These rebels can't have many real warriors with them. A determined assault by experienced veterans would be able to take that gate," Sogor said.

Rolf, standing behind Sogor, shook his head and then flashed Hussa a look which said 'what a load of bollucks.'

"Even poorly trained fyrd with rocks could kill fifty of our men before they reached those gates. Do you want to lead the way?"

Sogor glared at Rolf and bristled. "I might do that just to show everyone that the great Hussa is not as great as he might think he is!"

Then he studied the gatehouse for a while and as time went by seemed somewhat less confident than his outbourst had implied. Eventually, he spoke again.

112

"Still, if they are just fyrd, there is little glory in that victory, is there? Not much point in me going."

"Of course not," Hussa replied dryly. Sogor stared at him, apparently trying to work out if Hussa was mocking him or not.

Rolf coughed to draw everyone's attention.

"What is it?" Sogor asked irritably.

Rolf did not reply at first but just pointed. "I think there is a chance for glory here, I just noticed what banners are flying beside the royal standard of Rheged."

They all turned to look at the fortress.

Hussa saw first the Stag of Rheged, then he spotted a banner with a red dragon.

"That is a Gwynedd banner. They must have sent help."

Rolf pointed at a third banner that flapped above the stone battements. The wind caught it and it unfurled showing a running wolf. They all watched it in silence for a moment, taking in the implication.

"My brother is there. Or, at least, some of his company. Gwynedd must have sent him to help Rhoerth. How poetic that he goes to save the kingdom whose king he killed."

"So, it is not just a fyrd rabble within. The Wicstun company is there." Rolf said. "That means it will not be an easy fight, Lord Sogor."

"Plenty of glory for you, then," Hussa suggested to Sogor. "After you."

"Your bloody family are a pain in the arse, Hussa," Sogor said.

"Now you and I agree on something at last," Hussa replied without smiling.

Sogor scratched at his beard whilst he thought. "If an assault will be hard going, what other ideas are there?" Sogor asked.

113

"I think, in this case, I can be of help," Rowenna said.

They all turned to look at her.

"How?" Hussa asked.

She moved forward to peer at the fortress, shielding her eyes from the sun which was now low in the western sky.

"By getting up there and taking a look," she replied, glacing north along the edge of the woods, looking for something.

"What! No, that is an insane idea," Hussa said.

"Why insane, Lord Hussa? As I understand it, this is exactly what she used to do," Sogor replied. "Is this not the reason she was instructed to come with us? The king wanted her to be of service to us."

"That is different. She was meant to just give us advice. Not risk her life sneaking into the fortress. It is a crazy idea."

"Why?" Rowenna asked, her eyes glittering with irritation. Hussa felt Rolf take a step back.

"I won't send you into that sort of danger; what sort of a man would that make me?"

Rowenna laughed. "I used to be sent into all sort of places far more dangerous. Why is this any different from when you sent me into that villa in South Seax?"

"There is an army up there. My brother … his company…."

"Your brother and his company were both at the villa three years ago. You did not care then, why now?"

Hussa shook his head.

"We were not married then and you were not…"

"Not what?" Rowenna asked.

Sogor cleared his throat loudly to gain their attention.

"The point is that the king sent Rowenna because she has certain skills you don't have. Nor do any of us. We have all heard the tales of the Nightjar. If anyone can get in and find a weakness up there, it is her. She is going," Sogor insisted.

Hussa opened his mouth to argue but could think of nothing to say. So, he shut it again.

Sogor clearly took his silence as assent. "Then it is decided. We will rest the men, and then establish patrols into these woods. Rowenna will scout out the fortress and return with a report on weaknesses and options for getting us inside. Then we will plan the assault."

That evening, Bridget and Rowenna cooked for the family. Rolf had managed to spot a brace of hare in the woods and dispatched both with a slingshot. He knew that Hal loved the rich, thick stew that the ladies could prepare from them and handed her the fruits of his hunting expedition. He turned to leave but Rowenna called him back.

"Plenty here for us five to share", she said and gestured that Rolf should join them at the table. He did so and, after a cup or two of mead, the four were soon laughing over a tale of how Rolf had once snagged his britches on a palisade he was climbing over and, having left them behind on the nail, had to fight for an hour with nothing from the waist down. In the end, he had driven his opponents off and captured the fortress.

"I think the enemy were so impressed by what they saw that they ran away," he said.

"Oh, and who were the enemy, if I may be so bold as to ask?" Bridget had said.

Rolf frowned at Hussa. "Who were they? I forget."

Hussa scatched his face as he tried to remember. "Scots, I think – your people, I mean," Hussa said, gesturing at her.

"Huh, Scots men might have been impressed by your physique, but I dare say Scots women would not," she said.

"I will let you do your own appraisal, if you behave yourself."

"If I behaved myself, what would be the point?" Bridget said.

Rowenna coughed and tilted her head toward Hal who was listening intently with a puzzled but fascinated expression on his face.

"Right, and on that note, you two can leave and continue this outside. It is time to put the lad to bed," Hussa said.

Rolf and Bridget shuffled out of the door. As he left, Rolf turned back to Hussa.

"Twenty shillings?" he asked

"Twenty shillings," Hussa replied. "So, behave yourself!"

After they had left, Hal lapped up the last of the broth and Rowenna played with him for a while and then, as he grew drowsy, took him into the small hut that Hussa had been allocated for himself and his family. Hussa followed her in and watched in silence as she lay down beside the boy, singing softly to him of ships sailing over an eternal sea, seeking new lands and adventures as he dropped off to sleep. She then sat up and looked at Hussa.

"Well?" she asked.

"What?" he replied.

"What do you mean, what?"

Hussa shook his head. "I don't know what you are asking me, Rowenna."

She got up and moved over to the low hearth and poked the glowing embers.

"I am waiting for you to say something. You have said bugger all since we got back from the woods."

116

"I am not sure what there is to say. You have made your mind up to do this thing. What does it matter what I say?"

"So, now you just plan to sulk?"

"I am not sulking."

Rowenna snorted in derision. "Yes, you bloody well are!" she said. Hal stirred in his sleep, so she stroked his hair and then dropped her voice to repeat the words. "Yes, you bloody are!"

Hussa stomped over to the fire and took the stick from Rowenna to poke at the logs himself.

"Think about Hal. What if something happens to you? He would not have a mother. I would have lost a wife."

"Every time you go to a battle the same risk is run. More so, in fact, because I try to avoid any fighting."

Hussa looked around the small hut and sighed.

"You know, sometimes I just wish we were a boring family in a boring hut like this one, living out our boring lives, not thinking about kings and princes. Just the pigs and the wheat. Don't you?"

Rowenna's face softened. She laughed a soft little laugh. "No, I don't. You know why?"

Hussa shook his head.

"Because we would be awful at it. We came from huts like these and we left them behind. . Neither of us wanted to live like this. This was never a life we would lead. We both had our reasons. Things we have told each other and things we have maybe not. But we left this behind."

They were interrupted by a snore from the bed. They both turned and watched Hal as he slept, oblivious to their concerns.

"Do you ever worry about what world we are leading him into?" Hussa asked.

"Not while there is one of us to do the leading. He has our blood in his veins. He belongs in the life we lead. Kings and princes, dynasties and kingdoms. Not pigs and wheat."

"'*A share of the glory...*'"

She frowned. "What do you mean?"

He shook his head. "It is something Rolf once said. He was talking about us all wanting a share of the glory about us, my glory he meant, but in truth we, too, seek a share of the glory of Aethelfrith or the other kings and princes."

"What is so wrong about that? We would be awful growing wheat, and even more terrible at rearing pigs. The world needs pig farmers, fishermen and men and woman to sow the wheat and harvest it. But that is not us. What are we good at? We are good at this." She waved her hand about her. "Kings and princes, plots and intrigue. It is the world you found me in. Palaces and fortresses. It is the world I want our children part of."

He looked about the hut. "If you say so," he said.

She patted the bed beside her. "Tonight, this is palace enough for me. Come, sit here."

"As you wish," he said sitting down beside her as he pulled her into his arms to kiss her.

Chapter Eleven
The Nightjar
Summer 611

Carpenters and blacksmiths had sets of implements and equipment with which they plied their trade. This was just the same for Rowenna. Whilst a journeyman's tools consisted of hammers and lathe, adze or anvil, hers were designed to aid her own craft. When they had ridden out from Bebbanburg, she had thrown a wooden chest on the back of one of the supply wagons that accompanied the army.

Now, as dusk turned into full night, Rowenna opened up her travelling chest and examined the contents. The clothing was dark. Not fully black, for night was rarely totally black. The tunic was dark green and the britches, which allowed more mobility than a dress, the same shade – both almost grey, in fact. After she had dressed, she considered her footwear. The thin leather boots she selected were well worn –in and had long ago lost any squeaks and other noises that might betray her passage, and so both comfortable and almost silent.

She tucked a pair of light throwing axes into her belt and added a seax in its scabbard. She wore no armour for that would slow her down. If she found herself in combat, her aim would be to escape as quickly as possible. Mail shirts and cumbersome wooden boards would be of no benefit. Darkness would be her shield this night and flight her best strategy if she encountered opposition.

Finally, she smeared mud on her face to break up the reflection of moonlight on her pale skin and tied back her raven hair to keep it out of the way. Her bracelets and necklaces which again might catch the silver light of moon or star were removed and stored in the chest. She considered her reflection in a piece of polished metal and nodded with satisfaction.

When she had plied her trade for West Seaxe and other lands in the past, she had acquired a name that fitted her admirably. They called her 'Nightjar' after the nocturnal bird which had mottled grey –brown plumage granting ideal camouflage which, coupled with an ability for almost silent flight, made it a superb hunter in twilight and darkness.

"I had not thought to see you like this again," Hussa observed from the far side of the room where he had been watching her in silence. "Well, I will give you this, you look the part once more. The Nightjar is back amongst us. However, I cannot say I am happy about it."

She frowned but then relaxed and put a hand on his cheek.

"There was a time when you found this garb enticing as I recall. Arosuing even…"

He smiled.

"That has not changed."

"What has changed is you are not happy for me to pursue my vocation any –more. You once were, don't you recall? You encouraged it even. We were lovers and enjoyed each other's company but when I had need to become the Nightjar, you never blinked or hesitated, not even if I had to kill in service of West Seaxe. You also could be just as ruthless and focused in pursuit of your goals. That seems not the case any –more. I would not be surprised if I heard you say to Rolf 'Pull up a stool, old companion, pour yourself some mead and let us old men tells our tales.'"

Hussa blinked and took a step back.

"Have you been talking to Rolf?"

120

She shook her head.

"What do you mean?"

"It is just that you sound like him. Never mind. Look I still care about my rank and power but there is more now. Since Hal came along, since we married and now since I learnt you were once more with child. Believe me, I am surprised as any of the rest of you that I care so much," he laughed. Then he took her hands in his.

"Let the Nightjar be about her business tonight. Just make sure Rowenna returns to me with the dawn."

"Do not worry, husband, I will return to my nest," she said and then moved over to embrace him briefly before, after a glance at their son, they both left the hut leaving Hal fast asleep beneath the furs.

Hussa had insisted on accompanying her through the village and the woodlands until they were within sight of the hill fort and had reached the line of patrols that he and Sogor had established to watch the enemy position. As they walked along, she noticed Hussa looking at her.

"What is it?" she asked.

"I was just thinking that I know little about you before I came to Witanceastre. I know you came from the west but nothing else? Were you always so adventurous? What about your family?"

She laughed at that.

"My family?" She shook her head. "Far from it. My mother you know."

"Nina," he said. The old woman had been with Rowenna when he first met her, a former slave in the household of Boyden in Witanceastre, freed now at Hussa's request after his part in the West Seaxe victories in the Thames Valley.

"Yes. Well, she had seven children and her life was always devoted to family and household in a quiet farmstead in the lands near the city of Badon. Most of my sisters never left the village, had married young and were mothers when I left, some are probably even grandmothers by now I guess and very content with it too. Almost half the village were related to my mother, all happily in and out of each other's huts all day, all knowing everything about each other. That life was all about the latest marriage, the latest birth or death, the passing of each season to the next and the celebration and maintaining of traditions passed down by our ancestors from before the Romans had come to the island from all accounts. No one was curious about what went on beyond their little valley. Kings and queens and their affairs were of no interest. They barely knew even which kingdom they lived in and were not bothered at all about their ignorance. In fact, it seemed to be a matter of pride that that they new nothing of the world a few miles away."

They had left the village now and were approaching the trees.

Hussa pursed his lips.

"You seem resentful of their happiness."

Rowenna stopped and looked at him. She slowly shook her head.

"No, not resentful. Maybe I don't understand them but if they were happy with that life, good luck to them. But I had seen it all and by the age of ten I just knew that I wanted more than that. I started going on long walks – something completely unheard of. The furthest my family travelled was to the nearest market less than five miles from the village. When they did, they treated everyone outside the village with suspicion, avoided conversation other than that necessary in relation to buying what they needed and selling what they had brought with them. They would leave as soon as they could and were most glad to return home at the end of the day."

"You felt differently, I gather?" Hussa asked as they carried on down the path through the woods.

She smiled at him.

"I loved those journeys, just loved them. I would listen eagerly to any tales from the travelling merchants that attended, or the stories and songs of bards and poets. Any news of distant places fascinated me whether of this world or others. Then one day I really went too far."

Hussa raised his eyebrows.

"Indeed, tell me about it."

"Well, when we were at the market, I managed to slip away from the family and I persuaded a cloth merchant and his wife to take me with them to Badon and let me sleep on their workshop floor in exchange for doing chores. I stayed with them for several days. But what days they were!

She had stopped again and Hussa could see that her eyes glittered with the memories.

"The stone walled city – the first I had ever seen. Now thinking back, it was full of the crumbling remains of Roman buildings mostly used as warehouses, workshops and trading houses but still the same at the time I thought they were amazing. The crowds of people in a town of five thousand and more staggered me, as did the sight of all those people going about their life. The clatters and bangs from the workshops, mingled with the calls of market folk, assaulted my senses." She closed her eyes now, bringing the past back to life.

"Even more marvellous were the baths – large pools of steaming hot waters built inside yet more stone structures that seemed like temples to me. Then there were the languages I heard. Not just

Welsh but English, the first time I had heard it, and even Irish. The entire experience was overwhelming. The more I saw, the more I realised I was seeing part of a wider world, a world far bigger than my own little valley, and I desperately wanted to see more of it."

They were coming to the end of the path and up ahead the hill fort loomed dark and bulky against the stars, obscuring part of the Eagle constellation that was rising in the west. The moon was a faint sliver high above them, perhaps a quarter full and casting only a modest light. It was a good night for anyone wanting to pass unnoticed.

"You can tell me the rest later, but you have certainly seen a lot of it these last few years," Hussa said. Then he reached out and held her to him for a moment. "And I want you to see more of it with me. So be careful and come back safely."

She stood back from him nodded her head and then vanished into the woods, not west towards the hill directly but north-wards, aiming to circle the fortress from a distance of half a mile or more out. Her intention was to approach it from the north west, hoping that the enemy sentinels on watch would be less attentive in that direction. Her planned route should, she thought, lead to the hill fort from a direction more or less opposite the main gateway which she hoped might provide an access point which would be less well defended.

Rowenna needed to avoid being spotted by guards on the fort top or else encountering any roving patrol that Rheged might have sent out into the lands around the fortress. Therefore, her route took her in a long loop around the hill and, due to the need for stealth, would take her a full two hours. As she walked, the moon sank towards the east and Loki's Torch – the brightest star in the night sky – followed it. The Eagle was now high overhead, pursuing Dain the Deer through the heavens.

She was out alone at night, travelling lightly armed and close to an enemy fortress, moving through land where, at any moment, she might encounter a Rheged patrol. Leaving aside the dangers of human warriors, the woods were, most likely, haunted by spirits or inhabited by dark elves, trolls or ogres. No sane man, or woman for that matter, would do what she was doing. Yet, as she walked, despite the dangers or maybe even because of them, she enjoyed the freedom of doing this, leading her to questioning her own reason for being so keen to do it.

Her family had certainly never understood. When she returned home, her family were angry with her for staying away so long. They did not listen to her tales and showed no interest in her travels.

"Stay at home and we will get you married soon and then you will be happy," they told her.

"Let the girl be. She is still a child," her mother, Nina, had said to them.

"Not for much longer," her oldest sister had replied. "She should stay at home and get ready for that day."

That day proved to come along far too quickly for her liking. One of the village elders' wives had died that year and he was looking for a new wife. Rowenna's sisters had approached him and suggested her. He was more than happy to have as a wife the young, beautiful maiden who was then not even thirteen and had agreed to all the terms of the union. Rowenna discovered that the bride price, a payment to the bride's family intended to reflect the loss of her from the family and thus an assessment of her worth and value, was almost nothing.

"A man pays more for a night with a whore in Badon than that!" she said in outrage.

125

"That is probably what you have been doing in Badon and other places, from what I hear," her oldest sister had replied. "You will marry this man and he will make you respectful."

Her father had sealed the agreement with a shaking of hands with the elder and at the same time her fate was sealed, or so it seemed. That night the whole family got drunk celebrating the agreement about the wedding, so that Rowenna had been able to escape the village, taking with her whatever silver she could find including, and here she felt justified, the bride price which was on the table in front of her slumbering father. The only person who was not drunk that night was her mother who had run after her. Catching up with her at dawn the next day, Nina had tried to persuade her to return.

"I know you are not happy, but the man is not unkind and will give you a roof and status in the world. The world is not safe for a young girl." Rowenna recalled her saying.

Nina's words proved to be unfortunately true, for, whilst the pair stood on a hill arguing, they were attacked by a raiding party of Saxons from Badon. The two women were taken, their wrists bound and then, screaming in terror, were dragged away.

"Stop and give the password!" called a voice from the darkness. Rowenna, her mind still far in the past was startled. Whilst she had been walking, she had come round to the furthest sentry that Hussa had placed. She saw him standing across a small clearing, spear held at the ready as he peered towards her. She relaxed. The man was called Edgar and had been with Hussa a long time, although not as long as Rolf and had accompanied him to West Seaxe. She left the trees and emerged into the faint moonlight.

"The password is Firebrand."

She saw that he recognised her face though he glanced with curiosity at her clothing.

"I see the Nightjar takes flight this night," he said at last.

"She does, may I pass?"

He lowered the speak and stepped to the side to let her continue on her path.

"Any signs of enemy patrols away from the fort?" she asked. He shook his head.

"It is quiet tonight," he said. "But be careful."

She tilted her head in acknowledgment and continued on her route. Within moments the sentry was lost in the darkness behind and she was alone again. Alone with her thoughts and her memories.

After being captured, Rowenna and her mother were marched across West Seaxe to a city she later heard was called Witanceastre. The thegn leading the warband sold her to a certain Boyden who, then a young man, was a huscarl to King Ceawlin of West Seaxe.

That is how she had found her way into the household of the man who one day became Lord Boyden. At first, she and her mother were put to work in the kitchens as scullery maids. One day, one of Boyden's own warriors tried to take advantage of her near the bread ovens and Boyden had spotted this and thrown the man out. The man wanted revenge on his master and had plotted with other warriors to steal his silver. Rowenna had overheard the plotting and, in gratitude to the lord for protecting her, had told him. The men were caught, fined and exiled from the city.

Boyden had rewarded her with silver and then, appreciative of her talents, had paid her to find out secrets about other rivals and enemies. She provided him with all that he wanted and soon had left the scullery behind and became his most effective spy. Nina, whilst not possessing Rowenna's more unusual talents, was more than capable in the kitchens and was promoted to housekeeper. Captivity may not have been desirable, but they were together in the same household and fed, clothed and had a roof over their head and belonged to a master who rewarded skills and talents when he saw them. It could have been far worse.

In his employ she learnt to defend herself – skills that she eagerly absorbed as she did not want to be defenceless ever again. Knives and seax, throwing axes and the angon javelin soon became familiar to her and she became most skilled with them.

Boyden sent her on missions into neighbouring lands and even further afield. Spying came naturally to her, but her ability to extract information became enhanced if she used her good looks to influence men who she found were all too easy to sway. Sometimes things got out of hand however and on those occasions those skills with blade and missile came in handy. Soon she had honed all her skills, martial, subterfuge, stealth and seduction, using each as needed to get the job done. The person who men would soon call 'Nightjar' had come into being.

In all those years she had never felt affection for anyone, until, after fifteen years in Boyden's service, she found Hussa. She had been sent to spy upon him by Boyden and had treated him as any other target, to seduce and to use for the will of her master. The day that she realised that she had fallen in love with the Northumbrian and was not happy to carry on manipulating Hussa was a revelation. The day she found out she was with child was even more so.

Until that day she had been careful. Careful timing of encounters and when she needed it the cautious use of pennyroyal had stopped her getting pregnant before. She was never sure if she had just been careless or something more conscious was going

128

on but, in any event, she had kept the child despite Hussa's rejections of her. Those times had been hard. Why had she wanted the baby, given her earlier abhorrence of motherhood?

Hussa – what was it about the man that had attracted her to him and what was it about him that had made her fall in love with him, even want a child with him? The Nightjar had sneaked into a dozen kingdoms, spied on ten score nobles, had even assassinated a number. The Nightjar had become successful by being ruthless when she needed to be. But she was not always the Nightjar. Something about the man made her want to be Rowenna, just Rowenna, with him. Then at other times she missed her former life.

She stopped walking for a moment and recognised that all of this was why she had been so keen to come along on this expedition, why she wanted to come out alone this night. She wanted to be the Nightjar again, even if this was for the last time. The last time... why had she thought that? Was she also looking to hang up her axes and be a mother and wife? Is that what she wanted, truly?

"Woden's buttocks, what do I want?" she said out loud. Then she froze when she realised, she was now only a few hundred paces from Anwoth. She had finally reached the point she had been aiming for – a spot which was on the edge of the woods north west of the fortress. The sliver of moon was starting to sink on the far side of the hill and all about her was deep shadow. Somewhere nearby the rusting of leaves and the creak of branches betrayed the movement of a woodland creature – perhaps a fox out hunting. An owl hooted off to the north but, other than that, the night was silent.

Crouching, she surveyed the hill. The battlements atop it were illuminated by a couple of torches whose flames flickered in the gentle midnight breeze. She saw the silhouette of a warrior pass in front of one.

Closer to her, and a little lower down the northern slope, there was a terrace on which stood three buildings enclosed by a palisade where another torch burnt. Again, she saw movement that indicated a guard was patrolling there. Below the palisade the hillside dipped into a ditch. She frowned at that. An assault up this northern and western hillside would mean passing over that ditch which would be a big ask for any army. Was there any other way to get up to the fort? She would have to get closer to find out.

Slowly she stood up and half crouching, scampered across the open ground between the woods and the hillside. She paused for a moment, holding her breath and gazing up the slope, looking for any indication that she had been spotted. All was silent and she let her breath out. She started climbing the steep hill. It was hard going and slow work, but after a while she had reached the ditch. It was deep and its bottom filled with a foot or two's depth of muddy water so would be difficult to climb out of. She turned to her right, towards the west and followed the ditch. After a hundred paces it narrowed as it drew close to the steep western hillside. That hillside would also be impossible for a man in armour to climb.

"This is useless," she said quietly to herself. She was about to give up and turn away when she spotted something. The ditch did not in fact run the whole way to the western slope – there was a small gap a few feet wide between the two. At that point, the slope flattened somewhat and led into the lower terrace around the western end of the palisade. Now, if a body of men could get up there and gain access to that area, then the question was, could they then get into the main fort above? Was there communication from terrace to fortress? There surely must be but she needed to know.

"Well, only one way to find out." she muttered and started on her way around the ditch and the palisade, intending to move through the terrace above and then to explore the wall between it and the fortress.

Chapter Twelve
The camp
Summer 611

After we had settled in at Anwoth, the Wicstun company took part in the watch over the enemy encampment. From the vantage point of the high hilltop, we could see easily over the woodlands and rolling lands all the way to the settlement that straddled the river where dozens of campfires could be seen burning. Smoke also rose from the homesteads indicating that the Bernician commanders had billeted men in the town as well as had them camp out in the surrounding fields. I wondered if my brother was sat around one of the distant fires or was under one of those dark roofs which the firelight illuminated.

It was late at night, with what there was of the moon sinking eastwards and occasionally visible betweens scattered clouds, when I decided to check on the Wicstun men, all of whom were members of Aedann's 'swords.' He was with three of them watching the northern walls.

"Anything?" I asked, leaning forward against the stone battlements and gazing out over the forest.

"Nope," he said, shaking his head. "Quiet as mice out there. We occasionally see moonlight reflected by a spearhead or two we reckon in the woods over there, he pointed to the north east where the woods were three hundred paces away.

"Bernician patrols watching us as we watch them, I imagine," I said and Aedann nodded.

I stood in silence with them for a while, each of us staring towards the woods. After a long while I was rewarded by a faint glimmer of silver and maybe the shadowy hint of movement.

It was far away and there was no indication of any immediate threat to the fort.

"Well, keep an eye on it and I will check up on you later," I said and then stifled a yawn with my clenched fist.

He nodded and I left him to his vigil whilst I walked on around the walls to the west.

I passed over a wooden gate that was built into the stone battlement. It allowed access down to the terrace on the north side where there was a forge and workshops for a leather worker, a jeweller and a carpenter. All was quiet down there, with the fires of the forge banked with only a faint glow of residual heat and the blacksmith and his fellow workmen tucked up in their beds.

While I was crossing over the gateway, I happened to glance down and saw an odd shape on the ground. I stopped and leant over the wall to get a better look. After a moment my eyes adjusted to the darkness down below and I recognised the shape was that of a person crouched down by the side of the jeweller's hut. Whoever it was seemed to be staring straight at the gate beneath the archway I was standing on. Behind me, the night sky to the south was currently shrouded by clouds, obscuring the stars so that I must have been almost invisible – a grey form against a grey sky. A cloud which had been obscuring the setting moon drifted away and the moonlight fell upon the figure's face revealing that it was a woman I was looking at. A few moments later I realised that I had seen this face before. It was some years earlier and it had been dark, like tonight and I had had quite a bit to drink that night, but the image of a raven –haired woman came to me. This was the woman that I had once dismissed as a dream but who I had then found out had birthed a child and I was therefore the likely father.

This was Rowenna, the mother to my son.

As I watched, she turned away and started moving towards the outer wooden palisades that enclosed the terrace. I was about to jump down to the gateway and so head off in pursuit of her, when I noticed one of Rhoerth's guards coming down from the palisade and heading across the outer terrace, probably planning a visit to the privy. Pits had been dug over the western side of the terrace and that was where he was heading. His path would take him past the workshops. I could see him approaching the jeweller's hut, and due to my elevated position, I could also see the figure of Rowena heading towards the same corner from the direction of the gateway. It was clear that they would would encounter each other imminently. I thought about shouting out a warning ... but to whom?

Whilst I hesitated, Rowenna had reached the corner just as the guard did so from the other side. I heard a faint cry of surprise, although from which one I could not tell. They spotted each other too late to prevent a collision and so they walked into each other and went down in a tangle of arms and legs. Both must have been startled by the encounter and the fall but, moving more nimbly than I would have expected, it was Rowenna who was back on her feet first. There was a flash of steel and the guard's throat was ripped open.

Rowenna glanced down at the man who was writhing on the ground and bent down to finish him with a thrust to the body from her seax. Then she wiped her blade on the dead man's cloak, glanced about and carried on her way.

The whole incident had taken barely ten heartbeats and I just stood, frozen by the abruptness of it as well as the quiet efficiency and ruthlessness.

"Merciful Woden," I said to myself, feeling a chill pass up my spine. What kind of woman was this?

I stirred myself into action and glanced along the battlement towards where Aedann had been, but neither he nor his men were in sight. Maybe they were patrolling around the other side of the fort. There was no time to go looking for them, so I scampered down the steps to the gate, opened it and headed through in pursuit of Rowenna.

By the time I reached the terrace I could not see any sign of her. Another guard was walking towards the privy. I intercepted him and together we ran to the spot where the fallen guard lay. He was, as I expected, already dead when we got there.

"Go to the king, tell him Cerdic spotted an enemy spy in the camp and is going after ...her."

Even in the moonlight I saw the man's eyebrows rise in surprise.

"Her?"

"That is what I said."

He hesitated and I knew what was going through his mind.

"You are thinking that I killed the guard. I killed the former king, so who knows what I might do?"

He shrugged.

"That is not your main problem."

He frowned and looked confused. "What do you mean?"

I drew Catraeth. He stared at it.

"Your main problem is that I am armed with the sword that killed Owain. It's just you and me here. If you cry out and I am an enemy, how high do you rate your odds?"

He looked thoughtful.

I needed to end this quickly.

"Look, what's your name?" I said in a warmer voice.

"Cadoc, Lord."

Well, Cadoc, I need to go. The spy is already a distance away and I aim to catch her. So, I am going to walk that way," I pointed towards the palisade. "You can try to strike me down as I do that. Just be sure of your strike because, if you miss, I won't," I said. Then I raised Catraeth an inch to make my point. Cadoc stepped back and lifted his hands up to show he was not a threat.

I turned away and walked quickly. It was only when I got to the palisade that I let out a breath I had not realised I was holding. I glanced back. Cadoc was still watching me. I gesticulated violently towards the hilltop and he stirred into life and scampered off.

I examined the palisade, pondering how Rowenna had breached it. Then I noticed the narrow gap at its western end where a man could get around it. I went that way and stood, looking down the hillside towards the woods. The moon was now almost set. All was grey and black out there, ill formed and indistinct. I despaired of spotting her in that gloom and almost turned back. Standing there I cursed at the delay caused by dealing with Cadoc.

Then I heard the screech of a bird disturbed in the trees, followed by the flapping of wings and a barn owl erupted out of the foliage and shot away into the night. The bird had come out of some trees a little to the north and east. Maybe, just maybe, the route that Rowenna might take if she was circling around the fortress on her way back towards the Bernician camp.

It was a faint chance at best, I admit, but I took it. I headed down the hillside and across the open ground at its base taking a more angled route, one passing closer to the hill and that would place me in sight of the fortress, and this was intentional. I hoped Aedann or one of his 'Swords' might see me pass so someone up there knew where I was. In any event, I estimated that this course had a chance of intercepting Rowenna's longer path.

After reaching the trees, I darted into them and then blundered along, looking for some sign of my quarry, some indication that Rowenna had come this way. All the time I followed a track in my head that I expected would bring me to the village and the enemy camp. It took a good hour of walking through the woods before I heard a conversation close by.

"Halt and be identified," called out a voice in accented English, a Bernician accent.

"I am a friend. It is the Nightjar," I heard Rowenna answer. She could only be twenty paces ahead of me just beyond the trees.

"Password?"

"Firebrand."

"Approach, friend."

I peered around a tree trunk. Rowenna was talking to a spear-armed guard who was waving her past. Rowenna moved on towards the camp. She was dressed in practical dark coloured garb and yet she was, of course, an attractive woman. I was certainly not thinking about that, for the image in my head was still of her cutting the guard's throat. The guard, however, was not affected by such unpleasant thoughts and, no doubt, bored by his long time on duty turned to watch her walk by. That distraction allowed me to emerge from my hiding place and take a few steps towards him.

As Rowenna passed out of sight around a large beech tree, the guard turned back towards me. I was then just four paces away. He gawped at me in surprise and hesitated before he started to bring his spear down towards me. Moving faster than him, I stepped under the spear, grasping the stave with one hand whilst I punched him hard in the belly with the other, knocking the wind out of him. Then, as he struggled to breathe, I put my hand over his mouth and slammed his head back hard against the trunk of the beech tree. His eyes rolled up as he slumped forward, and I caught him in my arms. He was breathing, so clearly still alive, but out cold. Should I kill him, I wondered. An instant later I had decided not to. To kill a man in battle is one thing. To slay a helpless man, another thing entirely. He was just in the wrong place when I had encountered him. It was enough to disable him so he could not call for help. I took off his belt, pulled his arms around either side of the tree trunk and then used the belt to tie his hands. A sling that hung at his belt served as a makeshift gag that would prevent him yelling out. I inspected my work and then headed on after Rowenna.

I instantly regretted the mercy I had shown the man and so the time I had used in tying him to the tree, as it was obvious that Rowenna was once again out of sight. Cursing softly, I stood for a moment getting my bearings and then noticed that the sky in one direction was a fraction lighter than the rest. If that was east, then that was where the Bernician camp would be found. Dawn was not that far off, so I needed to move quickly.

I scampered on through the woods, forsaking stealth for speed and trusting that I had passed the line of scouts. This was either the case or the Norns were blessing me this night for I encountered no more sentinels. I finally emerged from the woodlands and could see the village up ahead. On the far bank of the river, a number of bivouacs and tents had been pitched but the fields to the west were empty. I used the cover of a hedgerow to approach the settlement unseen and entered the village, passing quietly by a few huts, searching for a sign of Rowenna.

I reached a ford where the river splashed over rocks and was no more than ankle deep, so I crossed it quickly.

On the other side of the river, I passed a makeshift corral that had been built by pulling together wagons and lashing them to each other, enclosing a dozen horses. One or two stirred as I passed, so I a made soothing noises to try to calm them, reaching out to stroke the flank of the nearest. It was then that I spotted Rowenna again. She was standing at the doorway of a hut to the north of the road just over the far side of the river talking to a man. I moved closer, staying under the shadows of the huts to get a better view. Closer now I recognised the man she was speaking to – Hussa. My hand went to draw Catraeth, but I realised I could not hope to kill him without a hullaballoo being raised with the whole Bernician army descending on me. I relaxed my arm and, keeping my sword out of the way of my legs, I crept closer.

Hussa and Rowenna went into the hut and I was able to cross over the road and then move by the door and around the side of the hut, passing into a narrow passageway that ran between the hut and its neighbour. The thin wooden walls and thatched roof of the hovel did not impede sound much at all and so I could hear what was being said.

"So, did you find what you were looking for?" Hussa asked.

"Yes. I think I have an idea. A hidden path which might allow us to approach and take them by surprise. Let us go and see Sogor," came the reply.

"What about you? Did you come to any harm?"

"None. I did bump into a guard I had to deal with."

"Deal with, how?"

"With my blade."

"I see. The old skills still work, then."

"They do," she replied.

"Had fun, did you?"

"What do you think?" she answered.

"Come on, then," Hussa said.

"Yes. But what about Hal? Has my son been quiet?"

"Our son you mean, and the answer is yes, he has not stirred."

'Son?' I thought. The lad was here? Why did Hussa think he was his son? That was nonsense, wasn't it?

"Come on, then. Shut the door quietly so we don't wake Hal."

'He is in the hut,'

I heard the door open with a creak and then shut. There was a blur of movement as Hussa and Rowenna passed by the little passageway and headed off towards the headman's hut. I waited a moment longer and then, peering around the corner, I crept back out. Opening the door quietly, I slipped inside.

Towards the back of the hut, a pile of furs was thrown on the ground on top of a low bed. Poking out from under the furs was a tiny pale face. I moved closer and looked down. A mop of light brown hair sat untidily atop the head. The boy's eyes were shut and he was breathing steadily.

"I have found you, son," I said softly.

Then I paused.

"Now I have found you, what in Woden's name do I do next?"

Chapter Thirteen
The boy
Summer 611

L ooking back on that moment, knowing what I know now, both about what happened more or less immediately after-wards, as well as later on as a direct consequence of my actions, I ask myself what do I now feel about what I did and also whether I would do the same again. The answer, of course, is that what I did was clearly insane. Not only was it sheer madness, but whilst it was not by my hand that the calamity about to unfold came to be, nor later events, I can hardly be thought of as blame-less for what happened.

Look at it through my eyes, however. Consider for a moment about what I was thinking before you judge me. Then ask your-self what you would have done. The truth is that I knew at that time, believed in any event, that Hussa could not be the boy's fa-ther. He had known many women and slept with them without consequences. He had not fathered any child with any of them. Not even one. I had children and so, in my mind, was capable of fathering more. Leaving all that aside, Rowenna had come to me that night at Fishbourne and we had lain together. An appropri-ate time later, lo and behold, along had come a baby. Having learnt of the boy's existence, I had thought about it often and it had been my main obsession since the previous summer.

I was the boy's father – it was as simple as that to me. I had hoped to find him but, having done so, I had no clear plans as to what to do next. I probably had imagined a fire –side chat, an introduction from Rowenna and then maybe games or hunting with him. He needed to know I existed and, more than that, that

I would be there for him. I had hoped Rowenna would welcome me as the boy's father. Not in terms of any relationship between me and Rowenna, I was not looking for that. I was married and enough hurt had been done to Aidith. However, it seemed to me that we could, and in fact should, both be involved with the child and his welfare.

That was about as far as my thought processes had taken me. Until tonight, that was. Tonight, I had seen Rowenna slaughter that guard without any thought or any evidence that she felt any guilt. Slash and thrust and he was dead. The image was etched into my memory and, with it, the beginning of a thought. The boy was not safe here. Certainly not with Hussa. I knew what he was capable of. Tonight, I had become aware of what Rowenna could do. To her it was just part of her role, presumably, as Hussa's spy.

My actions now seemed clear. I was going to have to take the boy with me.

The decision made, I gave the reason and justification no more thought. Maybe, even then, the madness of what I was about to do was apparent to me and my mind just needed to think about something else.

So, I turned to practicalities. I needed to act swiftly. I could not hope to get the sleeping boy all the way to the fort by carrying him. He was small and would be no burden, but it was still dark and it was a mile of woods and low hills populated by enemy patrols. He might wake at any moment and alert the guards. No, I was going to have to ride out and rely on speed over stealth.

I tentatively opened the door, poked my head out and looked around. The corral of horses I had spotted earlier was close at hand. Most of them had no bridle or saddle but one horse was fully equipped, presumably, in case an urgent message needed to be sent.

142

I moved over the roadway to the corral and, after finding a half-eaten apple in my belt pouch, offered it to the horse: a white stallion. He trotted over, took the apple and then allowed me to stroke his head. The improvised corral had a barrel pushed into place by way of a gate. I found that the barrel was only half full with rainwater and so not too heavy and that I was able to tug it to the side. I stepped inside and took the horse by the bridle to lead him out, all the time speaking softly and rubbing his head. I went to push the barrel back in place and so close the gate but then, on an afterthought, left it open. Several of the other horses started to follow and emerged out into the camp. I led my horse back to the hut, tied the reins to the door handle and then re-entered.

Inside, I found that the boy was still asleep. I looked about, spotted a small cloak that must belong to him and then gently pulled back the furs, lifted him out of bed, leaned his head on my shoulder, then threw the cloak about him. He stirred until I swayed and hummed into his ear and he drifted off again.

Having crept out of the door, I lifted him onto the horse and then, with the boy slumped against the neck of the beast, I untied him , pulled myself up and then shortened the reins, squeezed with my legs and steered the creature with my knees until it began to walk smoothly down the road towards the river.

We had already splashed across it when, behind me, a cry of alarm rang out. Three warriors had emerged from a hut and spotted the horses milling about. An instant later, one of them spotted me.

"Hey, who are you?" one shouted.

"Who is that on horse with him?" another asked. "It looks like a child!"

"Is that Hussa's lad?" the third said.

143

"Hussa!" the first cried out.

I gave the horse his head and dug in my heels; the horse whinnied in surprise and leapt away down the road. A horn rang out and then another and suddenly the road behind me was full of warriors pulling on tunics and grabbing spears. The horse galloped on. Just before I left the village, I looked back up the road again, saw my brother emerge from another hut. The first warrior was gesturing towards me and Hussa was roaring orders while he sprinted towards a horse. Without waiting to add saddle or bridle, he leapt onto the animal's back, grabbed its mane, drove in his heels and set off in pursuit.

I kicked my horse harder to urge it to go faster. The movement and noise woke the boy up. He twisted his head around to stare at me with a look of terror. He started struggling to get off the horse, so I held on to him tighter.

"Its alright boy, I am your father. I won't hurt you," I told him as I struggled to control boy and horse.

He shook his head and looked around. Behind us the pounding of hooves told me that Hussa was still coming after us and indeed was getting closer.

"Hal!" I heard him shout.

The boy heard it, too, and leant around me to look back down the road.

"Da!" he shouted and struggled even more.

"That is not your father! He lied to you. You are my son. Not his."

The boy looked confused, terrified and angry all at the same time. I ignored him. If I could escape there would be time enough to explain it all to him later.

We had reached the woods now and, knowing there was no hope of sneaking through them, I steered my mount down the

144

track that linked the town to the fort. Rounding a bend in the road, I was confronted by a patrol of three spearmen who were standing in the middle of the road.

Off to one side was a small camp site with a low burning fire and bivouac. They must have heard the uproar in the town and, uncertain of what was going on, emerged on to the road. As I came into view, they stared at me in astonishment. I rode straight on towards them without stopping. One of them started to lower his spear but the horse's speed and pace was just too great. Before he could complete his movement, we were upon him and so, with a cry of alarm, he dropped his spear, leapt out of the way, lost his footing, fell and went tumbling off to the side.

As we hurtled past the trio, I glanced back at them and spotted that another of the three had scampered back to the camp, picked up a bow and had already nocked an arrow. He assayed a shot, but I was moving too fast and the arrow was well wide of his mark, vanishing into the trees to my right. Up ahead I spotted the guards on the palisades and walls of the camp and steered towards the bottom of the slope that lead to the gate.

I glanced back and saw that Hussa was now passing the sentinels.

"Cerdic, you bastard!" he shouted.

"Da!" the boy Hal shouted and struggled even more.

"Be still!" I growled.

I pushed on to reach the bottom of the hill. Here a line of scouts watched me approach. One raised a bow and took aim.

"Put down that bow, man!" Cuthbert shouted from about fifty paces away. I remembered with some joy that, just as Aedann had been on watch up on the fortress, our best scout had been sent with some of his men out of the fortress as pickets. The man he was shouting at was not one of us Deirans, nor was he Cad-wallon's men of Gwynedd. He was one of Rhoerth's warriors and was looking very confused. Cuthbert had spoken in English and the man just didn't understand.

"I am a friend. It's Lord Cerdic!" I shouted in Welsh. For a moment I wondered if the man might release his arrow after all. Many men in the fortress would not consider me any kind of friend. He held his aim on me for several heartbeats but eventu-ally, as I galloped closer to him, he lowered the bow and I rode on past the picket line.

"Cerdic! What in the name of Thunor's arse are you up to?" Cuthbert asked as he came to join me as I slowed the horse and turned to meet him. Then he saw the child sitting in front of me and his eyes widdened.

"Is that the boy?" he asked. "Is that Hal?"

I nodded.

"Rider approaching!" the archer shouted. I looked back to-wards the woods. Hussa was still riding towards us.

"Take aim!" Cuthbert shouted. "Get ready to shoot the bas-tard full of arrows."

The scouts responded with a creak of bow string and stave. Hussa saw the dozen arrows aimed at him and veered away. He withdrew to longer range by which time a half dozen of his own scouts had reached him on foot and another warrior on horse-back.

"Come back, Hussa," the warrior shouted.

Hussa whirled round on the newcomer and fixed a wild – eyed glare on him. He thrust out a finger in my direction.

"He has got Hal, Rolf! He has got my boy."

The warrior glared at me, drew a seax and pointed it at me.

"You bastard, give the boy back to his father!"

146

"It is not his son," I yelled back. "He's my son. I won't leave him in my brother's hands. He is a murderer and so is the boy's mother."

Hussa rode back towards me. All around me the archers remained alert and ready to lose.

"Hussa, have care!" the man Hussa had called Rolf said, following up cautiously behind.

"Give me my son!" he snarled at me.

"No," I howled.

Hussa slid down from the horse and took three strides towards me. His man, Rolf, manoeuvred his horse so he could jump down next to him and put a hand on his shoulder.

"Don't go closer, they will kill you," he urged my brother.

Hussa turned his head and glared at Rolf.

"He has my boy!" he shouted at his companion.

"I know," he said, "but you are no use to your son dead, are you. You need to think straight."

"Da!" shouted Hal again, squirming in my arms.

"Keep still!" I hissed at him. "I am trying to help."

"I… don't want help. I want my da!" he said.

Hussa was watching me and stepped again towards me.

"If you harm him, if he has even a hair missing, I will gut Aidith and your children," he shouted.

"Hussa, I won't harm him, I promise, but I will kill you. Come and get him if you want and let these men perforate you!" I replied, gesturing at the archers. It meant I took one arm off Hal who pulled free of the grip of my other arm and jumped down from the horse. It was quite a drop for a three –year –old, and he landed heavily and then fell over, letting out a yelp of pain as he did.

Hussa looked at the boy, lying sprawled on the ground and set off again towards me. Rolf threw both arms around him and pulled him away again.

"They will kill you if you go closer. Come back!" Rolf pleaded with him.

Hussa struggled to get free but then eventually relaxed and
stood, limp in his huscarl's arms. For a long moment he just
glared at me and then he looked away at the line of archers and
up towards the men watching the spectacle from the battlements. He raised himself as high as he could and spoke clearly,
projecting his voice at the fortress.

"Hear me now, warriors of Rheged and Gwynedd and trai-
tors of Deira. Lord Cerdic has kidnapped my son. I will wait at
the camp yonder," he gestured to the fire a hundred paces back.
"Bring me my son and I promise mercy. If I do not have my son
returned to me safely within an hour, I will attack this fortress
and destroy it and you as well. No mercy will be given. No prisoners will be taken. Ask yourself, do you want to die for Lord
Cerdic?"

He paused for a moment and then spoke again. This time he
pointed at me.

"Men of Rheged, this is the one who killed your king, Owain,
who was a truly great man. Do you really want to be killed for
him?"

The scouts looked confused and seemed to not know whether
to stare at me or at Hussa.

"Da!" Hal shouted and made an attempt at climbing to his
feet. Cuthbert was by his side now and reached out a hand. Hal
looked wary but took the hand. Cuthbert pulled him up but
stood with one hand on a shoulder, keeping the boy from escaping.

Hussa again moved towards us a pace and the arrow strings
on our side creaked again, echoed by the bows belonging to the
Bernician pickets. Hussa halted.

148

"I will get you back, son!" Hussa said. "I promise, I will get you back."

Hussa threw another poisoned glance at me but then pulled away followed by Rolf and the rest of his party. The pair retrieved their horses, swiftly mounted and then withdrew to the fire in their small watch camp where they once more dismounted and took up a position watching us. Our own pickets relaxed their bows but did not move, each observing the enemy pickets closely, looking for any signs they were about to attack.

"Well, you certainly know how to make a s...s...scene" said Cuthbert, the stress of the moment bringing out his stammer.

"Your man is right about that, Lord Cerdic!" a voice addressed me. Cadwallon called out to me as he was coming down the path towards me.

"What is it, Prince Cadwallon?"

Cadwallon snorted at the question.

"What is it? What is it, you ask? I'll tell you what it is. King Rhoerth would like a chat, if you don't mind?"

"A chat?"

"Well, his exact words were, 'Get that bastard up here so he can tell me what the hell he thinks he is up to!'"

I slid down off my horse and glanced towards Hussa and his companions a few hundred paces away, gathered around their little campfire. Close by them, it looked like flying ants swarming on the day they take to the skies on the hottest day of summer, the Bernician warriors were scampering around, calling men to arms and sending messages back to the village. The huscarl Rolf was talking animatedly and gesturing towards me and then up at the fortress. In contrast, Hussa was standing dead still, eyes fixed on me, or so it seemed, watching me carefully. I could feel his hatred from here.

149

It was then that the magnitude of what I had done hit me like a hammer striking the red –hot rods of steel laying on the anvil of a weaponsmith forging a sword. From such an anvil sparks would fly skyward, an indication of the heat that lay in the iron. It did not require sparks for me to feel the fire of hatred inside Hussa. He was not a man given to false promises. Unless I handed back Hal, he would assault the fortress and kill anyone in his way. I needed to persuade Rhoerth to help me when every man in his army wanted him to throw me to the wolves and now they had the excuse to do just that.

I sighed and gestured at Cuthbert to lead Hal up the path.

"Let's go, then," I said, and followed them.

Chapter Fourteen
Trust
Summer 611

I walked into the fortress accompanied by Cuthbert who was still leading my son by the hand, the lad twisting his arm in a futile attempt to get free. The boy glanced around as we climbed the slope, taking in the weapons and armour of all the warriors, fear becoming evident on his face. I felt a jolt of guilt for the anxiety I was causing him but then told myself that, in the end, it was for his own good and he would, eventually, thank me for it. The man who pretended to be his father, Hussa, had burnt alive the boy's own grandmother, after all ... my mother. The child's mother had slain a warrior without remorse or any suggestion of guilt this very night and was a spy and a whore. Surely, it was right to take him away from them. I would be able to provide a far safer home for him. Wasn't that the right thing to do?

As I walked along, I was painfully aware of the staring faces belonging to, not just the men of Rheged, but those from Gwynedd and, as we turned off the main track into the high terrace where our company was camped, even my own spearmen. I turned to look at the boy who had stopped struggling, for the moment at least, and was now glaring at me.

"What is it, boy?" I asked him.

"I am Hal!" he said stubbornly.

I sighed. It was not a name I had chosen for him. Hussa, or maybe Rowenna, had given him that but that was the name he knew himself by.

"Very well, what is it, Hal?"

"Who are you?"

"I am your father."

He shook his head.

"No, you're not. I am Hal, son of Hussa," he said proudly. "He is a great warrior of the king, you know, and I am going to be one, too, one day."

Now it was my turn to shake my head. How could I make him understand what had happened?

"That is a mistake. I am your father and I have been looking for you for so long. Now I will look after you."

He started crying.

"I want to go back to my ma and my da! I want to go home."

I knelt down so I could look into his eyes. I reached out a hand and placed it on his shoulder. He flinched and retreated a few steps. I moved my hand back towards him but then withdrew it.

"I will keep you safe and take you to my house. I will take you to my home. I serve a king, too, you know. You can meet him."

He looked confused at that.

"Will Mother be there; will my da be there, too?"

"Your father will be there," I said to stop him asking awkward questions. Yet he asked one more.

"Can I take Wilbur with me, too? "

I frowned.

"I don't understand; who is Wilbur?" I asked him.

He opened up a clenched fist. Inside was a tiny wooden figure, roughly carved into the shape of a warrior.

"Where were you hiding that?" I asked him.

"I always have Wilbur," he answered.

"Why is he called that?"

He looked at me like I was a bit stupid.

"Cos that is the man who made him, of course"

"Where is he now? The man Wilbur, I mean," I added as he started to raise the figure to show me again.

"Oh him, he died", he replied sadly. "I liked him."

"I am sorry to hear that, Hal. Yes, you can take Wilbur along," I said.

"He was a hero, you know. Like I am going to be."

"I am sure you will be. Come and meet a friend of mine who is a hero, too…"

Over near the gate Cadwallon was watching us and, catching my gaze, gestured towards the king's hall.

"Hurry up, we are expected at once."

"Yes, yes I am coming. Just give me a moment, blast you," I growled and he glared back at me but said nothing.

I waved at Hal to follow me and, still accompanied by Cuthbert, we walked a bit further up the terrace until we had reached the camp where Eduard was sitting by a fire drinking mead and playing Hnefataflwith one of the other men. As I approached, he looked at me and then looked into his cup as if he had drunk too much or else, he was not sure if he liked it or not.

"What's up? Taste bad?" I said as I dropped myself down on a log that had been pulled up near the campfire and now acted as a substitute bench. I patted another log next to me and Hal sat down on it heavily and then stared open mouthed at the huge form of my friend. I had known him so long that I sometimes forgot how intimidating he could be.

"It tastes fine," he said with a shake of his head. "No, its just you and Cuth wandering in here with that child in your company was not something I was expecting to see. Is that the lad you have been looking for, or do you have other offspring stashed around the country?"

153

"It is him. Can you look after him? I need to go and see Rhoerth."

"Yes, I heard he had smoke coming out of his ears when you disappeared."

I shrugged and ran a hand through my hair. "It all just kind of happened, as these things do."

He snorted at that.

"What in Woden's name are you laughing at?"

"Cerdic, it seems to me that these things just have a habit of happening to you more than the rest of us. That's all."

"You can say that again," Cuthbert said quietly from behind me.

"You can shut up, too…" I muttered.

I turned to Hal.

"Hal, this is Eduard. I need to go somewhere and will be back soon, but you stay here and he will teach you this game."

Hal looked at the Hneftafel pieces and added the wooden figurine, Wilbur, to the board.

"Alright," he said. "My da plays this."

I bit back a response to that comment.

I got up and joined a frustrated looking Cadwallon who turned to follow me as I left the camp and carried on uphill towards the gates and Rhoerth's hall. Cadwallon was studying me as we walked along.

"Well, this should be interesting," he said, with a mirthless smile at me as we reached the doors to the hall.

After removing our blades, we entered.

The reception was as cool as the last time. On reflection, it was maybe even a little cooler. Every head was turned towards me, every gaze burning into me. When I got to the other end, Rhoerth was studying me.

"Lord king, how can I be of assistance?" I enquired with a

respectful bow. It may have been a bit of a frivolous comment because the king's face darkened like the summer sky when a thunderstorm was coming on. Around the hall there were whispered words that were silenced when the young king glared at the company. He returned his gaze, which had not lightened, upon me.

"You can explain to us all just what in the name of all the saints you were doing tonight?"

This was going to be hard to explain. I decided to start with the truth. "I was checking on my men on watch on the battlements."

"I mean, after that. You were spotted near a dead guard, and, when challenged, told some story about enemy agents in the fortress. Then, having threatened another of my guards with your sword, headed off at speed, hurtling down the hillside and disappeared into woods that we know are thick with Bernician scouts. A couple of hours later you come belting out of the woods pursued by some mad man that I am told by Prince Cadwallon is your brother…"

"Actually, he is my, half–brother…" I interrupted him and then having second thoughts, added an apologetic, "sorry, lord king."

"I don't care what the actual relationship is, Lord Cerdic. The point is, you burst out from the woods, pursued or, who knows, accompanied by several enemy scouts and carrying a young child…."

He trailed off and just glared at me while I tried to gather my thoughts and come up with an answer. If the truth be told, all the the time since I had spotted Rowena killing that guard and I had run off in pursuit had hurtled by in a blur. I had not really had time to gather my thoughts. Here we were and I did not know what to say.

155

"Lord Hussa was yelling something about the boy being his son," Cadwallon said.

My response was instinctive. "He's my, son not his!"

Around me, the king's lords and warriors gasped, and a dozen conversations leapt up before being silenced by another royal glare.

"So, if the boy is your son, what was he doing in their camp?"

"It's a long story. I got a woman with child. He later married the woman."

"Does not seem that long a story," Cadwallon muttered.

"So, was the woman in the camp as well?" Rhoerth asked me.

"The woman was the agent I spoke of earlier. She was the one who killed the guard. I had spotted her and followed her back to the enemy camp in the town. It was there that I found the boy."

"So, what … you decided to kidnap the boy?" Cadwallon asked incredulously.

"Look, it may have been a rash decision, but the boy is mine and I know what Hussa is capable off. He burnt my mother alive. When the woman killed the guard, I realised the boy was not safe there. So, I just grabbed him and ran."

"With half the Bernician army on your tail, it seems." the king said.

"That is a bit of an exaggeration. It is more the case that it was just Hussa and his huscarls."

"Hussa claims he is the father and you claim that you are. If this was a time of peace, I would call witnesses and take oaths. Then, I would have to make a judgement…"

He looked away for a while.

After a moment he turned back and saw me staring at him.

"Believe me, Lord Cerdic, I was just wishing it was, indeed, a time of peace and that I could have the luxury of a mere dispute

156

over a boy's fatherhood. Yet we are at war and at such times a king must use what weapons present themselves to him. It may be that this boy is such a weapon."

I did not like the sound of that.

"What do you mean?" I asked.

"We should threaten to kill the boy unless Hussa and the Bernicians withdraw," Cadwallon suggested.

"You touch him, and I will kill you, prince or not," I growled.

Cadwallon stepped towards me. "You dare threaten me, Lord Cerdic!" he snarled.

Rhoerth hammered his hand on the arm of his chair.

"Enough argument. Cerdic, don't worry. This boy will not come to harm. It may be, however, that if Hussa is concerned about his son, it may distract him from the task of capturing this fortress."

"Hussa threatened to attack unless we let this boy go," Cadwallon argued.

Rhoerth pursed his lips. "He would risk his army assaulting the fortress up the fortified path?" he asked.

"He seemed like a man who would set the world on fire to get him back," Cadwallon replied.

I thought about this and knew that Cadwallon was right. Yet Hussa was no fool. If he could attack in such a way that would minimise the risk, he would do so.

"Perhaps, Lord, I have news. Rowenna… the enemy agent I spoke of …told Hussa that she had a plan for entry. A way in that avoided the main gate. Hussa said that he felt such an attack would work best at night."

"It might be a trick," Cadwallon suggested. "Maybe they hope we will weaken our daytime defences to bolster the night

157

watch. Or taken men from the gate to elsewhere in the fortress. Maybe they knew you were listening."

I shook my head at that. "I was outside their hut, where the boy, Hal, was sleeping when I heard them talk about this. They went off and left me alone outside. If they knew I was there, they would surely not leave me near the boy and just go away."

"Perhaps not," Said Cadwallon through pursed lips. Then he raised a finger and pointed it at me. "Of course, we only have your word for any of this."

"What do you mean?" I asked.

"Yes, please explain your meaning, Prince Cadwallon," Rhoerth said.

"Just think about it. The last time Rheged fought Aethelfrith's men, Cerdic was a leader amongst the Deirans. Not long before that, he killed your uncle at Catraeth. He may have taken refuge with his exiled prince in my grandfather's land and that of others, but what if Edwin and Aethelfrith have come to terms?"

"Nonsense!" I said. "Edwin is going to kill Aethelfrith one day."

"So you say. What, though, if a deal has been brokered and you were sent here to help Aethelfrith's forces, led in part by your half-brother, gain entry into this fortress. You killed that guard to get out of the fortress, sneaked away to make your treacherous plans and then needed a way back in. What better ruse then to pretend you had stolen the man's son."

"Prince Cadwallon, you were at court when it was suggested by Rhun that I come here. It was not my idea."

Cadwallon snorted. "Your prince had already made the offer in private, even before the king's council. Knowing that Rhun was Owain's son, it might be expected that he did suggest you come. Whether through hope of his nephew enacting revenge or the convoluted logic he gave that day, it was not hard to ensure you came along."

"Lord king," I said to Rhoerth. "This is foolishness."

"Lord king," Cadwallon intervened, "Dare you take the risk?"

"What do you suggest I do?" Rhoerth asked.

Cadwallon looked at me. "Lock up his company. Make sure they can't break out to aid the enemy."

"Lord, please!" I gasped. "If you do that, you deny yourself the service of my veterans."

Rhoerth looked between us and then over at his nobles and huscarls. Most were nodding their heads, agreeing with the Prince of Gwynedd. He sighed and the turned to Cadwallon.

"Cadwallon, make the arrangements. I am sorry, Cerdic, but your actions today leave me no choice. I cannot take the chance that you are working with the Bernicians. If I am wrong, I will make amends, but that is my decision."

"You are wrong, lord king," I said, shaking my head. "I only hope you do not regret the decision."

"There is another matter, lord king," Cadwallon said, pacing forward so he stood between me and Rhoerth.

"What is that?"

"This boy … Hal is his name I believe. The boy Cerdic brought from the enemy camp. Hussa demanded we hand him over or he will attack and show no mercy. I think we should hand the boy back."

"I will not let you. If anyone tries to go near him, it will go badly for you," I growled.

"You threaten us here, in the king's hall with a hundred warriors all around and your infamous sword outside the doors yonder," Cadwallon asked, gesturing towards the hall entrance. "What stops us slaying you here and now."

159

"Yes, kill him now and be done with it," one of the lords shouted. There were many shouts of approval.

I turned to the king. "I came here in good faith and handed my weapon over to your guards. That was a sign of trust. Will you betray that trust? I did not threaten you, just anyone who came near my son. Would you do less for your own family?" I asked.

Rhoerth thought about that and shook his head.

"Allow Cerdic to return to his men, but make sure they stay on the terrace. I will consider what to do about this boy, but I will not just send him to the Bernicians until we know more about the truth of the matter."

Chapter Fifteen
Taken
Summer 611

Earlier that same evening, Hussa and Rowenna had been sitting in the headman's hall in the village. On the other side of the table, Sogor and other captains were looking down at a hide upon which, using charcoal, Rowenna had drawn a plan of the fortress. The Nightjar had just finished describing her night-time excursion and the route she had found into the fortress from the rear.

"It's a narrow gap between palisade and ditch but enough for a body of men, approaching in stealth, to gain entry to the terrace."

Hussa pointed at the few crude lines which represented the gate that blocked the path leading up the steep hillside into the inner fortress.

"If we can get to that gate, we are inside the fortress without having to risk a more costly fight up the hillside. Maybe we can open the gate, or perhaps we can cause a distraction which would be sufficient to draw men from the gateway. Then you can attack."

Sogor pursed his lips and pointed at the gap between the woods and the northern palisade.

"If you are spotted there, they could be waiting for you. You would be slaughtered."

Hussa shrugged. "If that is the case then we still provide a distraction, and you will have gotten rid of me."

Sogor appeared to be considering that. His sullen disposition brightened. Then he held up a finger.

"Yet, if you succeed you get the glory."

Hussa smiled. "Such are the stakes."

Sogor looked less happy now. "I need to think about this…"

He got no further as a horn rang out coming from the direction of the river. A moment later, another sounded and then a third. For an instant everyone stared at each other and then there was the cry of "Hussa!" from the same direction.

"That was Rolf!" Hussa shouted jumping to his feet. He took two large strides to reach the door and wrenched it open. A moment later he was outside on the road that ran towards the bridge. He stared that way trying to get a grasp on what was going on. He was looking at a scene of utter chaos.

The road was full of warriors tugging themselves into mail shirts, slapping on helmets and picking up spears and shields. Unbridled horses were milling about. Beyond them was a figure on a horse. The figure turned in his saddle and looked straight back at him. Even at night, Hussa could see that it was Cerdic. The horse turned a quarter circle so Hussa could now see that wrapped in furs and held fast in his half–brother's grasp was a small boy. An instant later he recognised his son… it was Hal.

"Hal!" he shouted, but Cerdic was fighting with his mount's reins and steered the beast so that the horse had now turned away again and started galloping towards the woods. Hussa set off at a sprint towards the nearest horse and, without pausing, leapt onto its back. He almost slipped right off again for the horse had no saddle and no reins. He lashed out and seized the horse's mane and tugging on it wildly, shouting at it and digging in his heels, set off after Cerdic.

"Hal" he shouted again, feeling the cold grip of terror in his guts. Hussa had killed Cerdic's mother. What revenge did he have in mind?

162

"Wait for me, I'm coming!" Rolf yelled as he ran awkward-ly toward another horse, saddle and bridle in his arms. Hussa shook his head. He was not waiting for anyone.

He rode on towards the woods where Cerdic had just van-ished and plunged into the darkness beneath their overhanging boughs. Some of the branches whipped at his face or snagged on his tunic as he passed, but he took no notice. The fort was not far away, so he pressed on knowing he had little time now to catch up. Emerging from the trees, he passed the camp of men from Rolf's company who were on watch that night. One of them loosed an arrow at his brother.

"Don't shoot, you bastard!" Hussa shouted. "He has my son."

The archer clearly did not hear him for he reached for another arrow and took aim once more. Hussa yanked on the reins and steered the horse so it knocked the archer sideways just as he released the missile, sending his arrow well to the right of his target. Then, with an angry glare at the man, he had passed the camp and was galloping on after his brother.

"Cerdic, you bastard!" he shouted after the man.

"Da!" Hal shouted from the back of Cerdic's horse.

The dark shape of the fortress was once more in view. In the light of the torches that burnt on its walls he could see guards. Beneath them, apparently alone on the dark grass at the foot of the fortress, Cerdic had reined in. He was bent over and was talking with another man. Hussa recognised him a moment lat-er.

"It's that little runt, Cuthbert" he hissed. Still, that meant only two of them. He drew his sword and steered a course that would take them between the rider and man on foot. Then cut and slash and they would die, and he would take back his son.

163

But then to his despair out of nowhere a dozen archers leapt up, each drawing a bead on him and gritting his teeth in frustration he was forced to back off. The next moments passed in a blur of anger and fear, anguish and futility. He tried to reach his son only to be stopped by Rolf. His friend was trying to talk sense into him but all he could see was his boy being taken by his brother.

He forgot how but he suddenly found himself on his feet, having abandoned his horse and stomping forward with a roar of rage. Around them the archers tensed and drew back on their bow strings. Somewhere in the back of his mind he knew that in moments he and many of these men could die but he did not care. Only Rolf, talking quickly and holding on to him at the same time, held him back.

"Give me my son!" he snarled at his brother.

Still that shake of the head. Damn it, Hussa thought. He assessed the odds, knowing that there was no hope of winning if he attacked. They were outnumbered. He glared at his brother and pointed his sword at him and made some futile threat. Cerdic replied but Hussa was not listening.

Then he saw Hal fall from the back of Cerdic's horse and moved back towards him only to be impeded again by Rolf who had thrown his arms about him and was urging him to come away.

"Damn it!" he said again and, with an immense effort of will, turned away. Then he turned back and projecting his voice so all could hear, he shouted out a threat to destroy the fortress if his son was not returned. Then, finally feeling a terrible gnawing inside him, he let Rolf lead him back to the camp.

A number of the men from his companies had now appeared, mustering around the small campfire. One of them, a man called

Edgar, was slumped against a tree and looked drowsy. Hussa did not have time to ask what had happened to him because he spotted Rowenna crouching beside the man. Rolf joined her and kneeling down, examined the man's wounds. As Hussa approached, he noticed that her face was ashen, and her eyes were wet with tears.

"My brother has Hal," Hussa said.

"I know…" she said weakly.

"The bastard must have sneaked into the camp whilst we were with Sogor. He found Hal and took him." Hussa shook his head. "What I don't know is how would he know where to look or what Hal looked like."

"I do…" she whispered.

Hussa did not hear at first.

"Maybe it was just blind luck or… what was that you said?" he asked, turning to face her.

Rowenna took a deep breath before she replied.

"I said I think I know how he found Hal."

She pointed down at slumped figure beside her. He looked at Edgar and spotted blood on the back of his head.

"This man was on guard in the woods and I came across him when I returned to the village. Edgar, tell Hussa what happened."

"After Lady Rowenna passed me, I was attacked. I only caught a brief glimpse of the man, but I recognised him, alright. It was your brother. It was Earl Cerdic. He was alone … I think, but he knocked me out cold before I could see for sure."

"What?" Hussa asked. "Why would he be in the woods… and why on his own?"

He thought for a moment and then turned to face Rowenna but before he could speak again, she did.

165

"He followed me. He must have done. He spotted me when I was up there and then came after me when I left the fortress. If he followed me into the camp and knew which hut we were in, that would lead him straight to Hal." More tears came to her eyes. "It's my ... it's my fault," she said in a hoarse voice.

He stared at her, lost for words.

"You were right. I should never have gone," she said in a forlorn voice.

Her sorrow cut through his own and he took her hand.

"It was Cerdic who did this, not the Nightjar, nor was it Rowenna."

She wiped her tears away then slumped back on to her heels shook her head again.

"But if I had not gone, Hal would be with us still."

Hussa shrugged and pulled her to her feet. She staggered slightly and he reached out two hands to steady her.

"We don't know that for sure. Anyway, it does not matter now. Let's concentrate on what we can do, now, to sort it out."

"Yes, you are right, I guess," she took a deep breath and when she spoke again her voice was clear and determined. "So then, what do we do now? We have to get him back."

Hussa stared up at the fort. "We will. That back route you suggested. Can you take us there? Half my men and I?"

"What, now?" she asked. "But Sogor said..."

"Sogor can go bugger Loki for all I care," he hissed. "I am not waiting any longer."

"I will come, too," Rolf said from where he was still tending to Edgar.

Hussa shook his head. "No, you won't."

Rolf stood up, looking puzzled. "Why not?" he asked.

"Because, for this attack to work, I need a distraction. I need

166

an assault that looks like you mean it against the front gates. Rowenna and I take the rest round the back and try to get in that way, locate Hal and then try to open the gates for you."

"Sounds a bit complicated to me," Rolf said, frowning.

"You will handle it, you dumb ox."

Rolf gestured with a thumb towards the village on the far side of the trees.

"What of Sogor? We could use his men. They are mustering in the village, awaiting a report from us."

"Get the attack under way and then have a messenger sent to tell him what we are doing.

Rolf's eyebrows raised an inch on his forehead. "You want to attack without telling him first?"

Hussa nodded. "I don't want the bastard interfering."

"Very well, I will get my company ready straightaway," he said.

Hussa looked down at Edgar. "You take it easy and rest that head."

The man climbed to his feet. "I am fine, Lord Hussa and if you don't mind me coming along, I fancy getting my own back on your brother. Reckon I owe him a lump or two."

A thin smile crept onto Hussa's face.

"Very well, you can come. Just be prepared for me gutting the bastard before you get a chance. Tell the rest of the men to get ready. We will muster...," he paused as he considered the order. Then he looked back at Edgar and smiled. "Why not make it your watch spot from earlier this night. Seems appropriate, don't you think? Tell the men to blacken their faces with mud and to tie furs and rags around weapons so we can travel quietly, unheard and unseen."

Edgar nodded and after rubbing the lump on his head a final time, trotted off.

Hussa looked towards the east. A faint sliver of light was visible above the trees. The dawn was not far off.

Rowenna looked at the signs of the coming sun too.

"You're sure about this? We are asking men to risk their lives for a small boy."

Rolf heard the question and came back over. "Lady Rowenna, my men and I are sworn to follow Hussa anywhere and to fight for him and his house. In exchange, he gifts us gold and silver and rewards of status and rank. His enemy and that of our king is up there, so, we attack. It's a question of our duty. To be honest though, even if that was not the case, Hal is an extra reason. Many of us are rather fond of him and rescuing him is the honourable thing to do," he said with a smile.

"So, this is about duty and honour? Just that?" Rowenna asked.

Rolf's smile broadened and there was genuine warmth in it. He raised his hands and gestured at the hilltop fortress. "Well, not just duty and honour, if we take that fort think of the glory and the loot!"

Rowenna laughed at that, despite her sorrow and fear for her son.

"So, duty, honour, glory and loot," she summarised. "Is that all? Seems reason enough I guess."

Rolf shook his head and looked up at the fort again. "No, that is not all. There is also revenge. I want a word with this half-brother of Hussa before the day is run."

He smiled again but this smile held no humour.

In almost no time, Edgar had assembled half of Hussa's men – a company's worth – at the spot where Edgar had been attacked by Cerdic just a couple of hours before. Rolf sent word that he had done the same with his company at the campfire that overlooked the entrance to the fortress.

As ordered, his men had wrapped furs and other rags around spears, shields, axes, swords and seaxes and now they made their way silently around the fort, following Rowenna who was retracing the steps she had taken earlier that night.

Soon they were lined up just inside the tree line that lay to the north of the hill. Rowenna took Hussa forward to show him the northern palisade and the route that lead up the steep hillside to the narrow path around its western edge.

Hussa examined the proposed route, bitting his lip as he did so.

"I can see how you got in, but it's a narrow gap and we have eighty men to get through. It won't be easy."

"With luck though," Rowenna said, "Rolf's attack will turn their attention south and then we go in."

"Agreed," he replied and crouched down to await the signs that an attack was starting on the far side of the fortress.

They waited in silence as the sun climbed the early morning sky. After a while, Rowenna asked a question Hussa was also thinking.

"Do you think he will be alright?"

He turned to look at her, but before he could think of an answer, they heard a cacophony of ox horns calling out through the still air. A few moments later it was answered by the clang of a bell and more horns calling out on the top of Anwoth fort. A few more moments passed and then the noise of battle reached them – voices roaring out in rage and challenge, and the clatter of axe or sword on shield.

Hussa turned to his men.

"Now," he said and he got to his feet. Stepping out of the tree line he started walking across the open space towards the slope that Rowenna had climbed. Rowenna followed and then the

169

company in single file behind her. Each man moved slowly and as stealthily as possible.

As he approached the bottom of the hill, Hussa peered up at the palisade above him. It was empty with no helmets or spears visible over the top. Higher still, the stone battlement of the fortress was also empty. Rolf's distraction appeared to be working.

Reaching the steep slope that angled up to the palisade, he started up it, legs and lungs soon protesting at the effort required to move his body, armour, shield and weapon up it. He settled into a repetitive pattern, stomping up the hill in a series of strides. Rowenna, wearing no armour and only carrying her daggers and seax passed him and moved towards the palisade.

"Be careful!" he hissed.

She turned to lift a finger to her lips and then carried on up the slope. She had just reached the gap at the side of the palisade when a pair of warriors appeared on the wall and spotted them.

For a moment the two guards just stared as they took in the snaking line of men labouring up the hillside. Then a mouth opened, and the words rolled down the hill side towards them.

"Under attack! North rampart!"

The other warrior had pulled out a horn and was preparing to blow it.

"Shit!" Hussa cursed and turning to his men shouted the order.

"We've been spotted! Move it!"

Chapter Sixteen
Escape
Summer 611

"Arse!" I cursed and kicked my shield. It had been leaning against a pile of firewood in the camp we had set up on the terrace but now rolled a few times, teetered on its edge and then toppled over and clattered onto the ground.

"You need to calm down before you burst something vital," Cuthbert commented.

I glared at him and then stomped over to the fire and poked at it with a half –burnt stick.

"It's not all that bad, is it?" Aedann asked from the other side of the fire.

"How did you work that out?" I asked, poking the ashes a few more times and then threw the stick into the branches.

"So, Rhoerth does not trust us and we are confined here. That means some other bugger will have to stand watch to-night. We have ale and some nice salted pork and some none –too - stale bread. Could be worse," he said, and to illustrate the point he bit off a chunk of the aforementioned bread and chewed at it.

"It also means you get to spend some more time with the boy," Cuthbert said inclining his head towards where Eduard was throwing Hal into the air and then catching him again leading to peals of laughter from Hal.

I nodded and wandered over to them. Eduard put the boy down. Hal looked at me warily.

"Are you taking me back to my da now?" he asked.

"Do you want anything to eat?" I asked, changing the subject.

He nodded eagerly and sat down on a rug under a cow hide that had been slung between four spears to create a temporary shelter from any rain that might come.

I went back to the fire and got some of the bread and salted pork and came back with it. I passed him some which he snatched and started munching away on. Sitting next to him under the awning, I ate as well. It did not take him long to complete the meal and having done so, he glanced around the camp at the rest of the company who were rousing from their night's rest and breaking their fast, too. After a while his eyes grew heavy and he slumped down against me. I looked down at him, then laid him down on the rug and pulled some furs over him.

When I emerged from the shelter, Eduard, Aedann and Cuthbert were all standing there.

"Are you sure about this?" Eduard said.

"What do you mean?" I asked.

"He means, he seems a nice boy. Is it right to take him away from his home?" Cuthbert put in.

"If your child was in the house of another man, would you not wish that he was with you?"

"Yes of course I would, but in this case, he was with his mother."

"A woman who last night murdered a guard."

"We have killed, Cerdic, many times," Aedann pointed out.

"Yes, but…" I started to say.

I did not get far because the sound of ox horns reached us from the land surrounding the fortress. We ran to the south palisade and looked down the steep hillside towards the woods. Emerging from the trees line was a loose skirmish line of archers and slingmen behind which a shield wall was assembling before, presumably, advancing towards the fortress behind the skirmishers. Several men amongst the shield wall raised horns to their lips and blew another signal, a challenge to the defenders and a rallying call to the attackers at the same time. Other warriors responded by clattering shield stave, axe handle and sword blade against the edges of their shields.

Above us, more horns alerted the defenders of the fortress who ran swiftly to take up their posts on the various battlements and gateways.

"The Bernicians are attacking!" Aedann said.

"How observant of you," Eduard said, "the rest of us might not have noticed."

"And we are stuck in here," I said, ignoring the banter.

"Do we help?" Cuthbert asked.

"I don't see how we can – they have shut the gate into the fortress." I shrugged, "I will go and tell them to let us reinforce the outer walls lower down. Not sure they will listen, though."

I marched off to where the wall of the southern terrace overlooked the narrow channel running from the engraved stone slab to the inner fortress gates where Cadwallon were lined up.

"You need to get them to let us out, Prince Cadwallon!" I urged him.

He just shook his head.

"They don't trust you. Come to that, I don't trust you, Cerdic. You go into the enemy camp the same day the enemy attacks… would you trust a man like that?"

"So, what are we supposed to do now, just sit here?"

"I don't care what you do. Just keep out of the way," he answered and turned back to his men.

Frustrated, I went back to the south wall where we could observe the approaching force. Above their ranks the coiled snake banner flew.

"It's your brother's men," Cuthbert said.

I joined him.

"Can you see him?" I asked. My sister's husband had the sharpest eyes of any man or woman I knew.

He stared for a while then slowly shook his head.

"No. I can see that Rolf man – his lieutenant – but not Hussa himself," he said finally.

We watched for a while. The skirmishers on both sides were exchanging shots. Some arrows and slingstones were finding their targets. Men were already falling and dying down on the low land around Anwoth, but all we could do from this distance was watch.

"Where is he?" I asked no one in particular.

"Maybe he is still in the woods, holding himself in reserve," Eduard suggested.

It was possible. This first attack appeared to be around company strength. It consisted of a high proportion of light troops. These were men armed with bow, sling or javelins and other throwing weapons like small –headed axes. Agile and mobile, they moved around in a dispersed formation, making it more difficult for our own light troops to target them. They concentrated a high volume of missiles at our outnumbered picket line. This first phase of the battle was favouring the Bernicians. It was forcing back our own skirmishers, but these light troops would never be able, on their own, to force their way up the slope to the fortress and would certainly need reinforcements to carry the fight beyond the surrounding land and capture the gate.

So, more men, heavy infantry wearing mail shirts and carrying heavy shields and spears would be called upon soon. We could only see a few of these, right now, and, therefore, more would be lurking somewhere in the woods, waiting on the sig-

174

nal to assault the fortress. Maybe Hussa was with them. It would take a good number and a well –organised attack to succeed, so perhaps my brother was preparing the next phase of their attack.

With the Wicstun company sitting it out, unable to do much to affect the outcome, only Rhoerth's men in the fortress above us and on the walls below and Cadwallon's company lining the passageway leading to the gate opposed them. Still, I would assume that this should be enough strength to hold the fortress against this attack.

Horns sounded and the men we had seen earlier forming up at the wood edge rolled forward in shield wall formation, following up their light troops and moving towards the fortress. I counted the numbers. Only about eighty spears were visible.

"Bit of a weak attack, don't you think," I commented.

"It is probably just a probing attack," Eduard suggested. "Testing our strength and Rhoerth's resolve."

We watched as the skirmishers exchanged more missiles and then fell back as the main body of the next, heavily armed company reached the foot of the path leading up towards the fortress. Here the cattle corral, now empty of animals as they had been led away into the woods to the west once the Bernicians had arrived, was lined by warriors. A cart had been pulled across the path up to the fortress and then tipped over onto its side, creating a barricade blocking it and this was also now held by Rhoerth's men.

The Bernicians advanced slowly, keeping in formation. Shields overlapped shields and men hunkered down behind them, maximising the protection that wooden board and iron helms gave them. The Rheged defenders pelted the approaching company with a shower of missiles. Some found their mark and a few men fell, injured or dead, but the veterans closed up the ranks and marched on.

175

Finally, the Bernicians reached the defenders and threw themselves at the stone –walled corral and the cart. The obstructions impeded the assault as well as lending shelter and protection to the defenders. Rhoerth's troops were mostly green men with little knowledge of battles. Rheged's best warriors had been left behind in the grave pits of Catraeth and Degsastan and these men were, for the most part, youths who had been just boys at those great battles. Yet, with the aid of the defences they manned, they put up a good fight and to begin with the Bernicians could not break though.

The struggle raged on with blow exchanged for blow but now the experience of the Bernician men started to tell. They had been part of the armies that had crushed Owain with us at that battle of Catraeth and then Mac Gabhrain at Degsastan, Aethelric of Deira at Godmundingaham and then gone on to expand its holdings towards Din Edin and elsewhere. Many of them had been with Hussa down in West Seaxe when he had conquered the Temese Valley. With the possible and debatable exception of my own company, they were the toughest and most experienced body of warriors in Britain. They showed it now.

One after another, a huge veteran would launch himself over the wall or leap onto the cart and then, not waiting for the defenders to react, set about them with a fury and brutality that, looking at things through the eyes of professional fighters, our own men could not but appreciate.

"Merciful Woden but those are tough bastards!" Eduard said expressing what we all felt.

The merciless onslaught first burst through the defences of the lower wall of the corral and, turning to the left, swung around toward the cart. Terrified of being cut off, the defenders now broke. They turned and fled up the slope, pursued by the

Bernicians who tugged the cart out of the way and then, flowing past it, charged after the men of Rheged and cut them down. Once through the wall, the Bernicians took no prisoners. I saw a young British spearman drop his shield and spear and hold out his hands in surrender. He was felled without hesitation by one of the men who then took two strides to another man. This man had also dropped his weapon and now, seeing the fate of the first, had turned to flee. He did not make it five paces before he, too, was killed. Most men who die in battle do so with wounds in the back, killed as they tried to escape. Some might think that wrong. Most warriors would not agree with that sentiment. After all, the same man, if he lived, might kill you in the next battle. Better to kill them first so they can't do that.

The Bernicians surged up the hill to where the path turned past a rocky outcrop. Here they passed out of our sight as they reached the part of the path running beneath the wall that Cadwallon held. Cadwallon yelled out an order and his men started dropping javelins and rocks and shooting arrows down at the attackers.

"Impressive attack but still only about a company," Aedann said thoughtfully. His eyes were on the woods. "Can't see any reserves as yet."

"So, either they are bloody sure of themselves or..." Eduard started so say.

"...Or this is a distraction. A decoy." I completed the sentence.

The image of Rowenna killing that guard was on my mind and her secret way into the fortress. A way up past the northern palisade and up on to that northern terrace! The way I had tried to tell Rhoerth about but had been ignored. I could try again to talk to Cadwallon but, looking at things, he had his hands full and, anyway, would not listen to me. Clearly, I needed to persuade Rhoerth myself.

177

I turned and sprinted towards the gate connecting our enclosure to the fortress. It was shut. A group of Rhoerth's warriors glared at me as I approached.

"I need to see Rhoerth quickly!" I shouted.

"He is busy, Deiran. The fortress is under attack, in case you had not noticed."

"That is what I need to see him about. This attack is a decoy. Another attack is coming from the back of the hill…"

"Go away from here with your deceptions!" the captain of the guard replied.

I kicked the gate in frustration.

"Let me in!" I insisted.

"If you don't go away, I will have you shot," growled the captain.

One of the other guards brought a bow into sight. An arrow was nocked upon the string. I backed away and held out my hands.

"Alright… alright. Don't let me in if you don't believe me. But would it hurt to send a man to go and look?"

The captain considered this. "I am not sure…" he said.

"Listen. If I am wrong, you can still shoot me. If I am right, though, and you did not look and it got out you had been warned, think how that would be for you."

He glared at me and then turned to the man beside him. "Go and check the north wall."

The man nodded and turned away, scampering around the battlements and out of sight. We waited on his return. The noise of the assault by the Bernicians and the shouts and cries of Cadwallon's men as they threw or dropped missiles and rocks down upon the Bernician warriors below them, washed over us. I noticed a fingernail was rather long and bit through

178

it, spat it out then chewed at it impatiently. I looked up at the captain.

"Well?" I asked.

He was about to answer when the strident calling of horns echoed out from the north end of the hill. He turned to look behind him, down at the northern gate.

"Mary, preserve us!" he gasped.

"What is it?" I asked.

In answer, the gate in front of me swung open and I was able to step through into the inner fortress. To my right the insistent hammering and heavy blows against the main gates told of the attack we knew of. So far, the gates were holding, for now, anyway.

I turned my attention past the hall of Rhoerth to the northern gate beyond and opened my mouth to swear.

"Bugger me!" Eduard standing beside me said, beating me to it.

The gates were being forced open. I had been right. The attack on the south side, dramatic and full of examples of muscular valour that it had been, was not expected to succeed by itself. Hussa had sent another company around the back of the fortress and, under cover of the distraction afforded by the earlier assault on the gates, had broken through, up onto the north terrace and was now forcing the northern gate. That gate was a light internal gate, not intended for defence and I could see that it was already being slowly forced ajar.

There was a splintering sound close at hand. I whipped my head around to see an axe head bursting through the main gate just a few paces away from me. They were solid enough to hold a while yet, but not for long. I shook my head. If the enemy broke though both ways, it would be a slaughter. I spotted Rhoerth in

179

the centre of the fortress, gathering his men for a counterattack on the main gate. He did not seem to have that many men up here. Those holding the northern gate were being forced back, step by step, as I watched several Bernicians now inside the gate forming a small shield wall and pushing at the shields of Rhoerth's defenders. Behind me, there was another crashing sound as the axe hacked through the gate once more.

I looked up at the skies above, half expecting to see the Valkyries gathering, for surely there would be many fallen for them to carry to Woden's halls or to Freya's Volkvangyr this day. Mind you, many of the fallen would be Christians. Would they be gathered up to this Christian heaven they speak of? I guessed so. Either way, many would die here. I shook my head. Thoughts of the afterlife could wait for a while, at least.

"Rhoerth!" I bellowed, running towards him. He turned to me.

"What is it, Lord Cerdic? Come to say you told me so?" he asked.

I shook my head. "No – come to get you out of here!"

He frowned. "What do you mean? I can't leave my fortress."

"Look at what is going on! You can't win. That main gate won't hold much longer and they are already in the north gate. We need to get out...now!" I said.

He shook his head. "Get out, how? They have us surrounded."

I gestured towards the small gate that led to the southern terrace.

"We go that way and then around to the north terrace behind them and then down the hillside. We use the same route they used to get in. That path up the hillside is a narrow one. If we

180

can reach it, it is easy to hold and we can escape. Then we get away into the woods and head west to our ships. We live today and fight another day."

He frowned and then shook his head. "I will not abandon my men."

There was another crash against the outer door. More splintering of timber, another axe head bursting through. The gate was weakening.

"They will all die here if you don't. Let's get as many out as we can, along with your family. You have other fortresses, other land. You can't win here today but if you live there is always hope to win another day."

To the north end of the small fortress, there was a roar. We looked that way. Hussa had just come through the gate. He had spotted me and now pointed his sword at me. It was that sword he had won in that duel long ago in the days of our youth. He clearly intended to renew the fight between us and was pushing his men forward. Rhoerth's spearmen were holding for now but the impetus was on the side of my brother.

"It's now or never, lord king." I said.

He glanced around at his captains. They were all nodding in agreement with me. What a difference a few hours and imminent defeat made to their view of me. His shoulders slumped down.

"Very well, let's go," he assented. "Fetch my family!" he added to one of his warriors who scampered over to the hall. Moments later, his wife carrying his infant daughter, princess Rhianmelth, emerged with a gaggle of her companions.

He turned back to me. "Lead us on, Lord Cerdic."

I turned away, passed back through the gate and found Cadwallon.

"Lord Prince, we are leaving," I nodded towards the king.

He shrugged and looked over the wall and down to the pathway below. "That gate won't hold much longer. The Bernician captain down there is driving them on like fury. All our missile and slings have failed to slow him. I think a few moments at most and they will be through. Very well, you lead, and my company will bring up the rear."

I nodded and ran back over to my company.

"We are leaving. We are travelling light so leave everything you can't carry," I announced and as they hurried to comply, I turned to Hal who was with Eduard.

"Come with me, Hal, we need to go now."

"Are you sure of this, Cerdic?" Eduard asked "You're sure you want to take the boy? You could leave him here and Hussa will find him."

Aedann was at his elbow and looked at me expectantly.

"What are you two staring at? You, of all people, know what that bastard is capable of. I am not leaving the boy to him. I know what I am doing. You two just get the men ready. Let me worry about the boy."

Aedann held up his hands. "Alright, alright, nothing to agitate yourself about."

I glared at him and he wisely turned away and shouted orders to his men. "Swords to me, gather on me!" he commanded and soon his men were around him with Eduard's axes forming around him.

"This way!" I shouted and led the way around the fortress to the west, then we passed two men abreast along the narrow strip connecting the south terrace to the north terrace. Where the north terrace opened up before me, I halted and glanced around. As I had hoped, Hussa and his men had already passed

182

by and had forced their way into the fortress via the north gate. The terrace was empty save for a score of bodies, mostly Rho-erth's defenders but also some of Hussa's Bernicians. One of the craft buildings on the terrace was burning, but otherwise there was no activity. The battle had moved on inside the fortress. I looked towards the gate and considered a change of plan. Why not lead the companies through the gate and attack Hussa from behind? Even as I pondered this, there was a roar of triumph from somewhere inside the fortress, followed by shouting and cries of alarm from behind me.

"What is it?" I asked of Cuthbert who was just behind me. He listened to the shouts of men further back along the trail.

"They are saying the main gates are down. The Bernicians are through."

"Time to leave, then," I said and, abandoning thoughts of the gate and any change of plan, I ran towards the edge of the ter-race and found the path down the hillside. Then I turned and gestured for Cuthbert to join me.

"Go! Take Hal and get the ships ready" I shouted at him and he set off at once leading my men down the path and the steep slope. When Eduard reached me, I halted him.

"Form up here, just in front of the path down. We must let the rest past before we escape."

He nodded, halted and formed his shield wall at the edge of the terrace. Aedann's men passed by, then Rhoerth. Finally, Cadwallon's company emerged onto the terrace at the same mo-ment that I spotted that Hussa had come back out the north gate and spotted us. He bellowed an order and in a heartbeat his men were streaming back out the gate towards us.

"Shit!" I cursed.

This was going to be touch and go.

"Run, Cadwallon!" I yelled.

He spotted my brother, nodded at me and set off at a sprint for the spot where Aedann was standing at the top of the path gesturing at him. Hussa spotted him and set off in an attempt to intercept him.

"Get a bloody move on!" I bellowed at Cadwallon. He and his men ran. Hussa and his men ran and, by a hair's breath, Cadwallon and his men reached us and passed by us, before Hussa arrived in front of us. His Bernicians drew up sharply a few paces away rather than run unformed into Eduard's tightly packed shield wall. Hussa spat towards us.

"Where is my son?"

"Start falling back," I ordered Eduard, ignoring my brother.

"Shield wall!" Hussa ordered and his men moved to obey, but it takes a few moments to form a shield wall and, in that time, we had retreated to the top of the path.

"Where is our son?" Hussa asked again, and now I saw that the raven –haired woman was by his side, seax drawn and looking angry.

Around me, the men started to disengage, rear rank first to pass on down the path.

"Where is he?" Rowenna asked.

"He is safe," I replied and then took my turn, followed by the rest of Eduard's Axes. Last of all, Eduard stood at the head of the path, axe and shield in his hands, like a tide break that no wave can overcome.

"Fancy trying me?" he bellowed.

The enemy hesitated and we ran on down the slope. Finally, he turned and ran after us.

"Get them!" I heard Hussa yell and his men started down the slope. The first men tried to run after us, but this meant they could not seek the protection of their shields nor hold any formation. When he reached the bottom, Cuthbert had positioned his skirmishers with their bows and slings. The first three of Hussa's warriors fell to arrows and after this the pursuit slowed as they walked slowly down the slope, shields held up for protection. We, meanwhile, abandoned any formation and just ran for the woods, seeking the shelter it afforded and the paths to our ships and the hope of escape.

Chapter Seventeen
Wrath
Summer 611

"Cerdic, you bastard!" Hussa bawled from the top of the path and then, seizing a spear from a nearby warrior, launched it down the slope towards the fleeing Deiran warriors. He let out a loud roar as he released the missile but despite this, or maybe because of his loss of control, it was a futile gesture and the missile came to earth twenty -five paces down the hillside , ricocheted into the air, bounced once more and then slid on another ten yards before it finally came to rest. He stood breathing hard, glaring at the spear which had come nowhere near the fleeing figures at the base of the hill, and certainly nowhere near his brother who by now had vanished into the treeline to the west of the fortress.

Cursing, he moved to head off in pursuit of his brother and his captive son, but Rolf thrust an arm around him and pulled him back from the precipitous incline.

"Let me go, Rolf!" he hissed.

Rolf held on firmly. "You'll break your neck hurtling down there. Your brother's men used a rope but that big bastard cut it when he jumped. He is a bloody lucky sod or else tough as an auroch. Could easily have cracked his ankle on that tumble."

Hussa ignored him and struggled against the grip, but Rolf was one of the strongest men he knew and it was hopeless. He finally gave up, letting out a deep breath.

"He is speaking truth, husband," Rowenna said. "I will go. I have been down the path already today and I am not weighed down by armour."

Hussa whipped his head round to stare at her.

"On your own? I don't think so," he said. "Rolf, you can release me now."

He had stopped struggling and Rolf finally let him go. Hussa shot his friend a poisonous glare and then went over to the west side of the terrace and looked towards the woods.

"They are going cross country. If we go down the road, we may be able to cut them off. Come on!" he ordered and headed back into the fortress, past the bodies of the fallen. He looked about him as he did, hating the place and the uprising that had brought him here. If it had not been for the Rheged king's rebellious ways, he would not be here and his son would still be with him. He felt the anger returning like a pot of stew boiling again when put back on the fire to warm up.

"Damn this place, a curse on it!" he spat.

In the centre of the fortress a brazier was burning low. It was a fire which had been lit to help the men of the watch combat the chill air that could blow over the fortress in the middle of the night.

A wave of rage came over Hussa and, with a shout, he kicked the brazier over and it crashed against the side of Rhoerth's hall where a pile of fire wood was stacked. In an instant, a sack full of bark and dry leaves that had been collected to serve as kindling had caught fire, igniting, in turn, the smallest branches piled up next to the logs and the flames quickly spread so that the wooden walls of the hall began to smoulder.

A group of warriors who had been guarding the remnants of Rhoerth's warriors hurried to the water butts and began to fill buckets stacked nearby. One of the men took off his helmet and scooped up water with that and ran along with his companions toward the blaze. Hussa glared at them.

"Let it burn, let the whole fort burn!" he commanded.

The men hesitated and looked at Rolf. Rolf, in turn, was staring at Hussa.

"Have you lost your mind?"

"Don't question me, just do it. Let the whole place burn."

The men holding the buckets halted and stared at the flames. The firewood was dry, and the stack was engulfed by flames quickly. These spread unhindered and the hall was soon ablaze with fire now licking at the battlements of the fortress. The outer walls were made of large stones, but the stone was laced with a timber framework and that timber in turn soon started to smoulder.

Hussa spotted another fire over near the wall next to the hall. The flames flickered below a cauldron suspended over it on a cast iron frame. He stomped over to it and saw that the cauldon was full of pine tar, sourced no doubt from the ample forests around the fortress and in peaceful times used to seal the timbers of boats or houses. The defenders must have put it on to heat up when the attack had begun but had been unable to use it due to the speed of their defeat. He hurtled into the frame, shoulder first and the whole frame tipped over sending the caludron crashing to the ground and then over onto its side. A wave of hot tar gushed out and splashed up the wall which was already smouldering. The tar caught fire and the lattice –like arrangement within the walls channelled the blaze through the stones with a rapidity that took Hussa by surprise. Nevertheless, the destruction felt good and a suitable channel for his anger.

"Feel better now?" Rolf asked him and the words brought him back to his senses. He reminded himself that he had more important matters to deal with and that Cerdic was still out there with his son. So, gesturing at Rowenna and Rolf to follow him, he left the fort ablaze and strode towards the gate, determined to continue the pursuit. He did not get far because he found Sogor standing in the gateway surrounded by his huscarls staring around the fortress in disbelief.

"Just what in the name of Woden's balls are you doing, Hussa!" Sogor roared.

Hussa recovered from the initial surprise at seeing Sogor and stomped on towards the gate.

"Out of my way. I'm leaving."

"You're doing no such thing. You are going to tell me what has gotten into your head!"

Hussa shook his head and moved to push himself between two of Sogor's men.

"Stop him," Sogor ordered and the men raised their spears to point at Hussa's chest.

"Let me through," Hussa demanded, but Sogor just shook his head.

He glanced up at the fire that had now spread in an arc around the outer fortress battlements. The wooden framework was burning, driving flames along dozens of channels. The stonework, held together by the timber, was now heated to a ferocious level, giving Hussa the sudden thought that this was like a vision of Muspelheim, the fire world wherein Sutyr the fire giant ruled as king. The very rocks were now cracking and splintering with the heat.

"Shall we fight the fire, Lord?" one of Sogor's men asked him.

Sogor shook hs head. "Too late now I reckon," he said. He turned back to Hussa. "Well, you certainly arsed this up, didn't you?"

"I don't have time to argue with you. I need to go find my son," Hussa said.

"Your son?"

"My brother came to the village and took him last night."

"Your brother is here?" he asked warily glancing around the hilltop.

Hussa threw up his hands in exasperation. "Was! He was here. He has gone with my son and Rhoerth."

Sogor's eyes bulged. "So, you let him escape?"

"I did not let him escape, he escaped with Cerdic."

"Where did he go?"

"That is what I am trying to find out, you idiot. He went off to the west through the forest. I was going to go down the coast road and try to intercept him."

"You are not going anywhere," Sogor said, shaking his head. "My men will do it. Your men will secure the prisoners on the lower terraces and wait for orders."

"What about me? Let me and Rowenna go."

Sogor glanced around. "Where is she?"

Hussa span round. His wife was nowhere to be seen.

"Where is she?" he asked Rolf who just shrugged. "I have no idea she was here a moment ago."

Sogor snorted. "So, you have lost not only the king of Rheged and his family, but also your son and your wife, and you have burnt down a fortress that could have been a useful base. All in all, not one of your best days is it, Lord Hussa?"

Hussa did not reply except to whisper to himself.

'Where is she?'

When Hussa had waved at her to follow him towards the gateway, Rowenna had spotted Sogor coming up the path towards the fortress with a face like a thunderstorm. She realised at once that as speed was important and any delay was not acceptable, she could not get entangled with him and his men. Therefore as Hussa strode towards the main gate, she made a snap decision and had slipped through the side gate into the empty south terrace and, hurrying past the now abandoned camp, quickly reached the battlements that lined the terrace. She climbed up onto the battlements and then lowered herself over edge and dropped down into the cattle corral beneath.

Picking her way past the bodies of Rheged's warriors who had fallen defending the empty corral, she reached the wall that encircled it and again climbed over and so gained the hillside beneath. From here she passed steathily into the western woods and soon found herself near a makeshift corral containing animals she assumed had been driven out of the way of the imminent Bernician assault earlier in the day. She found a horse in the corral slipped on a saddle from a pile in the corner and mounted, setting off along the road to the west.

Behind her smoke was rising in a dense cloud and the flames encircling the fortress leapt into the skies. It was an impressive blaze, but she turned her gaze away and dug in her heels, urging her mount onwards. Soon she left the rolling land around Anwoth and entered the forest that lay along either bank of the river. She reached the ford and splashed through it. To her left, to the south, the river widened into a harbour and emptied into the sea. At anchor in the river were several fishermen's boats and against the quay lay two larger ships. Clustered on the quayside were dozens of men, warriors of Deira, Gwynedd and also of Rheged. They were clearly boarding the larger craft. Sails were being unreefed from the mast of one of the ships in readiness for departure. She did not have long.

"Come on!" she urged her horse and turned south on the road. It curved inland behind a small hill crowned by beech trees and she lost sight of the harbour.

Bending forward she urged the beast on to even more exertion and, with no regard to her surrounding they plunged on, tree branches whipping her face and tugging at her clothes.

Finally, they burst out of the trees and she saw that they had reached the harbour. The quayside was empty, and the first ship had pulled away from the dock and was turning seaward. The second ship was still beside the quay but even now men were pushing it away with poles and the sails were unfurling. She jumped down from her horse and ran towards it.

"Hal!" she shouted.

All faces turned to stare at her. She desperately searched them all.

"Hal," she repeated.

The ship was pulling away now, turning with the wind southwards towards the open sea. She ran along the quayside, frantic now.

"Hal, are you there?" she asked.

"Ma?" a reply came, faint at first from the men clustered around the stern of the ship. Then louder it was repeated. "Ma, Ma, I am here!"

She searched the stern of the vessel and at last she spotted him. Hal was standing beside a great brute of a warrior, one of Hussa's brother's companions, she thought. He was the man who had stood alone at the top of the path back at the fortress, holding back Hussa's men with that axe that even now he held. On Hal's other side was Cerdic himself. He was staring at Rowenna with surprise.

"Give me back my son," she shouted at him.

Cerdic glanced down at the boy. Then he shook his head. "I can't. I will care for him now. He will be safe, I promise you that."

"Ma!" Hal cried again.

Cerdic shouted an order and more sails unfurled and filled with wind and the ship pulled away from the shore and passed out to sea

"Hal!" Rowenna screamed in a voice that the men on the boat must have heard, yet the boat sailed on.

"Hal," she repeated this time in a whisper that only she could hear.

At the bottom of the path leading up Anwoth hill, Hussa was arguing with Sogor. As the fire had spread they had evacuated the fortress and retreated down to near the base of the hill. Here the prisoners were now enclosed in the corral and set under guard. Meanwhile, Hussa's men had gathered around him, surrounded by Sogor and his companies.

Hussa had both hands on his hips and was glaring at the other man.

"You must let me go after them, Sogor."

"You are not going anywhere except back to Aethelfrith to explain your actions," Sogor replied.

"My son is with my brother and his men."

Sogor shrugged. "Not my problem, Hussa."

Hussa drew his seax and lunged towards the other man.

Sogor pulled out his own blade and in an instant all the men under both Sogor and Hussa were armed and staring warily at each other.

"Say the word, Hussa, and I will cut you a way out of these bastards so you can go after your son," Rolf said, his voice low.

Hussa glanced around at Sogor's men. There were more of them, and, whilst Hussa and Rolf's men had just assaulted a fortress and fought a battle, these men were fresh. If he did give the order, the odds were against his men. Yet he was desperate

193

to pursue his son and desperation gave men strength. His men were loyal to him and many like Rolf loved Hal almost as much as he did. So, he did not doubt that Rolf would cut a bloody swathe through Sogor's ranks, whatever the odds. It would, of course, mean that he would be an outlaw, almost certainly declared a criminal by Aethelfrith. Yet, at that moment, he did not care. He drew his sword and turned towards Rolf, ready to give the order.

"Stop," commanded Rowenna as she pushed through Sogor's men. "It is too late."

Hussa frowned at her. "What do you mean, too late?" he asked.

She looked up at him. Her eyes were wet. "He has gone.... they reached the ships and cast off from the quay."

"Hal?"

"Your brother has him. The ships went out to sea. Maybe turning west, maybe going south – I am not sure."

Hussa looked up at Sogor. "If they have gone west, they might be taking Rhoerth to another fortress further down the coast."

"It is possible.' Sogor agreed. "There are other fortresses they may have reoccupied."

"So, we go west and pursue."

Sogor shook his head. "There is no we, Hussa. I will send two companies on under one of my captains. They will scout the other fortresses and, if they are occupied, report back to me." He paused a moment as he stared at Hussa. "We, though, will return to Bebbanburg. Aethelfrith must hear of your incompetence. You are finished, Hussa. If I have my way, your head will be on a spike above Bebbanburg by the end of the summer. At the very least, your days leading Aethelfrith's companies are over."

194

"You bastard!" Hussa said and stepped forward. At once swords and spears were raised once more on both sides and his company moved forward with him. Rolf was at his side. The battle rage was upon him, the heat was in his blood and he gripped his blade and raised it, ready to strike down at Sogor.

He felt a hand upon his own, gently pulling it down. It was Rowenna's.

"Not today. Not like this. Think about Hal," she said softly.

He turned his head and looked at her. Around her, the men's eyes burned with bloodlust. Men ready to do murder out of loyalty to their lord. Her eyes had none of that. There was a yearning there to see her son again and an appeal to him to let that happen.

"Please, Hussa, give in today."

Then, just like that, he felt the rage leave him and he let his blade fall.

"Leave it," he commanded Rolf and his men, turning fully to face them. "No more fighting today."

Rolf reluctantly sheathed his sword. His men, one by one, did the same or else dropped their spears' butts onto the ground.

Then he turned back to Sogor who was watching him intently.

"Very well, I will come with you. But you let my men return to my estates in Bernicia with Rolf."

Sogor considered this. He looked like he might argue but then glanced around at the faces of Hussa's veterans and appeared to decide not to push the matter too far. He had more men than him, Hussa was well aware, but not that many more. He seemed content enough with the potential prize of his rival's head. He nodded slowly and gestured to his own men who now also relaxed.

"Very well, it is you that will answer for your actions this day to the king. You are my prisoner. Hand over your sword, Lord Hussa. You are coming with me."

Chapter Eighteen
Consequences
Autumn 611

After our ships had pulled away from the harbour, Hal began to cry.

"I want to go back to Ma and Da!" he said.

"As I said before, Hussa is not your father, Hal. I am. I am going to look after you."

He looked up at me, his face a mask of absolute confusion and bewilderment.

"I don't understand. What do you mean, he is not my father?"

"I mean, that before you were born I...your mother. Well ... we were together, and you came along as a result."

He looked even more confused. He was only three, after all, I reminded myself. I took a deep breath and tried again.

"Hussa married your mother after you were born."

"Did you marry her first?" he asked.

I shook my head. "No. I did not know about you until later. I was already married so I could not have married her, anyway."

His confusion returned, then dropped away and left a sceptical expression of doubt.

"I don't believe you," he said and, breaking away from me, he rushed to the side of the ship. We were a fair way out at sea by now. The wind was strong and it was driving the waves towards us. We were tacking to make progress against the head wind and the boat was tossing up and down on the swell. Hal stumbled as the vessel heaved to one side and reached out to seize the sideboard and steady himself. He stared at the waves and then, turning towards the bow, started climbing up on the side of the prow nearest the shore.

"Hal, stop that." I ordered and grabbed his shoulders and pulled him back down.

I became aware that around me the men were studying me. Some looked disapproving, one even shook his head. I glared at him.

"What are you looking at? I know what I am doing."

He lifted up his hands in submission and turned away. Eduard joined us and Hal readily went to him. I experienced a moment's irritation that the boy clearly trusted my friend more than he trusted me. I drove the thought away. For now, whatever calmed him down was welcome. Time enough to sort this all out later.

"I know what I am doing," I said to myself. But it did not sound that convincing, even to me.

The boats pushed further out to sea. I made my way over to where Rhoerth and his companions were crowed along the steerboard side of the ship. The king was staring back at the land where smoke could be seen rising from the inferno that was destroying Anwoth's fortress, visible even here, several miles away. Rhoerth looked ashen faced. He glanced at me when I arrived by his side.

"What wrath have you brought upon us, Cerdic?"

"What do you mean?"

He gestured towards Eduard and Hal. "That boy you have there. You claim he is your son."

I nodded. "Yes, I do."

"Yet, he believes your half brother Hussa to be his father."

I shook my head. "That cannot be the case, Lord, Hussa has never fathered a child. The child was born after I lay with his mother once."

"You seem so certain," he said.

I looked at Hal. Why, indeed, was I so certain?

"Whether I am right or not, I will not leave him with Hussa – he will be safer with me. Hussa is a monster. I will protect him."

Rhoerth snorted. "Because you are not a monster? Slayer of the golden king of Rheged. Many of my people would see you as a monster."

Rhoerth studied me and I looked away, staring instead at the dark smudge above the ashes of the fortress.

"Whichever of you is the boy's father, it seems that you both are sure it is you. How ironic is that?"

"I don't understand what you mean," I said.

He laughed but it held no humour.

"When a man has made a woman pregnant and learns about it, it is often the case that they are reluctant to acknowledge the fact, maybe even fleeing the responsibility. Yet this woman has not one but two brothers claiming to be father. Monsters or not, you have more in common with your brother than you think, perhaps. Both will take whatever action they feel is neccesary for those they love. Your action, and his, means that my fortress burns today." He gestured at the distant smoke.

I made a face. "He was going to attack anyway. I did try and warn you that he had a plan and an alternative way in, did I not?"

He shrugged. "You did, I admit that. Maybe if I had listened, we could have stopped him."

I pursed my lips. "Always easy to tell after the event, but maybe. No point pondering what might have been," I said.

We watched the smoke rise together for a while and then a thought occurred to me.

198

"Now the fortress is burnt, what will you do? Your forces are depleted and many captured."

He pointed west along the coast. "We have other fortresses. We can reach them, fortify them and call for more men."

"I don't think you have the time," I said, pointing towards the coast.

Hundreds of spearmen could be seen marching along it, emerging from the forests and heading west. They appeared to be Sogor's warriors, pushing on along the coast.

"Aethelfrith will occupy your forts. You may reach one by sea faster than he can march, but most of your land will be occupied by his men. I don't think you have a hope now, not for the present, anyway. Maybe you never had a hope. It was quite a gamble you took. You would have been better waiting until Aethelfrith attacked Mercia as we expected him to do."

He looked glum. "I suppose I was too eager. My people's honour was wounded by the defeats at his hands. We saw a chance to free ourselves from him and get our homeland back."

"I can understand that desire," I said thinking of the Villa.

"What can I do now? What do you think?"

I looked over at the other boat where Cadwallon and his men, along with some more of the Rheged survivors, were visible. The flight from the fortress had been chaotic and the companies were mixed across both vessels.

"Gwynedd will shelter you. Your father is there, and Iago would not refuse a request from him. Come back with us and, maybe, a day will come when you can return," I told him.

I thought about it more and then nodded to myself.

I gave the order to pull the ship over to Cadwallon's.

"Cadwallon!" I shouted. "We need to talk."

I was right that Iago welcomed Rhoerth, his family, and his forces into his court. Soon, a song had been written by Aneirin about the uprising and the heroic, but tragic, defence and ultimate destruction of the fortress. As with all these Welsh songs, it seemed to revel in the fight against terrifying odds and to emphasise the sense of loss of yet another British stronghold falling to the English invader. Rhoerth had a verse to himself full of references to his youthful valour. Even Cadwallon got a line about going to the aid of this royal brother and distant kin, descendants together as were most of the Welsh kings from Coel, king of the north in the years just after the Romans had left. The English, the Angles of Bernicia or Deira on either side, got little mention, other than a general reference to the enemy's swords and spears being dipped in the blood of the valorous defenders.

"Why do most of your songs focus on defeat?" I asked Aneirin when we sat by the hearth in Iago's hall. "Doom and gloom, I mean."

He looked at me under his dark eyebrows, now showing the first flecks of grey and white. "Doom and gloom make better songs," he said simply.

Doom and gloom certainly surrounded me at that court. Whilst Rhoerth was welcomed and sheltered and given rooms in the king's fortress, the court regarded my conduct in a less than heroic light.

My situation was not helped, of course, by Cadwallon. He did his best to pour all the blame on me. It suited his purpose to shed doubt on the continuing wisdom of Gwynedd allying with Mercia and, in particular, fostering and sponsoring Edwin and his claim upon the crown of Northumbria.

"Lord King, grandfather," he addressed Iago a few days after our return from Rheged. "Lord King, the disaster at Anwoth can

200

be laid firmly at the door of Lord Cerdic. His actions in bringing the wrath of his brother down upon us all led directly to the destruction of the fortress and the defeat of the uprising. However, I want to ask a question. Does it not strike you as convenient that the attempt to free a Welsh kingdom from Angle domination failed and he was at hand?"

Iago, now looking increasingly old and frail, said nothing but his son, Cadfan, spoke instead. Cadfan stood up from his seat at the right hand of the king.

"My son, I cannot see that it suits Prince Edwin for this rebellion to fail. It only aids his rival, Aethelfrith."

Cadwallon shrugged. "Maybe, though Edwin is thinking that if and when he regains the throne of Deira and, probably, also Bernicia, then he as king in Northumbria would not wish a powerful Rheged to exist. Why not help Aethelfrith sort out this problem so he would not need to when he becomes king?"

Rumbles of agreement rolled around the court. Cadwallon smiled. He knew he had won a point. Sabert, sitting beside Edwin, raised a hand.

"Lord King, may I be permitted to speak?" he said in Welsh. He was pretty fluent in the language having had Anneirin teach him in the years we had lived in Gwyedd. He said that speaking in another man's language implied respect of that man and that only helped whatever embassy and diplomacy he was embarked upon.

Cadfan glanced at his father who, after a moment's pause, nodded. Prince Cadfan gestured at Earl Sabert and sat back in his seat. Sabert rose.

"Lord King, I assure you and all your lords," he gestured around the hall, "that we have only honourable thoughts towards you and your ally." He bowed toward Rhoerth who sat near Cadfan. Edwin nodded firmly.

"It is true my prince's main aim is to reclaim the crown of Deira which was wrongly taken from him. Maybe what prince Cadwallon says is truthful and a powerful Rheged would be a a challenge to him. However, let me assure you that Cadwallon is thinking far too far ahead. Unless Edwin becomes king in Northumbria, none of that would matter. So, helping Aethelfrith defeat his enemies, our allies, makes no sense at all. In any event, you are forgetting one thing – Aethelfrith killed Aethelric, Prince Edwin's brother."

He paused for a moment after saying those words.

"I say again, Aethelfrith killed his brother," he repeated. "I ask all the men here. If a man killed your brother, would you contemplate any action that helped that man? Instead, would your blood not burn for revenge?"

He paused again to look each man in the hall in the eyes. Challenging them to say something. None did.

"Lord Prince," he said to Edwin, "Does your blood not burn for revenge on Aethelfrith?"

Edwin nodded. "Yes, Earl Sabert, it burns," he said in a low voice, yet one that everyone heard.

Cadwallon looked around the hall and glowered. He knew his attempt to blame Edwin for the defeat at Anwoth had failed. Yet he was not finished. He glanced at me.

"Very well. Let's accept that Prince Edwin's aim was genuine, and he had no part in the triumph of his rival at Anwoth. That still leaves the actions of Cerdic. What does Earl Sabert have to say about what he did?"

Sabert, who was still standing, pivotted to look at Edwin, who said nothing and lowered his head to look at the reed strewn floor beneath his boots. Edwin was not able to help defend me, or not willing.

202

"Well?" Cadwallon asked.

"My Lord King," Rhoerth interrupted. "Lord Cerdic did try to warn me about his brother's surprise attack. Rushing off on his own into the town and bringing that boy back with him was not wise but, had I listened to him, we may have averted defeat. I would not have the blame placed upon him when some should be shared with me."

Cadwallon was clearly not at all happy with this intervention. His face fell. He looked angrily at Rhoerth and then at me. He appeared ready to speak again but now, finally, Iago spoke.

"If King Rhoerth judges that blame does not lie upon Earl Cerdic, then I accept that. The matter occurred in his lands, after all. Lord Cerdic appears to have acted rashly and his judgement is questionable, but no censure or punishment will ensue. The matter is closed."

With that, he rose and retired towards his own rooms. Everyone stood out of respect and then, once he had gone, the company broke into dozens of groups, each debating and discussing what had happened. Many a scornful glance was directed at me. Rhoerth may have made his decision and Iago closed the matter down, but it was clear that many present were not happy with me, not happy at all.

Edwin and Sabert were also less than pleased at me when we gathered in the old hall which had again been given over to us during our stay.

"You were supposed to help Rhoerth defend his fortress, not provoke your brother as part of your ongoing feud. All this seemed to have been triggered off by some dispute over a boy," Edwin said.

"Not just any boy, my lord prince, but my son," I said.

"Or his son," Sabert commented. "Hussa's son, I mean."

"He is mine and I will protect him." I said, "You don't understand Sabert, you don't have a son."

The old advisor shook his head. "I know enough to know that a man will do what he needs to for his family, but you also have a higher duty to Prince Edwin. You swore an oath to him. This alliance was important, and you jeopardised that for your own personal reasons."

"I do have a son," Edwin said. Cwenburg had bore him his first child whilst we had been away in Rheged. The news had reached Deganwy a few days before. "So, whilst I have not seen him yet, I do understand the bond of father and son. Yet, this matter has put me, and my alliance with Gwyedd and the other Welsh lands at risk. I need to repair that damage. I can't do that with you here."

"So, what do you want me to do?" I asked.

"Go back to Mercia and your estates there and guard that border. I will stay here and see what I can do. I will follow you later."

So, I went home, and I took Hal with me.

When we arrived back at Souekesham, the welcome was warm from the villagers and families of the warriors. Our experience of the battle at Anwoth had been peripheral at best and whilst there had been a few minor wounds, all of these had healed on the voyage to Gwyedd and the march back through Mercia. Our return, therefore, was accompanied by relief and the whole incident treated by our men as a confusing but ultimately irrelevant distraction from the main aim – of one day returning home to Deira and Edwin or perhaps Hereric gaining the throne.

This was not, however, my own experience. To me the whole episode had been much more profound. The failed attempt to

204

support rebellion against Bernician control over Rheged as part of an overall alliance may have been some sort of justification that I spoke about when Eduard, Cuthbert or Aedann mentioned the trip but I was fooling neither them nor myself that that had been the main thing on my mind.

We left the company at Souekesham and walked across the fields to the lodge on the island to the south of the town that lay in the bend of the Temese. There we were met by my family. Cuthwine was first, running across the fields to meet us halfway to the lodge. He had filled out that summer whilst we had been away, his former scrawny arms showing more muscle, he had grown an inch or two and the stubble on his chin was darker.

"Who are you and where is my son?" I asked him as he reached us.

Cuthwine frowned at me.

"You are not still angry with me, are you?" I asked.

Cuthwine, along with the youngest lads in the company, had been left behind when we had gone north. I had not felt that they were ready and had chosen to leave them in Grettir's hands with a smattering of the oldest veterans. He had been most unhappy with me.

"When will I ever come to war with you?" he had asked.

"The day will come sooner than you wish, my son," I had answered solemnly.

"And hopefully, very soon," Eduard put in cheerfully with a wink at him.

I had scowled at my friend but knew there was no point trying to explain to Cuthwine why a man might not wish for war. He would never understand and, for that matter, when I was Cuthwine's age, neither would I. It took a summer of war to make me see the truth. Eduard never had. For him, war was his purpose.

205

Cuthwine shook his head at my question. "No, I am not angry. Grettir has kept us busy, the old bastard. He even took us out after some bandits that had raided the abbey in those hills north of here."

"Oh, really? What happened? Was Ealdwig hurt?" I asked, realising I was bothered about the monk.

"Nothing much. The monks had fled into the woods. In fact, your friend, Ealdwig, had taken charge of that. There was a trapper's hut in the woods, and he took them and hid them there."

"He did tell me once that he had been a hunter and a trapper before becoming a monk."

"Yes, turns out he knows the woods all around here for miles around the abbey and the hunting lodge. Anyway, after we chased off the bandits, he found us and showed us the hiding spot and we escorted the monks back to the abbey. No one got hurt. Bit boring, to be honest," he replied trying to sound as casual as he could, but I could tell he had found the experience exciting.

"Alright, well, if you were not angry at me, why were you frowning?"

He gestured at Hal. "It was seeing him walking besides you. Is he... who I think he is?"

I glanced down at Hall. "What do you know about it?" I asked instead of answering the queston.

"Oh, come on, Father! You and Mother don't exactly argue quietly. The entire household knows about it."

I stuck out my lip. "Really?"

"So, is this my brother?"

Hal frowned at him. "I don't think I have a brother."

Cuthwine pointed at me. "If he is your father, you do, and a sister, too,"

"Sister?" Hal looked even more confused.

"Yes!" squeaked an excited voice from behind Cuthwine and five –year –old Sian burst past Cuthwine and ran up to Hal. "I am your sister."

Hal looked unsure how to react and, I have to say, I was also dumbstruck. I had given no thought at all to the implications of having another son. How foolish was I? If Hal was my son then, yes, Cuthwine and Sian had a new sibling.

A shadow fell over Hal and Sian. Aidith had arrived and was looking down at the boy.

"You did not think this through, did you?" she said quietly to me.

Hal looked up at her at that moment. "If you are my father, is this my ma?" he asked.

I felt a sudden chill as if the first winter winds were arriving. I patted Cuthwine on the shoulder.

"Take the lad and your sister and show him the lodge. I need to talk to your mother." I said.

Cuthwine gave me a knowing look that said, without words, 'You are in trouble now, it was nice knowing you' and then put his arm around Hal's shoulders.

"Come along, lad. Let's go get you some food."

Hal nodded enthusiastically about that idea and, as if he had known Cuthwine for his whole life and not just moments, allowed himself to be led away.

I found myself smiling as I turned to face Aidith. Yet the sight of her icy cold face, which was like another reminder of the coming winter, made my smile drop away.

"Look, love…" I started. It was perhaps not the best start.

"Don't 'look love' me, Cerdic son of Cenred," she addressed me very formally. "Did you give all this any thought at all?"

"Of course, I did…" I replied hesitantly then I winced. I did not even convince myself.

"No, you bloody didn't, you idiot!" she shouted. "You just charged in without thought acting like, I don't know, Eduard at a shield wall, with no thought for the consequences. You kidnapped a boy we don't even know is your son, and certainly is not mine, and drag him halfway across Britannia. For what? Why?"

"I didn't think Rowenna was a suitable mother and we know for certain Hussa is not a suitable father. Besides, he is my son, Hussa can't have children."

"Do we know that with certainty? No, we don't."

"I…" I stumbled to reply. Then I just gave up. I stepped over to a tree stump in the field and sat down on it heavily.

"As for Rowenna not being a suitable mother, how can you make that judgment?"

"She killed a guard…" I said and told her the story of that night when I had spotted her, seen her kill the guard and then, following her back to the camp, had found Hal and taken him away. She listened and then shook her head, her expression softening slightly as she came and knelt beside me. She laid a hand on my knee.

"So, you saw her sneak into the camp as a scout, kill a guard she encountered and then… like a scout, you followed her and in turn attacked a guard yourself."

"Well, yes, but I didn't kill him, I think…"

"No, you just smacked his head against a tree and ran on. He may have died, you don't know. Did that action make you unsuitable as a father, or just a man acting to defend himself? Yet, from her action there, you decided she was no good as a mother. Can you explain to me the difference?"

208

"Well, I am not sure…" then I shook my head. "I see your point."

She laughed. "You idiot!" she said this time without venom. She got up and dusted down her smock. "Well, what is done is done, I guess. The boy is your kin, whether son or nephew, and the children's, too, whether brother or cousin, so, we will make him welcome and keep him safe."

She turned towards the lodge then stopped after a few steps and glanced back at me.

"Cerdic," she added. "I want this sorted by the spring. Somehow work out if he is your son or not and what you are going to do about it. He is welcome here through the winter, after that I need this resolved."

I nodded and watched her walk away leaving me on the meadow sitting on the stump as the autumnal evening light faded.

Chapter Nineteen
Back at court
Summer to Autumn 611

Heavy storms had descended upon the area soon after Sogor's scouts had returned confirming Rowenna's report that the boats carrying Rhoerth, Cerdic and Cadwallon had left the port. The rain fell upon the flames that were consuming the hilltop fort. At first, they did little to combat the fire, but gradually the raindrops' persistence won the day and finally, the inferno which had destroyed the fortress on top of Anwoth was quenched. As the smoke cleared, the Bernicians could see there was but little left of the smouldering ruin.

In the days after the assault on the fortress, Sogor consolidated his hold on the area around Anwoth by occupying nearby villages and towns. He also sent his light cavalry scouts and small numbers of spearmen west into Rheged with orders to investigate other fortresses and try to establish if Rhoerth had set himself up in one of them in preapartion for renewing the rebellion. Despite further entreaties to be allowed to puruse his brother, Hussa, along with Rowenna and his companies, was told to prepare to march east, first to Luguvalium and then across to Bebbanburg. Sogor and Eanfrith returned with Hussa and Rowenna to the king's court. Hussa was permitted to disperse his own men back to his estates under the command of Rolf whilst he and Rowenna were taken to Bebbanburg where they would be called upon to defend their actions.

Hussa had hoped to be able to present his arguments to the king soon after arriving in Bebbanburg, yet, to Rowenna's and his intense frustration, they were kept waiting, confined to their rooms, for well over a week before being summoned and escorted by armed guards to the king's hall.

"This will not be easy," Hussa murmured. "Sogor has had ample opportunity to poison the king against us."

When they entered the hall, they were greeted with silence. Every lord watched them walk up to Aethelfrith's chair and bow. The king's gaze followed them up the hall and then, without saying anything to either of them, he gestured to a pair of stools set to one side. Once they had taken their seat, she nodded at Sogor to begin. Right from the start the odds were set against them. Sogor's portrayal of the events was damning.

"Lord Hussa acted without a plan, Lord," he told Aethelfrith, who continued to listen to the report without interruption or comment. "Before we had opportunity to properly scout out the lay of the land, or assess the strength of the enemy, and without any discussion with myself or your son, he acted on his own initiative. Indeed, it seems that he hardly discussed the plan with his own men but just attacked."

"My men agreed with me…" Hussa interrupted.

"Oh, indeed. If there is one thing I do not fault here, it is the loyalty of your men. A loyalty born of stupidity and blind faith in whatever they see in you, I am sure, but whilst loyalty on their part may be a virtue, it does not excuse your actions. Indeed, it even makes it worse as you knew they would follow you and act in this most risky way. More than risky, in fact. This was perilous in the extreme and, to be frank, should not have worked. You attacked a fortress that was well defended and alerted to our presence."

"The attack succeded," Rowenna put in.

Sogor scowled at her. "You had some success based on the valour of Rolf's companies and the surprise the alternative as-

211

sault route allowed you. In the end, though, it was a fire that defeated Rhoerth and that fire destroyed the fortress and denied it not only to him but to us as well. That will impede our further conquest of the area. It was rash and unnecessary. We had sufficient numbers to take the fortress by siege or force of arms in a more controlled way."

"So, it appears that Hussa acted rashly. Is that your main complaint?" Aethelfrith asked, stirring at last.

Sogor shook his head. "Not just that, Lord. His actions were rash, but the reason was a result of his own son being captured by his brother, Earl Cerdic."

Aethelfrith raised his eyebrows. "Indeed, you criticise him for acting in defence of his own son, is that it?"

"No, Lord, I do not. I criticise him for acting without thought, risking the lives of hundreds and our own strategy affecting a kingdom over the life of one small boy."

Sogor held out his hands. "Everyone knows I have no love for Hussa, but I am not cold. Had he confided in me, I would have, of course, understood his loss and his need to find his son."

"Liar!" Hussa snarled. "When I asked to pursue him, you denied me the request."

"You had already forfeited the right to my trust at that stage," Sogor shouted and then turning back to the king added, "my lord king, my point is, that Hussa acted for personal reasons without thought for your kingdom, strategy or men. In the future, what is the likelihood that he can be trusted to act in your best interests?"

"I always have acted in the interests of my king," Hussa objected.

"When it suits you!" Sogor retorted. "Lord, your son was witness to these events, can I suggest you ask him."

Hussa groaned and glanced at Rowennna before he could stop himself.

Eanfrith heard and stared at him. "What are you saying? Are you suggesting I would not speak my own mind?"

Hussa hesitated. That was exactly what he was thinking but he dared not say it. He was sure that Sogor had already encouraged Eanfrith to back him up. The prince stood up and walked to stand in the centre of the court.

"Well, I can speak my own mind, Lord Hussa," he said. "I have taken time to think about it, unlike yourself that night. You did act as the Lord Sogor says, in haste, and without taking good counsel or consulting myself or Sogor, whose command you were under."

"Very well," Aethelfrith said, turning to his son. "What then should I do about Lord Hussa?"

"He has betrayed his oaths to you and his life is forfeit if you judge it so, or else banishment is also a worthy punishment." Eanfrith replied.

Athelfrith studied Hussa for a while. Then he shook his head.

"No, I will not kill you or banish you. You have proven to be of value in the past and may again in the future. For now, though, you have lost my trust."

"I understand, my king. What should I do? Return to my lands?"

"What, so you can go off in pursuit of your son and, maybe, fall into your brother's hands with all the secrets of my kingdom? I think not. No, you will stay in Bebbanburg and Rowenna, too, until I call you."

"Please, my lord, I must go after my son!"

"I have decided. Do not question my will or I may change my mind on your punishment."

213

"Then let me go, lord king," Rowenna asked.

Aethelfrith shook his head again.

"And have the 'Nightjar' fall into enemy hands instead? That is not something I want either. You will both remain in the fortress. Go now to your quarters and await my call."

Hussa and Rowenna stood and walked out of the hall and across to the living quarters they had in another building. They did not speak until the door was shut behind them. Then they were alone in their room. Alone except for each other, their bed and, next to it, the small bed that Hal used. It was Hussa who started crying first.

Slowly, so very slowly, the days slipped by. Each day, each week that passed they were forced to endure with the knowledge that their son was somewhere out there. Had he forgotten them already? Whilst they were not allowed to leave the fortress and remained under guard whenever they left their quarters, they were both allowed exercise for a short while each day. In addition, sometimes Acha sent for Rowenna. Whilst Hussa visiting the queen might attract suspicion, neither Sogor nor Eanfrith seemed bothered about Rowenna going to see her.

"Men are predictable you know, Lady Rowenna," Acha said to her the first time the two were together in the queen's hall. She pointed at the square of fabric in Rowenna's hands which Rowenna was embroidering with a bronze needle and thread which had been dipped in wax as proof against water. "If your husband had come here in his warrior's garb, my stepson and his cousin would have intervened. Yet I send for you and you come armed only with needle and thread and they think nothing of it."

Rowenna laughed, laying the cloth on her lap.

"I take it something other than needlecraft is on your mind this day."

Acha smiled.

"Indeed," she said putting down her own needlework on the table. She picked up a cup of mead and passed it to Rowenna before she poured herself another. Rowenna sipped some of the sweet honey –favoured liquor whilst she waited for the queen to talk.

"This business is unfortunate as it removes your husband from power, power I need access to in order to advance my own family's cause," she said looking across the room where the young Oswald was playing with a set of small wooden warriors. Close at hand, the queen's warrior, Ecgfrith, was watching over him. Acha laid a hand on her stomach which bore a swelling that was evidence that her next child would soon arrive. Rowenna felt stirrings in her own belly, the first signs of her second child's life.

"Yet, there is more to it than just ambition. I am very sorry for the sorrow you must both be feeling." Again, her gaze passed over the young prince. "Only another mother can surely know."

Rowenna nodded.

"So, it is in my interest to help you find your son so that, when the time comes for Hussa to regain my husband's trust and again regain power, he is able to act with his full strength, unimpeded by the pain he now is under."

"What are you suggesting?" Rowenna asked, feeling hope rise inside her.

"I am suggesting that, whilst you are unable to leave or pass messages on, I can. I can have Ecgfrith visit your man Rolf and suggest to him that he send scouts out seeking news of your son. Let us find him first. Then, we can decide how to act."

Rowenna looked at the queen. "May the goddess Freya shower you with her blessings, my queen," she said with heartfelt gratitude.

Acha laughed,

"I am already pregnant. I think I would like a break from the attention of the fertility god after this one!" she said.

When Rowenna had told Hussa about the queen's plan, they had quickly acted upon it. Hussa had given Ecgfrith several secret words that only he and Rolf knew, words they had long ago agreed upon so messages could be passed between them with the certainty of knowing the origin of them. Armed with these words, Ecgfrith left the fortress under the guise of visiting one of the queen's own estates in preparation for the following summer when the court would leave the fortress and visit the various lord's estates. It was a longstanding tradition where the king would be assured of the loyalty of his thegns as well as enjoying their hospitality and familiarising himself with the readiness of Bernicia for war when it should come again.

Ecgfrith did have a genuine message to pass on – instructions regarding stocking the estate with beer and ale. Once done, he was to return home to Bebbanburg. On the way, however, he was instructed to take a small detour from the most direct road. A few miles off that road lay Hussa's estates, home to Rolf and his most loyal men.

Ecgfrith had returned to Bebbanburg with the message passed on, the queen was able to confirm to Rowenna when she next was invited to visit to share in another needlework session. Her own fabric now showed the outline of a wyvern, the queen's had the beginnings of Mjolnir, the thunder god's hammer. The queen's design seemed most appropriate this day as outside the autumn storms were lashing the rooftops of the halls and winds blowing in from the north east were driving on the waves of the inhospitable sea which charged like cavalry into the harbour. The fire burning in the hall flickered in the wind which found entry to pound and buffet at the shutters and doors.

Rowenna listened to the gale and pondered where in this windswept land her son was.

"Now, we wait," she said quietly.

The queen nodded,

"Now we wait," she agreed and returned to her needlework.

Days became weeks and weeks slipped into months. The days shortened and darkness lingered longer each night. Yuletide came and left, along with the shortest days. Prayers were said to Freya and Frey, brother and sister gods of fertility for the return of the light and the the coming of new life to the fields and woods.

One day, a week or so after Yuletide had ended, with snow lying thick on the ground and the stony paths of Bebbanburg icy and slick, a messenger came to see the queen, brought in by Ecgfrith when Rowenna was present. The wyvern pattern on her embroidery was now detailed and the beast leapt skyward from a rocky precipice. The queen was stitching the last lightning bolt to her own design. The messenger bowed and then glanced at Rowenna in hesitation.

"You may speak, warrior, the Lady Rowenna has my trust."

He nodded and spoke. The news sent Rowenna hurrying to Hussa despite her own growing pregnancy.

Hussa was sitting on steps down from the upper enclosure, close to the new well which was nearing completion but work on which had been abandoned during the winter. He was sharpening his sword on a whetstone. He was, like most days, practicing with his sword with some of the king's warriors. It had been a way to pass the hours and take his mind off other, darker thoughts.

"He was been found!" she said.

Hussa jumped to his feet and dropped the sword. It landed with a heavy clang on the stony ground and slid down the steps. He ignored it and took hold of Rowenna's hands in his own.

"Well?" he said.

"Rolf sent a message. His men have all this time been searching for news of Cerdic. What took the time was a rumour that he had been seen in Gwynedd, so they had to first infiltrate there. Eventually, they learnt that he had been sent, in some disgrace, to estates in Mercia. It then took time in turn to track down those estates. Just a couple of weeks ago they found Cerdic's lands and, Hussa, then they found Ha. He is with Cerdic and his family and he appears to be safe and unhurt."

Hussa let out a deep breath which hung white in the cold air.

"Could they not get him out?"

Rownenna shook her head. "No, Rolf says the place is teeming with warriors – Deiran and Mercian."

"Where… where is he?"

"A place on the Temese called Souekesham."

Hussa nodded.

"You know it?"

"I know it. Not many miles from Doric where I was a year or two ago."

"What do we do?" Rowenna asked.

"Do? We go get him, of course."

"How will you get out?"

Hussa shrugged

"I will ask the king," he said.

The request to be allowed to leave the fortress and go in search of his son fell on deaf ears with the king. This was not assisted by the fact that when he had visited the king, under guard, Sogor and Eanfrith had been present.

"The lord Hussa must feel that we have short memories, Lord if he expects us to so easily forget his disobedience of the summer or his reckless behaviour," Sogor said.

Eanfrith nodded and Aethelfrith just shook his head.

"No, Hussa, I am not willing to trust you yet enough to let you depart. I will send for you when I am. You may go now."

"But, Lord, my son!" Hussa entreated.

"The king has spoken. You are dismissed," Sogor shouted and Hussa was forced to leave.

He stomped back across the enclosure to their lodging. The outer chamber was empty and he was about to call out to Rowenna when he heard a sudden cry of pain from the direction of his and Rowenna's bedroom. Fumbling at the handle of his seax as he rushed towards it, he opened the door.

Rowenna was kneeling by the bed, groaning. He glanced around the room looking for a hidden enemy but saw none.

"What is it?" he asked.

"The baby is coming, fetch Bridget," she shouted.

He stared at her.

"Move your arse!" she added, and he leapt into action, calling out for his servants.

Bridget came running in first and she, in turn, sent for one of the local women who acted as midwife to the fortress and she accompanied by two assistants soon took charge.

What followed was a sudden bustle of activity and Hussa found himself pushed out of the room by the officious midwife. Standing outside, he was not sure what to do. Should he leave as clearly the woman expected? Then he thought about

Hal and how he had been away, fighting in the Temese Valley, when his son had been born. Whether the woman agreed or not, he wanted to be part of this birth. He opened the door again and entered. Most of the women ignored him, one or two were disapproving of this man's presence but Rowenna saw him and nodded that he should come to her side. Then she let out another cry of pain. Hussa knelt down and took Rowenna's hand gently. She suddenly squeezed it violently and shouted again.

Hussa stayed with Rowenna whilst the hours passed, not sure if his presence was helping but trying to comfort her and encourage her as best as he could. Around them, the women and even the midwife seemed to have accepted his presence.

"You can push now, my lady," the midwife said at last and Rowenna gritted her teeth and did so.

"Come on, love, push. It won't be long now," Hussa said.

The next moments were a blur until, suddenly, he heard a baby crying. The midwife was holding a small form, wrapped in a woollen blanket. At first all he could see were two small hands complete with tiny fingers protruding from the blanket. Then, as the midwife handed the bundle to Rowenna and she took it in her arms, the baby's head came into view. He looked down at a pair of dark eyes staring up at him.

"What is it?" Rowenna asked.

"A boy, my lady," the midwife said smiling at them.

"Can I hold him?" Hussa asked, feeling oddly nervous.

Rowenna leant over and handed him the bundle. Hussa took the baby in his arms and he held him, and father and son studied each other.

"What shall he call him?" he asked her.

Rowenna thought for a moment before answering. "Huw, son of Hussa and brother of Hal."

She smiled and then flopped back down on the bed, clearly exhausted. After a few moments, she closed her eyes and, from her steady breathing, he could tell she had drifted off to sleep.

Hussa stayed by her side as she slept, holding his new son but thinking also of his other son.

"Don't worry, Huw. I will get your brother back home! He will want to meet you."

It was just a few days later that news came that created a buzz of excitement across all of Bebbanburg. The queen had given birth to her second child and mother and child were apparently both well. The child was also a boy who was given the name of Oswiu. Hussa and Rowenna accompanied by Huw were permitted to attend the court when Acha first presented the boy.

The queen was clearly happy but also appeared thoughtful and somewhat distracted, Hussa thought. She kept looking first at Rowenna and then at Huw who was sleeping on her lap. Finally, she turned and whispered something to Aethelfrith.

The king looked surprised, appeared to argue but then held up his hands and nodded. Then he rose to his feet and as he did so conversations across the hall ceased.

"My lords, I am delighted to show you my new son...." he began to say.

He had to wait then as everyone cheered and hammered hands on tabletops or benches or stamped their feet. The noise was like thunder.

He held up his hands and the uproar died away.

"My queen has asked that on this day I exercise compassion. That I allow some of the joy I feel to pass to others. So, Lord Hussa, please will you step forward."

Hussa noticed that Sogor looked up sharply from where he had been deep in conversation with Eanfrith as he stumbled forward to the king and bowed.

"Lord king," Hussa said. "How may I be of service?"

"Today, at my queen's request, I release you from the state of arrest you have been under. You may return to my council. Moreover, I have a need to soon send a message to our ally in West Seaxe. I am conscious of your request to be allowed to visit the Temese Valley in search of your son. So, I agree to your request, providing you accompany Lord Sogor on the embassy to the south."

Hussa nodded.

"Thank you, my king," he replied.

Returning to his bench, he saw that Rowenna was smiling at him and he returned the smile. Then he noticed that Sogor was scowling at him and, feeling happy with developments and so disposed to an attempt at peace, he flashed a friendly smile at the man. If anything, Sogor looked even more angry at the gesture.

When he got back to Rowenna, she placed a hand on his.

"Sogor does not look happy," she said.

"Who cares?" he replied. "I am finally going to look for our son."

Chapter Twenty
Winter distractions
Winter 611

Three hundred and more miles away, the winter had also passed slowly at Souekesham. Cuthwine and Sian had made Hal welcome. For his part, Hal worshipped Cuthwine and followed him around like a little dog. He called him "Clothwind" but that did not seem to bother Cuthwine who would pick him up and carry him on his shoulder or let the small boy use the woden practice sword that Cuthwine now used daily under the tutelege of Grettir. Hal would charge in with the sword flashing all over the place, reminding Cerdic of earlier years when he and his companions had been taught by Grettir. He and his friends were sitting in the lodge hall, drinking together whilst Cuthwine played with the boy near the fire pit.

"Cuth," I said to Cuthbert, "he takes after you."

"Thanks, Cerdic," Cuthbert had replied. Aedann laughed and gulped his ale.

Eduard shook his head. "That's not fair," he interjected.

They all turned to look at their friend in surprise at him apparently rushing to the defence of Cuthbert.

Then Eduard grinned. "Not fair on Hal, I mean, he is already better than Cuth ever got!"

"Bugger off!" Cuthbert said but he could not help laughing.

Sian had taken to adorning the little boy with necklaces and bracelets or placing winter flowers in his hair and, whilst Hal did not mind, Cuthwine complained most severely.

"I am trying to train him to be a warrior, Sian. He hardly looks the part with those bloody petals there, does he?"

"I think he looks very nice," Sian replied.

I smiled but then my smile dropped because Hal was looking at me and the glance bore none of the warmth the boy held for Cuthwine or Sian. Whist the children were his kin, whether cousin or sibling, Hal clearly still believed that Hussa was his father and resented beng taken from him and his mother.

Hal's hair was changing colour now, becoming redder and his eyes even more green, just like Hussa. 'Could I be wrong?' I asked myself.

"Still think he is your son, do you?" Aedann asked quietly, clearly reading my mind.

"I …" I said, hesitating. Then I spotted Aidith at the door of the lodge, looking over at them all. She must have heard Aedann's words because she seemed to be waiting for his reply. I nodded emphatically. "He must be mine," I replied, and I got up and went over to a pile of logs that lay near the side of the lodge. I picked up an axe and began chopping at the wood. I enjoyed the work; it was simple and repetitive and took my mind away from other thoughts.

Aidith, however, was not put off, judging by the determined expression on her face. She sat down on a log and folded her arms.

"Well?" she asked, looking up at me, her lips draw tightly together.

"Well, what?"

"Do you really think the boy is yours?"

"Hussa can't have children. He has had enough women in his time, by all acounts, but none that he fathered a child with," I said, throwing the axe down and I slumped down on a log opposite Aidith.

"You know that means nothing. Some people become pregnant with ease. To others, it comes far harder. Is that your only reason for wanting this boy to be your son and not his?"

"I don't understand."

"There is something else, isn't there?"

"What do you mean?"

"This is about you and him, isn't it. It's not about Hal himself at all."

"No..."

"Yes, it is. You can't abide the thought of Hussa having a family. You can't cope with the idea that he might be happy."

I stared at her.

"I am right, aren't I?"

I looked down at the ground and absentmindedly picked up a chip of wood and threw it away.

"Well, Cerdic?"

I finally looked up at her. "He betrayed the kingdom, he killed so many people...he killed my mother, he burnt the Villa and destroyed our home, and drove us into exile. He does not deserve a family. He caused so much harm... and now he knows how that feels..."

I stared at her, suddenly surprised at what I had just said. Had that been inside me this whole time? Was this all about vengeance on my brother?

"Cerdic... he is just a boy," she said.

I looked over at Hal who was now playing with Eduard. The big man was carrying him around on his shoulders, galloping along like a horse to guffars of laughter from the small boy.

"You may be right..." I said. What should I do? Should I try to contact Hussa? Should I try to return the boy? Yet, if I ever saw Hussa, I would try to kill him. So, what should I do about the boy?"

I sighed, pushing the thought from my mind and then stood up and reached for one of the wooden practice weapons and handed it to Aidith. After I had returned to the family, I had taken steps to ensure that Aidith and Sian knew how to use a sword and a seax. Female warriors – shield maidens – were fairly rare but not unknown and whilst a battle in a shield wall may rely on strength and a brutality few women had, a one on one fight in the open required a certain agility and dexterity that many women possessed in greater abundance than men. Whatever I felt about Rowenna, it was clear she was most skilled with weapons. Regardless of whether I was comfortable with the idea of my own wife and daughter fighting in a battle, it made sense that they should be able to defend themselves and, so, having recognised that I had been slow in this matter, I had now rectified things. I swung at my wife with my own training sword but Aidith deftly stepped to one side to avoid the attack and jabbed at me with her own weapon. I was forced to retreat to avoid the blow.

Nearby, Grettir clapped in appreciation and came to join us.

"Good reaction, pushing Lord Cerdic onto the defensive in turn, my lady, but be sure to use the moment to break and run or else do not give him the time to come at you again. Follow up. That seax is a shorter weapon than a longsword, so you need to keep close."

"So that I have the reach to strike him?" she asked, waggling the seax from left to right.

The old man nodded. "Yes, but also because a long sword needs room to swing and slash or thrust and stab. Either way, the closer you are, the more you deny him that. His sword is larger, heavier and longer, so, in almost all cases, he has the advantage, yet right up close you tilt the odds in your favour."

Aidith nodded and practised a few stabbing motions.

Grettir watched her and grunted. "Yes, a seax can be useful as a close in stabbing weapon, but armour and shield may turn it aside. Look for the opportunity to slash across an exposed throat or at an area not protected by armour, like a man's hands or legs."

Aidith looked pale at the thought. "I am not sure I would be able to do that," she said and stared intently at the wooden practice blade which now hung limply in her hand.

"If your life is in danger, you will find a way. Even more so if it is the life of someone you love," I said.

She looked unconvinced by this argument at first but then brought the blade back up so the point was towards me.

"Attack me again," she said and prepared to defend herself.

Chapter Twenty-One
Going south
Spring 612

"This is what I need you to do, Hussa," Aethelfrith began. It was a few weeks later. Hussa had been eager to depart immediately, now that the king had given him permission to leave and seek for his son. However, for a variety of reasons, this had proven to be impossible. The main reason was the inclement weather for, soon after Aethelfrith had told Hussa he could travel south, snowstorms rolled in and winter gales battered the fortress. The winter was one of the worst any of them could remember with driving snow drifts which at times were ten feet or more deep in places. More than a few stories reached Bebbanburg of travellers being lost in the hills. Some fell to their deaths having stumbled off the edges of hidden drops. Others became so disorientated by the blinding storms that they could not find or keep on the roads and sometimes only a few hundred paces from a village they froze to death.

Hussa got up each morning and went to the battlements to gaze over the wilderness beyond. A white, inhospitable land greeted him. Sometimes the storms abated and he would find Sogor and Eanfrith and encourage them to get ready. Always they would stare at him like he was mad and tell him they were not going anywhere, that it was not safe to travel. What frustrated him was that they were correct. It was simply not a sensible time for a journey.

The snow lasted several weeks, lying deep on the fields and roads. Clearing the snow just revealed paths that iced over in a matter of an hour or less. One of the king's warriors slipped on steps leading down towards the harbour and broke his hip, crippling him. A trader trying to reach the fortress lost control of his cart which slid off the pathway and plunged into the ocean, carrying his cargo of ale into the icy depths.

Rolf was now back at his side at Bebbanburg after returning from his journey south. It was clear that he and Bridget were spending a lot of time together and, whilst Hussa was frustrated by each day he had to stay in the fortress waiting for the winter to abate, Rolf and Bridget certainly appeared to be enjoying this time.

Even if the weather had permitted his departure, Hussa had decided not to leave straight away as Rowenna developed a fever some days after the baby was born, along with pains in her belly. He had been concerned that she might die, as many mothers did.

The healing woman from the nearby village, armed with herbs, arrived and concocted a medicament brewed from feverfew, agromony and burdock. Rowenna screwed up her face in disgust as she swallowed the acrid –smelling mixture. Hussa braved the winter pathways to visit the temple to the gods in the village near Bebbanburg and handed over a precious gold ring that had been part of his share of plunder in the wars near Din Edin. The priest seemed more interested in the ring than he was in Rowenna but prayed to Eir the goddess of healing that Rowenna should recover.

Whether through the old woman's concoction, the intervention of the gods, or simply the workings of fate, Rowenna revived a few days later, the fever broke, and the pain subsided. She smiled for the first time in weeks and was able to feed Huw herself rather than relying on a wet nurse.

229

Nevertheless, he stayed with her night and day for another fortnight, during which the winter weather finally abated, and the snow melted in the warmth of the late winter sun. Eoster approached and the start of spring loomed when Aethelfrith sent for him once more and told him his plan.

"How can I serve, my king?" Hussa answered in reply to the king's summons.

They were gathered in the king's hall – the king, Sogor and Eanfrith were there as well as Rolf.

"I have decided to delay my attack upon Mercia one more year whilst we consolidate the position in Rheged. This year, once the campaign season begins, I will go to Rheged myself with the bulk of the army. We will subdue what remains of the rebellion and restore order. This will mean that we have insufficient men to risk an attack into Mercia."

Hussa nodded. This made sense. It took time to arrange a campaign and more time to carry it through. Mercia and Northern Reged were a significant distance apart. No king would wish to fight wars on two borders at the same time if it could be avoided.

"But, you still want me to go south?" He glanced around at Sogor and Eanfrith. "All of us, I mean. You want us to go south to Mercia?"

Aethelfrith shook his head. "No, to West Seaxe and yes, you will go with Sogor and Eanfrith. You can each take a choice of your best men – a company each. I need you to see Ceolwulf and to coordinate the attack for next year. We need him to attack up the Temese when we go across into Mercia. I will give you the full details of my plan later. Ensure he is ready to attack on midsummer's day next year so we can cause more confusion by coordinating the attacks."

Hussa nodded. "And my son?"

Aethelfrith hesitated and glanced at Sogor. Was he about to change his mind? Maybe he been softened by the birth of Oswiu and now, with a few weeks distance from that decision, changed his mind. Or had Sogor and Eanfrith been speaking to him and exerted their influence?

"You may make enquiries and scout out the area where your son is. Our spies inform us that your brother, along with his companies, those vagabond refugees from Deira, are in Soueke-shame along with companies loyal to Ceorl of Mercia. "

"Thank you, Lord."

The looks of disappointment on the faces of Sogor and Eanfrith suggested that they had indeed argued that Hussa's role and freedom of action should be limited.

"Thank you again, Lord. If I can find my son, I can bring him home."

"You may look, but," Aethelfrith interjected and raised a finger, "you will take no action without the order being given by Sogor or Eanfrith. I don't want a repeat of what happened in Rheged. Do you understand?"

"Yes, my king, of course I understand," he said with a glance at Rolf. Rolf read something in that glance for, whilst he said nothing, he rolled his eyes skyward.

Rowenna had wanted to come with him to West Seax, but Hussa had refused her.

She looked up from where she was sitting, Huw at her breast feeding eagerly, loudly. "I want to come and find our son," she had argued. "You know I could be useful doing that. As the Nightjar, I mean…"

Hussa gestured at their baby. "The Nightjar could be very useful, I won't try to deny it, but Huw needs Rowenna, right now. He needs his mother."

"He could come with us."

The sudden image of Rowenna and Huw lying dead, blood spreading in a pool around them, leapt into his mind. He shivered.

Hussa shook his head. "If I find him, it will be too dangerous. He will be with Cerdic and his men. There might be fighting." He shrugged. "There will be fighting." he added.

"I am no fool with a blade, husband," she protested. Huw had finished feeding and was now snoring gently. She rose, carried Huw to his crib and laid him down, covering him with furs.

Hussa followed her and laid his hands on her shoulders and stood, gazing over her head at the sleeping infant below them.

"This may not be a matter of stealth, an area with which you are, without a doubt, an expert. This may be the brutality of the shield wall. There, it is all about rage and strength. Agility and subtlety play little part," he said softly.

Rowenna turned in his arms to face him.

"But..."

Hussa held up a hand. "I will not take you, wife. That is final."

For a moment her eyes flared with anger and he thought she would argue further, but she dropped her head and then turned away.

"As you wish, husband. I will stay here and care for Huw."

He regretted his abruptness and once again put his hands on her shoulders.

"I cannot lose you two, and I cannot do my job if I am worrying about what might happen to you. Stay here, keep him safe, and I will get Hal and bring him home."

She reached up and placed a hand on his hand and then turned back to look into his eyes.

"Alright. I will do as you ask."

"Thank you," he said and relaxed. "Come, let us eat before I leave."

After their meal, he hugged her one more time and then leaned over Huw's crib to place a kiss on his forehead. Then he left his wife and the boy in their rooms and descended from the northern gateway to the harbour. Here, a half dozen boats were at anchor, bobbing up and down on the swell. Rolf, who had arrived the day before from Hussa's estate, was supervising his men loading their gear and their weapons along with supplies for the journey that would take several days – down the east coast past the kingdoms of the East Angles and the East Seaxe, the estuary of the River Themese that lead to the port of Lundenwic , the lands of Cantia and Suth Seaxe before finally arriving in West Seaxe. It would have shortened their journey to go up the Temese to the upper Temese valley, newly acquired by Ceolwulf's West Seaxe, but Lundenwic lay in the hands of Cantia and its king, Aethelbert, who was an ally of Edwin and his nephew, Hereric, Aethelfrith's enemies. Hereric was married to a Breguswith, who was a princess of Suth Seaxe, Cantia's ally. They would not permit a Northumbrian fleet to pass through the city. So, Sogor, Eanfrith and Hussa had to risk the passage along the Cantish coast as speedily as possible so as to avoid any engagement with Cantia or Suth Seaxe, and on to West Seax.

"How are we doing?" he asked Rolf.

"Well enough. This will be finished soon. The winds are good. If they hold, we can be on our way tomorrow."

Hussa looked further down the quay where Sogor could be heard issuing instructions to his own men undertaking a similar procedure. Sogor gave him a dark look but Hussa walked over to him nonetheless.

233

"We will be finished soon, Lord Sogor. How goes it with your preparations?"

"Well enough," Sogor grunted.

"So, do we depart on the morning tide?"

Sogor nodded.

The following day dawned cold but dry and with strong winds that filled the ship's sails.

Hussa stood in the prow of his ship, gazing south over the waves as the vessel rose and fell. The men chatted and joked with each other behind him but Hussa said nothing. Hal lay this way and he was going to get him back.

The ships slid into the harbour at Hamwic and tied up to the docks. Hussa jumped out of his vessel and landed with a thump on the wooden quay. It had been eighteen months since he had last been in West Seaxe. He had spent three years in the kingdom and in the surrounding territories. Arriving under orders from Aethelfrith to secure an alliance with West Seaxe, he had first needed to gain the trust of Ceolwulf and his lords. This had not been easy and, indeed, the first attempt to prove his merit to West Seaxe had failed with an aborted assault he had led on Suth Seaxe. There he had been repelled at a ruined old Roman villa held by Cerdic, Edwin, and the rest of the exiled supporters that his brother led like a bunch of vagabonds trailing around Britannia, looking for support. That defeat had led to Edwin and Hereric gaining support from Cantia and Hereric marrying into the Suth Seaxe royal house.

At that stage, with a failed diplomatic visit to Cantia and then the defeat in Suth Seaxe behind him, the whole enterprise had seemed doomed to failure. However, Ceolwulf gave Hussa a second chance. He sent him and his men to the Temese Valley where he embarked on a campaign that in turn, and over two years, captured Doric, Garinges, Readingham and Wochinoes and a number of other settlements and brought the Temese valley Saxons under control of West Seaxe. Then, the previous spring, he led his victorious companies south to destroy the last British kingdom in the south east, Celeminion. The campaign had cost him a close friend, Wilbur, but had secured the alliance with Ceolwulf and an agreed intention to one day cooperate with Northumbria in the destruction of a joint rival, Mercia, the campaign that was now delayed by over a year because of the uprising in Rheged.

However, Sogor and Hussa were to begin the coordination with Ceolwulf. To strengthen the alliance and the resolve of West Seaxe, it had been decided that Sogor's and Hussa's companies would accompany the forces of Ceolwulf up the Temese and meet up with Aethelfrith somewhere around the Mercian capital, Tamwerth.

To that end, Hussa's and Sogor's men gathered on the quayside and then marched north to Witanceastre to find Ceolwulf and agree a plan with him.

Arriving in Witanceastre the following day, Hussa found that Ceolwulf, his nobles and several companies were actually in the Temese Valley, encamped at Readingum. Boyden, one of his advisors and a friend to Hussa, was left in the city and, having offered Sogor, Eanfrith and Hussa hospitatilty, explained further.

"There have been a few uprisings against the king's rule that needed supressing," he said. "The king also led a raid against the Chiltenae – villages in the hills to the north of Readingum. That is where you will find him."

"How is Rowenna's mother, by the way? Is she in the city still?" Hussa asked.

Boyden had been master to both Rowenna and her mother. Hussa had bought Rowenna's freedom and then, following Hussa's service to West Seaxe, Boyden had released her mother from his service at Hussa's request.

"No," Boyden said with a shake of his head. "She left to go back to her family home near Badon. I sent two warriors to make sure she got there. She is safe. You can tell your wife that. Come, let us eat, then you can rest before journeying on."

The next day, they marched north east, passing through the ruins of Calleva to Readingum. Most of the buildings, damaged during the assault, were already starting to collapse and Hussa noticed that the locals had begun robbing away the stones of the walls that had surrounded what had once been a large, bustling Roman city. The gateway which had caused them so much grief and loss of blood, and near where Wilbur had died, still stood. Most of Hussa's men had fought here and now stood around in clusters, quietly recalling incidents from the fateful day to each other. Some pointed out the features to the new recruits and described the battle whilst a number who had lost close companions said nothing and sat on the ruins in silence, lost in their own thoughts.

Rolf and Hussa found Wilbur's grave and Hussa knelt to add a pendant shaped in the form of Molnir to it, pushing it into the top soil.

"Give our regards to Woden and Thunor, old friend," Hussa had said as he got back up from his knees.

"And keep us a space on the benches in Valhalla, and don't drink all the bloody ale before we get there," Rolf added.

They reached Readingum a few days later and Hussa, Sogor and Eanfrith went to see Ceolwulf. The king, however, was away from the city.

236

"He is expected back any day now," one of the captains of the king's companies explained. "Right now, he is away to the east dealing with a little trouble with a village of British who don't seem so keen on his overlordship for some reason. Make yourself at home while you wait."

Wait… was that what he was expected to do? Hussa thought to himself as they left the collonaded stone buildings and were led to rooms nearby. The men were quartered in other parts of the city and were soon happily investigating the ale houses and brothels. Yet, only a few miles away, upriver, lay Souekesham, his brother, Cerdic, and his son.

"I am going to go and look for my son, tomorrow, whether the king has returned or not," he told Rolf.

"Not alone, you bloody ain't," Rolf said,

"We can't all go; someone needs to be here when Ceolwulf arrives."

"That has to be you, surely. You know the king and he knows you."

"I don't give a shit. I am going for my son."

Rolf shrugged. "Alright, but who will talk to Ceolwulf?"

Hussa pointed at him, "You will. You have met him."

"Me? Bollocks to that. I am going with you. I care for Hal, too. Try to stop me and I will land this on you." He raised a fist.

"I thought you said something to me once about families getting in the way of our pursuit of glory?"

Rolf shrugged. "Glory and power are important, of course, but you want your son back and that is more important."

"Alright, but someone has to be here when Ceolwulf comes who was with us before,"

They called through Edgar.

"Me, you want me to talk to the king?"

237

"Yes, you. Just keep an eye on Sogor and that fool Eanfrith and stop them from saying anything too stupid. Explain what I am doing and that I will be back in a few days."

"Arse!" said Edgar by way of expressing his feelings on the matter. Then he gave Hussa a sharp look. "Just don't go and get killed alright."

"That is the plan," Rolf said.

So, they asked permission of Sogor for their company to leave at dawn to 'go hunting in the woods' by way of giving them some exercise and Sogor yawned and agreed, disinterested.

"Sogor will not be happy when we don't come back tonight," Rolf pointed out as they quietly left the city as the gates were opened at sun rise.

"Well… easier to ask forgivenees later than permission now. Which he would not give."

"True," Rolf said once they'd turned north out of the gates and were on the road towards Souekesham. "That's the kind of philosophy I can get behind."

They marched north up the Temese Valley to Doric, the first city they had captured in that earlier campaign, and then pushed on beyond it, following overgrown, grassy tracks that cut across the neck of the land that was looped around by the river . From Doric it was another two -day journey past farmlands where the fields were being ploughed and the first seeds sown. At the end of the second day they reached an abandoned farmhouse which had lost its roof. Ahead of them was a marshy land with scattered copses and low scrub. Through the trees they could see smoke rising from a small settlement and, beyond that, the smudge of smoke from a larger town.

When they had been here before, they had scouted north from Doric and Hussa now recalled his understanding of the geography.

"Souekesham is over there, beneath that more distant smoke. It is on the other side of the river from us. There is no direct route and certainly no Roman road, so any attack upon it needs to be up the river and also along the west bank to attack it from the land side," Hussa said.

"If we go that way and try to infiltrate the town, we will get stopped and you and I are certainly sufficiently well known to your brother and his men to be recognised," Rolf pointed out.

Hussa agreed.

Rolf studied the evidence of a smaller settlement, closer to them, and on their side of the river.

"The island of Andersey has hunting lodges and connects to the town via a ford over the river. What if we cross to Andersey and try to sneak into the town that way?"

Hussa thought about that idea.

"Makes sense." He squinted up at the sky. "The sun will set soon. I don't fancy crossing the stream and bogs in the dark, do you? We'll go back to that abandoned farmhouse and camp for the night. If we make an early start tomorrow, I guess many of Cerdic's men will be fast asleep or hung over. Dawn, or soon after, we should be able to get in and find wherever he is staying, house or hall."

They retraced their steps and led the men back to the farm. Despite the loss of most of its roof, it provided an adequate shelter from the winds as well as a brief shower of rain that arrived soon after they had reached it. Rolf sent some men to a nearby tree. They felled it and chopped it up for fuel and soon got a fire going.

Several of the warriors produced skins of ale or wine, but Hussa did not drink any. He was not in the mood.

"You alright?" Rolf asked him as they huddled around the fire.

239

Hussa shrugged. "He is close, Rolf. Hal, I mean. I just want the dawn to come so I can go and find him."

"Try to sleep, Hussa. You will need your strength in the morning."

"I am not sure I can sleep," he replied but laid down and closed his eyes. He then discovered just how exhausted he was. And despite his anxiousness to get on with the day ahead, he was soon fast asleep.

"Hussa," Rolf's voice called him. He felt someone shaking him by the shoulders and opened his eyes. Rolf was leaning over him. Confused, he rubbed his eyes and sat up. Around him the rest of his company were still sleeping. It was dark, the only illumination provided by the flickering light of a single tallow candle over in the corner of the farmhouse.

"What is it?" he asked drowsily.

"Edgar is here."

"What?" Hussa said, throwing back his furs and jumping to his feet.

"Come quickly."

Hussa wrapped his cloak around him and crept outside.

The fire was now little more than glowing embers. Edgar was kneeling beside it, throwing on a few branches which caught after a few moments. In the glow of the firelight, Hussa saw the man turn to look at him.

"What is it?" Hussa asked him.

"It is Sogor. He and Ceolwulf are coming to Souekesham with their men. They will be here tomorrow."

"What the bloody hell are you talking about?"

Edgar held up his hands. "I am sorry, Hussa I tried to talk them out of it but they would not listen."

"What happened?"

The man took a deep breath. "Soon after you left, the same morning in fact, Ceolwulf arrived back. Sogor sent for you and when I turned up instead, Sogor lost his temper and started shouting that you had learnt nothing and that you were going to do it all again."

"Do what?"

"He has got it into his head that you are going to attack Souekesham."

"What, with just a single company."

"I said that to him, but he would not listen. He told Ceolwulf what you had done in Rheged and that, chances are, you would try to steal all the glory here."

"I would not give one of Thunor's balls for glory'" Hussa said. "I came here to look for my son. That is all."

"Which is what I said, but he would not listen. It did not seem to help."

Hussa bent down and picking up a stick from the ground, poked the fire with it.

"So, what is he going to do?"

"He is already doing it. Sogor suggested to Ceolwulf that they join forces and attack Souekesham. He ordered my company to follow along. They are all camped over the river to the west just south of Sudestone. I snuck out at dusk and, knowing where you were aiming for, trusted in fate to find you. I saw the fire and headed this way."

"What? He said nothing about Aethelfrith's planned delay until next year?"

"No."

"And what about Eanfrith?"

Edgar laughed. "Eanfrith wants to prove himself the son of the great warlord. He will do whatever Sogor says, if he has a chance to win his own fame."

241

"They will be here tomorrow?" Rolf asked.

Edgar nodded. "Hussa, if they attack, anything might happen to Hal," his friend said.

Hussa poked the fire again.

"Then we go in first, across the island. Wake the men and tell them to get ready. We are going as soon as there is enough light to see our way. I will find Hal and get him out. If anyone tries to stop me...I will kill them."

"I am with you, my lord. We will find your son, and may the gods have mercy on anyone who tries to stop us. Let's get him back and go home."

Hussa looked over at his friend, Rolf. "You have changed you know, all this talk about family and home. Think you're getting soft in your old age."

Chapter Twenty-Two
Converging paths
Spring 612

"The master will not be happy, my lady," said Bridget. She was looking disapprovingly at Rowenna who was dressing in her Nightjar garments.

"He won't just be not happy, he will be livid," Rowenna replied. "However, I cannot just stay here and wait for news that may never come. I am going after him."

"But you told me he said…"

Rowenna picked up her seax and thrust it into the scabbard on her belt. "It does not matter what he said," she interrupted the other woman.

Bridget pouted and then tried a different tack.

"You can't go after him; his ship has sailed and there are no others in the harbour."

Rowenna shrugged. "That matters not. I am not going by boat. I am going by land."

Bridget stared at her. "Through Mercia? You can't be serious, my lady!"

Rowenna nodded.

"Won't you get caught? You are bound to."

"I was … am, the Nightjar, you know. I don't think so."

Bridget laughed and pointed. "The Nightjar never took a baby along, did she?"

They looked over to where Huw was sleeping on a linen sheet. Rowenna picked up the sheet, baby and all, and held it to her and then wrapped it around her, tied a couple of knots. Huw opened his eyes, gave her a puzzled look but then, obviously not concerned with developments, fell back asleep.

"Not just any baby. My son. He is not a grumpy baby. If I keep him fed, he will be fine."

Bridget shook her head in resignation. "Oh alright. I can't stop you. Just be sure to tell Lord Hussa that I am not to blame. I am after all to be part of the deception."

Rowenna nodded and allowed Bridget to drape a cloak over her shoulders and fasten it with a broach shaped as a bird.

"Is that a Nightjar?"

Rowenna glanced down at it. "It is."

"I will pray to the gods that you can fly like the real thing, swift and safe to Lord Hussa."

Bridget, also dressed in travelling clothes albeit a more usual feminine fashion befitting a companion of a noble lady now wrapped herself in a cloak. The two women now left the rooms were Rowenna and Hussa lived in and walked over to the stables. There they had a stableboy saddle their horses. They mounted and mother, child, maid and beasts trotted out of the stable toward the gatehouse. At the gatehouse the guards enquired where they were going.

Rowenna looked down at them.

"I am going to visit my husband's estates in his absence and will return in a few weeks."

The guards let them pass and they descended the steep path to the village below. They rode together side by side at a gentle pace, making no attempt at stealth as they headed west from the citadel to the Roman road which lay some miles to the west. Here they prepared to go their separate ways.

"Once you reach the estates inform the steward that if any enquiry from court comes about me, he is to say I am indisposed with some illness but will return as soon as I am able."

Bridget nodded at her. "I will, my lady," then she looked thoughtful and seemed to make up her mind about something. "Can you carry a message to Rolf for me?" she asked. "I hope you will not be angry with what I need to tell him."

She looked around and then, despite them being alone on the open road, she whispered her words into Rowenna's ear.

Rowenna stared at her for a moment, smiled and leaned over and embraced her.

Then she turned her mount south dug in her heels and as the horse leapt into a gallop, Rowenna murmured a prayer for a safe journey. With the help of the gods and despite the need for stealth, she, travelling lightly and on horseback across the shorter land route, would catch up with her husband and her other son.

"Come on, Huw," she murmured to the child wrapped to her front, "let's go and find your father and brother."

She travelled south as fast as she could, only resting at roadside taverns after it was already almost dark and departing most days before it was fully light. The pace was exhausting, and this is why her attention was waning when late on the third day, not long before sunset, she was ambushed in the dying light.

As she came round the bend, several shapes moved out onto the road ahead of Rowenna, startling her horse which shied and turned away from them, taking a few steps towards the trees that lined the road. She glanced behind, looking for an escape route but another two figures now blocked that path.

As she struggled to control her beast, she saw more details of the shapes. They were men, each wearing dirty, ragged tunics and torn cloaks and armed with axes and long-bladed seaxes. In an instant, her skills as the Nightjar snapped into life.

"Bandits," she hissed under her breath. Masterless men, devoid of a lord and worthy of derision and pity, possibly in equal measure. Belonging nowhere, they wandered the wild places where they preyed upon travellers such as merchants or settlers pushing westwards, expanding the lands under the rule of Angle or Saxon. The merchants were often old and fat and were invariably slain and their wealth taken. Settlers, in contrast, usually had few valuables but were often young and healthy, suitable for the slave fairs of Badon or Lundenwic.

The sun was already falling in the west when she passed a tavern some time before but, as Huw was asleep inside her cloak, she had elected to press on to the next whilst the twilight lingered. On reflection, this appeared to have been the wrong choice.

The Nightjar assessed the situation. Ahead of her the men were speading out into a horseshoe –shaped formation, looking to prevent her flight, whilst those behind were armed with spears and had these braced in such a way that a horse would be reluctant to charge them down. Off to the west, dark silhouettes of houses visible through the trees revealed the settlement she believed to be Oxenforda, just a few miles north and east from the village Hussa and his men would be heading for. Could she possibly make it to this riverside town and seek shelter and protection there?

"I have a bow, so if you try to get away, you will grow a crop of arrows before you get thirty paces," a man said apparently reading her intent.

He was a weasel –faced man with an evil expression. The bow was in one hand, strung but with no arrow nocked. He had a few arrows in a loop hanging from his belt. One hand now reached for one, his fingers resting around the flight. He stood just to the left and slightly in front of her horse's head. Another man matched his stance on the other side of the horse. Ahead of them each, another pair moved forward to flank her.

The weasel –faced man peered through the gloom at her.

"Freya's tits but it's a woman," he said and then, having studied her a little longer added, "And a good looking one, at that. Reckon we can have fun with her before we sell her on, what do you say, boys?"

At that moment Huw stirred and let out a cry as he started to wake up.

"By Asgard," the weasel said, "she has a pup, too. We can take our turns with the woman then sell her and the babe at the slave markets. Two for the price of one, eh?"

One of the men, the one moving around to her left, looked barely out of childhood, appeared frightened and said nothing. The two other men sniggered at the weasel's comments.

Well, I was going to get away from you all and let you live, she said to herself. Now, though, I think you need to learn a lesson'

There were four of them, each armed and apparently stronger than her with two more not far away. They had each, she assumed, killed before, apart, perhaps, from the young one. Having killed, they seemed at ease with the situation whilst they must think her a soft and easy victim. They had her almost surrounded. All the odds appeared slanted heavily in their favour. In that confidence were the foundations of their destruction.

She needed room to manoeuvre, so she struck first at the man to her right. She swifty drew a knife from its scabbard hanging from her belt. Even as she was doing this, she kicked out hard with her boot and landed him a blow in his guts. As the air left his lungs, he bent forward with a groan and now she smashed the hilt of her knife onto the back of his head. His eyes rolled upwards, and he toppled forward.

The weasel's eyes widened, and his mouth formed into a shape, ready to utter a shout of alarm. Before the sound emerged, she had dug her heels in hard and the horse jumped towards him. As the beast crossed the few paces between them, she brought her hand back upwards and tossed the knife at the man to the weasel's side. He never even saw the blade before, with a squelch, it was protruding from his throat. As he collapsed, blood pouring from his mouth, she had reached the weasel and he was struck by the horse's shoulder throwing him onto his back. He lost his grip on the bow which span away into the bushes.

She turned in the saddle, drawing another knife as she did, and stared at the young man who was the only one of them still left on his feet. His expression was one of shock and utter terror. He dropped his axe and stepped back a few paces.

"Run!" she hissed, "and tell everyone it was the Nightjar that spared you."

He must had heard the name before because, if anything, he now looked even more terrified. He turned and ran as fast as he could.

"The nightjar? That's just a story!" she heard the weasel say.

He was climbing back to his feet, reaching for a seax.

He was not fast enough. The blade left her hand and thudded into his chest just above his heart. As he collapsed, she rode past him.

"Then a story just killed you," the Nightjar said and left him to die in the road as she trotted onward to the south. She thought about going back for her blades, expensive ones too she thought. But there were still the other two men further back who had been taken by surprise by her sudden attack but had recovered and were advancing towards the scene, spears at the ready. With a sigh at the loss of her knives she picked up the pace and put distance between herself and the bandits.

Huw cried again and Rowenna bent to kiss him on the top of his fuzzy head.

"It's alright, child. I will find a safe place to stop soon and I will feed you and rest till dawn."

Then, tomorrow, she would find Hussa and Hal, and also Rolf, of course, for whom she had a message.

Souekesham

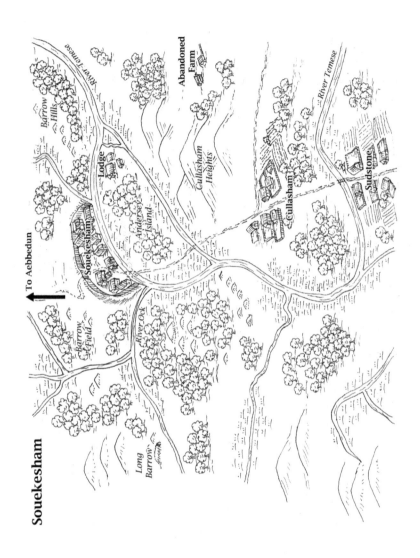

Chapter Twenty-Three
The Norns gather
Spring 612

The sun had risen only a little while before, but I had been awake before the first rays had filtered through the trees. I had walked out to the edge of the buildings around the hunting lodge and, once more, I had found myself absently chopping firewood. What was on my mind that morning and every morning of late was Hal. In the autumn, when I had returned from the expedition north, I had promised Aidith that I would decide what to do about the boy. At the time it had seemed that I had forever to think about this.

Yet, Yuletide had come and gone, the winter snows had fallen and melted and now the flowers of lily and primrose were evident across the woodlands. Yet the normal promise of returning life did not excite me as it once would. Birds who had left these islands during the coldest months had returned. Now the songs of swallow, cuckoo and turtledove, cheerful and strident with each approaching dawn, proved to bring little of the comfort it would normally do. The coming of new life and the returning of the old just served as a reminder of how I still had to make a decision and that my time was running out to do so.

I heard the sound of approaching footsteps and looked up to see Aidith walking towards me, her cloak wrapped around her this cool spring morning. She sat on the pile of logs and shivered. I gathered up some wood shaving and chips and piled few twigs and branches together over them and then reached inside my belt pouch for my strike –a –light and a small piece of flint. Moments later I had the beginning of a fire crackling and popping, and I joined her on the logs and put my arm around her. She rested her head on my shoulder and we both watched the fire grow.

"I know what you are thinking about," she said.

"Is it that obvious?" I replied.

"To me, yes,." she said with a slight smile and then rubbed my arm and spoke softly. "Look, Cerdic, what you did was rash, stupid even, but at the time you took Hal, you did not do so for malicious reasons. You thought you were saving a boy you thought was your son…"

"Maybe I still think he is," I replied, sharply.

She sighed.

"Even now?"

"Well, maybe…" I stumbled, knowing I sounded unconvinced.

"Cerdic, look at me," she said

I did and she was staring at me with an expression so determined it actually frightened me a bit.

"I need you to think hard about this today. Go for a walk if you need to, or a beer with Ealdwig or even pray to the gods if you think they will listen. Whatever it takes to make up your mind. If the boy is yours and you truly believe it then, perhaps, he must stay," she hesitated before going on to say, "…he must stay as our son."

"Really?" I asked.

She nodded.

"Really. Though, even then, we must think about his mother. I would have reasons of my own to dislike her, the woman who slept with my man, but the boy's mother she still is and must be told, at least, where he is."

I nodded slowly. Maybe she was right.

"But…," she held up a finger and tapped me on the chest, "if in your heart you truly believe he is your brother's son and not yours then, whether we hate Hussa or not, the boy must return to him."

She stood up and took the cloak off and folded it over one arm. The sun was rising, and the air was warmer than when she had first joined me. She looked down at me.

"Today then, husband, you must decide."

I stood up and nodded and then gestured at the sky.

"Before the sun sets, I will tell you what I will do about the boy."

She smiled and she held out her hand. I took it and she led me back to the lodge.

Eduard and Aedann were up now and were practising with their weapons, laughing and teasing each other as one got an advantage over the other.

"Shall we spar, too?" I said, gesturing at them. "A little exercise would help to clear my mind."

Aidith nodded before draping her cloak on the ground and she took a wooden seaxe and a wicker shield from the rack near the lodge. She then advanced towards me but got no further. From the woods to the south of the island upon which the lodge stood there sounded a horn blast. It was joined by another and then a third. The signal was clear and loud and was blown with urgency. Were we under attack?

A moment later a runner arrived at the lodge, saw me and changed direction to come to me.

"My lord, I have a message from Prince Edwin. West Seaxe is attacking up the river and on either shore. He asks that you rally the Wicstun company in the town at once."

I glanced at Aidith.

253

"Get rid of that wooden blade and get your seax," I said, and she nodded.

"I will take Hal and Sian, and the other youngsters and secure them in the lodge with Cwenburg and her son. Then I will gather Mildrith and the other women and come and care for the wounded."

She looked at Cuthwine and pulled him towards her to hug him. He looked surprised and, as many youths are, a little awkward but did not protest. Eventually, she let him go and held him at arm's length whilst she looked into his eyes.

"Don't let him die," she said to him and gestured at me.

"I won't, Mother," he said and then ran away to find his spear and shield.

She then turned to me.

"As for you, don't let our son die," she said and they kissed. She turned and ran away to gather up her charges.

I was left with my friends. I turned to them both.

"Muster the company. We will form at the ford first and then join the prince to see what is going on," I ordered, and went to get into armour and to find my swords, spear, helm and shield.

The companies of West Seaxe spearmen came on in great strength along the west side of the Temese, heading for the Ock and ultimately the gates. I had joined my men at the ford connecting the little island to the town of Souekesham. Leaving the company there under Aedann's command with orders to follow when fully formed, Cuthbert, Eduard and I headed towards the west gate into the town where I expected to find Edwin and Sabert.

On the way we passed a dozen of Ealdwig's monks who were preparing their infirmary to be ready to treat the wounded just behind the battlelines.

"Hope there are not too many customers for you today," I shouted as we ran past.

"Indeed, I pray that it is so," Ealdwig said emphatically.

There were, along with Sabert's company of Edwin's royal guard, the commanders of Cwenburg's companies who had come here the previous spring and were still garrisoned in the town. All were looking south at the oncoming forces.

"They don't seem to have learnt much from a year ago," Sabert observed.

He was right, the plan of attack more or less duplicated that which they had tried at the end of the previous winter. Skirmishers emerged from the tree line beyond the stream first and were soon engaged with our own missile troops. A vigorous exchange of slingshot and arrows ensued supplemented, once they had closed the range, with angons, javelins and light throwing axes.

Our pallisde protected our men for the most part whilst the enemy, out in the bare open fields, suffered the first losses of the battle. Still, the exchange of missiles was, so far, inconsequential. Its aim, rather than to cause much harm, was to keep our heads down and prevent us being able to direct any significant attention to the main body of heavy infantry who were now advancing in a formed body, spears hammering against shields with the rhythm and beat of the call to arms that preceded every battle and acted to facilitate both the summoning of courage and to distract the men of West Saexe from the fear that the thought of impending injury and potential death might bring them.

The shield wall manoeuvred ponderously across the stream as men slid down the far bank, waded across it and then dragged themselves up the near bank. There was a pause as they reformed on our side and then they were off again, swinging to their right as they directed their march towards our gates.

Now, as they closed in upon us, the skirmishers fell back around their flanks and, taking their own shields and spears from their companions, they re-joined the rear ranks of the shield wall.

"Won't be long now," Eduard observed, hefting his axe from hand to hand in readiness. "Get ready, Cuth, my friend, we're going to kick them in the balls. I don't think they brought enough men. Still, a shame to tell them that when they are making a mistake. It would be rude."

Something in the back of my mind woke at these words. Like a faint voice trying to warn me about something.

"They don't seem to have learnt much from a year ago," Sabert had said. "I don't think they brought enough men." Eduard had commented. I studied their ranks and counted numbers. They outnumbered us, but not by much. Given we held fortifications, I did not think they had enough to take the town by this frontal assault. What, though, if that was not their plan? What if they had something else in mind? Unable to shake the thought, I looked to the south, past the assaulting companies, and further down the river. Was that movement there, a couple of miles distant?

"Cuth," I called my friend over. "What can you see there?"

Cuth squinted. Then his eyes opened wide.

"I see spearmen crossing the river, maybe two hundred. Maybe more. They are some miles away, but I can just about make them out. I think they are coming over from Sudestone and then going south of Cullasham."

"Thunor's arse!" I cursed and found Edwin where he was standing close to Sabert.

"What is it?" he asked. "I need your company here."

"I came to see what was happening, my prince. But now I need to go back to the island."

"Why?"

"They are tricking us," I said, pointing down the river. "They attack us here to pin us whilst they outflank us. They plan to gain the island and then cross the ford into the town and get in behind us."

"Here they come!" Sabert shouted. "King's guard, make ready."

"Go!" Edwin ordered, drawing his sword and gesturing with it towards the south. "We will hold them here. You go and stop them there!"

"My lord!" I obeyed with a nod. Then, with a jerk of the head to my friends to tell them to follow me, I headed back towards the ford.

Chapter Twenty-Four
Preparation
Spring 612

Having returned to the company, which was gathered around the ford, I felt a sudden stab of anxiety about Aidith and the children. Cuthwine was here amongst the company. I searched the ranks for a sight of him and spotted him showing his shield to Aedann. It showed the sword symbol the Welshman's warriors used. The night before, Cuthwine had told me that he had chosen to join Aedann's Swords. So, he was safe. As safe as anyone when a battle was about to begin, at least, I thought. But Aidith, Sian and Hal were back at the hunting lodge which was just a mile away at the eastern edge of the island. Whilst the flanking companies of Ceolwulf's West Seaxons were coming up towards the ford, across the western side of the island where the ford lay, I could not be sure how safe the lodge would be. I wanted them in the town and out of harm's way.

I was about to ask Cuthbert to run to the lodge and summon them when I saw Aidith emerging through the trees. With her was Cwenburg, several children including Hal, but not Sian. I ran over to them.

"I am going to join my companies," Cwenburg said.

"But, my lady, that may not be safe," I said.

"That is what I told her," Aidith said.

"I may not be a warrior, but a princess of Mercia should not be hiding in a hunting lodge when her warriors are fighting for the protection of her father's kingdom."

"I cannot argue with that," I said with a resigned shrug. "Let me send two warriors with you as escort."

She nodded and I summoned two of my veterans and ordered them to get her to Edwin and then return to us.

After they had left, I turned to Aidith. She was armed with the long seax I had given her.

"I decided to get the children into the town – I expect they will be safer there in your sister's house, in case any enemies get onto the island," Aidith said to me before I could speak.

"They are already on the island," I replied. "They crossed the river south of here. They are heading towards us now. They could be here any moment in fact."

"What?" she asked and turned to look back through the woods towards the lodge.

"Where is Sian?" I asked feeling anxiety rising in my chest.

"She set out with me but went back – she had forgotten her comb and refused to leave with out it."

"Alone?" I asked.

Aidith nodded.

"I didn't know the West Seaxe were on the island. I will go back and get her."

She turned to leave but I stopped her with a hand on her shoulder.

"No! It's too dangerous. I will send Cuthbert. He is the fastest man I have."

I searched the nearby ranks and spotted my friend examining an arrow with another of his skirmishers. Cuthbert was pointing at the flights and were clearly deep in conversation about some obscure detail of archery.

"Cuth!" I yelled.

He handed the arrow to the other man and scampered over. I explained what I needed him to do and with an expression of urgency on his face, he ran off east. I turned back to Aidith.

"Best get into the town with Hal," I said. "Go to Mildrith and lock the children in there. Stay with them."

"I will take them there but then I will come back for Sian. Once she is safe, I will go and join brother Ealdwig and help him."

I nodded and she moved towards the ford, but I could see her glancing towards the lodge, clearly as worried about Sian as I was. I was going to go back to her and hurry her along but, at that moment, a scout appeared from the south. He looked around at us, spotted the banner close to me and ran over.

"My lord," he said, "Ceolwulf is coming this way. With him are companies from Northumbria under Sogor and their prince, Eanfrith."

"Sogor and Eanfrith, here?" I asked. "How soon will they be here?"

"Not very long – maybe a count of three hundred."

I turned to Eduard and Aedann.

"If Northumbria is attacking with West Seaxe, this could mean Aethelfrith is attacking Mercia from the north. We need to tell Edwin at once." To the south I thought I heard a distant shout. The enemy was close. "I can't spare either of you. I will send Grettir." I said and found the old veteran.

He listened to my message then shook his head.

"I can't leave the company. My place is here. Are you trying to spare me the battle? I am not that old."

"You are a bloody old git, but that is not the point. I need a messenger I can rely on and one who Edwin and Sabert will trust. Go now!"

"At once my lord," he said with a quick bow of the head, and jogged away. Not as fast as Cuthbert, but good enough for a man who was not far off sixty winters.

I looked around at the field the company was deployed in which ran along the south side of the ford. There were woods to the west and east of us and open land to our front for the hundred paces between us and the nearest trees. I glanced at Eduard and Aedann.

"This is as good a place as any to stand," I suggested.

"We have cover on the flanks to stop an encircling move. The trees also give the skirmishers somewhere to hide. Then there is open space in front so we can see the buggers coming. It's rocky land around this ford so we have a decent grip under foot whilst the field around is boggy which will slow them down," Eduard summarised succinctly.

"And if all goes wrong, a ford to retreat across to the town beyond," Aedann added.

"Always the pessimist," Eduard grunted, "but you are not wrong."

"Right then. Let's get ready!" I said.

The Wicstun company had formed up lining the southern bank of the Temese. Standing on the rocky ground adjacent to the ford, they faced away from the river over the boggy meadow which, at present, was empty of the enemy. A dozen or so skirmishers had taken up positions in the wooded land to each flank. These light troops made their weapons ready, testing the strength of the ash staves and stringing their bows. Others counted sling stones and sorted through them, assessing the balance and weight of their missile. One or two more stacked javelins against tree trunks where they would be close at hand when the moment came.

Between the woods, the company had formed a shield wall in three ranks. In the front rank were the best warriors, men in the prime of their life. They were the strongest and healthiest.

261

Warriors now full grown whose musculature and power was at the peak of development, men who had fought from Degsastan in the wild lands north of the great Roman wall to the villa in the Suth Seaxe kingdom and from Godmundingham , the royal hall of Deira to the City of the Giants in Lleyn. Amongst these men were Aedann and Eduard.

Behind the front rank were the youngest warriors, some only three and ten summers old. Cuthwine was amongst them and he now looked eagerly around, wide eyed with a mix of thrill and fear for what was about to happen.

The rear rank consisted of a line of veterans, companions of Grettir who was right now absent on his errand to Edwin. When he returned, he would rejoin them. They were forty and, in some cases, fifty -year -olds. They were, perhaps, weaker and less lean than the front rank warriors but full of wisdom that went back even before my first battle. Some, like Grettir, had fought in the wars that created Deira and the campaigns of Aelle that led to the capture of Eboracum, now renamed Eoforwic. That wisdom was accompanied by endurance, determination and even a certain cunning that could at times save the day if the front ranks were breached.

The company may have left Deira years before lacking all but a few weapons but now the men were well equipped thanks to sponsors in both Gwynned and Mercia, along with the loot from a dozen battlefields. Most wore mail shirts and strong iron helms. Every man had spear and seax but many of them had swords taken from slain foes or given as a reward for loyalty. Each, too, had broad wooden shields – the heart of the defence that a shield wall allowed. These were heavy and strong and each featured an iron butt in the centre.

262

The shields were painted green and each also bore designs that identified the captain they served. On the left the shields were painted with the red axe of Eduard's men. Many had axes like him as well as spears. Eduard stood at their heart and a step or two to their front and surveyed the woodland to the south, looking eager to get on with the battle.

To the right of the company the shields boasted white swords. Aedann himself paced up and down examining the men, adjusting the arrangement of the ranks and chatting to each man in turn, wishing them well. To some, fellow Christians and, in many cases, Welshmen who had joined our ranks in Gwynnedd, he added an extra blessing.

"God be with you," he said.

"God be with you," many replied. Some kissed crosses worn on chains at their neck.

In the centre, a small number of shields bore the running wolf symbol. These men had been selected by me as my personal guard as well as a useful reserve, which included Grettir. I looked back over the company and over the ford. Grettir was still not in sight. Had his message reached Edwin yet? I would feel happier knowing that he had, and even more so knowing that Grettir had returned and literally had my back. For I trusted him to watch over me like no other, save my three closest friends. Two were now in command of their own men. I thought about the third, Cuthbert. My small friend had not yet returned either. He must have reached the lodge by now. What was keeping him?

Over the heads of the company flew our banners, three in number. Alongside Eduard's and Aedann's and larger than either, the running wolf of Wicstun running on its field of green billowed in the breeze. It was a banner that had been carried at

Catraeth, had fallen with its lord – Wallace – in that battle but had been retrieved after and carried with the company everywhere we went. At times of danger or flight, it had to be removed from its pole and carried wrapped around men's chests or hidden beneath tunics after the disasters of the aftermath of Degsasatan and the fall of Godmundingham. Now it stood over us again.

"How long now?" I heard Cuthwine ask.

"Not long, lad," Eduard replied to my son.

He was right because a horn sounded now very close and, a few heartbeats later, the bushes moved to one side and a half dozen scouts emerged, spotted us and halted abruptly. Then they shouted back something into the trees and crouched down to study the Wictsun company who, to a man, stared back at them.

"Not long now, indeed," I said under my breath and drew Catraeth.

Chapter Twenty-Five
On to the island
Spring 612

At first light, Hussa and his men decamped from the ruined farmhouse and headed out across the fields towards the trees that marked the little island of Andersley. At first, they saw no sign of anyone and Hussa felt, with luck, they could easily reach the island and infiltrate the town without interferance. As the dim first light of the new day brightened in the east and visibility across the fields increased, however, it was Edgar who first saw that their approach to the town was not going to be so easy.

"There, Lord!" he pointed west towards the Temese. Hussa was able to see companies of men marching up the west bank of the river, angling around for an attack against the town's western defences.

"So much for surprise, but they will at least serve as a distraction," he commented. "Whilst Ceolwulf is battering away at the palisades, we can attempt to get into the town this way, maybe even undetected."

Edgar was shaking his head.

"Ceolwulf is not there," he gestured at the town. "He is over here!"

Hussa craned his neck round to his left to see where Edgar was indicating. Men, lots of them, were emerging from a copse of trees on this side of the river close to where smoke was rising from the small village of Cullasham and swinging around to their left to head north. They were still some distance away but there was no mistaking Ceolwulf's banner flapping about above the men alongside the battle pennants of Sogor and Ean-frith. They were this side of the river, barely a mile distant and marching with determination towards the same objective Hussa was aiming for. They were marching towards Andersley island and the ford into the town.

"Bollocks!" Hussa said.

"We need to get there first," Rolf said. "Not one of them knows Hal, apart from maybe Sogor and Eanfrith, and even they may not recognise him. In any event, somehow, I don't see them taking special care to look out for him, do you?"

Hussa shook his head grimly. "Come on, follow me!" he ordered.

He set off at a jog and the men picked up their own pace, shields and spears and the rest of their gear rattling and clattering as they ran along. They reached the small stream that trickled along the southern edge of Andersley island and splashed through it, squelched up the muddy bank beyond onto the marshland, disturbing a crane that was nested in reeds. It flew off, squarking in outrage at the intrusion. There they halted and took stock. To the southwest the glittering sunlight reflecting from spear points and brief glimpse of colour from the battle standards betrayed the approach of Ceolwulf . They had not reached the stream yet but could not be far away. Up ahead, smoke rose from a small settlement on the island. Hussa was keen to drive on to the village but it was sensible not to open themselves up to a potential ambush from any warriors who might be there.

"There first," Hussa said, and headed off.

Hussa's company reached the settlement and found it to consist of a cluster of six buildings. One had the appearance of a

266

mead hall, whilst the others were out –buildings such as a barn, smaller dwellings and a stables. As they approached, he noticed the smoke which had earlier been rising from various hearths had thinned out and then dispersed. The fires had been put out.

"What do you think?" Rolf asked. "Have the occupants abandoned the place and run away to the town?"

"Makes sense," Hussa grunted. "But let's go and check."

They left the men in a clearing nearby and the two of them sneaked forward through the trees until they reached a spot where they could see the buildings. They observed for a while. There were no signs of movement.

"No one there, I reckon." Rolf said.

"Come on," Hussa said and lead the way out of the trees and into the nearest building. This was indeed a stable, but there were no horses inside and no men either. The barn, like the two adjacent hovels, was empty. The fires in the dwellings had been dowsed some time before and only a faint heat radiated from them. The workshop appeared to be a small smithy whose forge was cold. Finally, they searched the main hall.

Here they found evidence of abandoned meals but again no occupants.

"Well, that is that," Rolf said as he chomped on a wedge of cheese and washed it down with some ale he had found on a table.

"You are right, let's go to the town," Hussa said.

At that moment the door opened with a loud creak and a small girl of around eight entered and crossed the hall, heading towards the other end where a door lead to living chambers. Halfway across she spotted them and froze.

"Who are you, child?" Hussa said gently as he circled around the benches towards the exit, looking to cut her off from any possible escape route.

"Sian," she said.

Hussa stopped and stared at her.

"Your father, is he Lord Cerdic?" Hussa asked, forcing himself to speak as calmly as he could. He was aware Rolf was watching him.

"Yes, Lord. Who... who are you?"

"My name is Hussa, child. I am your uncle." he answered.

Sians' eyes opened wide and she bolted towards the exit but Hussa was ahead of her and threw his arms around her. She squealed and fought to get free, but he held her firm until she gave up.

"Hussa...what are you doing?" Rolf asked.

Hussa glared at his friend. "I am going to find out what she knows." Then he knelt down and looked the girl in the eyes. "Now, niece. Tell me were I might find my son."

"Do...do you mean Hal?" Sian said, biting her lip.

Hussa nodded.

"Father says he is our brother. Ouch, stop that..." she cried because Hussa had shaken her by the shoulders.

"Hussa!" Rolf protested but Hussa ignored him.

"Your cousin he is, but not your brother. He is my son, not your father's." Sian looked terrified and said nothing. "So, niece...where is he?"

Sian still said nothing so Hussa squeezed her shoulders.

"You are hurting me," she cried.

"Just tell me what I want to know."

Sian nodded, eyes wide now with fear. "He is in the town – in Souekesham, with my mother. We were going to my aunt's house."

"Lady Aidith is taking him to Mildrith's house?" Hussa asked. Sian nodded. "Well, the Lady Aidith and the Lady Mildrith are

268

old friends of mine," he said with a mirthless smile. "Show me where this house is," Hussa said and led the child towards the exit with a reluctant Rolf trailing along in their wake.

Chapter Twenty-Six
The battle at the ford
Spring 612

The scouts continued to observe us, and we them for some time. In the distance, off to our right, we could hear the sounds of battle at the western palisade. How was it going, I wondered? It sounded as if West Seaxe were fully engaged there now. The trees that ran along the riverbank as well as the town of Souekesham obscured the view and I could only guess how the battle faired. Come on Grettir I growled to myself, for I craved news of what was going on over there. If the enemy broke through, they could appear behind us at any moment. Then, with an enemy deployed to our front, there would be no escape for us.

To my front the heavy foliage twitched and swayed, and a large warrior emerged in full armour: a veteran of West Seaxe. A moment later there was more movement and a half dozen more arrived and then almost at the same moment still more came until over two hundred stood there. Almost twice our number.

"Bugger, this won't be easy," I muttered under my breath.

Then, with a crash, still more poured out next to the existing warriors. At their head was a man with a fine mail shirt and an impressive helm decorated with strips of bronze and gold and adorned by garnets. Accompanying him were two men I remembered from when I had spent time in Bernicia's court – Sogor, the son of the late Theobald who had died at Degsastan and nephew to Aethelfrith, and Eanfrith, the king's son.

I walked over to Eduard. Aedann saw us together and joined us.

"So, that is Ceolwulf, I assume," he said when he reached us.

"Nice armour and helm. Fancy that, I do," Eduard commented.

"I think he might object to that," Aedann commented.

"Well, I will just have to be persuasive in my argument, won't I?" he replied.

I opened my mouth to say something but then spotted Cuthbert emerge from the trees to the east. He studied the gathering army and then turned to find me and scampered over. I noticed that he was alone, and I felt a sudden stab of anxiety.

"Where's Sian?" I asked when he had reached us.

Cuthbert shook his head regretfully. "Sorry, Cerdic, but she was not at the lodge. No one was, in fact. I searched each building and then the surrounding woods."

"Are you saying there was no sign of her?"

He reached into the pouch at his belt and pulled out a white object and passed it to me. . It was a bone comb with silver decorations. Sian's comb.

"That was in the clearing to the south of the lodge," he said.

"She went back for this. She had left it at the lodge which meant she had got there and collected it and then… something happened," I said.

"I went further south to see if I could pick up a trail, but you know the woods on this island… how many paths there are. I saw no sign of anyone but could hear the horns. I decided to come back and tell you."

I thought back something like fifteen years to the summer before the battle of Catraeth. That year it had been my sister, Mildrith, who had gone missing. Now it was my daughter. I felt again that tension in my throat that I had then. Where was she? Was she alive? Had anything else happened to her? She was still young, still a child, and yet I knew what some men could be like. Some were, by nature, prone to evil, but others, who in normal life were gentle, might still fall prone to the worst of lusts or cruelty in the times surrounding a battle.

Whilst I was lost in my fears, there was a sudden bellow and roar from two hundred throats that echoed across the clearing. Ceolwulf was walking along in front of his men who were now crashing spears against shields or waving swords and axes over their heads.

"Woden...Woden," some shouted "Tiw ... Tiw," others added. The gods were being called to aid them this day and I had to put aside fears for Sian. Now we had to call to the gods ourselves. Then it would be down to a man's wyrd or fate to decide if he lived or died this day.

"Eduard, lead the chanting. Let us shout louder and let the gods come to our aid."

Eduard nodded and waved energetically at the men and they too hammered weapons against wooden boards or thudded spear butts against the stony ground beneath our feet. Our pleas to the gods blended with those of the enemy. To these, other calls were made to the Christian God by some of the men in Aedann's band. I did not care which god helped us this day. I added a prayer to any that would listen to let me live so I could find my daughter.

"Here they come!" Eduard observed as the enemy shield wall formed up and began inching across the open ground towards us. Ahead of them skirmishers spread out and took aim. I nodded at my friends and rejoined my huscarls under the running wolf banner. Aedann and Eduard joined their own men whilst Cuthbert ran over to the woods to the right of our company and waved forward our own skirmishers. One of them handed him his bow. He nocked an arrow on the string, took aim and re-leased it towards the enemy skirmishers. The missile pierced a slingman's shoulder and he cried out in pain and dropped his sling then struggled to pull out the arrow.

"Let fly!" Cuthbert shouted and our skirmishers and those of the enemy started exchanging arrows and stones.

"Shield wall!" I shouted as the missiles started to fall around us.

We locked shields with our neighbours and hunkered down behind the boards. Stones pelted the wooden walls we had erected, and arrows slammed into them.

"Ut...ut...ut!" bellowed the West Seaxe shield wall as it closed in upon us. It was an ancient war cry of our peoples and it meant "out...out...out!"

They were telling the enemy to get out of their way.

Flee now whilst you can. This is your last chance before we destroy you. Go on, run now, get out.

"Ut... ut...ut!" our own men replied indicating that they would not be running. We were pinning ourselves to this land.

If you want it, you will have to go through us.

"Ut...ut...ut!" Eduard bellowed louder than anyone on the battlefield.

The enemy had adopted a formation as wide as our own. To an extent, the woods on either side dictated that. To be formed up in close order as they were, they had to stay in the open space. They had more men than us, however, so were deeper – formed in six ranks to our three. That meant that we needed to kill two of their men for each of ours that fell, if we were to keep pace.

The shield wall closed upon us and the skirmishers scattered on either side. They were twenty paces away now. Both shield walls now opened up an exchange of javelin and angon missile.

273

Men fell on both sides. The ranks shuffled together and closed up. Ten paces away now.

"Shields overhead!" I commanded. Spears held mid shaft could be directed down so that their points attacked the enemy's heads and necks.

Five paces now…

"Brace yourselves," I ordered and we tightened our grips on the shields and shifted our weight forward a little, anticipating the coming blow.

Then, with a mighty crash, the shield walls met.

In a shield wall a man's view narrows down to just encompass that space between the man to his left and that to his right and the distance from the warriors behind the three of them as far as those of the enemy to their front. Thus, his knowledge of the fight was perhaps the same as a piece on a tafl board might have about the eight spaces around it. Beyond and outside this brief area, all was noise and chaos, fury and rage, with no form or shape.

Beorma was the man to my left. He grunted as a spear point from the dark -haired warrior to his front reached over the shield and scrapped across his shoulder, drawing blood but causing little damage. I angled my own spear over and drove at the man, but he flinched out of the way and the point missed his throat. The act of recoiling, however, meant that he lost his grip on his own spear and Beorma seized it pulled it over his own shield and out of the way before passing it behind him where it was seized by the rear ranks. Beorma's opponent shouted some abuse and then fumbled with a baldrick, trying to draw a sword.

To my right was Dudda, a huge man of similar size to Eduard and he would have joined Eduard's axes had it not been for me inviting him to join my personal guards. Eduard had moaned about that, but I had got used to an axeman to my flank and, as Eduard could no longer serve that function, Dudda and his huge axe filled the gap. Dudda made use of it, heaving the axe over the top of the shield in front and pulling down hard. This opened up the man to his front to attack and, sure enough, Leom who stood behind Dudda thrust forward with his spear and took the man in the throat. He fell choking on his own blood and after a heartbeat he was forgotten as another man stepped into his space on the tafl board of our battlefield.

I realised with a start that I had been focussing on Dudda and Beorma to the extent that I was neglecting my immediate opponent. I looked up at him. He was a well armoured brute with a cruel mocking half –smile. He pushed at my shield with all his weight and I found myself staggering backwards several steps. I dug my heels in, taking purchase on the rocky ground, and leant forward. Behind me I could feel Ror pushing me forward, lending his weight and strength to my own. The enemy brute grunted, and I saw his jaw clenched with the effort of the push of shield on shield. He spat and the saliva hit my cheek, dribbled down my face and ran on inside my tunic. He grinned at me. I stepped forward and felt his foot under my own, so I kicked hard, and the grin dropped off his face as he winced in pain. I kicked again but he had moved position and my boot found no target.

"Push, boys!" I shouted. "All together now, heave!"

We pushed and were rewarded by the enemy giving ground some paces before their sheer numbers stopped our drive.

"Ut, ut, ut!" one of them started up the chant and his companions joined in. They bellowed their war cry and pushed back at us. Dudda took a spear point in his chest and collapsed. Was he dead? I was not sure. Leom took his place but almost at once was forced back himself. I could feel our wall giving way, foot by foot, yard by yard. A moment later I felt water inside my left boot and realised I was now standing in the river, ten paces behind where I had started the battle. The river's plant –covered rocks were slippery under foot and we could not brace our weight as well on the rocks as we could on the land beyond.

The enemy continued to push and we gave way. I risked poking my head up to look to the left and right and then just as quickly ducked back down as an axe almost decapitated me. In that brief glimpse, I had seen that the flank warbands under Eduard and Aedann were holding firm on the river back, whilst the enemy was directing the bulk of their efforts in the centre. Half their men were pushing us back whilst Aedann and Eduard were facing even numbers and, as a result, holding their own. I saw now the danger we were in. They planned to crack our shield wall by breaking through it at the ford. Once that was done, they could finish Aedann and Eduard at their leisure.

"Ut, ut ut!" they bellowed and in that chant was a new tone, a note of imminent triumph mingled with the threat of the horror that would then be unleashed upon us. I could see that around me my men were exchanging worried glances. The same danger had been seen by them, too.

Another cry came from the enemy as they called out their lord's name, chanting the name of their king and shouting their alliegance. "Ceolwulf, Ceolwulf, Ceolwulf! ," they called and "West Seaxe, West Seaxe, West Saexe!" They wanted any of us who survived to remember who had beaten us.

Then suddenly, Ceolwulf was there. He was just yards away a few ranks back in the enemy shield wall with his banner near to him.

"West Seaxe!" he shouted and raised his sword high above his head. His men roared and heaved at us and we fell back. Ceolwulf pushed through his own ranks, eager to lead his men across the ford. Once across, he could burst into Souekesham and fall upon Edwin from behind.

Beneath me I felt the sand of the track on the north side of the river. Ceolwulf's plan was working. He was almost over the river and our company was breaking.

"West Seaxe!" Ceolwulf shouted. Next to him, I spotted Sogor and Eanfrith. They saw me at the same moment and headed towards me.

"Stand!" I tried to shout but my voice was weak and my throat bone dry. None of my men heard me and they continued to fall back. To my left, Beorma was bleeding heavily from a wound on his temple and seemed to be swaying, close to collapse. I had lost track of Leom, and Dudda was somewhere on the ground amongst the enemy ranks, most likely dead.

"Stand!" I shouted and reached out to steady Beorma. We locked shields and tried to rally the men as Ceolwulf, Eanfrith and Sogor approached us.

"Stand!" I shouted again, this time with more conviction. Somewhere to the rear I heard horns sounding. My fears, it seemed, had come to pass. West Seaxe must have broken through at the western gate and were now coming to take us from behind.

It was over, the battle was lost!

Chapter Twenty-Seven
Intervention
Spring 612

Ceolwulf arrived in front of me in a rush and, without a pause to breathe or take stock, swung mightily with his sword, the blow aimed at cleaving my head from my body. I was panting hard with the exertion of the battle so far and already feeling exhausted, so my fatigued body reacted slowly. I only just managed to get my own blade in the way and parried but the force behind the blow was immense and the shock numbed my sword arm. I had no control over my unfeeling hand, and I dropped Catraeth. By now, Eanfrith and Sogor had reached the king's side and all three prepared to strike at me. In desperation, I fumbled at the hilt of Wreccan, my long sword, and drew it, knowing I could not hope to bring it to bear before one of the three blows connected with me.

Sogor's blade swung first and, even whilst I fought to bring Wreccan into play, I brought up my shield to deflect the blow. Eanfrith saw the movement and shifted position to angle his own attack at my exposed legs. I reacted to the attack, stepping to the side, but knowing that I was moving too slowly and, in a moment, I would feel the bitter pain of steel cleaving my muscle and bone. Then, out of nowhere, a spear thrust, coming from somewhere to my flank, intervened and whilst the spear point buried itself uselessly in the sandy river bank, the spear shaft got[NG1] in the way of the attack upon me and so saved my legs. Eanfrith's sword hacked into the spear shaft and sheared it through, but the force had been taken out of the blow. I glanced to my right and saw that Leom had joined with Beorma and myself. He locked shields with me and, throwing away the now useless spear, he pulled a seax from his belt. He had lost his axe somewhere in the battle.

Leom's arrival had surprised our opponents and made them step back and reassess the situation. I did the same. My warband, the heart of the company, was in complete disarray. A significant number were clearly dead, their corpses in heaps out on the grass or dotted here and there across the ford. Like Beorma, Leon and myself, small groups were gathered together, trying to reform a shield wall, but there were wide gaps and Ceolwulf's men were heading for these gaps, looking to break through to the the town, then fall on the rear of our company. Behind me, the horns I had heard earlier were more strident and now I could hear the bellowing of warcries. I felt my heart leap in my chest – my fears were coming true. West Seaxe had broken Edwin on the western palisade and were swinging around behind us.

Around me, the men had thought the same thing, and many were backing off, ready to run. I felt Beorma take a step back and fought the urge to do the same. Why, though? If we were surrounded, I should run. It was the only sensible thing to do. Should I give the order to flee? Every moment I hestitated more men were injured or killed. Why did I hesitate?

Unless...

Unless the horns did not belong to West Saexe. What if Ceolwulf's men had not beaten Edwin but the outcome had been the other way around? What if the weaker West Seaxe attack had foundered and Edwin had won? What if Grettir had gotten through and told Edwin about the attack from the south. In that case ...

At that moment there was a loud bellow as a huge warrior bearing a shield emblazoned with Cwneburg's Mercian Wyvern

279

jumped into the gap beyond Leom, challenging any foe that would dare to try their luck in combat with him. A few heart-beats passed and suddenly dozens of warriors were running past me out of the town and throwing themselves at the enemy. Ceolwulf took in the new arrivals and then turned his head back to glare at me and his face twisted in rage as he swung again, but, this time, Wreccan was ready and I parried his blow with ease. Sogor surged forward on Ceolwulf's left and smashed his shield into mine with such brutality that I was knocked over and landed on my back, a fall which took the wind from me. At the same time, Wreccan fell out of my grip and I clawed at the sand, trying to retrieve it. Sogor loomed over me, a cruel smile of an-ticipation playing across his face. I abandoned the futile search for my sword and tried to find the seax that I wore at my waist.

Then a shadow fell over me and I arched my head back to see Grettir stepping over me. The aged veteran left the ground as he launched himself at Sogor, smashing his shield against that of his enemy. Sogor's shield shattered and the blow took him off his feet so he now tumbled back through the ranks coming up behind him. In the respite, Grettir turned and pulled me to my feet.

"Get off your arse!" he growled and I rushed to obey him as if I was once again that eight – year –old boy a lifetime ago, practising with wicker shields and wooden swords in the fields around the Villa. I spotted Catraeth and Wreccan just a few pac-es from where I stood and quickly retrieved them both.

Around me, the Wicstun company was shattered but the at-tack by Grettir and, now I could see, a company of Cwenburg's Mercian warriors, had flung back West Seaxe. The blow had stunned the enemy, but they would recover unless we acted im-mediately. Cwenburg was suddenly next to me with the captain of the company by her side and I gave her a grateful nod which earnt me the thinnest of smiles in response. I pointed forward and she nodded, agreeing with the unspoken plan and turned to her commander.

"Wicstun company, form up!" I shouted and the men reacted to the command and gathered around me. The banner reappeared from only the gods knew where and was just to my rear where I was grateful that Grettir was now standing in his customary position once more.

"Wicstun company, advance!" I bellowed and Grettir shouted the order in echo of my own command. Off to the left I heard Eduard shouting it also and, a few moments later, to my right, Aedann also took up the call. I felt a surge of relief that my friends still lived. I wondered about Cuthbert, was he still living? I had lost track of him. The thought that was uppermost on my mind was What about Sian? What had become of her?

I pushed the thoughts to the back of my mind as our attack got underway. As we moved forward, Cwenburg shouted out the order, too, and our depleted ranks were swelled by Cwenburg's militia. I was suddenly anxious again to see that the princess herself was accompanying her men. Brave though she was, even to be here, she was unarmed and unarmoured and would surely make a tempting target for our enemies. Her death here would shatter our alliance with Mercia.

"Please, princess, stay back, I implore you!" I shouted to her and she shot me an angry glance before turning back, though only as far as the ford. She then turned again and watched the battle unfolding from a safer distance.

"What is it with me and strong –willed women!" I muttered to no one in particular. Then I heard someone shouting from behind me. I glanced back and saw that Cuthbert was running flat out behind the company from the right flank where he had been deployed with his light troops in the woods, behind Aedann's Swords, my own guard, and Eduard's Axes and off to the left.

I heard the words, "Watch the flank!" as he ran by. Puzzled, I pulled out of the shield wall and ran around in Cuthbert's wake, behind the company to the left flank which was almost at the eastern edge of the clearing. When I reached him, he was gesturing into the woods and, a moment later, nocked an arrow and released it into the woods. With a cry of pain and a crash of branches, a warrior fell out of the bushes at the edge of the clearing. His shield hit the ground and rolled ten feet before falling over. In that moment I spotted the symbol upon it – Hussa's snake symbol. I stared wide eyed at Cuthbert before turning and bellowing the command.

"Wicstun company, halt! Eduard, swing your company around! Face the flank!"

Eduard stared at me over the ranks of his men but shouted the order and his warband angled back to face south east. The rest of the company stumbled to a halt. They had been marching forward with conviction, and now they stood looking confused and uncertain. They were not happy with the change of plan and neither was I, but we had acted only just in time.

I pushed through the ranks to the hinge of the Wicstun men, where Eduard's company angled away from my own. Barely a handful of yards away, Ceolwulf was studying me with Sogor and Eanfrith at his side. There was puzzlement on his face. Then puzzlement changed to surprise as he started to the right.

At that moment a company emerged from the wood around the spot where Cuthbert's victim had fallen out of the trees. A company of Bernician spearmen with the Loki serpent on their shields. At their centre was my brother, Hussa.

Hussa spotted me immediately and I glared at him and he, in turn, at me. He held the gaze for a few moments and then his face flickered into a smile. There was knowledge in that smile. Whatever he knew that I did not know, I did not like the feeling. I felt my hand tighten around Catraeth's hilt and a tension leap into my throat. Then I realised to some irritation that I was playing the game by his rules. He wanted me to feel uneasy, but I realised Cuthbert's sharp eyes had removed some of his advantage. He and his men had expected to hit us in the flank and in taking us by surprise, cut us to pieces. Even now I could see some of them looked perturbed by the fact Eduard's company was angled towards them. No flank presented itself and the advantage which they had been expecting was no longer theirs. They would be feeling frustration and disappointment.

And in that disappointment lay an opportunity for us ... if we acted at once. I shifted my gaze over to Ceolwulf and saw in his face surprise at Hussa's arrival. He had not expected it and, even though it was clearly to his advantage and a threat to us, he and his men were put on the back foot for a few moments. I needed to sieze this one chance Cuthbert had given me.

"Wicstun company.... Charge!" I bellowed and, without waiting to see if they obeyed, I ran straight at Ceolwulf, Catraeth at the ready in my hand. Ceolwulf had still been looking over at Hussa and took a few instants to react. Sogor had seen me first and shouted a warning. Ceolwulf turned back to see me almost upon him and started to bring his own sword up. It was still only half raised when I crashed into him, shield first. He was unbalanced and fell backwards. I let my momentum carry me forward, so I stood over him. Around me I was dimly aware of the clash of armies as my men followed me into the West Seaxe ranks. All I focussed upon was Ceolwulf, king of West Seaxe. I thust Catraeth at his throat and he parried with his own blade as he struggled to get back to his feet. My momentum was still moving me forward and I used it to push my shield at his face. He brought his own shield up to intervene and the two crashed together again. He was pushed onto his back once more and I was now on my knees straddling him, pushing shield and sword down with all my weight.

Another shadow fell over me and, as I struggled with Ceolwulf, I glanced up to see Sogor above me, bearing a new shield and with his spear point aimed at my throat. I was helpless to intervene but bent away to my left to try to avoid the thrust. But it never fell because Grettir had arrived and, without pausing again, crashed into Sogor. They both went down in a heap next to me and Ceolwulf. Beneath me the king was struggling and I felt his knee in my belly only a few inches from a rather softer and more vulnerable spot. , I groaned anyway, and leant back slightly, making him think he had landed his blow where he intended. He must have fallen for it because he relaxed and tried to use the time to get up off the ground. In the effort of that attempt, his shield and sword moved apart and now I could see his throat. I reacted to the opportunity and thrust forward with my sword point. It pierced skin and cartilage and bone, and pinned him to the ground as it thrust into the muddy soil beneath his neck. His eyes widened in shock, surprise and pain and then the light in his eyes faded and he was gone, his soul carried to Valhalla by the Valkyries who even now swooped and flew around us, taking the dead away.

I looked over at Sogor and Grettir and saw that they were still locked in each other's clutches, weapons and shields abandoned as the young man and the almost sixty –year –old veteran wrestled in the mud. Youth and agility battled wisdom and experience. I staggered to my feet and turned to help my own retainer when he gave a sudden grunt and headbutted Sogor. Sogor's eyes rolled up into his head and he slumped down on the ground, knocked unconscious by the blow. I felt a smile come to my lips. Grettir had picked up a few dirty tricks over the years.

I thrust out a hand and pulled Grettir to his feet and then stared around. The Wicstun company had slammed into Ceolwulf's and Sogor's ranks like a hammer on an anvil and it was the anvil that shattered. The charge had unnerved them but what really shook them was what happened next.

One of the king's huscarls took in the visage of me with a blood stained Catraeth standing over the broken body of Ceolwulf with Sogor, the Bernician lord, also at our feet and shouted, "The king is dead... save yourselves!"

An army is bound by common loyalty to its lord whether earl, prince or king. We are sworn to our lord's service with promises made touching their sword and paid for in wealth, gifts and status. Bound thus, a warrior will fight till death rather than suffer the dishonour of flight. This contract, though, is shattered when that man falls. The commanders of the armies of West Seaxe and Northumbria lay on the ground, and whilst the young Eanfrith remained, he had yet to gain the loyalty that the older men had commanded. The ranks of West Seaxe and Bernicians started to step back. In these moments, morale cracks like an acorn under a boot and weapons and shields were now dropped as the call "Save yourselves!" spread down the ranks like a summer fire through a wheatfield.

Eanfrith did not run. He stepped towards me, full of the mad impetuosity that twenty years into the future I would see set Northumbria briefly on fire. But that would be another Eanfrith, fighting at my side against another enemy and a tale not

285

for today. This day only a few of his huscarls accompanied him whilst, around him, the enemy army melted away. I stepped towards him, sword already swinging, to end the young prince's attempt at rallying the army and saving the day.

His courage did not help him, for even whilst he came at me, he slipped in the mud and, with a cry, fell to the ground. In a moment, I was over him, just as I had been over Ceolwulf. Catraeth lunged forward, point aiming at his heart, yet my blow never connected because Hussa's blade was in the way, deflecting my blow. He had arrived just in time to save the prince. I turned towards my brother, thinking that this day was the day I would end our rivalry and, finally, I would be rid of this thorn in my side.

Then I gasped in horror because it was then that I saw that, whilst his one arm was extended in front of him, his priceless blade thrust out and getting in my way, his other arm was coiled around the neck of my daughter Sian and in that hand he was holding Sian's own little seax, point angled under her chin. Her eyes were wide with terror.

"Brother," he said. "We need to talk."

Chapter Twenty-Eight
An innocent face
Spring 612

"Let her go, you bastard," I hissed at Hussa as I leapt to my feet. I took a few steps towards him and then froze as I saw the point of the little blade touch the skin at her throat.

"Careful, Cerdic, careful," my brother said. "I am feeling more than a bit agitated today and it would be so easy for my hand to slip."

I backed off; hands held out in submission.

Then I swallowed hard and forced myself to speak more softly. "Just calm down, Hussa."

"Papa, help me," Sian said. Her eyes were wide with terror.

"It is going to be alright, Sian" I said, trying to sound as reassuring as possible. In truth, I was as terrified as she was. Hussa might be my brother, but he had burnt my mother alive in revenge. What would he do to my daughter?

Around us the battle was continuing. My company was pursuing the West Seaxe off the battlefield whilst the Bernicians were still formed up – Hussa's company off to the side and around Sogor and Eanfrith their own men. One of them was helping Eanfrith back to his feet. He glared at me a moment and then nodded thanks at Hussa. Sogor, still lying prostrate at our feet, groaned and then opened his eyes and looked about him before dragging himself upright.

He swayed slightly and then looked sharply at Hussa, and me.

"What is going on?" he asked.

I ignored him and spoke instead to Hussa.

"Well, you have my attention …brother, what do you want to discuss?"

Hussa studied me for a while and then let his gaze drift over the battlefield and over towards the ford and the town beyond.

"Where is he?"

I did not have to ask who the 'he' was.

"He is not your concern anymore."

"He will always be my concern; he is my son."

I shook my head. "No, he is not!" I replied but even I could hear the doubt in my voice, the doubt I had started to feel.

Hussa heard the tone of my voice and his eyes narrowed. "You know this to be true… don't you?"

I shook my head again. "He cannot be your son. You can't have children."

Hussa laughed. "Always so sure of yourself, aren't you, Cerdic? But you are wrong. Rownenna and I have had another son."

"What?"

"Now, what do you think?"

That news stunned me, and I did not know what to say.

"Just let my daughter go…" I managed after a few moments.

"When I have Hal back," Hussa said. "Then I will free her unharmed, you have my word."

"I might still be Hal's father…" I said.

"Enough of this nonsense!" Sogor shouted. "If this is your brother's daughter, Hussa, kill her now and then we will kill her father."

Hussa and I both stared at Sogor.

"Wait…" I said.

"Kill her!" Sogor repeated.

"Father!" Sian screamed.

"Pa!" another voice said. It was a boy's voice. Hal's voice.

We all turned in its direction. Hal was standing next to Eduard. Eduard had a hand on his shoulder, holding him back just as Hussa was holding Sian back. Except, of course, Hal had no knife at his throat. Where had he come from suddenly, I wondered. He had been with Aidith, hadn't he? Where was she, then?

"Let him go, Eduard!" Hussa shouted.

"He won't be harmed.," Sogor said. "Your brother thinks he is Hal's father, so he won't harm the boy. We have the advantage. Kill his daughter, now!"

Sogor clearly believed that if Sian died, I would be destroyed and unable to act and he could still win the battle. The thing was... he was probably right. As it was, I could not move. Terror had taken hold and my limbs were like lead.

Hussa looked at me and I saw indecision there and also fear. If he killed Sian, what might I do to Hal. I might lash out at him in anguish and revenge. Would I do that? I did not know, if I was being honest. And if I didn't know, then he certainly didn't, and that is why he hesitated.

"Hussa..." I said. "We don't have to do this. Not today..."

Sogor stepped towards my brother. His own seax was now in his hand, glittering point levelled at Sian.

"If you will not do it, I will!" he hissed.

My numb limbs finally responded, and I started to move towards them. Even as I did so, I knew he was too close to Sian and I could not reach her in time to save her.

Then, as despair rose in my chest, Sogor's eyes widened in shock. His mouth opened and he made a choking sound as blood welled up in his throat and then gushed out of his mouth. I stared at him in shock, almost matching his own. Then the shock turned to utter astonishement as Aidith appeared by his shoulder, bloody seax in her hand. Just beyond her, I also spotted brother Ealdwig, panting hard, his tunic mud splattered and torn as if he had just been running through the woods.

"I won't let you touch my daughter, you bastard!" Aidith shouted and I turned my gaze back to her just as she slashed her blade back across his throat.

No one moved and no word was spoken as he fell first to his knees, wobbled there a moment, hands clutching his throat and then toppled face forward onto the mud.

Aidith moved over to Hussa and now her blade was at his throat.

"Let her go, Hussa" she said dangerously.

"Where in the name of Thunor's balls did she come from!" I heard Grettir say.

Behind Aidith, Sogor's huscarls were as stunned as we were. Then one recovered and stepped towards her and Ealdwig

"Watch out, my lady!" Grettir shouted and jumped forward so he stood between her and the huscarl. The unarmed Ealdwig scampered around behind the old veteran who fixed the huscarl with a murderous glare.

"Just try it, bastard!" Grettir hissed, his own sword now in plain sight between them.

The threat of renewed bloodshed hung in the air. Around me my own men were tensing, ready to strike as Sogor's huscarls shifted weight and eased forward a pace or two. Hussa's hand still held a blade at Sian's throat even while he glared down at the knife at his own.

This could go badly wrong very quickly, I thought.

May the merciful gods help us now, I prayed fervently but feeling very little hope in the appeal.

The gods, you see, rarely concern themselves in the affairs of men. They are too busy with their own buisiness, with their seemingly interminable wars with the giants of Jotunheim, as well as with their own divisions and rivalries, to waste much attention on mortals.

Yet, I knew the Valkyries would still be flying above us, choosing those fated to die this day and carrying them to Woden's halls or maybe to the folkvangr – the fields of Freya. They would be letting the gods know of this battle. Or maybe Munin and Huginn, Woden's ravens who flew daily over our world, Midgard, and reported back to him were whispering in his ear and his one eye was turned upon us. Or perhaps the mischevious god Loki, who my brother served, was watching over his follower.

Something like that must have occurred because you know sometimes the gods do pay attention and sometimes, rarely perhaps, but sometimes they intervene...

... and this was one of those days.

"Stop!" a voice called out. A female voice.

I glanced over at my wife, even though the voice did not sound like hers. I turned towards the sound and, as I expected, saw that it was not Aidith who looked as surprised as the rest of us, but close to her, the woman with whom I had spent that fateful night in that distant villa close to the sea in Suth Seaxe, the woman I believed had born me a son. The same woman I had followed that night at Anwoth and who had led me to Hal. Rowenna pushed out from beside Rolf and came to stand between me and Hussa. She was, again, today wearing her assassin's clothes and so it was the Nightjar I saw in front of me, the same one who had struck down that guard in Anwoth fort. Except, today, the Nightjar was carrying, close to her body, wrapped in her cloak, a child. The baby's eyes opened, and I saw that a baby now stared out at us.

"Ma!" Hal's voice called out, breaking the stunned silence.

Hussa blinked at her. "Rowenna, what are you doing here?"

The Nightjar looked around at the battlefield, at the bodies of Ceolwulf and Sogor and across at Aidith, then over at Hal, and finally at Hussa. She shrugged at him.

"Well, husband, I have come to sort everything out," she said. "and it seems not a moment too soon..."

"Rowenna, get away from here," Hussa shouted.

The raven –haired lady took no notice of him. I certainly took notice of her. Indeed, everyone on our part of the battlefield did. Further away, there were sounds of fighting, out in the woods and down by the river but here, in the bloodstained clearing, all the fighting had ceased and everyone stared at her as if she were a poet about to recite a saga, or a lyre player whose fingers were reaching for the first note.

"What foolishness is going on here?" Rowenna asked Hussa.

He glared at her. "I have come for our son like I said I would, wife!"

She let out a gasp of exasperation. "And you plan to get him back by threatening to cut your niece's throat, do you?" she asked.

"If my brother does not let Hal go, I will do it."

She did not respond but turned to look at me.

"What about you?"

I frowned. "What about me?"

Rowenna snorted. "Don't play the fool, Lord Cerdic, you must know that much of what has happened here has only happened because of what you did at Anwoth. Taking our son away from us that night."

"My son, you mean?" I replied.

"Do you really believe that?"

"We did lie together," I answered. "Hussa cannot have children. So, it is obvious."

"How do you know?" she asked.

"Know what?"

"How do you know that Hussa cannot have children?"

I shrugged. "He never has in the past."

"Maybe that is true," Rowenna agreed, "he has been with other women before me, I know that and we know of no children from any of those times but, even then, we cannot be sure. He has travelled a lot, after all."

I shrugged and then thought of something. I pointed at my brother.

"He did send that message through Lilla saying the child was mine."

"Were those the words he used?" she asked.

I thought back two years. I was not sure now.

"I think so… I am not sure now. Maybe it was just inferred."

Hussa laughed. "Or you believed what I wanted you to believe, idiot! Maybe I sent words intended to cause you trouble, to bring mistrust and shame to your oh, so wonderful marriage and life, dear brother."

I glanced at Aidith. She was focusing on Hussa, her eyes unreadable. Then she looked over at me, confusion apparent on her face.

Hussa laughed again. "I see that my plan worked," he said and then looked at Hal and his smile dropped away. "Maybe too well. I did not think you would actually believe you were the father. Or that you would take the actions you have done."

I rubbed my face and then pinched my nose then pointed at Hal.

"So, how do we know who is father is? It could be either of us."

Aidith came to my side, her hand laid on my forearm. I looked at her.

"What is it?" I asked.

"Look, Cerdic... just look."

She nodded her head towards Rowenna. I frowned at her, not understanding what she was trying to tell me. . She saw the doubt on my face.

"Not the woman, Cerdic, look at the child."

I looked at Rowenna again, this time once more at the small form wrapped at her side. I could not see much of the child, but I could see dark eyes and dark hair, the shape of his nose, the curve of his chin. It was familiar. I looked at Rowenna. There was something about the face and, in particular, the hair which he shared with her, there was no doubt about that. I looked back at him and this time paid more attention to his eyes, those eyes that even now were fixed upon me. The colour of these eyes were a shade of green that I had only seen in one other person. I realised with a shock that I was looking at the face of Hussa. Something, at least, close to Hussa's face and sharing with him features Hussa himself shared with his mother. There was indeed very little in my brother's appeareance that he owed to his father and my father, Cenred.

I could not deny that the child was without a doubt Hussa's son.

"Now look at Hal," she said.

I did so, aware, in fact, there was a creak of leather and mail armour as everyone on our part of the battlefield turned at the same time and did so. Hal was aware of all the attention and blushed but did not flinch or turn away. Indeed, he stared back with the same beligerant, somewhat angry expression I had seen on Hussa's face on dozens of occasions. Same eyes, same nose and chin.

"Woden's balls," I said. "Hal is his son."

The realisation of what I had done washed over me. I had let myself get carried away with this obsession that Hal was my son and justified everything that I had done because of this. I looked around me. How many men had died today because of those actions?

I tuned back to my brother.

"I was wrong to take Hal. The boy can leave with you."

I was suddenly aware that everyone nearby was letting out a deep breath of relief at the same time, as if in the tension of the moment they had not dared to make a noise.

"I was wrong," I repeated. "Please let my daughter go."

Hussa studied me for a moment and I wondered if he would have revenge on me even now. The feeling of relief I had felt around me seemed to melt away and everyone watched to see what he would do. A swift move of the hand, a stab with the seax and Sian would die here, and the battle would erupt once more. I felt my chest tighten again and my hand grip, Catraeth.

Then, he let the hand holding Sian's seax fall away from her throat. He turned the blade around and handed it to her. Without saying a word, she took it and stepped away from him. I felt Aidith relax next to me and then step forward, arms held out as our daughter rushed over to us. Sian sobbed as she fell into her mother's arms. The pair turned away to the rear where I noticed that Cwenburg had joined them and was leading them to the town and safety.

"Now, release my son," Hussa said with a tilt of the head towards Hal.

"Eduard, let him go," I said and Eduard removed his hand from the boy's shoulder. Hal scampered away from my friend and rushed to his mother and father. I saw Hussa embrace him and Rowenna join them. There was love in that embrace. I had been wrong about that, too. He belonged with them. I looked at Aidith and saw she was still holding the bloody knife which had killed Sogor. I took it from her and passed it to Grettir.

"Hussa," I said, turning back to my brother.

He looked up at me. "Yes, Cerdic?"

"I was wrong to take the child. I thought he was mine and … I thought you two were unfit to be parents after I had seen Rowenna kill the guard at Anwoth. Today, I realise that we all do what we must."

He nodded at me. "So, what now?" he asked, gesturing at the Bernician warriors and the Deiran ones just yards from each other. Do you still want to fight today?"

I looked around the battlefield, at the men who had witnessed this remarkable moment, a time when even the gods and Valkyries may have been watching and shook my head.

"One day we will settle our differences, brother. Many here owe you death. But today is not the day for that. Withdraw your men and we will not pursue for an hour. Get down the river and away from here before dark and there will be no more killing. For today, anyway…."

He nodded at me and held my glance for a moment. We knew that one day there would not be families gathered about us, no reason not to fight and not to kill. Today, though, we were both fathers and our families were safe.

"Goodbye, Cerdic," he said and turned away.

Hal looked back at me.

"Farewell, Hal,"

Hal nodded. "Farewell, uncle," he said.

Hussa led his men south towards the ruined farmhouse as the first leg of their journey towards Bebbanburg. Once they had reached the farm, Rowenna had hugged them all, all four members of his family in one big embrace for the first time. Then she had thrust Huw at his father and moved over to the horses which Rolf and Edgar had just started to get ready for the road. She drew Rolf to one side and spoke to him. Rolf looked shocked but then, when she returned to Hussa he smiled.

"What was that about?" Hussa asked.

"Oh, nothing to concern you for now. Come here, Hal and tell me what you have been up to."

Before Hussa could ask anything else, Hal was holding her hand as they walked and was talking non -stop about everything he had seen since they had last been together.

Chapter Twenty-Nine
Moving on
Summer 612

"Well, Lord Hussa. You certainly have some explaining to do. What in the name of Thunor's balls happened?" Aethelfrith bawled.

His voice echoed and rebounded off the walls of the great hall at Bebbanburg like the bellow of a giant auroch might around the mountains of Gwynedd.

The hall was crowded. Eanfrith sat at the king's right hand and every stool, chair and bench in the room was occupied. Indeed, clearly sensing that they might witness Hussa's final fall from greatness, the whole of the witan was present along with many of the various lord's house troops. In Hussa's mind, they were a flock of carrion birds all hunched over a corpse. The only problem was, he was the corpse. He thrust away the thought and tried to ignore everyone else apart from the king.

"Things got a bit out of hand, I admit that," Hussa said. "But, believe me, when I say I just went there to look for my son."

The king's eyes bulged in outrage and he thust a finger at Hussa so violently that Hussa took an involuntary step away from him. .

"'A bit out of hand'," Aethelfrith quoted. "A bit out of hand, you call it?"

"Yes, lord king," Hussa replied with a nod of the head.

Aethelfrith, though, was shaking his head and waggling a finger in front of Hussa.

"No, Hussa. It did not just get a bit out of hand. 'A bit out of hand' is a pot of briw boiling over. A bit out of hand is burning flatbread or inviting one too many guests to a wedding. This was on a whole different level, Lord Hussa. This was a catastrophe."

Hussa chewed his lip. "That is not how I see things. I don't think it particularly changes anything."

Aethelfrith leapt to his feet, his face red with anger and once more thrust out a finger and this time jabbed it into Hussa's chest.

"You let Ceolwulf get killed. Cynegils, his son, is furious. He is not minded at all to honour his father's agreement with me that you spent three years arranging. How is it that things are not changed? We just lost an important ally."

Hussa spoke quietly and slowly, trying to calm Aethelfrith down.

"It is true that we – at least for the moment – have lost West Seaxe as an ally. But, in that battle, unplanned though it was, the Mercian fyrd got mauled. They were not the strongest in terms of spears and now, maybe a third of its warriors are dead, or wounded so much as to be unable to fight. Mercia is weakened which, in the end, was all you were trying to achieve. For fear of further aggression up the Temese Valley, they must now divert, maybe, half of what they have in the north of Mercia, on our border, in fact, towards the south. Indeed, West Seaxe is more likely, not less likely, to attack Mercia, seeking revenge for its slain king. Whether or not that is in alliance with us or an independent act, really makes little difference to us, does it?"

Aethelfrith pondered this.

"I had hoped that such an attack would be coordinated with our own attack planned for next year. It may be that I need to gather more men before attacking. It may delay us still longer."

"Maybe," Hussa agreed, "yet it is easier for us to find four hundred more men than Mercia forty as our realm is much larger and more popoulated, with cities like Eoforwic. Mercia has no city of that size."

Aethelfith sat back down. He was calmer now, yet was still glaring at Hussa, his ire still not fully extinguished. He tilted his head to one side and considered Hussa.

"There is still the matter of how this got so out of hand in the first place. You were sent with Sogor to plan an attack with West Seaxe for next year. I agreed that you could look into the matter of your son, but I did not expect you to cause a war or trigger off a major battle."

"He did not cause a war, Father," Eanfrith said suddenly. All around the hall, whispered conversations broke out at this intervention, but the king silenced them all with a glare.

Aethelfrith turned to look at his son, sitting on a chair at his side. "What did you say?"

"It was Lord Sogor, Father."

Around the room the king's council erupted into shouts of surprise and confusion. This time the king did nothing to stop them.

"Sogor?" he asked.

Eanfrith nodded. "He believed that Hussa was using this search for his son as a ruse. He thought that he was going to try to win some fame by capturing Souekesham to gain your trust and more influence. It was Sogor who talked Ceolwulf into the attack."

Aethelfrith stared at him. "What about you?"

"Me, Father?"

"What did you do to try to stop him?"

Eanfrith looked confused.

"Stop him? Nothing. I went along with it. I ... thought there was a chance of glory."

"Why are you admitting to this now?"

Eanfrith nodded at Hussa. "He saved my life in the battle. I would have died if it was not for his intervention. I owe him for that."

Aethelfrith tilted his head and looked again at Hussa. "So, you did not start the battle."

"No, Lord. I admit I went to look for Hal and then, when the battle started, I got involved but I had hoped to sneak in and out. That proved impossible. I arrived at the meadow near the river just before Ceolwulf died but was not in a position to prevent that."

Aethelfrith studied him for a while then pursed his lips and nodded. "It seems I have blamed you wrongly. I am grateful for the life of my son."

Hussa nodded, letting out a deep breath in relief. "And I am grateful, lord king, that you let me go and find my own son and bring him home."

The king nodded. "As I am glad that you found him." He then turned back to stare at his son. "You and I need to talk. This rashness is not a trait suited for a future king. I am displeased with you and your lack of control over Sogor."

"I am sorry, Father," Eanfrith said.

"Yet, I am glad you are here for me to rebuke. Come, let us retire and talk in private," Aethelfrith said and father and son left through the doors that lead to their private quarters.

Many of the witan appeared disappointed that they had not seen Hussa's fall from grace. However, now that his position seemed, if anything, stronger, others came up and congratulated him on his saving of the prince's life. The council broke up soon after that and it was a relieved Hussa who returned to his own lodgings and his family.

He kissed Rowenna, patted Hal on his head and sat down with a great sigh in his favourite chair and for a moment watched Hal play with the wooden warrior toy, Wilburh. Then he reached for a tankard of ale that Bridget had brought him. There was something hesitant, perhaps even apprehensive, about the way she placed the drink on the side table that caught his attention.

"Bridget, is everything alright?" he asked her. Now that he thought about it, she had been like this since they had returned to the fortress the night before.

"Master, I need to tell you something," she said.

"Oh, what?"

"I am … I am with child, master."

Hussa always thought of himself as a bright, intelligent man but now several things fell into place – Bridget's recent hesitancy in talking to him but also Rowenna's secretive conversations to Rolf on the way back from Souekesham and then, of course, some things Rolf had said to him which hinted that Rolf's world view had changed, implying a newly found intimacy. Bridget was Hussa's slave and, as such under the law, whoever had made her pregnant had committed a crime and owed him money. It was pretty bloody obvious who that was. With a splash of ale, he slapped his tankard back down onto the table, crossed to the door, tugged it open and stuck his head out the door. He twisted his neck around for a moment, spotted the man he was looking for and bellowed out across the courtyard.

"Rolf, get your arse in here! You owe me twenty shillings!"

Rolf had been sitting on a bench near the blacksmith's, apparently pretending to sharpen his sword, but it was clear from his expression that he was expecting this summons. He got up, sheathed his blade, and made his way over to Hussa's door. Hussa blocked the way for a moment and glared at the man be-

302

fore gesturing that Rolf should follow him. Rolf, looking very sheepish, duly did so. He and Bridget shared an anxious glance as Hussa sat back down and then they both stood, heads bowed in front of him.

"Well, what have you got to say for yourselves?" he asked.

"I am sorry, my lord," they both said.

"So, what am I to do with you both?"

"Husband..." Rowenna started to say something but Hussa shook his head at her. She frowned but said nothing.

"By rights, I am entitled to my weregild. But that still leaves me with a pregnant maid. What am I supposed to do with her? I could throw her out, let her fend for herself in the wilds I guess..."

Rolf's head snapped up and an angry expression had leapt onto his face.

"No, lord I won't let you!"

So, I was right, he thought.

"Oh, you won't let me, eh? I am her master, after all." Hussa leaned back, beginning to enjoy himself, but careful not to let it show in his face. "Well, now, I imagine I could be persuaded to be lenient; I might keep her on in my service if she was wed to someone sworn to me. Eadgar, perhaps, or Frithwulf my steward out on my estates, even, although he is a bit fat and old and has a wife already, of course."

"I will marry her!" Rolf burst out then looked surprised at what he had said. A moment later the surprise had turned to determination. "I will marry her, if she will have me and with your permission, my lord."

"You're sure? I thought a wife and family got in the way of one's pursuit of glory. Sure, you said that."

"Well, when I said that, I meant ..." he stumbled.

"Anyway, I can't have my lieutenant married to a slave."

"But my lord!" Rolf protested but Hussa was lifting up a hand.

"So, I suppose I will just have to free her and then you can marry her."

Rolf stared at Hussa, jaw open in shock and then he grinned. "You bastard! You complete and utter bastard! You called me in here knowing you were going to say that, didn't you?"

"Not entirely. I needed to know first that you cared for her. So, the question is, will Bridget have you as her husband?"

Bridget looked over at Rolf and nodded. "I will, my lord and gladly, too!"

Hussa lifted his tankard. "Well then, Bridget, I need more ale and bring more for everyone. We have a wedding to toast. Oh, and Rolf, you still owe me twenty bloody shillings!"

An hour later, Rolf and Bridget had left to tell the company the news. Rowenna came over carrying Huw.

"You are one of the most confusing men I have ever met. But I just want to say, I love you." and she leant forward and kissed him.

He had just taken up Huw from Rowenna and placed him on his lap when there was a knock at the door which Rowenna opened to admit a waiting Queen Acha. She gestured at him to remain seated when he tried to rise and joined him and Rowenna at the table, her own baby, Oswiu, on her own hip.

"I have heard what happened in Souekesham and in council just now."

"Oh."

"I am pleased."

Hussa and Rowenna echanged a glance of mutual confusion. "Why so? I would have thought you would be disappointed that I had saved Eanfrith's life. Surely, your cause and that of your sons would have been strengthened if I had let him die."

"Eanfrith's position is weakend in his father's eyes and your own position is stronger again. Which helps me and my own children," she said looking at the baby.

"Even so" Rowenna said, "I would have thought at least part of you regrets that Eanfrith lives."

"I don't wish for a man's death," she said. "Indeed, Eanfrith dying now would push too much attention on Oswald and even Oswiu here, "she replied, looking at her son. She paused for a moment and after a moment shook her head. "Both of them are too young for that. It is best for the present if they and I remain in the background. I just wanted the best chance for my sons to have life and their future secure. Your trip south helped that."

Hussa laughed. "As I told the king, I just went there for my son."

Acha inclined her head. "Where you encountered your brother?"

Hussa nodded. "There is no surprise there. He had taken my son, after all."

"Indeed, and yet, how remarkable that you two seem to come together at many of the important moments of our times. Big battles and the places that witness the deaths of kings."

Hussa considered this. "It's my brother who has killed not one but now, two kings. Cerdic just seems to have an annoying habit of being, by chance, in the wrong place at the right time."

"I am not so sure that either of you get anywhere by chance. I think fate plays a role in whatever happens to you both." Acha said. "And I don't think that is over yet. You will meet again, at least once more, that seems inevitable, as does the fact that your little familial dispute has a wider impact. "

305

Hussa considered that.

"Fate plays its part in all our lives. It seems, at times, we all must entertain the gods. But as it is out of our control, it is not something I worry much about. In any event, I am not going anywhere now for some time, not if I have anything to do with it. I want some peace and quiet and time to spend with Rowenna and with both my sons and see them grow."

Acha smiled benignly. "Then I will pray that the gods look elsewhere for their entertainment, and you get the peace you desire."

Chapter Thirty
A story
Summer 612

"Now, that is a story I will delight in telling from the southern waters to the Northern Isles," Lilla said with a laugh, glancing around at Aidith and I, as well as all my friends including Brother Ealdwig who sat around on benches in the hall of the hunting lodge sipping at ale and finishing off the meal we had enjoyed together.

The bard had arrived for the midsummer celebrations some weeks after the battle of Souekesham. He brought news that the new king of West Seaxe had been forced to take his companies west to secure the frontier with Dumnonia where tribesmen had taken advantage of the death of Ceolwulf to raid east. So, the Temese Valley was safe for the present. However, mindful of the threat from the south from a vengeful West Seaxe, Ceorl had reinforced the garrison at Souekesham. For now, it seemed we would have a quiet year. Lilla pressed us for all the details we were willing to give him of the battle and his eyes shone when Sian spoke of her mother's intervention.

"I hardly did anything apart from deal with that Sogor bastard when he threatened my daughter." Aidith had said but I could see from the excitement on Lilla's face that much embellishment of her role would ensue in future tellings of the tale.

Aidith tried to explain a bit more what had happened.

"I had left the children at Mildrith's house and came back looking for Brother Ealdwig. I found him near the ford where he was seeing to the wounded. Then I saw Sian in Hussa's clutches, and I knew I had to do something. I knew that the sight of Hal might make Hussa hesitate and so I sent for him to be taken to Eduard and then I asked Ealdwig to lead me through the woods to get behind the git, and just in time, too."

"By the time I am done with you, Aidith my dear, you will be a Valkyrie thundering to the rescue."

"Oh, please don't," Aidith said weakly but I could tell she actually quite liked the idea. She took a long drink from her ale and her eyes were distant. I laughed at her and she thumped me on the arm.

"What about Ealdwig? He deserves a part in this saga, surely?" I suggested as I rubbed my arm.

Lilla looked at the monk mischievously.

"As for Ealdwig, he will take the role of Woden, the *all-father*, master hunter as he leads the wild hunt through the woods. What do you say to that, monk?"

Ealdwig considered the suggestion.

"I am not sure Father Abbot will approve of a Christian brother being cast in the role of the patriarchal god of a pagan religion, no offense to all those present. Although," he added with a wink, "I rather like the sound of it."

"We won't tell him if you don't" Eduard said. "We will just call you Brother Woden from now on!"

Everyone laughed at that.

"What news from Cantia?" I asked Lilla, realising how much I had missed him and relished this opportunity to catch up on all his news.

Lilla had spent most of the last year away in the south with Hereric, nephew to Edwin, who was married to a Cantian princess and was pursuing his own attempts to get the crown of Northumbria.

Lilla shook his head and a shadow came across his face.

"That concerns me, if truth be told."

"Why?" I asked, concerned by his tone.

"Prince Hereric grows impatient with life at the court of Aethelbert. The Bretwalda is aging and seems reluctant to risk an expedition north. I fear Hereric is impetuous and may act prematurely one of these days. He speaks of being son to Aethelric, the last king of Deira and so the duty being his."

I grunted. "Just being the son of a king is not enough."

Lilla nodded. "Indeed, yet he seems convinced he can rally support from the people of Deira for what he says would be the rightful heir to Aethelric returning."

"If he steps foot in Deira, Aethelfrith will slaughter him," Eduard commented.

Lilla nodded. "He knows that but he and Guthred seem to have some other plan. Something about a local ally that will provide a safe base."

"Where?" I asked.

Lilla shrugged. "He would not tell me," he replied, sounding rather hurt at being left out of the deliberations of this princeling. "So, what of your own plans, those of prince Edwin, I mean?"

"At times he gets frustrated at the lack of progress," I said with a sigh, "yet, I think he knows that, in the end, it all depends on Aethelfrith. His attack has been delayed several times but will come eventually and when it does, I think the fact that Mercia and Deira – Edwin and Cwenburg – fought side by side here will help our alliance. I think Edwin might finally have his chance to take action. I sometimes hear my prince pray to the gods to give him that chance for what he most desires. For revenge and a crown."

"What about you, my friend?" the bard asked, gesturing at me, "Do you also pray for what you most desire?"

I looked around at my family gathered around the hall, at my friends and companions.

"What I most desire I have here. If I do speak to the gods, I tell them to bugger off and leave us alone for once."

Lilla laughed.

"What is so funny?"

"You are Cerdic, son of Cenred, earl and hero of many battles. You have killed not one but two kings and had more glory than most men could dream of and yet you hope and pray for a quiet life."

I frowned. "Are you suggesting my chances are not high?"

He reached over and poured me an ale and passed me the tankard. "I am saying, don't think too far ahead. Enjoy what you can get today!"

I picked up the tankard and looked down at the frothy brown liquid and then winked at him.

"I will drink to that!" I said and clashed it against his own tankard. "To a simple life," I said and the whole company echoed my toast.

The End

Historical Notes

As with all the books in the Northern Crown series, there is a paucity of contemporary source material that can be relied up. To be honest, there is a paucity even of unreliable sources and accounts and, in virtually no cases do any of the references date to anywhere near the years this tale covers – circa 610 to 612 A.D.

The only entry in the Anglo –Saxon Chronicle (ASC) for this period is in the year 611 when it records the death of King Ceolwulf of Wessex. There is much ambiguity on dates in the ASC during this period and so there is a good reason to assume that date is only approximate. I have the death in early 612. The ASC goes on to say Ceolwulf is succeeded by Cynegils which it states was the son of a Ceol – who reigned before Ceolwulf. Probably then Cynegils was the nephew of Ceolwulf who may have been brother to Ceol. As Ceolwulf became king of Wessex around 597, Cynegils may have been too young to succeed his father at that time.

Did Ceolwulf die in battle? We simply do not know. It is by no means unlikely given the violence of these times but the incident I describe and, for that matter, the battle at Souekesham is fictional. Battles up and down the Thames Valley were not unusual so whilst I cannot say this particular battle did occur, it is not too far a stretch that it did.

What do we know about Souekesham where this story starts and ends? Well, Souekesham is believed to be the original name for what is now called Abingdon. What is strange about the modern name is that it evolved from Abbendun which literally means 'hill of Aebba'. Yet Abingdon is a riverside town and not on a hill. There is a reference in a manuscript (MSS 933) at Trinity College Cambridgewhich contains entries about the year 688 referring to the foundation of the Abbey at Abingdon. This talks about the monks under the then King Cissa's command, bringing the abbey of Abbendun down from a hill to a village called Souekesham. So, Abbedun was the name given to this town in memory of an earlier hilltop religious site founded by a certain Aebba. The site is believed to be Boar's Hill a few miles north of Abingdon. According to tradition, Aebba may have been a British monk who fled to this hill in the 5th century to escape the so called *'night of the long knives'* when the first Anglo –Saxon king of Cantia, Hengist, was supposed to have slain the court of Vortigern, high king of the Britons. It seems that some form of abbey or monastery could then have survived through the 5th, 6th and 7th centuries and so would have been on Boar's Hill at the time of the events in this tale.

If Abbedun, later Abingdon, was the name this town was given in the later 7th century what do we know about the earlier place, called Souekesham?

Well, Souekesham would mean the dwelling of a person called Soueke. There is another place name in the area with a similar origin – the modern day Seacourt (Old English Seuecurda) – so maybe this is evidence of a couple of locations named after the same figure. Maybe Soueke was a 5th century Saxon who settled in the area. Quite a few digs have been undertaken in the area and we know from the archaeology of the Saxton Road site at Abingdon that this place was settled by Saxons as early as the mid 5th century. The Thames river provided an easy route for Saxons to migrate into the heart of Britain and many Thames valley locations show early evidence of this settlement.

Abingdon claims to hold the record of being Britain's oldest town in that it shows continuous occupation from the Iron Age onwards. Outer ditches were dug at this period and may have been used by the Romans who also built structures in the town, some of which would have survived into the Anglo –Saxon period to be seen by Cerdic and his companions. Little or nothing from this period is visible above ground but one of the modern roads – West St Helen's street which follows a curved course – is believed to follow the route of the original ditch. To the south of Abingdon, Andersley Island lies between the Thames and a side branch, today called the Swift Ditch. In Saxon times the Swift Ditch may have been the main water way and the Thames, as it passes Abingdon, may be a lesser branch, expanded and widened by monks when the abbey was built. The area is a boggy, marshy flood plain with dotted trees. It once did feature an Anglo –Saxon era hunting lodge built by King Offa. I figured that if Offa felt it was a good site for a royal hunting lodge in the 8th century, maybe earlier generations thought so, too, and thus this provided a location for Cerdic's family to stay in.

There is close to Abingdon the village of Sutton Courteney which had the original name of Sudstone. Recently, evidence of a very large Saxon hall was discovered there and the Sylva Foundation has reconstructed the structure, now given the name 'The House of Wessex' as a living history project which comprises an 'Anglo –Saxon Trail' you can follow to discover some of the history of the area.

Another significant site in this book is the hill fort of Trusty's Hill at Anwoth in Dumfries and Galloway about a kilometre west of Gatehouse of Fleet. This fort is believed to be a significant, probably royal site, of the Kingdom of Rheged. In recent years historians have concluded that Rheged ruled lands north of the Solway Firth, not just to the south of it as had previously been the belief. The engraved stone I mention in this book is still present and it is possible to make out bizarre shapes on it, some abstract in nature and others possibly sea creatures. It is believed to probably have ceremonial significance, perhaps like the footprint in the rock of Dunadd , the fortress that was once the capital of the Kingdom of the Dal Riata Scots a little further north and west in Argyll and Bute.

The hill itself is very steep and the climb up to the stone takes you through a channel and past terraces that must have provided a highly defensible location. There is evidence of vitrification of what is left of the stone battlements at the summit. These walls were believed to have been a lattice of timber surrounding stones. The fire that destroyed them is believed to have been ferocious and intense and would have been visible for miles around as well as burning for a long time.

What caused the fire is unknown for the incident is unrecorded, but it is believed to have occurred in the first half of the seventh century. Could this have been during an uprising by an occupied Rheged? It is possible. The kingdom of Rheged eventually merges officially with Northumbria when Rhiainmelt, daughter to Rhoerth (who is king at the time of this book) married the then king, Oswy but that is not for around twenty –eight years from the date of the events I relate here.

The final location where many of the events in this novel takes place is Bebbanburg. This is today the castle of Bamburgh in Northumbria. Bamburgh itself is a tiny though quite pretty village totally overshadowed by the stone medieval castle that dominates the coastline, standing high on its rocky platform.

This is a natural site for a fortress that would rule the surrounding area for centuries. It was once the British citadel of Din Guarie before falling to King Ida who founded the kingdom of Bernicia which took its name from the original British Kingdom of Bryneich. He captured it in the year A.D. 547.

What was the fortress like in Anglo –Saxon times? The modern castle is a Norman construction. Accounts from earlier writers record that the entrance in Anglo –Saxon times was at the north west end, unlike the modern castle whose gateway is at the southern end. The Bernicians would come and go through what later became known as St Oswald's gate. It would have been a steep approach from the village and harbour below which is believed to have wrapped around the north side of the fortress much closer than the current silted up bay does. We don't really know what the pre Norman castle looked like although writing in the years after the Norman conquest but before the Norman castle was built, the monk Simeon of Durham wrote about the place *'The city of Bebba is exceedingly well fortified, but by no means large, containing about the space of two or three fields, having one hollowed entrance ascending in a wonderful manner by steps.'*

The Bamburgh Research Project (BRP) is an independent, not for profit archaeological project investigating Bamburgh Castle in association with various universities. Their archaeological studies suggest a large wooden hall was present as well as forges and workshops and considerable evidence of industry such as metal working.

The well which Hussa builds in the novel does exist deep down in the vaulted chambers of the oldest part of the stone castle. It was there long before the Normans built their arched pillars which you can see today, however. Again, Simeon of Durham records 'There is on the west and highest point of this citadel, a well, excavated with extraordinary labour, sweet to drink, and very pure to the sight...'

We don't know when the well was made although Simeon includes this detail in his entry for the year 774 but that does not mean that was when the well was made. As for the method Hussa uses, using fire and cold water, I took that from a method suggested on a sign next to the well itself. It is a method that might explain how a well could be made in the thick hard dolerite rock that lies beneath the fortress.

What about the references to twenty shillings? We do not know for certain what the law pertaining to slaves in Bernicia was at this time, but we do, for once, at least have a reference that comes from the time period. Aethelberht was king of Kent at this time as readers will know. He was the first Anglo –Saxon king that we definitely know of to establish a law code because the code survives. One clause stipulates that 'if someone lies with a nobleman's serving maid, he shall pay in compensation 20 shillings.' It is believed that these codes were based upon traditional laws coming into the land from the Germanic homelands or the lands of the Franks.

So then, in the end, given the paucity of documented events, I chose to focus in this novel on a number of locations that existed at this time and which at this period or others certainly played their part on the battle board of history. This book has also focused on the families of Cerdic and Hussa whose disputes have, after all, been the catalyst behind much of what has gone on in the Northern Crown series. If the history books failed to present us with a story, I figured that the two brothers could provide enough drama and issues to work through themselves.

In future novels in this series we start to emerge from the shroud of ignorance and guess work I have laboured under into years when at least some documentation exists.

Hussa and Cerdic will come together again in more than one of these historical locations and be present at more than one of these significant events that changed history and which would become pivotal both in the history of the north of England and Britain generally.

Their story will continue in Book 6 of the Northern Crown Series.

Also by the same author

The Nineworlds series

The Nine Worlds series is a Historical Fantasy Adventure for Children of Ages 9+

The historical world of Anglo -Saxon England meets the mysterious world of myths and legends, gods and monsters our ancestors believed in.

This is the world as it might have been had those stories been true…

An excerpt from The Nineworlds Series Book 1: Shield Maiden

Chapter One - Anna

"It's not fair!" the girl shouted as she stabbed her short sword down into the oak table, leaving it vibrating in the wood. Her deep green eyes fixed the man on the far side with a furious glare.

"Father, it's not fair! Why can Lar train as a warrior and not me?" she asked him, her arms folded in front of her chest and her foot tapping the reed -strewn floor in impatience.

The man she was talking to sighed, as if this was an almost daily argument, which it was, and as if he despaired of ever getting his way with this, his twelve -year -old daughter, which he did. He stepped forward, pulled the knife out of the table and held it out to the girl, handle first.

"Anna, we have been through all this before. Your brother, Lar will follow me as headman of the village one day and must

318

be a warrior. You in turn will marry a warrior or a lord of another village and raise children."

"Lar is younger than me. I don't see why he should be the leader. Raedann tells me there have been warrior women before now – shield maidens – and even queens and ladies who have led their folk in battle. Why not me?"

Her father, Nerian, looked at her helplessly and, as was his habit when he was at a loss for words he scratched the bald patch in his brown hair.

"Your father has many cares, child.' These words were spoken by a man standing further down the hall, staring at the embers that burned in the fire pit running the length of the building. 'You should not distress him with these ideas. Nor should you take note of what that tinker, Raedann, says."

This was Iden, the priest of Woden, a fat man with grey hair, who enjoyed mead a little too much and as a result had a large belly and red cheeks. Anna, as well as the other children, thought him stuffy and when he preached found him boring and dull. Nothing like Radeann's fun tales of the gods, of great heroes, of the monsters that lived in the woods and hills and of the adventures he had supposedly had in the world outside their tiny village of Scenestane.

Iden was right in that Raedann was a tinker: he sold trinkets as he travelled around the villages of Mercia. But he sold stories too – anything for a bed for the night and maybe some food and mead. His stories were good ones and the children loved them.

"Are you saying that Raedann lies?"

"Child," Iden replied as he came to join them at the table, "he is a spinner of tales. He exaggerates. He makes stories seem more than they really are."

319

"But there have been shield maidens," Anna insisted, "women who fight alongside the men."

Iden nodded, but Anna could see he was reluctant to admit it. "Maybe,' he agreed, 'but not many and only when something unusual happens, when special times come along and they are forced to take up arms. It is best to forget such tales. You will soon be old enough to marry. You should be thinking about that and not this nonsense."

"I can be a warrior. I will prove it to you one day!"

"Please, Anna," her father pleaded with her. "Take back your seax and go help Udela prepare the evening meal."

Fists clenched, teeth gritted, Anna glowered at him for a while and then finally let her shoulders drop. Reaching out she removed the long knife which he offered her and slid it into the scabbard on her belt. With a nod she left the headman's hall and walked out into the village. Once there though, she did not go as ordered to the cookhouse to find the elderly cook, but looked around the village, past the wooded path that led up to the rocky outcrop upon which Iden's small temple was built, to the hut that lay beyond. This was home of the healing woman, Julia. Outside it Anna could see her friends loitering, playing a game of Tafel on the ground, with pebbles and a board they had created by cutting lines into the sun –baked mud. She joined them.

Her brother Lar looked up from the game as she approached. He gave her a kindly smile.

"So how did your talk with father go?" he asked, tilting his head towards the headman's hall.

She stuck out her lower lip and frowned at him, "What do you think? You are the boy so you will be leader and a warrior, whilst I have to have babies."

"Sorry, sister, but that is just the way it is," Lar said. "Shield maidens are all well and good in stories, but in the real world we all have to accept what fate has in store for us. If it helps I don't feel any better about it than you, but you can't fight fate."

Anna snorted. "Maybe I can. Maybe I can prove I am worthy to be a warrior and defend the village."

But Lar was not listening to her. He had turned back to the board, smiled and moved one piece.

"My game, pay up Wilburh!"

His opponent, ten –year –old Wilburh, gave Lar a dark look from under a fringe of blond hair, his blue eyes darkened, suddenly seeming almost black.

Wilburh's twin sister, Hild, gurgled with laughter. "Come on, pay him," she said. Her own eyes, whilst also blue, seemed lighter somehow, just like Hild herself – bubbly and happy in a way that gave Anna headaches sometimes and contrasted with Wilburh's more gloomy nature.

Wilburh shrugged and reaching into a pouch at his belt brought out a tarnished old ring and handed it over. Lar held it up to the late afternoon sun and examined it.

"Should be able to sell that to Raedann for a new knife," he boasted.

"A knife? Why in Woden's name do you think that dirty old ring is worth the same as one of my knives," a man's voice cut in.

They turned around and saw the tinker looming over them. Tall, almost gangly, with curly brown hair and a hook nose, Raedann grinned at them. "I will give you this seashell bracelet for it," he said with wink, and Lar and Raedann were soon bargaining and trading.

Listening to her brother Anna shook her head in despair. Lar had no interest in swords and fighting. He had passed on to her all he had learnt after she badgered him into going off to the woods to teach her how to fight with a sword and how to fire a bow. No, Lar was a trader at heart and a good one at that, but he was no fighter. She sighed. If only her father could see that.

"Well, I must be off," Raedann said, after he and Lar had finally agreed a fair exchange for the ring and Lar had got his knife, although not as fine a one as he would have hoped. "I want to reach Wall before the sun sets and that's a couple of miles to go."

The tinker set off towards the Roman road that ran past the west side of the village. Anna beckoned at the children and they all trailed along with Raedann, passing between the blacksmith's house and the one next to it, crossing a field and finally stepping onto the cobbled road beyond.

"We will go to just past the old Roman house with you, Raedann," Anna said. "Tell us about shield maidens again."

Lar groaned. "Not again, sister. Raedann, tell us something different. Tell us about giants."

"Giants? Ah, now there are many sorts of giants in this world. There are hill giants and cliff giants and fire giants and frost ones too. They come from other worlds you know, places like Jotunheim, Niflheim and the fire world, Muspelheim. They visit our world of Midgard from time to time."

He went on telling a tale about how he had once been chased by a fearsome fire giant and had escaped by swimming a river. By the time he had finished they had crossed the ford north of the town where a brook trickled over the old road, and soon they were passing the crumbling ruins of a Roman farm beyond.

"Did the giants build that?" Wilburh asked, gazing at the stone structure.

Raedann smiled at him. "You ask me that because it is made of stone, don't you? But no, the Romans were not giants, just men. They built many houses like that, walls and cities too, all over this land. Then they left because their empire was under attack. That was two hundred years ago. When our own people, the Saxons, came here across the Eastern Sea they gazed on such buildings, and because they could not build them, they assumed the Romans must have been giants. That is why those ruins and many others like it make our people feel scared and why we keep away from them."

The children stared at the ruins and Raedann, chuckling at the expressions on their faces, said, "Well, I'll be on my way. I will be back in a couple of days. You'd best be getting home to the village, children. The sun is sinking. You don't want evil spirits to find you out in the dark, do you?"

He pointed to where the old fort on the hills to the west was silhouetted against the setting sun. Then he was off, singing a song and strolling up the road.

"Come on, let's go home," Hild said, turning to head back down the road.

Anna moved to join her and then abruptly changed her mind. "No! Let's go and look in the ruins," she said.

"The Roman ruins? In the dark?" Lar asked, studying the decaying structure.

"Indeed, why not?"

The others stared at her. Lar opened his mouth to speak but did not get a word out. Around them the twilight was gathering, the evening air warm but quiet. Into that silence they heard a noise that made them all jump: the sound of running footsteps

323

coming along the road from the direction of the village. They spun around to glance back towards the ford, but could see nothing apart from deep shadows at the bases of the trees.

No, there was something else there.

A shape was moving in the shadows....

The Hourglass Institute Series

Book One - Tomorrow's Guardian

Time Travel Sounds like fun until you try it!

Tom Oakley experiences disturbing episodes of déjà -vu and believes he is going mad. Then, he discovers that he's a "Walker" – someone who can transport himself to other times and places.

Tom dreams about other "Walkers" in moments of mortal danger: Edward Dyson killed in a battle in 1879; Mary Brown who perished in the Great Fire of London; and Charlie Hawker, a sailor who drowned on a U -boat in 1943. Agreeing to travel back in time and rescue them, Tom has three dangerous adventures before returning to the present day.

But Tom's troubles have only just begun. He finds that he's drawn the attention of evil individuals who seek to bend history to their will. Soon, Tom's family are obliterated from existence and Tom must make a choice between saving them and saving his entire world.

The Praesidium Series

Book One - The Last Seal

Gunpowder and sorcery in 1666...

17th century London – two rival secret societies are caught in a battle that threatens to destroy the city and beyond. When a truant schoolboy, Ben, finds a scroll revealing the location of magical seals that binds a powerful demon beneath the city, he is thrown into the centre of a dangerous plot that leads to the Great Fire of 1666.

"an awesome array of characters which definitely included the good, the bad and the ugly, and an amazing plot! This young adult historical fantasy had me totally engrossed and I would recommend it to anyway who loves historical fantasy/fiction (especially British) whether you're a teen or an adult."
The Slowest Bookworm

"Denning has a real thirst for historical knowledge and this certainly shines through in his books, with his descriptions of London in 1666 making you feel as if you were in the middle of the raging fire."
YA Yeah Yeah

Winner of a B.R.A.G. Medallion